HERETICS
OF DUNE

BOOK FIVE IN THE DUNE CHRONICLES

FRANK HERBERT

With an Introduction by Brian Herbert

ACE
New York

ACE
Published by Berkley
An imprint of Penguin Random House LLC
penguinrandomhouse.com

Copyright © 1984 by Herbert Properties LLC
"Introduction" by Brian Herbert copyright © 2009 by DreamStar, Inc.

The excerpt from "The Vigil," copyright © 1953 by Theodore Roethke,
from *The Collected Poems of Theodore Roethke*, is reprinted by permission
of Doubleday & Company, Inc., and Faber and Faber Ltd.

ISBN: 9780593098264

G. P. Putnam's Sons hardcover edition / April 1984
Berkley trade paperback edition / March 1985
Berkley mass-market edition / April 1986
Ace mass-market edition / August 1987
Ace hardcover edition / February 2009
Ace premium edition / June 2019

Printed in the United States of America
19   21   23   25   26   24   22   20   18

INTRODUCTION
BY BRIAN HERBERT

Frank Herbert wrote much of the first draft of *Heretics of Dune* in Hawaii, a few miles outside the village of Hana on the eastern shore of Maui. He had not expected to be writing there, because the Pacific Northwest was his Tara, the place of his heart. But difficult circumstances led him to a distant, tropical isle.

When my father signed the contract for the novel in 1981, it was the largest science fiction book deal in history. World famous, he was at the top of his profession, having risen from poverty to success in a fashion that was reminiscent of the works of Horatio Alger, Jr. But Dad's remarkable achievement was bittersweet. The actual process of writing the fifth book in his classic Dune series would prove to be exceedingly arduous and much slower for him than usual, because of all the time he had to spend out of his study tending to the medical crises of my mother, Beverly Herbert.

She was seriously ill at the time, and for years had been battling valiantly for her life. The original diagnosis in 1974 had been terminal lung cancer from a lifetime of smoking cigarettes, sometimes as many as two packs a day. At the time of the discovery of the dread disease, the most optimistic prognosis had given her only a 5 percent chance of surviving beyond six months. Our family was devastated.

Under a rigorous program of chemotherapy and cobalt radiation treatments, my mother beat the cancer, but radiation seriously damaged her heart, which was inadequately shielded because of the limitations of medical technology in the 1970s. After these treatments, she suffered several life-threatening episodes, but Beverly Herbert was a fighter, and my father did everything possible to save her. He was her champion, and in true heroic fashion he sacrificed himself for her, just as she had done for him more than two decades earlier—when she gave up her own creative writing career in order to become the breadwinner for our family, thus enabling him to write. When she became gravely ill, he took time away from his writing to find the latest treatments for her and tended to her every need. He became her personal nurse, maid, and cook, preparing the low-salt meals required for her. Under his loving attention, she kept beating the odds, kept rising like Lazarus from ICU hospital beds and going on with her life. As soon as she was able, she continued to help Dad with his business operations, handling his accounting, scheduling, and management. But over the years, she had weakened physically and was slipping away from us, and from him.

Stretching their financial resources to the limit, in 1980 my parents purchased an incredible piece of property in a remote area of Maui and proceeded to have a wonderful home built there. Frank Herbert did this for my mother because she could breathe much easier in the warm air of Hawaii, far from the cold, damp Pacific Northwest, where she had been born and had lived more than thirty-five years of her life.

By late 1982, the home was still under construction but could be occupied. They arrived in October of that year. A swimming pool was being built for Mom on the property so that she could get some much-needed exercise, but work was progressing slowly, frustrating her and my father. Even so, she loved the eastern side of Maui, with its warmth, stunning beauty, and relaxed pace of life. It was a very spiritual, old-Hawaiian region, inhabited by a people reminiscent of a bygone, less-hectic time, and it was the perfect spot for her to recuperate.

Having researched old records, my mother had already found a map showing their property. It was five miles from Hana, in an area that used to be called "Kawaloa," which means "a nice long time" in the Hawaiian language. She said she hoped to spend a long time there herself and that it was a magical place, unlike anything she had ever seen. A five-acre piece of paradise, the land fronted an aquamarine sea with dancing whitecaps and a surf that pounded against the black lava shoreline. The property had palms, papayas, mangoes, bananas, breadfruit trees, and a graceful kamani tree overlooking the water. The flowers on the gentle slopes around the home were spectacular, with bougainvillaea, blue lilies, orchids, torch gingers, heliconias, bird-of-paradises, poinsettias, and huge hibiscus blossoms.

"It's warm here," my mother said to me over the telephone, "and there are flowers everywhere."

In Hawaii, Frank Herbert set to work on *Heretics of Dune.* I spoke with him by phone in early January 1983, and he told me he was putting in long hours on the new novel, pressing to complete it as soon as possible. Each morning he rose before dawn and worked out on a rowing machine and an Exercycle. Then he took a quick shower and made a light breakfast of toast and guava juice, which he carried to his loft study on the second floor of the house.

After writing for three hours, he would help Mom get ready for the day. He made her Cream of Wheat with sliced bananas on top, found books and knitting materials and art supplies and whatever else she needed, and sometimes adjusted the louvers in the walls to allow just the right amount of trade winds to enter, naturally ventilating the interior of the house. By nine thirty he was back at his desk upstairs, but he was always going to the interior railing and looking down into the living room to make sure she was comfortable. Under the circumstances, it was difficult for him to find the time or the energy to write, but he did the best that he possibly could. The novel, as important as it was, had to be secondary to Beverly Herbert, his loving wife and companion since 1946.

For the new book project, he was using a Compaq word processor since it was much faster than his customary electric typewriter. Each night he put the new machine away in a sealed "dry room" by the kitchen to prevent it from being damaged so quickly in the caustic, salty air that blew in from the ocean. By the middle of February, he told me he'd been having plot problems with the novel, but he was a little over halfway through the first draft. Only a few days later, he was interrupted by yet another of my mother's medical emergencies, one that forced them to return to a home they still owned in

Port Townsend, Washington. Choosing to stay there instead, a short distance from Seattle, they could more easily obtain the best medical treatment for her. It was the practical thing to do, though they would return to Hawaii later in the year.

By early June, they were still in Port Townsend, and Dad had the first draft completed—around 200,000 words, which would eventually be cut to 165,000. I remember visiting them at their home on the Olympic Peninsula and seeing my mother reading the manuscript. A slender brunette woman, she was seated on a dark yellow recliner in the sitting area adjacent to the kitchen, with manuscript pages spread out on the table beside her. She said the story was great, that she couldn't put it down. Mom felt that each book in the series was superior to the one before, with plots and characterizations that were even better than *Dune*.

The strong characterizations of women in the series—and particularly in *Heretics* and *Chapterhouse*—appealed greatly to my mother. In fact, Dad based the Lady Jessica on her, creating a memorable literary character who had my mother's beauty and grace. Remarkably, even though Beverly Herbert passed away years ago, she continues to live through the ages . . . a significant testimonial to the love that Frank Herbert felt for her.

It is interesting to note the progression of women in my father's Dune novels. Female characters get stronger and stronger as the series develops, and in *Heretics of Dune* and *Chapterhouse: Dune*, women are running most of the important planets in the Dune universe. By that time, the Bene Gesserit Sisterhood is the most important political power, although it is a more austere age, without the grandeur and pomposity of the Imperium back in the days of Shaddam Corrino IV, the Emperor Paul Muad'Dib, or the tyrannical God Emperor, Leto Atreides II. The glories of the desert planet Arrakis are long gone as well, and the sandworm species has been moved off world, where it may not survive.

Thousands of years before the events described in *Heretics of Dune*, the God Emperor set mankind on his "Golden Path" and scattered civilization across countless star systems, as if sprinkling human seeds in the wind. But now, in *Heretics of Dune*, evil, supremely powerful women have emerged from the Scattering and threaten the Sisterhood. They call themselves "Honored Matres," which is ironic because there is nothing honorable about them. Individually and collectively, they can outfight the Sisters, so that the Sisterhood—like the sandworms—seems in danger of being wiped out. The brutal Honored Matres appear to be unstoppable, and there are rumors about their origins. Could they possibly be descended from failed Reverend Mothers, making them the dark side of the Sisterhood? Or could something else be at play, something even more sinister that has been generated in the secret breeding laboratories of the fanatical Tleilaxu?

Heretics of Dune is a remarkable, cerebral excursion through the most fantastic universe in science fiction. In this novel, as in *God Emperor of Dune* before it and *Chapterhouse: Dune* afterward, the author explored layers that he originally interwove into the action of the first novel in the series, *Dune*—layers containing important messages about politics, religion, ecology, and a host of other interesting, timeless subjects. The last three novels he wrote in the series are intellectually stimulating, and sometimes the action almost seems secondary. Huge battles, and even one that is environmentally catastrophic, occur behind the scenes.

As I wrote in *Dreamer of Dune*, the biography of my father, *Heretics of Dune* was actually intended to be the first book of a new trilogy that would complete the epic story chronologically. It is set thousands of years in mankind's future, long after the events in *Dune*. Before his untimely death in 1986, Frank Herbert wrote the first two books of the trilogy (*Heretics* and *Chapterhouse*), but he left the third unwritten. Using my father's outline and notes, I eventually co-wrote the grand climax with Kevin J. Anderson, but it required two novels for us to do so— *Hunters of Dune* (2006) and *Sandworms of Dune* (2007).

Heretics of Dune is the beginning of that extraordinary, climactic adventure, a giant leap in time and space beyond the novels preceding it. In this novel, you will meet a diverse and complex cast of characters, inhabiting worlds that stretch the imagination. It is a journey into what my father liked to call one of humankind's "possible futures," showing where we might very well be headed, into a tableau that is at once terrifying and exhilarating. Even with its complexities, *Heretics* is a page-turner, a novel that will not disappoint the most critical of Dune fans. After reading the last page of the book, you will want to go back and read it again, revisiting old friends in a fantastic realm that never quite leaves your thoughts.

Brian Herbert
Seattle, Washington
June 24, 2008

Most discipline is hidden discipline, designed not to liberate but to limit. Do not ask *Why?* Be cautious with *How? Why?* leads inexorably to paradox. *How?* traps you in a universe of cause and effect. Both deny the infinite.

—THE APOCRYPHA OF ARRAKIS

"Taraza told you, did she not, that we have gone through eleven of these Duncan Idaho gholas? This one is the twelfth."

The old Reverend Mother Schwangyu spoke with deliberate bitterness as she looked down from the third-story parapet at the lone child playing on the enclosed lawn. The planet Gammu's bright midday sunlight bounced off the white courtyard walls filling the area beneath them with brilliance as though a spotlight had been directed onto the young ghola.

Gone through! the Reverend Mother Lucilla thought. She allowed herself a short nod, thinking how coldly impersonal were Schwangyu's manner and choice of words. *We have used up our supply; send us more!*

The child on the lawn appeared to be about twelve standard years of age, but appearance could be deceptive with a ghola not yet awakened to his original memories. The child took that moment to look up at the watchers above him. He was a sturdy figure with a direct gaze that focused intently from beneath a black cap of karakul hair. The yellow sunlight of early spring cast a small shadow at his feet. His skin was darkly tanned but a slight movement of his body shifted his blue singlesuit, revealing pale skin at the left shoulder.

"Not only are these gholas costly but they are supremely dangerous to us," Schwangyu said. Her voice came out flat and emotionless, all the more powerful because of that. It was the voice of a Reverend Mother Instructor speaking down to an acolyte and it emphasized for Lucilla that Schwangyu was one of those who protested openly against the ghola project.

Taraza had warned: "She will try to win you over."

"Eleven failures are enough," Schwangyu said.

Lucilla glanced at Schwangyu's wrinkled features, thinking suddenly: *Someday I may be old and wizened, too. And perhaps I will be a power in the Bene Gesserit as well.*

Schwangyu was a small woman with many age marks earned in the Sisterhood's affairs. Lucilla knew from her own assignment-studies that Schwangyu's conventional black robe concealed a skinny figure that few other than her acolyte dressers and the males bred to her had ever seen. Schwangyu's mouth was wide, the lower lip constricted by the age lines that fanned into a jutting chin. Her manner tended to a curt abruptness that the uninitiated often interpreted as anger. The commander of the Gammu Keep was one who kept herself to herself more than most Reverend Mothers.

Once more, Lucilla wished she knew the entire scope of the ghola project. Taraza had drawn the dividing line clearly enough, though: "Schwangyu is not to be trusted where the safety of the ghola is concerned."

"We think the Tleilaxu themselves killed most of the previous eleven," Schwangyu said. "That in itself should tell us something."

Matching Schwangyu's manner, Lucilla adopted a quiet attitude of almost emotionless waiting. Her manner said: "I may be much younger than you, Schwangyu, but I, too, am a full Reverend Mother." She could feel Schwangyu's gaze.

Schwangyu had seen the holos of this Lucilla but the woman in the flesh was more disconcerting. An Imprinter of the best training, no doubt of it. Blue-in-blue eyes uncorrected by any lens gave Lucilla a piercing expression that went with her long oval face. With the hood of her black aba robe thrown back as it was now, brown hair was revealed, drawn into a tight barette and then cascading down her back. Not even the stiffest robe could completely hide Lucilla's ample breasts. She was from a genetic line famous for its motherly nature and she already had borne three children for the Sisterhood, two by the same sire. Yes—a brown-haired charmer with full breasts and a motherly disposition.

"You say very little," Schwangyu said. "This tells me that Taraza has warned you against me."

"Do you have reason to believe assassins will try to kill this twelfth ghola?" Lucilla asked.

"They already have tried."

Strange how the word "heresy" came to mind when thinking of Schwangyu, Lucilla thought. Could there be heresy among the Reverend Mothers? The religious overtones of the word seemed out of place in a Bene Gesserit context. How could there be heretical movements among people who held a profoundly manipulative attitude toward all things religious?

Lucilla shifted her attention down to the ghola, who took this moment to perform a series of cartwheels that brought him around full circle until he once more stood looking up at the two observers on the parapet.

"How prettily he performs!" Schwangyu sneered. The old voice did not completely mask an underlying violence.

Lucilla glanced at Schwangyu. *Heresy.* "Dissidence" was not the proper word. "Opposition" did not cover what could be sensed in the older woman. This was something that could shatter the Bene Gesserit. Revolt against Taraza, against the Reverend Mother Superior? Unthinkable! Mother Superiors were cast in the mold of monarch. Once Taraza had accepted counsel and advice and *then* made her decision, the Sisters were committed to obedience.

"This is no time to be creating new problems!" Schwangyu said.

Her meaning was clear. People from the Scattering were coming back and the intent of some among those Lost Ones threatened the Sisterhood. *Honored Matres!* How like "Reverend Mothers" the words sounded.

Lucilla ventured an exploratory sally: "So you think we should be concentrating on the problem of those Honored Matres from the Scattering?"

"Concentrating? Hah! They do not have our powers. They do not show good sense. And they do not have mastery of melange! That is what they want from us, our spice knowledge."

"Perhaps," Lucilla agreed. She was not willing to concede this on the scanty evidence.

"Mother Superior Taraza has taken leave of her senses to dally with this ghola thing now," Schwangyu said.

Lucilla remained silent. The ghola project definitely had touched an old nerve among the Sisters. The possibility, even remote, that they might arouse another Kwisatz Haderach sent shudders of angry fear through the ranks. To meddle with the worm-bound remnants of the Tyrant! That was dangerous in the extreme.

"We should never take that ghola to Rakis," Schwangyu muttered. "Let sleeping worms lie."

Lucilla gave her attention once more to the ghola-child. He had turned his back on the high parapet with its two Reverend Mothers, but something about his posture said he knew they discussed him and he awaited their response.

"You doubtless realize that you have been called in while he is yet too young," Schwangyu said.

"I have never heard of the deep imprinting on one that young," Lucilla agreed. She allowed something softly self-mocking in her tone, a thing she knew Schwangyu would hear and misinterpret. The management of procreation and all of its attendant necessities, that was the Bene Gesserit ultimate specialty. Use love but avoid it, Schwangyu would be thinking now. The Sisterhood's analysts knew the roots of love. They had examined this quite early in their development but had never dared breed it out of those they influenced. Tolerate love but guard against it, that was the rule. Know that it lay deep within the human genetic makeup, a safety net to insure continuation of the species. You used it where necessary, imprinting selected individuals (sometimes upon each other) for the Sisterhood's purposes, knowing then that such individuals would be linked by powerful bonding lines not readily available to the common awareness. Others might observe such links and plot the consequences but the linked ones would dance to unconscious music.

"I was not suggesting that it's a mistake to imprint him," Schwangyu said, misreading Lucilla's silence.

"We do what we are ordered to do," Lucilla chided. Let Schwangyu make of that what she would.

"Then you do not object to taking the ghola to Rakis," Schwangyu said. "I wonder if you would continue such unquestioning obedience if you knew the full story?"

Lucilla inhaled a deep breath. Was the entire design for the Duncan Idaho gholas to be shared with her now?

"There is a female child named Sheeana Brugh on Rakis," Schwangyu said. "She can control the giant worms."

Lucilla concealed her alertness. *Giant worms. Not Shai-hulud. Not Shaitan. Giant worms.* The sandrider predicted by the Tyrant had appeared at last!

"I do not make idle chatter," Schwangyu said when Lucilla continued silent.

Indeed not, Lucilla thought. *And you call a thing by its descriptive label, not by the name of its mystical import. Giant worms. And you're really thinking about the Tyrant, Leto II, whose endless dream is carried as a pearl of awareness in each of those worms. Or so we are led to believe.*

Schwangyu nodded toward the child on the lawn below them. "Do you think their ghola will be able to influence the girl who controls the worms?"

We're peeling away the skin at last, Lucilla thought.

She said: "I have no need for the answer to such a question."

"You *are* a cautious one," Schwangyu said.

Lucilla arched her back and stretched. *Cautious? Yes, indeed!* Taraza had warned her: "Where Schwangyu is concerned, you must act with extreme caution but with speed. We have a very narrow window of time within which we can succeed."

Succeed at what? Lucilla wondered. She glanced sideways at Schwangyu. "I don't see how the Tleilaxu could succeed in killing eleven of these gholas. How could they get through our defenses?"

"We have the Bashar now," Schwangyu said. "Perhaps he can prevent disaster." Her tone said she did not believe this.

Mother Superior Taraza had said: "You are the Imprinter, Lucilla. When you get to Gammu you will recognize some of the pattern. But for your task you have no need for the full design."

"Think of the cost!" Schwangyu said, glaring down at the ghola, who now squatted, pulling at tufts of grass.

Cost had nothing to do with it, Lucilla knew. The open admission of failure was much more important. The Sisterhood could not reveal its fallibility. But the fact that an Imprinter had been summoned early—that was vital. Taraza had known the Imprinter would see this and recognize part of the pattern.

Schwangyu gestured with one bony hand at the child, who had returned to his solitary play, running and tumbling on the grass.

"Politics," Schwangyu said.

No doubt Sisterhood politics lay at the core of

Schwangyu's *heresy*, Lucilla thought. The delicacy of the internal argument could be deduced from the fact that Schwangyu had been put in charge of the Keep here on Gammu. Those who opposed Taraza refused to sit on the sidelines.

Schwangyu turned and looked squarely at Lucilla. Enough had been said. Enough had been heard and screened through minds trained in Bene Gesserit awareness. The Chapter House had chosen this Lucilla with great care.

Lucilla felt the older woman's careful examination but refused to let this touch that innermost sense of purpose upon which every Reverend Mother could rely in times of stress. *Here. Let her look fully upon me.* Lucilla turned and set her mouth in a soft smile, passing her gaze across the rooftop opposite them.

A uniformed man armed with a heavy-duty lasgun appeared there, looked once at the two Reverend Mothers and then focused on the child below them.

"Who is that?" Lucilla asked.

"Patrin, the Bashar's most trusted aide. Says he's only the Bashar's batman but you'd have to be blind and a fool to believe that."

Lucilla examined the man across from them with care. So that was Patrin. A native of Gammu, Taraza had said. Chosen for this task by the Bashar himself. Thin and blond, much too old now to be soldiering, but then the Bashar had been called back from retirement and had insisted Patrin must share this duty.

Schwangyu noted the way Lucilla shifted her attention from Patrin to the ghola with real concern. Yes, if the Bashar had been called back to guard this Keep, then the ghola was in extreme peril.

Lucilla started in sudden surprise. "Why . . . he's . . ."

"Miles Teg's orders," Schwangyu said, naming the Bashar. "All of the ghola's play is training play. Muscles are to be prepared for the day when he is restored to his original self."

"But that's no simple exercise he's doing down there," Lucilla said. She felt her own muscles respond sympathetically to the remembered training.

"We hold back only the Sisterhood's arcana from this ghola," Schwangyu said. "Almost anything else in our storehouse of knowledge can be his." Her tone said she found this extremely objectionable.

"Surely, no one believes this ghola could become another Kwisatz Haderach," Lucilla objected.

Schwangyu merely shrugged.

Lucilla held herself quite still, thinking. Was it possible the ghola could be transformed into a male version of a Reverend Mother? Could this Duncan Idaho learn to look inward where no Reverend Mother dared?

Schwangyu began to speak, her voice almost a growling mutter: "The design of this project . . . they have a dangerous plan. They could make the same mistake . . ." She broke off.

They, Lucilla thought. *Their ghola*.

"I would give anything to know for sure the position of Ix and the Fish Speakers in this," Lucilla said.

"Fish Speakers!" Schwangyu shook her head at the very thought of the remnant female army that had once served only the Tyrant. "They believe in truth and justice."

Lucilla overcame a sudden tightness in her throat. Schwangyu had all but declared open opposition. Yet, she commanded here. The political rule was a simple one: Those who opposed the project must monitor it that they might abort it at the first sign of trouble. But that was a genuine Duncan Idaho ghola down there on the lawn. Cell comparisons and Truthsayers had confirmed it.

Taraza had said: "You are to teach him love in all of its forms."

"He's so young," Lucilla said, keeping her attention on the ghola.

"Young, yes," Schwangyu said. "So, for now, I presume you will awaken his childish responses to maternal affection. Later . . ." Schwangyu shrugged.

Lucilla betrayed no emotional reaction. A Bene Gesserit obeyed. *I am an Imprinter. So . . .* Taraza's orders and the Imprinter's specialized training defined a particular course of events.

To Schwangyu, Lucilla said: "There is someone who looks like me and speaks with my voice. I am Imprinting for her. May I ask who that is?"

"No."

Lucilla held her silence. She had not expected revelation but it had been remarked more than once that she bore a striking resemblance to Senior Security Mother Darwi Odrade. "A *young Odrade*." Lucilla had heard this on several occasions. Both Lucilla and Odrade were, of course, in the Atreides line with a strong backbreeding from Siona descendants. The Fish Speakers had no monopoly on *those* genes! But the *Other Memories* of a Reverend Mother, even with their linear selectivity and confinement to the female side, provided important clues to the broad shape of the ghola project. Lucilla, who had come to depend on her experiences of the Jessica persona buried some five thousand years back in the Sisterhood's genetic manipulations, felt a deep sense of dread from that source now. There was a familiar pattern here. It gave off such an intense feeling of doom that Lucilla fell automatically into the Litany Against Fear as she had been taught it in her first introduction to the Sisterhood's rites:

"I must not fear. Fear is the mind-killer. Fear is the little-death that brings total obliteration. I will face my fear. I will permit it to pass over me and through me. And when it has gone past I will turn the inner eye to see its path. Where the fear has gone there will be nothing. Only I will remain."

Calm returned to Lucilla.

Schwangyu, sensing some of this, allowed her guard to drop slightly. Lucilla was no dullard, no *special* Reverend Mother with an empty title and barely sufficient background to function without embarrassing the Sisterhood. Lucilla was the real thing and some reactions could not be hidden from her, not even reactions of another Reverend Mother. Very well, let her know the full extent of the opposition to this foolish, this *dangerous* project!

"I do not think their ghola will survive to see Rakis," Schwangyu said.

Lucilla let this pass. "Tell me about his friends," she said.

"He has no friends; only teachers."

"When will I meet them?" She kept her gaze on the opposite parapet where Patrin leaned idly against a low pillar, his heavy lasgun at the ready. Lucilla realized with an abrupt shock that Patrin was watching her. Patrin was a message from the Bashar! Schwangyu obviously saw and understood. *We guard him!*

"I presume it's Miles Teg you're so anxious to meet," Schwangyu said.

"Among others."

"Don't you want to make contact with the ghola first?"

"I've already made contact with him." Lucilla nodded toward the enclosed yard where the child once more stood almost motionless and looking up at her. "He's a thoughtful one."

"I've only the reports on the others," Schwangyu said, "but I suspect this is the most thoughtful one of the series."

Lucilla suppressed an involuntary shudder at the readiness for violent opposition in Schwangyu's words and attitude. There was not one hint that the child below them shared a common humanity.

While Lucilla was thinking this, clouds covered the sun as they often did here at this hour. A cold wind blew in over the Keep's walls, swirling around the courtyard. The child turned away and picked up the speed of his exercises, getting his warmth from increased activity.

"Where does he go to be alone?" Lucilla asked.

"Mostly to his room. He has tried a few dangerous escapades, but we have discouraged this."

"He must hate us very much."

"I'm sure of it."

"I will have to deal with that directly."

"Surely, an Imprinter has no doubts about her ability to overcome hate."

"I was thinking of Geasa." Lucilla sent a knowing look at Schwangyu. "I find it astonishing that you let Geasa make such a mistake."

"I don't interfere with the normal progress of the ghola's instructions. If one of his teachers develops a real affection for him, that is not my problem."

"An attractive child," Lucilla said.

They stood a bit longer watching the Duncan Idaho ghola at his training-play. Both Reverend Mothers thought briefly of Geasa, one of the first teachers brought here for the ghola project. Schwangyu's attitude was plain: *Geasa was a providential failure.* Lucilla thought only: *Schwangyu and Geasa complicated my task.* Neither woman gave even a passing moment to the way these thoughts reaffirmed their loyalties.

As she watched the child in the courtyard, Lucilla began to have a new appreciation of what the Tyrant God Emperor had actually achieved. Leto II had employed this ghola-type through uncounted lifetimes—some thirty-five hundred years of them, one after another. And the God Emperor Leto II had been no ordinary force of nature. He had been the biggest juggernaut in human history, rolling over everything: over social systems, over natural and unnatural hatreds, over governmental forms, over rituals (both taboo and mandatory), over religions casual and religions intense. The crushing weight of the Tyrant's passage had left nothing unmarked, not even the Bene Gesserit.

Leto II had called it "The Golden Path" and this Duncan Idaho–type ghola below her now had figured prominently in that awesome passage. Lucilla had studied the

Bene Gesserit accounts, probably the best in the universe. Even today on most of the old Imperial Planets, newly married couples still scattered dollops of water east and west, mouthing the local version of "Let Thy blessings flow back to us from this offering, O God of Infinite Power and Infinite Mercy."

Once, it had been the task of Fish Speakers and their tame priesthood to enforce such obeisance. But the thing had developed its own momentum, becoming a pervasive compulsion. Even the most doubting of believers said: "Well, it can do no harm." It was an accomplishment that the finest religious engineers of the Bene Gesserit Missionaria Protectiva admired with frustrated awe. The Tyrant had surpassed the Bene Gesserit best. And fifteen hundred years since the Tyrant's death, the Sisterhood remained powerless to unlock the central knot of that fearsome accomplishment.

"Who has charge of the child's religious training?" Lucilla asked.

"No one," Schwangyu said. "Why bother? If he is reawakened to his original memories, he will have his own ideas. We will deal with those if we ever have to."

The child below them completed his allotted training time. Without another look up at the watchers on the parapet, he left the enclosed yard and entered a wide doorway on the left. Patrin, too, abandoned his guard position without glancing at the two Reverend Mothers.

"Don't be fooled by Teg's people," Schwangyu said. "They have eyes in the backs of their heads. Teg's birthmother, you know, was one of us. He is teaching that ghola things better never shared!"

Explosions are also compressions of time. Observable changes in the natural universe all are explosive to some degree and from some point of view; otherwise you would not notice them. Smooth Continuity of change, if slowed sufficiently, goes without notice by observers whose time/attention span is too short. Thus, I tell you, I have seen changes you would never have marked.

— LETO II

The woman standing in Chapter House Planet's morning light across the table from the Reverend Mother Superior Alma Mavis Taraza was tall and supple. The long aba robe that encased her in shimmering black from shoulders to floor did not completely conceal the grace with which her body expressed every movement.

Taraza leaned forward in her chairdog and scanned the Records Relay projecting its condensed Bene Gesserit glyphs above the tabletop for her eyes only.

"Darwi Odrade," the display identified the standing woman, and then came the essential biography, which Taraza already knew in detail. The display served several purposes—it provided a secure reminder for the Mother Superior, it allowed an occasional delay for thought while she appeared to scan the records, and it was a final argument should something negative arise from this interview.

Odrade had borne nineteen children for the Bene Gesserit, Taraza observed as the information scrolled past her eyes. Each child by a different father. Not much unusual about that, but even the most searching gaze could see that this essential service to the Sisterhood had not grossened Odrade's flesh. Her features conveyed a natural hauteur in the long nose and the complementary angular cheeks. Every feature focused downward to a narrow chin. Her mouth, though, was full and promised a passion that she was careful to bridle.

We can always depend on the Atreides genes, Taraza thought.

A window curtain fluttered behind Odrade and she glanced back at it. They were in Taraza's morning room, a small and elegantly furnished space decorated in shades of green. Only the stark white of Taraza's chairdog separated her from the background. The room's bow windows looked eastward onto garden and lawn with faraway snowy mountains of Chapter House Planet as backdrop.

Without looking up, Taraza said: "I was glad when both you and Lucilla accepted the assignment. It makes my task much easier."

"I would like to have met this Lucilla," Odrade said, looking down at the top of Taraza's head. Odrade's voice came out a soft contralto.

Taraza cleared her throat. "No need. Lucilla is one of our finest Imprinters. Each of you, of course, received the identical liberal conditioning to prepare you for this."

There was something almost insulting in Taraza's casual tone and only the habits of long association put down Odrade's immediate resentment. It was partly that word "liberal," she realized. Atreides ancestors rose up in rebellion at the word. It was as though her accumulated female memories lashed out at the unconscious assumptions and unexamined prejudices behind the concept.

"Only liberals really think. Only liberals are intellectual. Only liberals understand the needs of their fellows."

How much viciousness lay concealed in that word! Odrade thought. How much secret ego demanding to feel superior.

Odrade reminded herself that Taraza, despite the casually insulting tone, had used the term only in its catholic sense: Lucilla's generalized education had been carefully matched to that of Odrade.

Taraza leaned back into a more comfortable position but still kept her attention on the display in front of her. The light from the eastern windows fell directly on her face, leaving shadows beneath nose and chin. A small woman just a bit older than Odrade, Taraza retained much of the beauty that had made her a most reliable breeder with difficult sires. Her face was a long oval with soft curved cheeks. She wore her black hair drawn back tightly from a high forehead with a pronounced peak. Taraza's mouth opened minimally when she spoke: superb control of movement. An observer's attention tended to focus on her eyes: that compelling blue-in-blue. The total effect was of a suave facial mask from which little escaped to betray her true emotions.

Odrade recognized this present pose in the Mother Superior. Taraza would mutter to herself presently. Indeed, right on cue, Taraza muttered to herself.

The Mother Superior was thinking while she followed

the biographical display with great attention. Many matters occupied her attention.

This was a reassuring thought to Odrade. Taraza did not believe there was any such thing as a beneficent power guarding humankind. The Missionaria Protectiva and the intentions of the Sisterhood counted for everything in Taraza's universe. Whatever served those intentions, even the machinations of the long-dead Tyrant, could be judged good. All else was evil. Alien intrusions from the Scattering—especially those returning descendants who called themselves "Honored Matres"—were not to be trusted. Taraza's own people, even those Reverend Mothers who opposed her in Council, were the ultimate Bene Gesserit resource, the only thing that could be trusted.

Still without looking up, Taraza said: "Do you know that when you compare the millennia preceding the Tyrant with those after his death, the decrease in major conflicts is phenomenal. Since the Tyrant, the number of such conflicts has dropped to less than two percent of what it was before."

"As far as we know," Odrade said.

Taraza's gaze flicked upward and then down. "What?"

"We have no way of telling how many wars have been fought outside our ken. Have you statistics from the people of the Scattering?"

"Of course not!"

"Leto tamed us is what you're saying," Odrade said.

"If you care to put it that way." Taraza inserted a marker in something she saw on her display.

"Shouldn't some of the credit go to our beloved Bashar Miles Teg?" Odrade asked. "Or to his talented predecessors?"

"We chose those people," Taraza said.

"I don't see the pertinence of this martial discussion," Odrade said. "What does it have to do with our present problem?"

"There are some who think we may revert to the pre-Tyrant condition with a very nasty bang."

"Oh?" Odrade pursed her lips.

"Several groups among our returning Lost Ones are selling arms to anyone who wants to or *can* buy."

"Specifics?" Odrade asked.

"Sophisticated arms are flooding onto Gammu and there can be little doubt the Tleilaxu are stockpiling some of the nastier weapons."

Taraza leaned back and rubbed her temples. She spoke in a low, almost musing voice. "We think we make decisions of the greatest moment and out of the very highest principles."

Odrade had seen this before, too. She said: "Does the Mother Superior doubt the rightness of the Bene Gesserit?"

"Doubt? Oh, no. But I do experience frustration. We work all of our lives for these highly refined goals and in the end, what do we find? We find that many of the things to which we have dedicated our lives came from petty decisions. They can be traced to desires for personal comfort or convenience and had nothing at all to do with our high ideals. What really was at stake was some worldly working agreement that satisfied the needs of those who *could* make the decisions."

"I've heard you call that political necessity," Odrade said.

Taraza spoke with tight control while returning her

attention to the display in front of her. "If we become institutionalized in our judgments, that's a sure way to extinguish the Bene Gesserit."

"You will not find petty decisions in my bio," Odrade said.

"I look for sources of weakness, for flaws."

"You won't find those, either."

Taraza concealed a smile. She recognized this egocentric remark: Odrade's way of needling the Mother Superior. Odrade was very good at seeming to be impatient while actually suspending herself in a timeless flow of patience.

When Taraza did not rise to the bait, Odrade resumed her calm waiting—easy breaths, the mind steady. Patience came without thinking of it. The Sisterhood had taught her long ago how to divide past and present into simultaneous flowings. While observing her immediate surroundings, she could pick up bits and pieces of her past and live through them as though they moved across a screen superimposed over the present.

Memory work, Odrade thought. Necessary things to haul out and lay to rest. Removing the barriers. When all else palled, there was still her tangled childhood.

There had been a time when Odrade lived as most children lived: in a house with a man and woman who, if not her parents, certainly acted in loco parentis. All of the other children she knew then lived in similar situations. They had *papas* and *mamas.* Sometimes only papa worked away from home. Sometimes only mama went out to her labors. In Odrade's case, the woman remained at home and no crèche nurse guarded the child in the working hours. Much later, Odrade learned that her birth mother had given a large sum of money to provide this for the infant female hidden in plain sight that way.

"She hid you with us because she loved you," the woman explained when Odrade was old enough to understand. "That is why you must never reveal that we are not your real parents."

Love had nothing to do with it, Odrade learned later. Reverend Mothers did not act from such mundane motives. And Odrade's birth-mother had been a Bene Gesserit Sister.

All of this was revealed to Odrade according to the original plan. Her name: Odrade. Darwi was what she had always been called when the caller was not being endearing or angry. Young friends naturally shortened it to Dar.

Everything, however, did not go according to the original plan. Odrade recalled a narrow bed in a room brightened by paintings of animals and fantasy landscapes on the pastel blue walls. White curtains fluttered at the window in the soft breezes of spring and summer. Odrade remembered jumping on the narrow bed—a marvelously happy game: up, down, up, down. Much laughter. Arms caught her in mid leap and hugged her close. They were a man's arms. a round face with a small mustache that tickled her into giggles. The bed thumped the wall when she jumped and the wall revealed indentations from this movement.

Odrade played over this memory now, reluctant to discard it into the well of rationality. Marks on a wall. Marks of laughter and joy. How small they were to represent so much.

Odd how she had been thinking more and more

about papa recently. All of the memories were not happy. There had been times when he had been sad-angry, warning mama not to become "too involved." He had a face that reflected many frustrations. His voice barked when he was in his angry mood. Mama moved softly then, her eyes full of worry. Odrade sensed the worry and the fear and resented the man. The woman knew best how to deal with him. She kissed the nape of his neck, stroked his cheek and whispered into his ear.

These ancient "natural" emotions had engaged a Bene Gesserit analyst-proctor in much work with Odrade before they were exorcised. But even now there was residual detritus to pick up and discard. Even now, Odrade knew that all of it was not gone.

Seeing the way Taraza studied the biographical record with such care, Odrade wondered if that was the flaw the Mother Superior saw.

Surely they know by now that I can deal with the emotions of those early times.

It was all so long ago. Still, she had to admit that the memory of the man and woman lay within her, bonded with such force that it might never be erased completely. Especially mama.

The Reverend Mother in extremis who had borne Odrade had put her in that hiding place on Gammu for reasons Odrade now understood quite well. Odrade harbored no resentments. It had been necessary for the survival of them both. Problems arose from the fact that the foster mother gave Odrade that thing which most mothers give their children, that thing which the Sisterhood so distrusted—love.

When the Reverend Mothers came, the foster mother had not fought the removal of *her* child. Two Reverend Mothers came with a contingent of male and female proctors. Afterward Odrade was a long time understanding the significance of that wrenching moment. The woman had known in her heart that the day of parting would come. Only a matter of time. Still, as the days became years—almost six standards of years—the woman had dared to hope.

Then the Reverend Mothers came with their burly attendants. They had merely been waiting until it was safe, until they were sure no hunters knew this was a Bene Gesserit–planned Atreides scion.

Odrade saw a great deal of money passed to the foster mother. The woman threw the money on the floor. But no voice was raised in objection. The adults in the scene knew where the power lay.

Calling up those compressed emotions, Odrade could still see the woman take herself to a straight-backed chair beside the window onto the street, there to hug herself and rock back and forth, back and forth. Not a sound from her.

The Reverend Mothers used Voice and their considerable wiles plus the smoke of drugging herbs and their overpowering presence to lure Odrade into their waiting groundcar.

"It will be just for a little while. Your real mother sent us."

Odrade sensed the lies but curiosity compelled. *My real mother!*

Her last view of the woman who had been her only

known female parent was of that figure at the window rocking back and forth, a look of misery on her face, arms wrapped around herself.

Later, when Odrade spoke of returning to the woman, that memory-vision was incorporated into an essential Bene Gesserit lesson.

"Love leads to misery. Love is a very ancient force, which served its purpose in its day but no longer is essential for the survival of the species. Remember that woman's mistake, the pain."

Until well into her teens, Odrade adjusted by daydreaming. She would *really* return after she was a full Reverend Mother. She would go back and find that loving woman, find her even though she had no names except "mama" and "Sibia." Odrade recalled the laughter of adult friends who had called the woman "Sibia."

Mama Sibia.

The Sisters, however, detected the daydreams and searched out their source. That, too, was incorporated into a lesson.

"Daydreaming is the first awakening of what we call simulflow. It is an essential tool of rational thought. With it you can clear the mind for better thinking."

Simulflow.

Odrade focused on Taraza at the morning room table. Childhood trauma must be placed carefully into a reconstructed memory-place. All of that had been far away on Gammu, the planet that the people of Dan had rebuilt after the Famine Times and the Scattering. The people of Dan—Caladan in those days. Odrade took a firm grip on rational thought, using the stance of the Other Memories that had flooded into her awareness during the spice agony when she had really become a full Reverend Mother.

Simulflow . . . the filter of consciousness . . . Other Memories.

What powerful tools the Sisterhood had given her. What dangerous tools. All of those other lives lay there just beyond the curtain of awareness, tools of survival, not a way to satisfy casual curiosity.

Taraza spoke, translating from the material that scrolled past her eyes: "You dig too much in your Other Memories. That drains away energies better conserved."

The Mother Superior's blue-in-blue eyes sent a piercing stare upward at Odrade. "You sometimes go right to the edge of fleshly tolerance. That can lead to your premature death."

"I am careful with the spice, Mother."

"And well you should be! A body can take only so much melange, only so much prowling in its past!"

"Have you found my flaw?" Odrade asked.

"Gammu!" One word but an entire harangue.

Odrade knew. The unavoidable trauma of those lost years on Gammu. They were a distraction that had to be rooted out and made rationally acceptable.

"But I am sent to Rakis," Odrade said.

"And see that you remember the aphorisms of moderation. Remember who you are!"

Once more, Taraza bent to her display.

I am Odrade, Odrade thought.

In the Bene Gesserit schools where first names tended to slip away, roll call was by last name. Friends and acquaintances picked up the habit of using the roll-call name. They learned early that sharing secret or private names was an ancient device for ensnaring a person in affections.

Taraza, three classes ahead of Odrade, had been assigned to "bring the younger girl along," a deliberate association by watchful teachers.

"Bringing along" meant a certain amount of lording it over the younger but also incorporated essentials better taught by someone closer to peer relationship. Taraza, with access to the private records of her trainee, started calling the younger girl "Dar." Odrade responded by calling Taraza "Tar." The two names acquired a certain glue—Dar and Tar. Even after Reverend Mothers overheard and reprimanded them, they occasionally lapsed into error if only for the amusement.

Odrade, looking down at Taraza now, said: "Dar and Tar."

A smile twitched the edges of Taraza's mouth.

"What is it in my records that you don't already know several times over?" Odrade asked.

Taraza sat back and waited for the chairdog to adjust itself to the new position. She rested her clasped hands on the tabletop and looked up at the younger woman.

Not much younger, really, Taraza thought.

Since school, though, Taraza had thought of Odrade as completely removed into a younger age group, creating a gap no passage of years could close.

"Care at the beginning, Dar," Taraza said.

"This project is well past its beginning," Odrade said.

"But your part in it starts now. And we are launching ourselves into such a beginning as has never before been attempted."

"Am I now to learn the entire design for this ghola?"

"No."

That was it. All the evidence of high-level dispute and the "need to know" cast away with a single word. But Odrade understood. There was an organizational rubric laid down by the original Bene Gesserit Chapter House, which had endured with only minor changes for millennia. Bene Gesserit divisions were cut by hard vertical and horizontal barriers, divided into isolated groups that converged to a single command only here at the top. Duties (for which read "assigned roles") were conducted within separated cells. Active participants within a cell did not know their contemporaries within other parallel cells.

But I know that the Reverend Mother Lucilla is in a parallel cell, Odrade thought. *It's the logical answer.*

She recognized the necessity. It was an ancient design copied from secret revolutionary societies. The Bene Gesserit had always seen themselves as permanent revolutionaries. It was a revolution that had been dampened only in the time of the Tyrant, Leto II.

Dampened, but not diverted or stopped, Odrade reminded herself.

"In what you're about to do," Taraza said, "tell me if you sense any immediate threat to the Sisterhood."

It was one of Taraza's *peculiar* demands, which Odrade had learned to answer out of wordless instinct, which then could be formed into words. Quickly, she said: "If we fail to act, that is worse."

"We reasoned that there would be danger," Taraza said. She spoke in a dry, remote voice. Taraza did not like calling up this talent in Odrade. The younger woman possessed a prescient instinct for detecting threats to the

Sisterhood. It came from the wild influence in her genetic line, of course—the Atreides with their dangerous talents. There was a special mark on Odrade's breeding file: "Careful examination of all offspring." Two of those offspring had been quietly put to death.

I should not have awakened Odrade's talent now, not even for a moment, Taraza thought. But sometimes temptation was very great.

Taraza sealed the projector into her tabletop and looked at the blank surface while speaking. "Even if you find a perfect sire, you are not to breed without our permission while you are away from us."

"The mistake of my natural mother," Odrade said.

"The mistake of your natural mother was to be recognized while she was breeding!"

Odrade had heard this before. There was that thing about the Atreides line that required the most careful monitoring by the breeding mistresses. The wild talent, of course. She knew about the wild talent, that genetic force which had produced the Kwisatz Haderach and the Tyrant. What did the breeding mistresses seek now, though? Was their approach mostly negative? No more dangerous births! She had never seen any of her babies after they were born, not necessarily a curious thing for the Sisterhood. And she never saw any of the records in her own genetic file. Here, too, the Sisterhood operated with careful separation of powers.

And those earlier prohibitions on my Other Memories!

She had found the blank spaces in her memories and opened them. It was probable that only Taraza and perhaps two other councillors (Bellonda, most likely, and one other older Reverend Mother) shared the more sensitive access to such breeding information.

Had Taraza and the other really sworn to die before revealing privileged information to an outsider? There was, after all, a precise ritual of succession should a key Reverend Mother die while away from her Sisters and with no chance to pass along her encapsulated lives. The ritual had been called into play many times during the reign of the Tyrant. A terrible period! Knowing that the revolutionary cells of the Sisterhood were transparent to him! Monster! She knew that her sisters had never deluded themselves that Leto II refrained from destroying the Bene Gesserit out of some deep seated loyalty to his grandmother, the Lady Jessica.

Are you there, Jessica?

Odrade felt the stirring far within. The failure of one Reverend Mother: "She allowed herself to fall in love!" Such a small thing but how great the consequences. Thirty-five hundred years of tyranny!

The Golden Path. Infinite? What of the lost megatrillions gone into the Scattering? What threat was posed by those Lost Ones returning now?

As though she read Odrade's mind, which sometimes she appeared to do, Taraza said: "The Scattered ones are out there . . . just waiting to pounce."

Odrade had heard the arguments: Danger on the one hand and on the other, something magnetically attractive. So many magnificent unknowns. The Sisterhood with its talents honed by melange over the millennia— what might they not do with such untapped resources of humanity? Think of the uncounted genes out there!

Think of the potential talents floating free in universes where they might be lost forever!

"It's the not knowing that conjures up the greatest terrors," Odrade said.

"And the greatest ambitions," Taraza said.

"Then do I go to Rakis?"

"In due course. I find you adequate to the task."

"Or you would not have assigned me."

It was an old exchange between them, going right back to their school days. Taraza realized, though, that she had not entered it consciously. Too many memories tangled the two of them: Dar and Tar. Have to watch that!

"Remember where your loyalties are," Taraza said.

The existence of no-ships raises the possibility of destroying entire planets without retaliation. A large object, asteroid or equivalent, may be sent against the planet. Or the people can be set against each other by sexual subversion, and then can be armed to destroy themselves. These Honored Matres appear to favor this latter technique.

—BENE GESSERIT ANALYSIS

From his position in the courtyard and even when not appearing to do so, Duncan Idaho kept his attention on the observers above him. There was Patrin, of course, but Patrin did not count. It was the Reverend Mothers across from Patrin who bore watching. Seeing Lucilla, he thought: *That's the new one.* This thought filled him with a surge of excitement, which he took out in renewed exercise.

He completed the first three patterns of the training-play Miles Teg had ordered, vaguely aware that Patrin would report on how well he did. Duncan liked Teg and old Patrin and sensed that the feeling was reciprocated. This new Reverend Mother, though—her presence suggested interesting changes. For one thing, she was younger than the others. Also, this new one did not try to hide the eyes that were a first clue to her membership in the Bene Gesserit. His first glimpse of Schwangyu had confronted him with eyes concealed behind contact lenses that simulated non-addict pupils and slightly bloodshot whites. He had heard one of the Keep's acolytes say Schwangyu's lenses also corrected for "an astigmatic weakness that has been accepted in her genetic line as a reasonable exchange for the other qualities she transmits to her offspring."

At the time, most of this remark was unintelligible to Duncan but he had looked up the references in the Keep's library, references both scarce and severely limited in content. Schwangyu herself parried all of his questions on the subject, but the subsequent behavior of his teachers told him she had been angry. Typically, she had taken out her anger on others.

What really upset her, he suspected, was his demand to know whether she was his mother.

For a long time now Duncan had known he was something special. There were places in the elaborate compound of this Bene Gesserit Keep where he was not permitted. He had found private ways to evade such prohibitions and had stared out often through thick plaz and open windows at guards and wide reaches of cleared ground that could be enfiladed from strategically positioned pillboxes. Miles Teg himself had taught the significance of enfilade positioning.

Gammu, the planet was called now. Once, it had been known as Giedi Prime but someone named Gurney Halleck had changed that. It was all ancient history. Dull stuff. There still remained a faint smell of bitter oil in the planet's dirt from its pre-Danian days. Millennia of special plantations were changing that, his teachers explained. He could see part of this from the Keep. Forests of conifers and other trees surrounded them here.

Still covertly watching the two Reverend Mothers, Duncan did a series of cartwheels. He flexed his striking muscles as he moved, just the way Teg had taught him.

Teg also instructed in planetary defenses. Gammu was ringed by orbiting monitors whose crews could not have their families aboard. The families remained down here on Gammu, hostage to the vigilance of those guardian orbiters. Somewhere among the ships in space, there were undetectable no-ships whose crews were composed entirely of the Bashar's people and Bene Gesserit Sisters.

"I would not have taken this assignment without full charge of all defensive arrangements," Teg explained.

Duncan realized that *he* was "this assignment." The Keep was here to protect him. Teg's orbiting monitors, including the no-ships, protected the Keep.

It was all part of a military education whose elements Duncan found somehow familiar. Learning how to defend a seemingly vulnerable planet from attacks originating in space, he *knew* when those defenses were correctly placed. It was extremely complicated as a whole but the elements were identifiable and could be understood. There was, for instance, the constant monitoring of atmosphere and the blood serum of Gammu's inhabitants. Suk doctors in the pay of the Bene Gesserit were everywhere.

"Diseases are weapons," Teg said. "Our defense against diseases must be finely tuned."

Frequently, Teg railed against passive defenses. He

called them "the product of a siege mentality long known to create deadly weaknesses."

When it came to military instructions from Teg, Duncan listened carefully. Patrin and the library records confirmed that the Mentat Bashar Miles Teg had been a famous military leader for the Bene Gesserit. Patrin often referred to their service together and always Teg was the hero.

"Mobility is the key to military success," Teg said. "If you're tied down in forts, even whole-planet forts, you are ultimately vulnerable."

Teg did not much care for Gammu.

"I see that you already know this place was called Giedi Prime once. The Harkonnens who ruled here taught us a few things. We have a better idea, thanks to them, of how terrifyingly brutal humans can become."

As he recalled this, Duncan observed that the two Reverend Mothers watching from the parapet obviously were discussing him.

Am I the new one's assignment?

Duncan did not like being watched and he hoped the new one would allow him some time to himself. She did not look like a tough one. Not like Schwangyu.

As he continued his exercises, Duncan timed them to a private litany: *Damn Schwangyu! Damn Schwangyu!*

He had hated Schwangyu from the age of nine—four years now. She did not know his hate, he thought. She had probably forgotten all about the incident where his hate had been ignited.

Barely nine and he had managed to slip through the inner guards out into a tunnel that led to one of the pillboxes. Smell of fungus in the tunnel. Dim lights.

Dampness. He peered out through the box's weapons slits before being caught and hustled back into the core of the Keep.

This escapade occasioned a stern lecture from Schwangyu, a remote and threatening figure whose orders must be obeyed. That was how he still thought of her, although he had since learned about the Bene Gesserit Voice-of-Command, that vocal subtlety which could bend the will of an untrained listener.

She must be obeyed.

"You have occasioned the disciplining of an entire guard unit," Schwangyu said. "They will be severely punished."

That had been the most terrible part of her lecture. Duncan liked some of the guards and occasionally lured some of them into real play with laughter and tumbling. His prank, sneaking out to the pillbox, had hurt his friends.

Duncan knew what it was to be punished.

Damn Schwangyu! Damn Schwangyu! . . .

After Schwangyu's lecture, Duncan ran to his chief instructor of the moment, Reverend Mother Tamalane, another of the wizened old ones with a cool and aloof manner, snowy hair above a narrow face and a leather skin. He demanded of Tamalane to know about the punishment of his guards. Tamalane fell into a surprising pensive mood, her voice like sand rasping against wood.

"Punishments? Well, well."

They were in the small teaching room off the larger practice floor where Tamalane went each evening to prepare the next day's lessons. It was a place of bubble and spool readers and other sophisticated means for information storage and retrieval. Duncan far preferred it to the library but he was not allowed in the teaching room unattended. It was a bright room lighted by many suspensor-buoyed glowglobes. At his intrusion, Tamalane turned away from where she laid out his lessons.

"There's always something of a sacrificial banquet about our major punishments," she said. "The guards will, of course, receive major punishment."

"Banquet?" Duncan was puzzled.

Tamalane swung completely around in her swivel seat and looked directly into his eyes. Her steely teeth glittered in the bright lights. "History has seldom been good to those who must be punished," she said.

Duncan flinched at the word "history." It was one of Tamalane's signals. She was going to teach a lesson, another boring lesson.

"Bene Gesserit punishments cannot be forgotten."

Duncan focused on Tamalane's old mouth, sensing abruptly that she spoke out of painful personal experience. He was going to learn something interesting!

"Our punishments carry an inescapable lesson," Tamalane said. "It is much more than the pain."

Duncan sat on the floor at her feet. From this angle, Tamalane was a black-shrouded and ominous figure.

"We do not punish with the ultimate agony," she said. "That is reserved for a Reverend Mother's passage through the spice."

Duncan nodded. Library records referred to "spice agony," a mysterious trial that created a Reverend Mother.

"Major punishments are painful, nonetheless," she said. "They are also emotionally painful. Emotion evoked by punishment is always that emotion we judge to be the penitent's greatest weakness, and thus we strengthen the punished."

Her words filled Duncan with unfocused dread. What were they doing to his guards? He could not speak but there was no need. Tamalane was not finished.

"The punishment always ends with a dessert," she said and she clapped her hands against her knees.

Duncan frowned. Dessert? That was part of a banquet. How could a banquet be punishment?

"It is not really a banquet but the idea of a banquet," Tamalane said. One clawlike hand described a circle in the air. "The dessert comes, something totally unexpected. The penitent thinks: *Ahhh, I have been forgiven at last!* You understand?"

Duncan shook his head from side to side. No, he did not understand.

"It is the sweetness of the moment," she said. "You have been through every course of a painful banquet and come out at the end to something you can savor. But! As you savor it, *then* comes the most painful moment of all, the recognition, the *understanding* that this is not pleasure-at-the-end. No, indeed. This is the ultimate pain of the major punishment. It locks in the Bene Gesserit lesson."

"But what will she do to those guards?" The words were wrenched from Duncan.

"I cannot say what the specific elements of the individual punishments will be. I have no need to know. I can only tell you it will be different for each of them."

Tamalane would say no more. She returned to laying out the next day's lessons. "We will continue tomorrow," she said, "teaching you to identify the sources of the various accents of spoken Galach."

No one else, not even Teg or Patrin, would answer his questions about the punishments. Even the guards, when he saw them afterward, refused to speak of their ordeals. Some reacted curtly to his overtures and none would play with him anymore. There was no forgiveness among the punished. That much was clear.

Damn Schwangyu! Damn Schwangyu! . . .

That was where his deep hatred of her began. All of the old witches shared in his hatred. Would the new young one be the same as the old ones?

Damn Schwangyu!

When he demanded of Schwangyu: "Why did you have to punish them?" Schwangyu took some time before answering, then: "It is dangerous for you here on Gammu. There are people who wish you harm."

Duncan did not ask why. This was another area where his questions were never answered. Not even Teg would answer, although Teg's very presence emphasized the fact of that danger.

And Miles Teg was a Mentat who must know many answers. Duncan often saw the old man's eyes glisten while his thoughts went far away. But there was no Mentat response to such questions as:

"Why are we here on Gammu?"

"Who do you guard against? Who wants to harm me?"

"Who are my parents?"

Silence greeted such questions or sometimes Teg would growl: "I cannot answer you."

The library was useless. He had discovered this when he was only eight and his chief instructor was a failed

Reverend Mother named Luran Geasa—not quite as ancient as Schwangyu but well along in years, more than a hundred, anyway.

At his demand, the library produced information about Gammu/Giedi Prime, about the Harkonnens and their fall, about various conflicts where Teg had commanded. None of those battles came through as very bloody; several commentators referred to Teg's "superb diplomacy." But, one datum leading to another, Duncan learned about the time of the God Emperor and the taming of his people. This period commanded Duncan's attention for weeks. He found an old map in the records and projected it on the focus wall. The commentator's superimpositions told him that this very Keep had been a Fish Speaker Command Center abandoned during the Scattering.

Fish Speakers!

Duncan wished then that he had lived during their time, serving as one of the rare male advisors in the female army that had worshiped the great God Emperor.

Oh, to have lived on Rakis in those days!

Teg was surprisingly forthcoming about the God Emperor, calling him always "the Tyrant." A library lock was opened and information about Rakis came pouring out for Duncan.

"Will I ever see Rakis?" he asked Geasa.

"You are being prepared to live there."

The answer astonished him. Everything they taught him about that faraway planet came into new focus.

"Why will I live there?"

"I cannot answer that."

With renewed interest, he returned to his studies of

that mysterious planet and its miserable Church of Shai-hulud, the Divided God. *Worms.* The God Emperor had become those worms! The idea filled Duncan with awe. Perhaps here was something worthy of worship. The thought touched a chord in him. What had driven a man to accept that terrible metamorphosis?

Duncan knew what his guards and the others in the Keep thought about Rakis and the core of priesthood there. Sneering remarks and laughter told it all. Teg said: "We'll probably never know the whole truth of it, but I tell you, lad, that's no religion for a soldier."

Schwangyu capped it: "You are to learn about the Tyrant but you are not to believe in his religion. That is beneath you, contemptible."

In every spare study moment, Duncan pored over whatever the library produced for him: the Holy Book of the Divided God, the Guard Bible, the Orange Catholic Bible and even the Apocrypha. He learned about the long defunct Bureau of the Faith and "The Pearl that IS the Sun of Understanding."

The very idea of the worms fascinated him. Their size! A big one would stretch from one end of the Keep to the other. Men had ridden the pre-Tyrant worms but the Rakian priesthood forbade this now.

He found himself gripped by accounts from the archeological team that had found the Tyrant's primitive no-chamber on Rakis. Dar-es-Balat, the place was called. The reports by Archeologist Hadi Benotto were marked "Suppressed by orders of the Rakian Priesthood." The file number on the accounts from Bene Gesserit Archives was a long one and what Benotto revealed was fascinating.

"A kernel of the God Emperor's awareness in each worm?" he asked Geasa.

"So it's said. And even if true, they are not conscious, not aware. The Tyrant himself said he would enter an endless dream."

Each study session occasioned a special lecture and Bene Gesserit explanations of religion until finally he encountered those accounts called "The Nine Daughters of Siona" and "The Thousand Sons of Idaho."

Confronting Geasa, he demanded: "My name is Duncan Idaho, too. What does that mean?"

Geasa always moved as though standing in the shadow of her failure, her long head bent forward and her watery eyes aimed at the ground. The confrontation occurred near evening in the long hall outside the practice floor. She paled at his question.

When she did not answer, he demanded: "Am I descended from Duncan Idaho?"

"You must ask Schwangyu." Geasa sounded as though the words pained her.

It was a familiar response and it angered him. She meant he would be told something to shut him up, little information in the telling. Schwangyu, however, was more open than expected.

"You carry the authentic blood of Duncan Idaho."

"Who are my parents?"

"They are long dead."

"How did they die?"

"I do not know. We received you as an orphan."

"Then why do people want to harm me?"

"They fear what you may do."

"What is it I may do?"

"Study your lessons. All will be made clear to you in time."

Shut up and study! Another familiar answer.

He obeyed because he had learned to recognize when the doors were closed on him. But now his questing intelligence met other accounts of the Famine Times and the Scattering, the no-chambers and no-ships that could not be traced, not even by the most powerful prescient minds in their universe. Here, he encountered the fact that descendants of Duncan Idaho and Siona, those ancients who had served the Tyrant God Emperor, also were invisible to prophets and prescients. Not even a Guild Steersman deep in melange trance could detect such people. Siona, the accounts told him, was a true-bred Atreides and Duncan Idaho was a ghola.

Ghola?

He probed the library for elaborations on this peculiar word. *Ghola.* The library produced for him no more than bare-boned accounts: *"Gholas: humans grown from a cadaver's cells in Tleilaxu axlotl tanks."*

Axlotl tanks?

"A Tleilaxu device for reproducing a living human being from the cells of a cadaver."

"Describe a ghola," he demanded.

"Innocent flesh devoid of its original memories. See Axlotl Tanks."

Duncan had learned to read the silences, the blank places in what the people of the Keep revealed to him. Revelation swept over him. He knew! Only ten and he knew!

I am a ghola.

Late afternoon in the library, all of the esoteric

machinery around him faded into a sensory background, and a ten-year-old sat silently before a scanner hugging the knowledge to himself.

I am a ghola!

He could not remember the axlotl tanks where his cells had grown into an infant. His first memories were of Geasa picking him up from his cradle, the alert interest in those adult eyes that had so soon faded into wary lidding.

It was as though the information so grudgingly supplied him by the Keep's people and records had at last defined a central shape: himself.

"Tell me about the Bene Tleilax," he demanded of the library.

"They are a people self-divided into Face Dancers and Masters. Face Dancers are mules, sterile and submissive to the Masters."

Why did they do this to me?

The information machines of the library were suddenly alien and dangerous. He was afraid, not that his questions might meet more blank walls, but that he would receive answers.

Why am I so important to Schwangyu and the others?

He felt that they had wronged him, even Miles Teg and Patrin. Why was it right to take the cells of a human and produce a ghola?

He asked the next question with great hesitation. "Can a ghola ever remember who he was?"

"It can be done."

"How?"

"The psychological identity of ghola to original pre-sets certain responses, which can be ignited by trauma."

No answer at all!

"But how?"

Schwangyu intruded at this point, arriving at the library unannounced. So something about his questions had been set to alert her!

"All will be made clear to you in time," she said.

She talked down to him! He sensed the injustice in it, the lack of truthfulness. Something within him said he carried more human wisdom in his unawakened self than the ones who presumed themselves so superior. His hatred of Schwangyu reached a new intensity. She was the personification of all who tantalized him and frustrated his questions.

Now, though, his imagination was on fire. He would recapture his original memories! He felt the truth of this. He would remember his parents, his family, his friends . . . his enemies.

He demanded it of Schwangyu: "Did you produce me because of my enemies?"

"You have already learned silence, child," she said. "Rely on that knowledge."

Very well. That's how I will fight you, damned Schwangyu. I will be silent and I will learn. I won't show you how I really feel.

"You know," she said, "I think we're raising a stoic."

She patronized him! He would not be patronized. He would fight them all with silence and watchfulness. Duncan ran from the library and huddled in his room.

In the following months, many things confirmed that he was a ghola. Even a child knew when things around him were extraordinary. He saw other children occasionally beyond the walls, walking along the perimeter road, laughing and calling. He found accounts of children in the library. Adults did not come to those children and engage them in rigorous training of the sort imposed on him. Other children did not have a Reverend Mother Schwangyu to order every smallest aspect of their lives.

His discovery precipitated another change in Duncan's life. Luran Geasa was called away from him and did not return.

She was not supposed to let me know about gholas.

The truth was somewhat more complex, as Schwangyu explained to Lucilla on the observation parapet the day of Lucilla's arrival.

"We knew the inevitable moment would come. He would learn about gholas and ask the pointed questions."

"It was high time a Reverend Mother took over his everyday education. Geasa may have been a mistake."

"Are you questioning my judgment?" Schwangyu snapped.

"Is your judgment so perfect that it may never be questioned?" In Lucilla's soft contralto, the question had the impact of a slap.

Schwangyu remained silent for almost a minute. Presently, she said: "Geasa thought the ghola was an endearing child. She cried and said she would miss him."

"Wasn't she warned about that?"

"Geasa did not have our training."

"So you replaced her with Tamalane at that time. I do not know Tamalane but I presume she is quite old."

"Quite."

"What was his reaction to the removal of Geasa?"

"He asked where she had gone. We did not answer."

"How did Tamalane fare?"

"On his third day with her, he told her very calmly: 'I hate you. Is that what I'm supposed to do?'"

"So quickly!"

"Right now, he's watching you and thinking: I hate Schwangyu. Will I have to hate this new one? But he is also thinking that you are not like the other old witches. You're young. He will know that this must be important."

Humans live best when each has his place to stand, when each knows where he belongs in the scheme of things and what he may achieve. Destroy the place and you destroy the person.

—BENE GESSERIT TEACHING

Miles Teg had not wanted the Gammu assignment. Weapons master to a ghola-child? Even such a ghola-child as this one, with all of the history woven around him. It was an unwanted intrusion into Teg's well-ordered retirement.

But he had lived all of that life as a Military Mentat under the will of the Bene Gesserit and could not compute an act of disobedience.

Quis custodiet ipsos custodiet?

Who shall guard the guardians? Who shall see that the guardians commit no offenses?

This was a question that Teg had considered carefully on many occasions. It formed one of the basic tenets of his loyalty to the Bene Gesserit. Whatever else you might say about the Sisterhood, they displayed an admirable constancy of purpose.

Moral purpose, Teg labeled it.

The Bene Gesserit moral purpose agreed completely with Teg's principles. That those principles were Bene Gesserit–conditioned in him did not enter into the question. Rational thought, especially Mentat rationality, could make no other judgment.

Teg boiled it down to an essence: If only one person followed such guiding principles, this was a better universe. It was never a question of justice. Justice required resort to law and that could be a fickle mistress, subject always to the whims and prejudices of those who administered the laws. No, it was a question of fairness, a concept that went much deeper. The people upon whom judgment was passed must feel the fairness of it.

To Teg, statements such as "the letter of the law must be observed" were dangerous to his guiding principles. Being fair required agreement, predictable constancy and, above all else, loyalty upward and downward in the hierarchy. Leadership guided by such principles required no outside controls. You did your duty because it was right. And you did not obey because that was *predictably* correct. You did it because the rightness was a thing of this moment. Prediction and prescience had nothing whatsoever to do with it.

Teg knew the Atreides reputation for reliable prescience, but gnomic utterances had no place in his universe. You took the universe as you found it and applied your principles where you could. Absolute commands in the hierarchy were always obeyed. Not that Taraza had made it a question of absolute command, but the implications were there.

"You are the perfect person for this task."

He had lived a long life with many high points and he was retired with honor. Teg knew he was old, slow and with all the defects of age waiting just at the edges of his awareness, but the call to duty quickened him even while he was forced to put down the wish to say "No."

The assignment had come from Taraza personally. The powerful senior of all (including the Missionaria Protectiva) singled him out. Not just a Reverend Mother but *the* Reverend Mother Superior.

Taraza came to his retirement sanctuary on Lernaeus. It honored him for her to do this and he knew it. She appeared at his gate unannounced, accompanied only by two acolyte servers and a small guard force, some of whose faces he recognized. Teg had trained them himself. The time of her arrival was interesting. Morning, shortly after his breakfast. She knew the patterns of his life and certainly knew that he was most alert at this hour. So she wanted him awake and at his fullest capabilities.

Patrin, Teg's old batman, brought Taraza into the east wing sitting room, a small and elegant setting with only solid furniture in it. Teg's dislike of chairdogs and other living furniture was well known. Patrin had a sour look on his face as he ushered the black-robed Mother Superior into the room. Teg recognized the look immediately. Patrin's long, pale face with its many age wrinkles might appear an unmoved mask to others, but Teg was alert to the deepened wrinkles beside the man's mouth, the set stare in the old eyes. So Taraza had said something on the way in here that had disturbed Patrin.

Tall sliding doors of heavy plaz framed the room's eastward view down a long sloping lawn to trees beside the river. Taraza paused just inside the room to admire the view.

Without being told, Teg touched a button. Curtains

slid across the view and glowglobes came alight. Teg's action told Taraza he had computed a need for privacy. He emphasized this by ordering Patrin: "Please see that we are not disturbed."

"The orders for the South Farm, sir," Patrin ventured.

"Please see to that yourself. You and Firus know what I want."

Patrin closed the door a little too sharply as he left, a tiny signal but it spoke much to Teg.

Taraza moved a pace into the room and examined it. "Lime green," she said. "One of my favorite colors. Your mother had a fine eye."

Teg warmed to the remark. He had a deep affection for this building and this land. His family had been here only three generations but their mark was on the place. His mother's touches had not really been changed in many rooms.

"It's safe to love land and places," Teg said.

"I particularly liked the burnt orange carpets in the hall and the stained glass fanlight over the entry door," Taraza said. "That fanlight is a real antique, I am sure."

"You did not come here to talk about interior decoration," Teg said.

Taraza chuckled.

She had a high-pitched voice, which the Sisterhood's training had taught her to use with devastating effectiveness. It was not a voice easy to ignore, even when she appeared most carefully casual as she did now. Teg had seen her in Bene Gesserit Council. Her manner there was powerful and persuasive, every word an indicator of the incisive mind that guided her decisions. He could sense an important decision beneath her demeanor now.

Teg indicated a green upholstered chair at his left. She glanced at it, swept her gaze once more around the room and suppressed a smile.

Not a chairdog in the house, she would wager. Teg was an antique surrounding himself with antiques. She seated herself and smoothed her robe while waiting for Teg to take a matching chair facing her.

"I regret the need to ask that you come out of retirement, Bashar," she said. "Unfortunately, circumstances give me little choice."

Teg rested his long arms casually on his chair's arms, a Mentat in repose, waiting. His attitude said: "Fill my mind with data."

Taraza was momentarily abashed. This was an imposition. Teg was still a regal figure, tall and with that large head topped by gray hair. He was, she knew, four SY short of three hundred. Granting that the Standard Year was some twenty hours less than the so-called primitive year, it was still an impressive age with experiences in Bene Gesserit service that demanded that she respect him. Teg wore, she noted, a light gray uniform with no insignia: carefully tailored trousers and jacket, white shirt open at the throat to reveal a deeply wrinkled neck. There was a glint of gold at his waist and she recognized the Bashar's sunburst he had received at retirement. How like the utilitarian Teg! He had made the golden bauble into a belt buckle. This reassured her. Teg would understand her problem.

"Could I have a drink of water?" Taraza asked. "It has been a long and tiresome journey. We came the last stage by one of our transports, which we should have replaced five hundred years ago."

Teg lifted himself from the chair, went to a wall panel and removed a chilled water bottle and glass from a cabinet behind the panel. He put these on a low table at Taraza's right hand. "I have melange," he said.

"No, thank you, Miles. I've my own supply."

Teg resumed his seat and she noted the signs of stiffness. He was still remarkably supple, however, considering his years.

Taraza poured herself a half glass of water and drank it in one swallow. She replaced the glass on the side table with elaborate care. How to approach this? Teg's manner did not fool her. He did not want to leave retirement. Her analysts had warned her about that. Since retirement, he had taken more than a casual interest in farming. His extensive acreage here on Lernaeus was essentially a research garden.

She lifted her gaze and studied him openly. Square shoulders accentuated Teg's narrow waist. He still kept himself active then. That long face with its sharp lines from the strong bones: typically Atreides. Teg returned her gaze as he always did, demanding attention but open to whatever the Mother Superior might say. His thin mouth was cocked into a slight smile, exposing bright and even teeth.

He knows I'm uncomfortable, she thought. *Damn it! He's just as much a servant of the Sisterhood as I am!*

Teg did not prompt her with questions. His manner remained impeccable, curiously withdrawn. She reminded herself that this was a common trait of Mentats and nothing else should be read into it.

Abruptly, Teg stood and strode to a sideboard at Taraza's left. He turned, folded his arms across his breast and leaned there looking down at her.

Taraza was forced to swivel her chair to face him. *Damn him!* Teg was not going to make this any easier for her. All of the Reverend Mother Examiners had remarked a difficulty in getting Teg to sit for conversation. He preferred to stand, his shoulders held with military stiffness, his gaze aimed downward. Few Reverend Mothers matched his height—more than two meters. This trait, the analysts agreed, was Teg's way (probably unconscious) of protesting the Sisterhood's authority over him. None of this, however, showed itself in his other behavior. Teg had always been the most reliable military commander the Sisterhood had ever employed.

In a multisociety universe whose major binding forces interacted with complexity despite the simplicity of labels, reliable military commanders were worth their weight in melange many times over. Religions and the common memory of imperial tyrannies always figured in the negotiations but it was economic forces that eventually carried the day and the military *coin* could be entered on anybody's adding machine. It was there in every negotiation and would be for as long as necessity drove the trading system—the need for particular things (such as spice or the technoproducts of Ix), the need for specialists (such as Mentats or Suk doctors), and all of the other mundane needs for which there were markets: for labor forces, for builders, for designers, for planiformed life, for artists, for exotic pleasures . . .

No legal system could bind such complexity into a whole and this fact quite obviously brought up another necessity—the constant need for arbiters with clout. Reverend Mothers had naturally fallen into this role within the economic web and Miles Teg knew this. He also knew that he was once more being brought out as a bargaining chip. Whether he enjoyed that role did not figure in the negotiations.

"It's not as though you had any family to hold you here," Taraza said.

Teg accepted this silently. Yes, his wife had been dead thirty-eight years now. His children were all grown and, with the exception of one daughter, gone from the nest. He had his many personal interests but no family obligations. True.

Taraza reminded him then of his long and faithful service to the Sisterhood, citing several memorable achievements. She knew the praise would have little effect on him but it provided her with a needed opening for what must follow.

"You have been apprised of your familial resemblance," she said.

Teg inclined his head no more than a millimeter.

"Your resemblance to the first Leto Atreides, grandfather of the Tyrant, is truly remarkable," she said.

Teg gave no sign that he heard or agreed. This was merely a datum, something already stored in his copious memory. He knew he bore Atreides genes. He had seen the likeness of Leto I at Chapter House. It had been oddly like looking into a mirror.

"You're a bit taller," Taraza said.

Teg continued to stare down at her.

"Damn it all, Bashar," Taraza said, "will you at least try to help me?"

"Is that an order, Mother Superior?"

"No, it's not an order!"

Teg smiled slowly. The fact that Taraza allowed herself

such an explosion in front of him said many things. She would not do that with people she felt were untrustworthy. And she certainly would not permit herself such an emotional display with a person she considered *merely* an underling.

Taraza sat back in her chair and grinned up at him. "All right," she said. "You've had your fun. Patrin said you would be most upset with me if I called you back to duty. I assure you that you are crucial to our plans."

"What plans, Mother Superior?"

"We are raising a Duncan Idaho ghola on Gammu. He is almost six years old and ready for military education."

Teg allowed his eyes to widen slightly.

"It will be a taxing duty for you," Taraza said, "but I want you to take over his training and protection as soon as possible."

"My likeness to the Atreides Duke," Teg said. "You will use me to restore his original memories."

"In eight or ten years, yes."

"That long!" Teg shook his head. "Why Gammu?"

"His prana-bindu inheritance has been altered by the Bene Tleilax, at our orders. His reflexes will match in speed those of anyone born in our times. Gammu . . . the original Duncan Idaho was born and raised there. Because of the changes in his cellular inheritance we must keep all else as close to the original conditions as possible."

"Why are you doing this?" It was a Mentat's data-conscious tone.

"A female child with the ability to control the worms had been discovered on Rakis. We will have use for our ghola there."

"You will breed them?"

"I am not engaging you as a Mentat. It is your military abilities and your likeness to the original Leto that we need. You know how to restore his original memories when the time comes."

"So you're really bringing me back as a Weapons Master."

"You think that's a comedown for the man who was Supreme Bashar of all our forces?"

"Mother Superior, you command and I obey. But I will not accept this post without full command of all of Gammu's defenses."

"That already has been arranged, Miles."

"You always did know how my mind works."

"And I've always been confident of your loyalty."

Teg pushed himself away from the sideboard and stood a moment in thought, then: "Who will brief me?"

"Bellonda from Records, the same as before. She will provide you with a cipher to secure the exchange of messages between us."

"I will give you a list of people," Teg said. "Old comrades and the children of some of them. I will want all of them waiting on Gammu when I arrive."

"You don't think any of them will refuse?"

His look said: *"Don't be silly!"*

Taraza chuckled and she thought: *There's a thing we learned well from the original Atreides—how to produce people who command the utmost devotion and loyalty.*

"Patrin will handle the recruiting," Teg said. "He won't accept rank, I know, but he's to get the full pay and courtesies of a colonel-aide."

"You will, of course, be restored to the rank of Supreme Bashar," she said. "We will . . ."

"No. You have Burzmali. We will not weaken him by bringing back his old Commander over him."

She studied him a moment, then: "We have not yet commissioned Burzmali as . . ."

"I am well aware of that. My old comrades keep me fully informed of Sisterhood politics. But you and I, Mother Superior, know it's only a matter of time. Burzmali is the best."

She could only accept this. It was more than a military Mentat's assessment. It was Teg's assessment. Another thought struck her.

"Then you already knew about our dispute in Council!" she accused. "And you let me . . ."

"Mother Superior, if I thought you would produce another monster on Rakis, I would have said so. You trust my decisions; I trust yours."

"Damn you, Miles, we've been apart too long." Taraza stood. "I feel calmer just knowing you'll be back in harness."

"Harness," he said. "Yes. Reinstate me as a Bashar on special assignment. That way, when word gets back to Burzmali, there'll be no silly questions."

Taraza produced a sheaf of ridulian papers from beneath her robe and passed them to Teg. "I've already signed these. Fill in your own reinstatement. The other authorizations are all there, transport vouchers and so on. I give you these orders personally. You are to obey me. You are *my* Bashar, do you understand?"

"Wasn't I always?" he asked.

"It's more important than ever now. Keep that ghola safe and train him well. He's your responsibility. And I will back you in that against anyone."

"I hear Schwangyu commands on Gammu."

"Against anyone, Miles. Don't trust Schwangyu."

"I see. Will you lunch with us? My daughter has . . ."

"Forgive me, Miles, but I must get back soonest. I will send Bellonda at once."

Teg saw her to the door, exchanged a few pleasantries with his old students in her party and watched as they left. They had an armored groundcar waiting in the drive, one of the new models that they obviously had brought with them. Sight of it gave Teg an uneasy feeling.

Urgency!

Taraza had come in person, the Mother Superior herself on a messenger's errand, knowing what that would reveal to him. Knowing so intimately how the Sisterhood performed, he saw the revelation in what had just happened. The dispute in the Bene Gesserit Council went far deeper than his informants had suggested.

"You are my Bashar."

Teg glanced through the sheaf of authorizations and vouchers Taraza had left with him. Already carrying her seal and signature. The trust this implied added to the other things he sensed and increased his disquiet.

"Don't trust Schwangyu."

He slipped the papers into his pocket and went in search of Patrin. Patrin would have to be briefed, and mollified. They would have to discuss whom to call in for this assignment. He began to list some of the names in his mind. Dangerous duty ahead. It called for only the best people. Damn! Everything on the estate here would have to be passed over to Firus and Dimela. So many details! He felt his pulse quicken as he strode through the house.

Passing a house guard, one of his old soldiers, Teg paused: "Martin, cancel all of my appointments for today. Find my daughter and tell her to meet me in my study."

Word spread through the house and, from there, across the estate. Servants and family, knowing that *The* Reverend Mother Superior had just conversed privately with him, automatically set up a protective screen to keep idle distractions away from Teg. His eldest daughter, Dimela, cut him short when he tried to list details necessary to carry on his experimental farm projects.

"Father, I am not an infant!"

They were in the small greenhouse attached to his study. Remains of Teg's lunch sat on the corner of a potting bench. Patrin's notebook was propped against the wall behind the luncheon tray.

Teg looked sharply at his daughter. Dimela favored him in appearance but not in height. Too angular to be a beauty but she had made a good marriage. They had three fine children, Dimela and Firus.

"Where is Firus?" Teg asked.

"He's out seeing to the replanting of the South Farm."

"Oh, yes. Patrin mentioned that."

Teg smiled. It had always pleased him that Dimela had refused the Sisterhood's bid, preferring to marry Firus, a native of Lernaeus, and remain in her father's entourage.

"All I know is that they're calling you back to duty," Dimela said. "Is it a dangerous assignment?"

"You know, you sound exactly like your mother," Teg said.

"So it is dangerous! Damn them, haven't you done enough for them?"

"Apparently not."

She turned away from him as Patrin entered the far end of the greenhouse. He heard her speak to Patrin as they passed.

"The older he gets the more he gets like a Reverend Mother himself!"

What else could she expect? Teg wondered. The son of a Reverend Mother, fathered by a minor functionary of the Combine Honnete Ober Advancer Mercantiles, he had matured in a household that moved to the Sisterhood's beat. It had been apparent to him at an early age that his father's allegiance to CHOAM's interplanetary trading network vanished when his mother objected.

This house had been his mother's house until her death less than a year after his father died. The imprint of her choices lay all around him.

Patrin stopped in front of him. "I came back for my notebook. Have you added any names?"

"A few. You'd better get right on it."

"Yes, sir!" Patrin did a smart about-face and strode back the way he had come, slapping the notebook against his leg.

He feels it, too, Teg thought.

Once more, Teg glanced around him. This house was still his mother's place. After all the years he had lived here, raised a family here! Still her place. Oh, he had built this greenhouse, but the study there had been her private room.

Janet Roxbrough of the Lernaeus Roxbroughs. The furnishings, the decor, still her place. Taraza had seen that.

He and his wife had changed some of the surface objects, but the core remained Janet Roxbrough's. No question about the Fish Speaker blood in that lineage. What a prize she had been for the Sisterhood! That she had wed Loschy Teg and lived out her life here, that was the oddity. An undigestible fact until you knew how the Sisterhood's breeding designs worked over the generations.

They've done it again, Teg thought. *They've had me waiting in the wings all these years just for this moment.*

Has not religion claimed a patent on creation for all of these millennia?

—THE TLEILAXU QUESTION,
FROM MUAD'DIB SPEAKS

The air of Tleilax was crystalline, gripped by a stillness that was part the morning chill and part a sense of fearful crouching, as though life waited out there in the city of Bandalong, life anticipating and ravenous, which would not stir until it received his personal signal. The Mahai, Tylwyth Waff, Master of the Masters, enjoyed this hour more than any other of the day. The city was his now as he looked out through his open window. Bandalong would come alive only at his command. This was what he told himself. The fear that he could sense out there was his hold on any reality that might arise from that incubating reservoir of life: the Tleilaxu civilization that had originated here and then spread its powers afar.

They had waited millennia for this time, his people. Waff savored the moment now. All through the bad times of the Prophet Leto II (not God Emperor but God's Messenger), all through the Famines and the Scattering, through every painful defeat at the hands of lesser creatures, through all of those agonies the Tleilaxu had built their patient forces for this moment.

We have come to our moment, O Prophet!

The city that lay beneath his high window he saw as a symbol, one strong mark on the page of Tleilaxu design. Other Tleilaxu planets, other great cities, interlinked, interdependent, and with central allegiance to his God and his city, awaited the signal that all of them knew must come soon. The twinned forces of Face Dancers and Masheikh had compressed their powers in preparation for the cosmic leap. The millennia of waiting were about to end.

Waff thought of it as "the long beginning."

Yes. He nodded to himself as he looked at the crouching city. From its inception, from that infinitesimal kernel of an idea, Bene Tleilax leaders had understood the perils of a plan so extended, so protracted, so convoluted and subtle. They had known they must surmount near disaster time and again, accept galling losses, submissions and humiliations. All of this and much more had gone into the construction of a particular Bene Tleilax image. By those millennia of pretense they had created a myth.

"The vile, detestable, dirty Tleilaxu! The stupid Tleilaxu! The predictable Tleilaxu! The impetuous Tleilaxu!"

Even the Prophet's minions had fallen prey to this myth. A captive Fish Speaker had stood in this very room and shouted at a Tleilaxu Master: "Long pretense creates a reality! You are truly vile!" So they had killed her and the Prophet did nothing.

How little all of those alien worlds and peoples understood Tleilaxu restraint. Impetuosity? Let them reconsider after the Bene Tleilax demonstrated how many millennia they were capable of waiting for their ascendancy.

"Spannungsbogen!"

Waff rolled the ancient word on his tongue: *The span of the bow!* How far back you draw the bow before releasing your arrow. This arrow would strike deep!

"The Masheikh have waited longer than any other," Waff whispered. He dared to utter the word to himself here in his tower fastness: "Masheikh."

The rooftops below him glittered as the sun lifted. He could hear the stirrings of the city's life. The sweet bitterness of Tleilaxu smells drifted on the air coming in his window. Waff inhaled deeply and closed his window.

He felt renewed by his moment of solitary observation. Turning away from the window, he donned the white khilat robe of honor to which all Domel were conditioned to bow. The robe completely covered his short body, giving him the distinct feeling that it actually was armor.

The armor of God!

"We are the people of the Yaghist," he had reminded his councillors only last night. "All else is frontier. We have fostered the myth of our weakness and evil practices for these millennia with only one purpose. Even the Bene Gesserit believe!"

Seated in the deep, windowless sagra with its no-chamber shield, his nine councillors had smiled in silent appreciation of his words. In the judgment of the ghufran, they knew. The stage upon which the Tleilaxu determined their own destiny had always been the kehl with its right of ghufran.

It was proper that even Waff, the most powerful of all Tleilaxu, could not leave his world and be readmitted without abasing himself in the ghufran, begging pardon for contact with the unimaginable sins of aliens. To go out among the powindah could soil even the mightiest. The khasadars who policed all Tleilaxu frontiers and guarded the selamliks of the women were right to suspect even Waff. He was of the people and the kehl, yes, but he must prove it each time he left the heartland and returned, and certainly every time he entered the selamlik for the distribution of his sperm.

Waff crossed to his long mirror and inspected himself and his robe. To the powindahs, he knew, he appeared an elfin figure barely a meter and a half tall. Eyes, hair, and skin were shades of gray, all a stage for the oval face with its tiny mouth and line of sharp teeth. A Face Dancer might mimic his features and pose, might dissemble at a Masheikh's command, but no Masheikh or khasadar would be fooled. Only the powindahs would be gulled.

Except for the Bene Gesserit!

This thought brought a scowl to his face. Well, the witches had yet to encounter one of the new Face Dancers.

No other people have mastered the genetic language as well as have the Bene Tleilax, he reassured himself. *We are right to call it "the language of God," for God Himself has given us this great power.*

Waff strode to his door and waited for the morning bell. There was no way, he thought, to describe the richness of emotion he felt now. Time unfolded for him. He did not ask why the Prophet's true message had been heard only by the Bene Tleilax. It had been God's doing and, in that, the Prophet had been the Arm of God, worthy of respect as God's Messenger.

You prepared them for us, O Prophet.

And the ghola on Gammu, this ghola at this time, was worth all of the waiting.

The morning bell sounded and Waff strode out into the hall, turned with other emerging white-robed figures and went onto the eastern balcony to greet the sun. As the Mahai and Abdl of his people, he now could identify himself with all Tleilaxu.

We are the legalists of the Shariat, the last of our kind in the universe.

Nowhere outside the sealed chambers of his malik-brothers could he reveal such a secret thought but he knew it was a thought shared in every mind around him now, and the workings of that thought were visible in Masheikh, Domel and Face Dancer alike. The paradox of kinship ties and a sense of social identity that permeated the khel from Masheikh down to the lowliest Domel was not a paradox to Waff.

We work for the same God.

A Face Dancer in the guise of Domel had bowed and opened the balcony doors. Waff, emerging into sunlight with his many companions close around, smiled at recognition of the Face Dancer. *A Domel yet!* It was a kin-joke but Face Dancers were not kin. They were constructs, tools, just as the ghola on Gammu was a tool, all designed with the language of God spoken only by Masheikhs.

With the others who pressed close around him Waff made obeisance to the sun. He uttered the cry of the Abdl and heard it echoed by countless voices from the farthest reaches of the city.

"The sun is not God!" he shouted.

No, the sun was only a symbol of God's infinite powers and mercy—another construct, another tool. Feeling cleansed by his passage through the ghufran the previous night, renewed by the morning ritual, Waff could think now about the trip outward to powindah places and the return just completed, which had made ghufran necessary. Other worshipers made way for him as he went back to the inner corridors and entered the slide passage that dropped him to the central garden where he had asked his councillors to meet him.

It was a successful foray among the powindah, he thought.

Every time he left the inner worlds of the Bene Tleilax Waff felt himself to be on lashkar, a war party seeking that ultimate revenge which his people named secretly as Bodal (always capitalized and always the first thing reaffirmed in ghufran or khel). This most recent lashkar had been exquisitely successful.

Waff emerged from the slide into a central garden filled with sunlight by prismatic reflectors on the surrounding rooftops. A small fountain played its visual fugue at the heart of a graveled circle. A low fence of white palings at one side enclosed a closely cropped lawn, a space near enough to the fountain that the air would be moist but not so close that the splashing water would intrude on low-voiced conversation. Around the grassy enclosure, ten narrow benches of an ancient plastic were arranged—nine of them in a semicircle facing a tenth bench set slightly apart.

Pausing at the edge of the grassy enclosure, Waff glanced around him, wondering why he had never before felt quite this intense pleasure at sight of the place. The dark blue of the benches was intrinsic to the material. Centuries of use had worn the benches into soft curves along the arm rests and where countless bottoms had planted themselves, but the color was just as strong in the worn places as it was elsewhere.

Waff sat down facing his nine councillors, marshaling the words he knew he must use. The document he had brought back from his latest lashkar, indeed, the very reason for that excursion, could not have been more exquisitely timed. The label on it and the words carried a mighty message for the Tleilaxu.

From an inner pocket Waff removed the thin sheaf of ridulian crystal. He noted the quickened interest of his councillors: nine faces similar to his own, Masheikhs of the innermost kehl. All reflected expectancy. They had read this document in kehl: "The Atreides Manifesto." They had spent a night of reflection on the manifesto's message. Now, the words must be confronted. Waff placed the document on his lap.

"I propose to spread these words far and wide," Waff said.

"Without change?" That was Mirlat, the councillor closest to ghola-transformation among all of them. Mirlat no doubt aspired to Abdl and Mahai. Waff focused on the councillor's wide jaws where the cartilage had grown over the centuries as a visible mark of his current body's great age.

"Exactly as it has come into our hands," Waff said.

"Dangerous," Mirlat said.

Waff turned his head to the right, his childlike profile outlined against the fountain for his councillors to observe. *God's hand is on my right!* The sky above him was polished carnelian as though Bandalong, the most ancient city of the Tleilaxu, had been built under one of those gigantic artificial covers erected to protect pioneers on the harsher planets. When he returned his attention to his councillors, Waff's features remained bland.

"Not dangerous to us," he said.

"A matter of opinion," Mirlat said.

"Then let us consider opinions," Waff said. "Have we a need to fear Ix or the Fish Speakers? Indeed not. They are ours, although they do not know it."

Waff let this sink in; all of them knew that new Face Dancers sat in the highest councils of Ix and Fish Speakers, the exchange undetected.

"The Guild will not move against us or oppose us because we are their only secure source of melange," Waff said.

"Then what of these Honored Matres returned from the Scattering?" Mirlat demanded.

"We will deal with them when it is required of us," Waff said. "And we will be helped by the descendants of our own people who voluntarily went out into the Scattering."

"The time does appear opportune," one of the other councillors murmured.

It was Torg the Younger who had spoken, Waff observed. Good. There was a vote secured.

"The Bene Gesserit!" Mirlat snapped.

"I think the Honored Matres will remove the witches from our path," Waff said. "Already they growl against each other like animals in the fighting pit."

"What if the author of that manifesto is identified?" Mirlat demanded. "What then?"

Several heads nodded among the councillors. Waff marked them: people to be won over.

"It is dangerous to be called Atreides in this age," he said.

"Except perhaps on Gammu," Mirlat said. "And the name Atreides has been signed to that document!"

How odd, Waff thought. The CHOAM representative at the powindah conference that had taken Waff away from the inner planets of Tleilax had emphasized that very point. But most of CHOAM's people were secret atheists who looked on all religion as suspect, and certainly the Atreides had been a potent religious force. CHOAM worries had been almost palpable.

Waff recounted this CHOAM reaction now.

"This CHOAM hireling, damn his Godless soul, is right," Mirlat insisted. "The document's insidious."

Mirlat will have to be dealt with, Waff thought. He lifted the manifesto from his lap and read the first line aloud:

"In the beginning was the word and the word was God."

"Directly from the Orange Catholic Bible," Mirlat said. Once more, heads nodded in worried agreement.

Waff showed the points of his canines in a brief smile. "Do you suggest that there are those among the powindah who suspect the existence of the Shariat and the Masheikhs?"

It felt good to speak these words openly, reminding his listeners that only here among the innermost Tleilaxu were the old words and the old language preserved without change. Did Mirlat or any of the others fear that Atreides words could subvert the Shariat?

Waff posed this question, too, and saw the worried frowns.

"Is there one among you," Waff asked, "who believes that a single powindah knows how we use the language of God?"

There! Let them think on that! Every one of them here had been wakened time after time in ghola flesh. There was a fleshly continuity in this Council that no other people had ever achieved. Mirlat himself had seen the Prophet with his own eyes. Scytale had spoken to Muad'Dib! Learning how the flesh could be renewed and the memories restored, they had condensed this power into a single government whose potency was confined lest it be demanded everywhere. Only the witches had a similar storehouse of experience upon which to draw and they moved with fearful caution, terrified that they might produce another Kwisatz Haderach!

Waff said these things to his councillors, adding: "The time for action has come."

When no one spoke disagreement, Waff said: "This manifesto has a single author. Every analysis agrees. Mirlat?"

"Written by one person and that person a true Atreides, no doubt of it," Mirlat agreed.

"All at the powindah conference affirmed this," Waff said. "Even a third-stage Guild steersman agrees."

"But that one person has produced a thing that excites violent reactions among diverse peoples," Mirlat argued.

"Have we ever questioned the Atreides talent for disruption?" Waff asked. "When the powindah showed me this document I knew God had sent us a signal."

"Do the witches still deny authorship?" Torg the Younger asked.

How alertly apt he is, Waff thought.

"Every powindah religion is called into question by this manifesto," Waff said. "Every faith except ours is left hanging in limbo."

"Exactly the problem!" Mirlat pounced.

"But only we know this," Waff said. "Who else even suspects the existence of the Shariat?"

"The Guild," Mirlat said.

"They have never spoken of it and they never will. They know what our response would be."

Waff lifted the sheaf of papers from his lap and again read aloud:

"Forces that we cannot understand permeate our universe. We see the shadows of those forces when they are projected upon a screen available to our senses, but understand them we do not."

"The Atreides who wrote that knows of the Shariat," Mirlat muttered.

Waff continued reading as though there had been no interruption:

"Understanding requires words. Some things cannot be reduced to words. There are things that can only be experienced wordlessly."

As though he handled a holy relic, Waff returned the document to his lap. Softly, so that his listeners were required to bend toward him and some cupped a hand behind an ear, Waff said: "This says our universe is magical. It says all arbitrary forms are transient and subject to magical changes. Science has led us to this interpretation as though it placed us on a track from which we cannot deviate."

He allowed these words to fester for a moment, then: "No Rakian priest of the Divided God nor any other powindah charlatan can accept that. Only we know it because our God is a magical God whose language we speak."

"We will be accused of the authorship," Mirlat said. The moment he had spoken, Mirlat shook his head sharply from side to side. "No! I see it. I see what you mean."

Waff held his silence. He could see that all of them were reflecting on their Sufi origins, recalling the Great Belief and the Zensunni ecumenism that had spawned the Bene Tleilax. The people of this kehl knew the God-given facts of their origins but generations of secrecy assured that no powindah shared their knowledge.

Words flowed silently through Waff's mind: *"Assumptions based on understanding contain belief in an absolute ground out of which all things spring like plants growing from seeds."*

Knowing that his councillors also recalled this cate chism of the Great Belief, Waff reminded them of the Zensunni admonition.

"Behind such assumptions lies a faith in words that the powindah do not question. Only the Shariat question and we do so silently."

His councillors nodded in unison.

Waff inclined his head slightly and continued: "The act of saying that things exist that cannot be described in words shakes a universe where words are the supreme belief."

"Powindah poison!" his councillors shouted.

He had them all now and Waff hammered home his victory by demanding: "What is the Sufi-Zensunni Credo?"

They could not speak it but all reflected on it: *To*

achieve s'tori no understanding is needed. S'tori exists
without words, without even a name.

In a moment, all of them looked up and exchanged
knowing glances. Mirlat took it upon himself to recite the
Tleilaxu pledge:

"I can say God, but that is not my God. That is only
a noise and no more potent than any other noise."

"I now see," Waff said, "that you all sense the power
that has fallen into our hands through this document.
Millions upon millions of copies already are being circu-
lated among the powindah."

"Who does this?" Mirlat asked.

"Who cares?" Waff countered. "Let the powindah
chase after them, seeking their origin, trying to suppress
them, preaching against them. With each such action,
the powindah inject more power into these words."

"Should we not preach against these words, too?"
Mirlat asked.

"Only if the occasion demands it," Waff said. "See
you!" He slapped the papers against his knees. "The
powindah have constricted their awareness to its tightest
purpose and that is their weakness. We must insure that
this manifesto gains as wide a circulation as possible."

"The magic of our God is our only bridge," the councillors intoned.

All of them, Waff observed, had been restored to the
central security of their faith. It had been easily managed. No Masheikh shared the powindah stupidity that
whined: "In thy infinite grace, God, why me?" In one
sentence, the powindah invoked infinity and denied it,
never once observing their own foolishness.

"Scytale," Waff said.

The youngest and most baby-faced of the councillors, seated at the far left as was fitting, leaned forward eagerly.

"Arm the faithful," Waff said.

"I marvel that an Atreides has given us this weapon," Mirlat said. "How can it be that the Atreides always fasten upon an ideal that enlists the billions who must follow?"

"It is not the Atreides, it is God," Waff said. He lifted his arms then and spoke the closing ritual: "The Masheikh have met in kehl and felt the presence of their God."

Waff closed his eyes and waited for the others to leave. *Masheikh!* How good it was to name themselves in kehl, speaking the language of Islamiyat, which no Tleilaxu spoke outside his own secret councils; not even to Face Dancers did they speak it. Nowhere in the Weklu of Jandola, not to the farthest reaches of the Tleilaxu Yaghist, was there a living powindah who knew this secret.

Yaghist, Waff thought, rising from his bench. *Yaghist, the land of the unruled.*

He thought he could feel the document vibrating in his hand. This Atreides Manifesto was the very kind of thing the masses of powindah would follow to their doom.

Some days it's melange; some days it's bitter dirt.

—RAKIAN APHORISM

In her third year with the priests of Rakis, the girl Sheeana lay full length atop a high curving dune. She peered into the morning distance where a great rumbling friction could be heard. The light was a ghostly silver that frosted the horizon with filmy haze. The night's chill still lay on the sand.

She knew the priests were watching her from the safety of their water-girded tower some two kilometers behind her, but this gave her little concern. The trembling of the sand beneath her body demanded full attention.

It's a big one, she thought. *Seventy meters at least. A beautiful big one.*

The gray stillsuit felt slick and smooth against her skin. It had none of the abrasive patches of the old hand-me-down she had worn before the priests took her into their care. She felt thankful for the fine stillsuit and the thick robe of white and purple that covered it, but most of all she felt the excitement of being here. Something rich and dangerous filled her at moments such as this.

The priests did not understand what happened here.

She knew this. They were cowards. She glanced over her shoulder at the distant tower and saw sunglint on lenses.

A precocious child of eleven standard years, slender and dark-skinned with sun-streaked brown hair, she could visualize clearly what the priests saw through their spying lenses.

They see me doing what they do not dare. They see me in the path of Shaitan. I look very small on the sand and Shaitan looks very big. They can see him already.

From the rasping sound, she knew that she, too, would soon see the giant worm. Sheeana did not think of the approaching monster as Shai hulud, God of the sands, a thing the priests chanted each morning in obeisance to the pearl of Leto II's awareness that lay encapsulated in each of the multi-ridged rulers of the desert. She thought of the worms mainly as "they who spared me," or as Shaitan.

They belonged to her now.

It was a relationship begun slightly more than three years ago during the month of her eighth birthday, the Month Igat by the old calendar. Her village had been a poor one, a pioneer venture built far beyond more secure barriers such as the qanats and ring canals of Keen. Only a moat of damp sand guarded such pioneer places. Shaitan avoided water but the sandtrout vector soon took away any dampness. Precious moisture captured in windtraps had to be expended each day to renew the barrier. Her village was a miserable cluster of shacks and hovels with two small windtraps, adequate for drinking water but with only a sporadic surplus that could be apportioned to the worm barrier.

That morning—much like this morning, the night's chill sharp in her nose and lungs, the horizon constricted by a ghostly haze—most of the village children had fanned out into the desert, there to seek bits and fragments of melange, which Shaitan sometimes left behind in his passage. Two big ones had been heard nearby in the night. Melange, even at modern deflated prices, could buy the glazed bricks to line a third windtrap.

Each searching child not only looked for the spice but also sought those signs which would reveal one of the old Fremen sietch strongholds. There were only remnants of such places now but the rock barriers provided a greater security against Shaitan. And some of the remnant sietch places were reputed to contain lost hoards of melange. Every villager dreamed of such a discovery.

Sheeana, wearing her patched stillsuit and flimsy robe, went alone to the northeast, toward the faraway smoky mound of air that told of the great city of Keen with its moisture richness lifting into the sun-warmed breezes.

Hunting scraps of melange in the sand was largely a matter of focusing attention into the nostrils. It was a form of concentration that left only bits of awareness attuned to the rasping sand that told of Shaitan's approach. Leg muscles moved automatically in the non-rhythmic walk that blended with the desert's natural sounds.

At first, Sheeana did not hear the screaming. It fitted intimately into the saltated friction of windblown sand across the barracans that concealed the village from her sight. Slowly the sound penetrated her consciousness and then it demanded her attention.

Many voices screaming!

Sheeana discarded the desert precaution of random strides. Moving swiftly as her childish muscles would carry her, she scrambled up the slipface of the barracan and stared along it toward that terrifying sound. She was in time to see that which cut off the last of the screams.

Wind and sandtrout had dried a wide arc of the barrier at the far side of her village. She could see the gap by the color difference. A wild worm had penetrated the opening. It circled close inside the remaining dampness. The gigantic flame-shadowed mouth scooped up people and hovels in a swiftly tightening circle.

Sheeana saw the last survivors huddled at the center of this destruction, a space already cleared of its rude hovels and tumbled with the remains of the windtraps. Even as she watched, some of the people tried to break away into the desert. Sheeana recognized her father among the frantic runners. None escaped. The great mouth engulfed all before turning to level the last of the village.

Smoking sand remained and nothing else of the puny village that had dared to claim a scrap of Shaitan's domain. The place where the village had been was as unmarked by human habitation as it had been before anyone walked there.

Sheeana took a gasping breath, inhaling through her nose to preserve the moisture of her body as any good child of the desert would do. She scanned the horizon for a sign of the other children but Shaitan's track had left great curves and loops all around the far side of the village. Not a single human remained in view. She shouted, the high-pitched cry that would carry far through the dry air. No response came back to her.

Alone.

She moved trancelike along the ridge of the dune toward where her village had been. As she neared the place a great wave of cinnamon odor filled her nostrils, carried on the wind that still dusted the tops of the dunes. She realized then what had happened. The village had been sited disastrously atop a pre-spice blow. As the great hoard far under the sand came to fruition, expanding in an explosion of melange, Shaitan had come. Every child knew Shaitan could not resist a spiceblow.

Rage and wild desperation began to fill Sheeana. Mindlessly, she raced down the dune toward Shaitan, coming up behind the worm as it turned back through the dry place where it had entered the village. Without thought, she dashed along beside the tail, scrambled onto it and ran forward along the great ridged back. At the hump behind its mouth, she crouched and beat her fists against the unyielding surface.

The worm stopped.

Her anger suddenly converted to terror, Sheeana broke off pounding on the worm. She realized only then that she had been screaming. A terrible sense of lonely exposure filled her. She did not know how she had come here. She knew only where she was and this gripped her with an agony of fear.

The worm continued quiescent on the sand.

Sheeana did not know what to do. At any moment, the worm could roll over and crush her. Or it could burrow beneath the sand, leaving her on the surface to be scooped up at leisure.

Abruptly, a long tremor worked its way down the worm's length from its tail to Sheeana's position behind the mouth. The worm began to move ahead. It turned in a wide arc and gathered speed on a course to the northeast.

Sheeana leaned forward and gripped the leading edge of a ring ridge on the worm's back. She feared that any second it would slide beneath the sand. What could she do then? But Shaitan did not burrow. As minutes passed without any deviation from that straight and swift passage across the dunes, Sheeana found her mind working once more. She knew about this ride. The priests of the Divided God forbade it but the histories, both written and oral, said Fremen rode thus in the ancient days. Fremen stood tall atop Shaitan's back supported by slender poles with hooked ends. The priests decreed that this had been done before Leto II shared His consciousness with the God of the desert. Now, nothing was permitted that might demean the scattered bits of Leto II.

With a speed that astonished her, the worm carried Sheeana toward the mist-dazzled shape of Keen. The great city lay like a mirage on the distorted horizon. Sheeana's threadbare robe whipped against the thin surface of her patched stillsuit. Her fingers ached where she gripped the leading edge of the giant ring. The cinnamon, burnt-rock and ozone of the worm's heat exchange swept over her on shifts in the wind.

Keen began to gain definition ahead of her.

The priests will see me and be angry, she thought.

She identified the low brick structures that marked the first line of qanats and, beyond them, the enclosed barrel-curve of a surface aqueduct. Above these structures rose the walls of terraced gardens and the high profiles of giant windtraps, then the temple complex within its own water barriers.

A day's march across open sand in little more than an hour!

Her parents and village neighbors had made this journey many times for trade and to join in the dancing but Sheeana had only accompanied them twice. She remembered mostly the dancing and the violence that followed. The size of Keen filled her with awe. So many buildings! So many people! Shaitan could not harm such a place as that.

But the worm plunged straight ahead as though it would ride over qanat and aqueduct. Sheeana stared at the city rising higher and higher in front of her. Fascination subdued her terror. Shaitan was not going to stop!

The worm ground to a halt.

The tubular surface vents of the qanat lay no more than fifty meters in front of its gaping mouth. She smelled the hot cinnamon exhalations, heard the deep rumblings of Shaitan's interior furnace.

It became apparent to her at last that the journey had ended. Slowly, Sheeana released her grip on the ring. She stood, expecting any moment the worm would renew its motion. Shaitan remained quiescent. Moving cautiously, she slid off her perch and dropped to the sand. She paused there. Would it move now? She held a vague idea of dashing for the qanat but this worm fascinated her. Slipping and sliding in the disturbed sand, Sheeana moved around to the front of the worm and stared into the fearsome mouth. Within the frame of crystal teeth flames rolled forward and backward. A searing exhalation of spice odors swept over her.

The madness of that first dash down off the dune and onto the worm came back to Sheeana. "Damn you, Shaitan!" she shouted, shaking a fist at the awful mouth. "What did we ever do to you?"

These were words she had heard her mother use at the destruction of a tuber garden. No part of Sheeana's awareness had ever questioned that name, Shaitan, nor her mother's fury. She was of the poorest dregs at the bottom of the Rakian heap and she knew it. Her people believed in Shaitan first and Shai-hulud second. Worms were worms and often much worse. There was no justice on the open sand. Only danger lurked there. Poverty and fear of priests might drive her people onto the perilous dunes but they moved even then with the same angry persistence that had driven the Fremen.

This time, however, Shaitan had won.

It entered Sheeana's awareness that she stood in the deadly path. Her thoughts, not yet fully formed, recognized only that she had done a crazy thing. Much later, as the Sisterhood's teachings rounded her consciousness, she would realize that she had been overcome by the terror of loneliness. She had wanted Shaitan to take her into the company of her dead.

A grating sound issued from beneath the worm.

Sheeana stifled a scream.

Slowly at first, then faster, the worm backed off several meters. It turned there and gathered speed beside the twin-mounded track it had created coming from the desert. The grating of its passage diminished in the distance. Sheeana grew aware of another sound. She lifted her gaze to the sky. The thwock-thwock of a priestly ornithopter swept over her, brushing her with its shadow. The craft glistened in the morning sunlight as it followed the worm into the desert.

Sheeana felt a more familiar fear then.

The priests!

She kept her gaze on the 'thopter. It hovered in the distance, then returned to settle gently onto a patch of worm-smoothed sand nearby. She could smell the lubricants and the sickly acridity of the 'thopter's fuel. The thing was a giant insect nestled on the sand, waiting to pounce upon her.

A hatch popped open.

Sheeana threw back her shoulders and stood her ground. Very well; they had caught her. She knew what to expect now. Nothing could be gained by flight. Only the priests used 'thopters. They could go anywhere and see anything.

Two richly robed priests, their garments all gold and white with purple trim, emerged and ran toward her across the sand. They knelt in front of Sheeana so close she could smell their perspiration and the musky melange incense which permeated their clothing. They were young but much like all the priests she could remember: soft of features, uncalloused hands, careless of their moisture losses. Neither of them wore a stillsuit under those robes.

The one on her left, his eyes on a level with Sheeana's, spoke.

"Child of Shai-hulud, we saw your Father bring you from His lands."

The words made no sense to Sheeana. Priests were men to be feared. Her parents and all the adults she had ever known had impressed this upon her by words and actions. Priests possessed ornithopters. Priests fed you to Shaitan for the slightest infraction or for no infraction at all, for only priestly whims. Her people knew many instances.

Sheeana backed away from the kneeling men and cast her glance around. Where could she run?

The one who had spoken raised an imploring hand. "Stay with us."

"You're bad!" Sheeana's voice cracked with emotion.

Both priests fell prostrate on the sand.

Far away on the city's towers, sunlight flashed off lenses. Sheeana saw them. She knew about such flashings. Priests were always watching you in the cities. When you saw the lenses flash that was the signal to be inconspicuous, to "be good."

Sheeana clasped her hands in front of her to still their trembling. She glanced left and right and then at the prostrate priests. Something was wrong here.

Heads on the sand, the two priests shuddered with fear and waited. Neither spoke.

Sheeana did not know how to respond. The crush of her immediate experiences could not be absorbed by an eight-year-old mind. She knew that her parents and all of her neighbors had been taken by Shaitan. Her own eyes had witnessed this. And Shaitan had brought her here, refusing to take her into his awful fires. She had been spared.

This was a word she understood. *Spared*. It had been explained to her when she learned the dancing song.

"Shai-hulud spare us!

"Take Shaitan away . . ."

Slowly, not wanting to arouse the prostrate priests, Sheeana began the shuffling, unrhythmic movements of the dance. As the remembered music grew within her, she unclasped her hands and swung her arms wide. Her feet lifted high in the stately movements. Her body turned, slowly at first and then more swiftly as the dance ecstasy increased. Her long brown hair whipped around her face.

The two priests dared to lift their heads. The strange child was performing The Dance! They recognized the movements: The Dance of Propitiation. She asked Shai-hulud to forgive His people. She asked God to forgive *them*!

They turned their heads to look at each other and, together, rocked back onto their knees. There, they began clapping in the time-honored effort to distract the dancer. Their hands clapped rhythmically as they chanted the ancient words:

> *"Our fathers ate manna in the desert,*
> *"In the burning places where whirlwinds came!"*

The priests excluded from their attention all except the child. She was a slender thing, they saw, with stringy muscles, thin arms and legs. Her robe and stillsuit were worn and patched like those of the poorest. Her cheekbones had high planes that drew shadows across her olive skin. Brown eyes, they noted. Reddish sun streaks drew their lines in her hair. There was a water-spare sharpness about her features—the narrow nose and chin, the wide forehead, the wide thin mouth, the long neck. She looked like the Fremen portraits in the holy of holies at Dar-es-Balat. Of course! The child of Shai-hulud would look thus.

She danced well, too. Not the slightest quickly repeatable rhythm entered her movements. There was rhythm but it was an admirably long beat, at least a hundred steps apart. She kept it up while the sun lifted higher and higher. It was almost noon before she fell exhausted to the sand.

The priests stood and looked out into the desert

where Shai-hulud had gone. The stampings of the dance had not summoned Him back. They were forgiven.

That was how Sheeana's new life began.

Loudly in their own quarters and for many days, the senior priests engaged in arguments about her. At last, they brought their disputations and reports to the High Priest, Hedley Tuek. They met in the afternoon within the Hall of Small Convocations, Tuek and six priestly councillors. Murals of Leto II, a human face on the great wormshape, looked down upon them with benevolence.

Tuek seated himself on a stone bench that had been recovered from Windgap Sietch. Muad'Dib himself was reputed to have sat on this bench. One of the legs still bore the carvings of an Atreides hawk.

His councillors took lesser modern benches facing him.

The High Priest was an imposing figure; silky gray hair combed smoothly to his shoulders. It was a suitable frame for the square face with its wide, thick mouth and heavy chin. Tuek's eyes retained their original clear whites surrounding dark blue pupils. Bushy, untrimmed gray eyebrows shaded his eyes.

The councillors were a motley lot. Scions of old priestly families, each carried in his heart the belief that matters would move better if *he* were sitting on Tuek's bench.

The scrawny, pinch-faced Stiros put himself forward as opposition spokesman: "She is nothing but a poor desert waif and she rode Shai-hulud. That is forbidden and the punishment is mandatory."

Others spoke up immediately. "No! No, Stiros. You have it wrong! She did not stand on Shai-hulud's back as the Fremen did. She had no maker hooks or . . ."

Stiros tried to shout them down.

It was deadlocked, Tuek saw: three and three with Umphrud, a fat hedonist, as advocate for "cautious acceptance."

"She had no way to guide Shai-hulud's course," Umphrud argued. "We all saw how she came down to the sand unafraid and talked to Him."

Yes, they all had seen that, either at the moment or in the holophoto that a thoughtful observer had recorded. Desert waif or not, she had confronted Shai-hulud and conversed with Him. And Shai-hulud had not engulfed her. No, indeed. The Worm-of-God had drawn back at the child's command and had returned to the desert.

"We will test her," Tuek said.

Early the following morning, an ornithopter flown by the two priests who had brought her from the desert conveyed Sheeana far out away from the sight of Keen's populace. The priests took her down to a dune top and planted a meticulous copy of a Fremen thumper in the sand. When the thumper's catch was released, a heavy beating trembled through the desert—the ancient summons to Shai-hulud. The priests fled to their 'thopter and waited high overhead while a terrified Sheeana, her worst fears realized, stood alone some twenty meters from the thumper.

Two worms came. They were not the largest the priests had ever seen, no more than thirty meters long. One of them scooped up the thumper and silenced it. Together, they rounded in parallel tracks and stopped side by side not six meters from Sheeana.

She stood submissive, fists clenched at her sides. This was what priests did. They fed you to Shaitan.

In their hovering 'thopter, the two priests watched with

fascination. Their lenses transmitted the scene to equally fascinated observers in the High Priest's quarters at Keen. All of them had seen similar events before. It was a standard punishment, a handy way to remove obstructionists from the populace or priesthood, or to pave the way for acquisition of a new concubine. Never before, though, had they seen a lone child as victim. And such a child!

The Worms-of-God crept forward slowly after their first stop. They became motionless once more when only about three meters from Sheeana.

Resigned to her fate, Sheeana did not run. Soon, she thought, she would be with her parents and friends. As the worms remained motionless, anger replaced her terror. The bad priests had left her here! She could hear their 'thopter overhead. The hot spice smell from the worms filled the air around her. Abruptly, she raised her right hand and pointed up at the 'thopter.

"Go ahead and eat me! That's what they want!"

The priests overhead could not hear her words but the gesture was visible and they could see that she was talking to the two Worms-of-God. The finger pointing up at them did not bode well.

The worms did not move.

Sheeana lowered her hand. "You killed my mother and father and all my friends!" she accused. She took a step forward and shook a fist at them.

The worms retreated, keeping their distance.

"If you don't want me, go back where you came from!" She waved them away toward the desert.

Obediently, they backed farther and turned in unison.

The priests in the 'thopter tracked them until they slipped beneath the sand more than a kilometer away.

Only then did the priests return, fear and trepidation in them. They plucked the child of Shai-hulud from the sand and returned her to Keen.

The Bene Gesserit embassy at Keen had a full report by nightfall. Word was on its way to the Chapter House by the following morning.

It had happened at last!

The trouble with some kinds of warfare (and be certain the Tyrant knew this, because it is implicit in his lesson) is that they destroy all moral decency in susceptible types. Warfare of these kinds will dump the destroyed survivors back into an innocent population that is incapable of even imagining what such returned soldiers might do.

—TEACHINGS OF THE GOLDEN PATH,
BENE GESSERIT ARCHIVES

One of Miles Teg's early memories was of sitting at dinner with his parents and his younger brother, Sabine. Teg had been only seven at the time, but the events lay indelibly in his memory: the dining room on Lernaeus colorful with freshly cut flowers, the low light of the yellow sun diffused by antique shades. Bright blue dinnerware and glistening silver graced the table. Acolyte servants stood ready at hand, because his mother might be permanently detached on special duty but her function as a Bene Gesserit teacher was not to be wasted.

Janet Roxbrough-Teg, a large-boned woman who appeared cast for the part of grande dame, looked down her nose from one end of the table, watching that the dinner service not be impaired by the slightest misplacement. Loschy Teg, Miles' father, always observed this with a faint air of amusement. He was a thin man with high forehead, a face so narrow his dark eyes appeared to bulge at the sides. His black hair was a perfect counterpoint for his wife's fairness.

Above the subdued sounds at the table and the rich smell of spiced edu soup, his mother instructed his father on how to deal with an importunate Free Trader. When she said "Tleilaxu," she had Miles' entire attention. His education had just recently touched on the Bene Tleilax.

Even Sabine, who succumbed many years later to a poisoner on Romo, listened with as much of his four-year-old awareness as he could muster. Sabine hero-worshiped his brother. Anything that caught the attention of Miles was of interest to Sabine. Both boys listened silently.

"The man is fronting for the Tleilaxu," Lady Janet said. "I can hear it in his voice."

"I do not doubt your ability to detect such things, my dear," Loschy Teg said. "But what am I to do? He has the proper tokens of credit and he wishes to buy the—"

"The order for the rice is unimportant at the moment. Never assume that what a Face Dancer appears to seek is actually what it seeks."

"I'm sure he's not a Face Dancer. He—"

"Loschy! I know you have learned this well at my instruction and can detect a Face Dancer. I agree that the Free Trader is not one of them. The Face Dancers remain on his ship. They know I am here."

"They know they could not fool you. Yes, but—"

"Tleilaxu strategy is always woven within a web of strategies, any one of which may be the real strategy. They learned that from us."

"My dear, if we are dealing with Tleilaxu, and I do

not question your judgment, then it immediately becomes a question of melange."

Lady Janet nodded her head gently. Indeed, even Miles knew about the Tleilaxu connection with the spice. It was one of the things that fascinated him about the Tleilaxu. For every milligram of melange produced on Rakis, the Bene Tleilax tanks produced long tons. Use of melange had grown to fit the new supply and even the Spacing Guild bent its knee before this power.

"But the rice . . ." Loschy Teg ventured.

"My dear husband, the Bene Tleilax have no need of that much pongi rice in our sector. They require it for trade. We must find out who really needs the rice."

"You want me to delay," he said.

"Precisely. You are superb at what we now require. Don't give that Free Trader the chance to say yes or no. Someone trained by the Face Dancers will appreciate such subtlety."

"We lure the Face Dancers out of the ship while you initiate inquiries elsewhere."

Lady Janet smiled. "You are lovely when you leap ahead of me that way."

A look of understanding passed between them.

"He cannot go to another supplier in this sector," Loschy Teg said.

"He will wish to avoid a go, no-go confrontation," Lady Janet said, patting the table. "Delay, delay, and more delay. You must draw the Face Dancers out of the ship."

"They will realize, of course."

"Yes, my dear, and it is dangerous. You must always meet on your own ground and with our own guards nearby."

Miles Teg recalled that his father had, indeed, drawn the Face Dancers out of their ship. His mother had taken Miles to the viewer where he watched the copper-walled room in which his father drove the bargain that won CHOAM's highest commendation and a rich bonus.

The first Face Dancers Miles Teg ever saw: Two small men as alike as twins. Almost chinless round faces, pug noses, tiny mouths, black button eyes, and short-cropped white hair that stood up from their heads like the bristles on a brush. The two were dressed as the Free Trader had been—black tunics and trousers.

"Illusion, Miles," his mother said. "Illusion is their way. The fashioning of illusion to achieve real goals, that is how the Tleilaxu work."

"Like the magician at the Winter Show?" Miles asked, his gaze intent on the viewer and its toy-figure scene.

"Quite similar," his mother agreed. She too watched the viewer as she spoke but one arm went protectively around her son's shoulders.

"You are looking at evil, Miles. Study it carefully. The faces you see can be changed in an instant. They can grow taller, appear heavier. They could mimic your father so that only I would recognize the substitution."

Miles Teg's mouth formed a soundless "O." He stared at the viewer, listening to his father explain that the price of CHOAM's pongi rice once more had gone up alarmingly.

"And the most terrible thing of all," his mother said. "Some of the newer Face Dancers can, by touching the flesh of a victim, absorb some of the victim's memories."

"They read minds?" Miles looked up at his mother.

"Not exactly. We think they take a print of the memories, almost a holophoto process. They do not yet know that we are aware of this."

Miles understood. He was not to speak of this to anyone, not even to his father or his mother. She had taught him the Bene Gesserit way of secrecy. He watched the figures in the screen with care.

At his father's words, the Face Dancers betrayed no emotion, but their eyes appeared to glitter more brightly.

"How did they get so evil?" Miles asked.

"They are communal beings, bred not to identify with any shape or face. The appearance they present now is for my benefit. They know I am watching. They have relaxed into their natural communal shape. Mark it closely."

Miles tipped his head to one side and studied the Face Dancers. They looked so bland and ineffectual.

"They have no sense of self," his mother said. "They have only the instinct to preserve their own lives unless ordered to die for their masters."

"Would they do that?"

"They have done it many times."

"Who are their masters?"

"Men who seldom leave the planets of the Bene Tleilax."

"Do they have children?"

"Not Face Dancers. They are mules, sterile. But their masters can breed. We have taken a few of them but the offspring are strange. Few female births and even then we cannot probe their Other Memories."

Miles frowned. He knew his mother was a Bene Gesserit. He knew the Reverend Mothers carried a marvelous reservoir of Other Memories going back through all the millennia of the Sisterhood. He even knew something of the Bene Gesserit breeding design. Reverend Mothers chose particular men and had children by those men.

"What are the Tleilaxu women like?" Miles asked.

It was a perceptive question that sent a surge of pride through the Lady Janet. Yes, it was almost a certainty that she had a potential Mentat here. The breeding mistresses had been right about the gene potential of Loschy Teg.

"No one outside of their planets has ever reported seeing a Tleilaxu female," the Lady Janet said.

"Do they exist or is it just the tanks?"

"They exist."

"Are any of the Face Dancers women?"

"At their own choice, they can be male or female. Observe them carefully. They know what your father is doing and it angers them."

"Will they try to hurt my father?"

"They don't dare. We have taken precautions and they know it. See how the one on the left works his jaws. That is one of their anger signs."

"You said they were com . . . communal beings."

"Like hive insects, Miles. They have no self-image. Without a sense of self, they go beyond amorality. Nothing they say or do can be trusted."

Miles shuddered.

"We have never been able to detect an ethical code in them," the Lady Janet said. "They are flesh made into automata. Without self, they have nothing to esteem or even doubt. They are bred only to obey their masters."

"And they were told to come here and buy the rice."

"Exactly. They were told to get it and there's no other place in this sector where they can do that."

"They must buy it from father?"

"He's their only source. At this very moment, son, they are paying in melange. You see?"

Miles saw the orange-brown spice markers change hands, a tall stack of them, which one of the Face Dancers removed from a case on the floor.

"The price is far, far higher than they ever anticipated," the Lady Janet said. "This will be an easy trail to follow."

"Why?"

"Someone will be bankrupted acquiring that shipment. We think we know who the buyer is. Whoever it is, we will learn of it. Then we will know what was really being traded here."

Lady Janet then began to point out the identifiable incongruities that betrayed a Face Dancer to trained eyes and ears. They were subtle signs but Miles picked up on them immediately. His mother told him then that she thought he might become a Mentat . . . perhaps even more.

Shortly before his thirteenth birthday, Miles Teg was sent away to advanced schooling at the Bene Gesserit stronghold on Lampadas, where his mother's assessment of him was confirmed. Word went back to her:

"You have given us the Warrior Mentat we had hoped for."

Teg did not see this note until sorting through his mother's effects after her death. The words inscribed on a small sheet of ridulian crystal with the Chapter House imprint below them filled him with an odd sense of displacement in time. His memory put him suddenly back on Lampadas where the love-awe he had felt for his mother was deftly transferred to the Sisterhood itself, as originally intended. He had come to understand this only during his later Mentat training but the understanding changed little. If anything, it bound him even more strongly to the Bene Gesserit. It confirmed that the Sisterhood must be one of his strengths. He already knew that the Bene Gesserit Sisterhood was one of the most powerful forces in his universe—equal at least to the Spacing Guild, superior to the Fish Speaker Council that had inherited the core of the old Atreides Empire, superior by far to CHOAM, and balanced somehow with the Fabricators of Ix and with the Bene Tleilax. A small measure of the Sisterhood's far-reaching authority could be deduced from the fact that they held this authority despite Tleilaxu tank-grown melange, which had broken the Rakian monopoly on the spice, just as Ixian navigation machines had broken the Guild monopoly on space travel.

Miles Teg knew his history well by then. Guild Navigators no longer were the only ones who could thread a ship through the folds of space—in this galaxy one instant, in a faraway galaxy the very next heartbeat.

The School Sisters held back little from him, revealing there for the first time the fact of his Atreides ancestry. That revelation was necessary because of the tests they gave him. They obviously were testing for prescience. Could he, like a Guild Navigator, detect fatal obstructions? He failed. They tried him next on no-chambers and no-ships. He was as blind to such devices as the rest of humankind. For this test, though, they fed him increased doses of the spice and he sensed the awakening of his True Self.

"The Mind at Its Beginning," a teaching Sister called it when he asked for an explanation of this odd sensation.

For a time, the universe was magical as he looked at it through this new awareness. His awareness was a circle, then a globe. Arbitrary forms became transient. He fell into trance state without warning until the Sisters taught him how to control this. They provided him with accounts of saints and mystics and forced him to draw a freehand circle with either hand, following the line with his awareness.

By the end of the term, his awareness resumed its touch with conventional labels, but the memory of the magic never left him. He found that memory a source of strength at the most difficult moments.

After accepting the assignment as Weapons Master to the ghola, Teg found his magical memory increasingly with him. It was especially useful during his first interview with Schwangyu at the Keep on Gammu. They met in the Reverend Mother's study, a place of shiny metal walls and numerous instruments, most of them with the stamp of Ix on them. Even the chair in which she sat, the morning sun coming through a window behind her and making her face difficult to see, even that chair was one of the Ixian self-molders. He was forced to sit in a chairdog, though he realized she must know he detested the use of any life form for such a demeaning task.

"You were chosen because you actually are a grand-fatherly figure," Schwangyu said. The bright sunlight formed a corona around her hooded head. *Deliberate!* "Your wisdom will earn the child's love and respect."

"There's no way I could be a father figure."

"According to Taraza, you have the precise characteristics she requires. I know of your honorable scars and their value to us."

This only reconfirmed his previous Mentat summation: *They have been planning this for a long time. They have bred for it. I was bred for it. I am part of their larger plan.*

All he said was: "Taraza expects this child to become a redoubtable warrior when restored to his true self."

Schwangyu merely stared at him for a moment, then: "You must not answer any of his questions about gholas, should he encounter the subject. Do not even use the word until I give you permission. We will supply you with all of the ghola data your duties require."

Coldly parceling out his words for emphasis, Teg said: "Perhaps the Reverend Mother was not informed that I am well versed in the lore of Tleilaxu gholas. I have met Tleilaxu in battle."

"You think you know enough about the Idaho series?"

"The Idahos are reputed to have been brilliant military strategists," Teg said.

"Then perhaps the great Bashar was not informed about the other characteristics of our ghola."

No doubt of the mockery in her voice. Something else as well: jealousy and great anger poorly concealed. Teg's mother had taught him ways of reading through her own masks, a forbidden teaching, which he had always concealed. He feigned chagrin and shrugged.

It was obvious, though, that Schwangyu knew he was Taraza's Bashar. The lines had been drawn.

"At Bene Gesserit behest," Schwangyu said, "the

Tleilaxu have made a significant alteration in the present Idaho series. His nerve-muscle system has been modernized."

"Without changing the original persona?" Teg fed the question to her blandly, wondering how far she would go in revelation.

"He is a ghola, not a clone!"

"I see."

"Do you really? He requires the most careful prana-bindu training at all stages."

"Taraza's orders exactly," Teg said. "And we will all obey those orders."

Schwangyu leaned forward, not concealing her anger. "You have been asked to train a ghola whose role in certain plans is most dangerous to us all. I don't think you even remotely understand what you will train!"

What you will train, Teg thought. Not *whom*. This ghola-child would never be a *whom* for Schwangyu or any of the others who opposed Taraza. Perhaps the ghola would not be a *whom* to anyone until restored to his original self, firmly seated in that original Duncan Idaho identity.

Teg saw clearly now that Schwangyu harbored more than hidden reservations about the ghola project. She was in active opposition just as Taraza had warned. Schwangyu was the enemy and Taraza's orders had been explicit.

"You will protect that child against any threat."

Ten thousand years since Leto II began his metamorphosis from human into the sandworm of Rakis and historians still argue over his motives. Was he driven by the desire for long life? He lived more than ten times the normal span of three hundred SY, but consider the price he paid. Was it the lure of power? He is called the Tyrant for good reason but what did power bring him that a human might want? Was he driven to save humankind from itself? We have only his own words about his Golden Path to answer this and I cannot accept the self-serving records of Dar-es-Balat. Might there have been other gratifications, which only his experiences would illuminate? Without better evidence the question is moot. We are reduced to saying only that "He did it!" The physical fact alone is undeniable.

—THE METAMORPHOSIS OF LETO II,
10,000TH ANNIVERSARY PERORATION BY GAUS ANDAUD

Once more, Waff knew he was on lashkar. This time the stakes were as high as they could go. An Honored Matre from the Scattering demanded his presence. A powindah of powindahs! Descendants of Tleilaxu from the Scattering had told him all they could about these terrible women.

"Far more terrible than Reverend Mothers of the Bene Gesserit," they said.

And more numerous, Waff reminded himself.

He did not fully trust the returned Tleilaxu descendants, either. Their accents were strange, their manners even stranger and their observances of the rituals questionable. How could they be readmitted to the Great Kehl? What possible rite of ghufran could cleanse them after all these centuries? It was beyond belief that they had kept the Tleilaxu secret down the generations.

They were no longer malik-brothers and yet they were the only source of information the Tleilaxu possessed about these returning Lost Ones. And the revelations they had brought! Revelations that had been incorporated in the Duncan Idaho gholas—that was worth all of the risks of contamination by powindah evil.

The meeting place with the Honored Matres was the presumed neutrality of an Ixian no-ship that held a tight orbit around a mutually selected gas giant planet in a mined-out solar system of the old Imperium. The Prophet himself had drained the last of the wealth from this system. New Face Dancers walked as Ixians among the no-ship's crew but Waff still sweated the first encounter. If these Honored Matres were truly more terrible than the Bene Gesserit witches, would the exchange of Face Dancers for Ixian crewmen be detected?

Selection of this meeting place and the arrangements had put a strain on the Tleilaxu. Was it secure? He reassured himself that he carried two sealed weapons never before seen off the Tleilaxu core planets. The weapons were the painstaking result of long effort by his artificers: two minuscule dart throwers concealed in his sleeves. He had trained with them for years until the flipping of the sleeves and the discharge of the poisoned darts was almost an instinctive reflex.

The walls of the meeting room were properly copper-toned, evidence that they were shielded from Ixian spy devices. But what instruments might the people of the Scattering have developed beyond the Ixian ken?

Waff entered the room with a hesitant step. The Honored Matre already was there seated in a leather sling chair.

"You will call me what everyone else calls me," she greeted him. "Honored Matre."

He bowed as he had been warned to do. "Honored Matre."

No hint of hidden powers in her voice. A low contralto with overtones that spoke of disdain for him. She looked like an aged athlete or acrobat, slowed and retired but still maintaining her muscle tone and some of her skills. Her face was tight skin over a skull with prominent cheekbones. The thin-lipped mouth produced a sense of arrogance when she spoke, as though every word were projected downward onto lesser folk.

"Well, come in and sit down!" she commanded, waving at a sling chair facing her.

Waff heard the hatch hiss closed behind him. He was alone with her! She was wearing a snooper. He could see the lead for it going into her left ear. His dart throwers had been sealed and "washed" against snoopers, then maintained at minus 340° Kelvin in a radiation bath for five SY to make them proof against snoopers. Had it been enough?

Gently, he lowered himself into the indicated chair.

Orange-tinted contact lenses covered the Honored

Matre's eyes, giving them a feral appearance. She was altogether daunting. And her clothing! Red leotards beneath a dark blue cape. The surface of the cape had been decorated with some pearly material to produce strange arabesques and dragon designs. She sat in the chair as though it were a throne, her clawlike hands resting easily on the arms.

Waff glanced around the room. His people had inspected this place in company with Ixian maintenance workers and representatives of the Honored Matre.

We have done our best, he thought, and he tried to relax.

The Honored Matre laughed.

Waff stared at her with as calm an expression as he could muster. "You are gauging me now," he accused. "You say to yourself that you have enormous resources to employ against me, subtle and gross instruments to carry out your commands."

"Do not take that tone with me." The words were low and flat but carried such a weight of venom that Waff almost recoiled.

He stared at the stringy muscles of the woman's legs, that deep red leotard fabric which flowed over her skin as though it were organic to her.

Their meeting time had been adjusted to bring them together at a mutually personal mid-morning, their waking hours having been balanced en route. Waff felt dislocated, though, and at a disadvantage. What if the stories of his informants were true? She must have weapons here.

She smiled at him without humor.

"You are trying to intimidate me," Waff said.

"And succeeding." Anger surged through Waff. He kept this from his voice. "I have come at your invitation."

"I hope you did not come to engage in a confrontation that you would surely lose," she said.

"I came to forge a bond between us," he said. And he wondered: *What do they need from us? Surely they must need something.*

"What bond can there be between us?" she asked. "Would you build an edifice on a disintegrating raft? Hah! Agreements can be broken and often are."

"For what tokens do we bargain?" he asked.

"Bargain? I do not bargain. I am interested in this ghola you made for the witches." Her tone gave away nothing but Waff's heartbeat quickened at her question.

In one of his ghola lifetimes, Waff had trained under a renegade Mentat. The capabilities of a Mentat were beyond him and besides, reasoning required words. They had been forced to kill the powindah Mentat but there had been some things of value in the experience. Waff allowed himself a small moue of distaste at the memory but he recalled the things of value.

Attack and absorb the data that attack produces!

"You offer me nothing in exchange!" he said, his voice loud.

"Recompense is at my discretion," she said.

Waff produced a scornful gaze. "Do you play with me?"

She showed white teeth in a feral grin. "You would not survive my play, nor want to."

"So I must be dependent upon your good will!"

"Dependency!" The word curled from her mouth as though it produced a distasteful sensation. "Why do you sell these gholas to the witches and then kill the gholas?"

Waff pressed his lips together and remained silent.

"You have somehow changed this ghola while still making it possible for him to regain his original memories," she said.

"You know so much!" Waff said. It was not quite a sneer and, he hoped, revealed nothing. *Spies!* She had spies among the witches! Was there also a traitor in the Tleilaxu heartlands?

"There is a girl-child on Rakis who figures in the plans of the witches," the Honored Matre said.

"How do you know this?"

"The witches do not make a move without our knowing! You think of spies but you cannot know how far our arms will reach!"

Waff was dismayed. Could she read his mind? Was it something born of the Scattering? A wild talent from out there where the original human seed could not observe?

"How have you changed this ghola?" she demanded. *Voice!*

Waff, armed against such devices by his Mentat teacher, almost blurted an answer. This Honored Matre had some of the witches' powers! It had been so unexpected coming from her. You expected such things from a Reverend Mother and were prepared. He was a moment recovering his balance. Waff steepled his hands in front of his chin.

"You have interesting resources," she said.

A gamin expression came over Waff's features. He knew how disarmingly elflike he could look.

Attack!

"We know how much you have learned from the Bene Gesserit," he said.

A look of rage swept over her face and was gone. "They have taught us nothing!"

Waff pitched his voice at a humorously appealing level, cajoling. "Surely, this is not bargaining."

"Isn't it?" She actually appeared surprised.

Waff lowered his hands. "Come now, Honored Matre. You are interested in this ghola. You speak of things on Rakis. What do you take us for?"

"Very little. You become less valuable by the instant."

Waff sensed the coldest machine logic in her response. There was no smell of Mentat in it but something more chilling. *She is capable of killing me right here!*

Where were her weapons? Would she even require weapons? He did not like the look of those stringy muscles, the calluses on her hands, the hunter's gleam in her orange eyes. Could she possibly guess (or even know) about the dart throwers in his sleeves?

"We are confronted by a problem that cannot be resolved by logical means," she said.

Waff stared at her in shock. A Zensunni Master might have said that! He had said it himself on more than one occasion.

"You have probably never considered such a possibility," she said. It was as though her words dropped a mask away from her face. Waff suddenly saw through to the calculating person behind these postures. Did she take him for some padfooted seelie fit only for collecting slig shit?

Bringing as much hesitant puzzlement into his voice

as possible, he asked: "How could such a problem be resolved?"

"The natural course of events will dispose of it," she said.

Waff continued to stare at her in simulated puzzlement. Her words did not smack of revelation. Still, the things implied! He said: "Your words leave me floundering."

"Humankind has become infinite," she said. "That is the true gift of the Scattering."

Waff fought to conceal the turmoil these words created. "Infinite universes, infinite time—anything may happen," he said.

"Ahhh, you are a bright little manikin," she said. "How does one allow for anything? It is not logical."

She sounded, Waff thought, like one of the ancient leaders of the Butlerian Jihad, which had tried to rid humankind of mechanical minds. This Honored Matre was strangely out of date.

"Our ancestors looked for an answer with computers," he ventured. *Let her try that!*

"You already know that computers lack infinite storage capacity," she said.

Again, her words disconcerted him. Could she actually read minds? Was this a form of mind-printing? What the Tleilaxu did with Face Dancers and gholas, others might do as well. He centered his awareness and concentrated on Ixians, on their evil machines. Powindah machines!

The Honored Matre swept her gaze around the room. "Are we wrong to trust the Ixians?" she asked.

Waff held his breath.

"I don't think you fully trust them," she said. "Come, come, little man. I offer you my good will."

Belatedly, Waff began to suspect that she was trying to be friendly and candid with him. She certainly had put aside her earlier pose of angry superiority. Waff's informants from the Lost Ones said the Honored Matres made sexual decisions much in the manner of the Bene Gesserit. Was she trying to be seductive? But she clearly *understood* and had exposed the weakness of logic.

It was very confusing!

"We are talking in circles," he said.

"Quite the contrary. Circles enclose. Circles limit. Humankind no longer is limited by the space in which to grow."

There she went again! He spoke past a dry tongue: "It is said that what you cannot control you must accept."

She leaned forward, the orange eyes intent on his face. "Do you accept the possibility of a final disaster for the Bene Tleilax?"

"If that were the case I would not be here."

"When logic fails, another tool must be used."

Waff grinned. "That sounds logical."

"Don't mock me! How dare you!"

Waff lifted his hands defensively and assumed a placating tone: "What tool would the Honored Matre suggest?"

"Energy!"

Her answer surprised him. "Energy? In what form and how much?"

"You demand logical answers," she said.

With a feeling of sadness, Waff realized that she was not, after all, Zensunni. The Honored Matre only played word games on the fringes of non-logic, circling it, but her tool was logic.

"Rot at the core spreads outward," he said.

It was as though she had not heard his testing statement. "There is untapped energy in the depths of any human we deign to touch," she said. She extended a skeletal finger to within a few millimeters of his nose.

Waff pulled back into his chair until she dropped her arm. He said: "Is that not what the Bene Gesserit said before producing their Kwisatz Haderach?"

"They lost control of themselves and of him," she sneered.

Again, Waff thought, she employed logic in thinking of the non-logical. How much she had told him in these little lapses. He could glimpse the probable history of these Honored Matres. One of the *natural* Reverend Mothers from the Fremen of Rakis had gone out in the Scattering. Diverse people had fled on the no-ships during and immediately after the Famine Times. A no-ship had seeded the wild witch and her concepts somewhere. That seed had returned in the form of this orange-eyed huntress.

Once more she hurled Voice at him, demanding: "What have you wrought with this ghola?"

This time, Waff was prepared and shrugged it off. This Honored Matre would have to be deflected or, if possible, slain. He had learned much from her but there was no way of telling how much she had learned from him with her unguessed talents.

They are sexual monsters, his informants had said. *They enslave men by the powers of sex.*

"How little you know the joys I could give you," she said. Her voice coiled like a whip around him. How tempting! How seductive!

Waff spoke defensively: "Tell me why you—"

"I need tell you nothing!"

"Then you did not come to bargain." He spoke sadly. The no-ships had, indeed, seeded those other universes with rot. Waff sensed the weight of necessity on his shoulders. What if he could not slay her?

"How dare you keep suggesting a bargain with an Honored Matre?" she demanded. "Know you that *we* set the price!"

"I do not know your ways, Honored Matre," Waff said. "But I sense in your words that I have offended."

"Apology accepted."

No apology intended! He stared at her blandly. Many things could be deduced from her performance. Out of his millennial experiences, Waff reviewed what he had learned here. This female from the Scattering came to him for an essential piece of information. Therefore, she had no other source. He sensed desperation in her. Well masked but definitely there. She needed confirmation or refutation of something she feared.

How like a predatory bird she was, sitting there with her claw hands so lightly on the arms of her chair! *Rot at the core spreads outward*. He had said it and she had not heard. Clearly, atomic humankind continued to explode on its Scatterings of Scatterings. The people represented by this Honored Matre had not found a way to trace the no-ships. That was it, of course. She hunted the no-ships just as the witches of the Bene Gesserit did.

"You seek the way to nullify a no-ship's invisibility," he said.

The statement obviously rocked her. She had not expected this from the elflike *manikin* seated in front of her. He saw fear, then anger, then resolution pass across her features before she resumed her predatory mask. She knew, though. She knew he had seen.

"So that is what you do with your ghola," she said.

"It is what the witches of the Bene Gesserit seek with him," Waff lied.

"I underestimated you," she said. "Did you make the same mistake with me?"

"I do not think so, Honored Matre. The breeding scheme that produced you is quite obviously formidable. I think you could kick out a foot and kill me before I blinked an eye. The witches are not in the same league with you."

A smile of pleasure softened her features. "Are the Tleilaxu to be our willing servants or compelled?"

He did not try to hide outrage. "You offer us slavery?"

"That is one of your options."

He had her now! Arrogance was her weakness. Submissively, he asked: "What would you command me to do?"

"You will take back as your guests two younger Honored Matres. They are to be bred with you and . . . teach you our ways of ecstasy."

Waff inhaled and exhaled two slow breaths.

"Are you sterile?" she asked.

"Only our Face Dancers are mules." She would already know that. It was common knowledge.

"You call yourself Master," she said, "yet you have not mastered yourself."

More than you, Honored Matre bitch! And I call myself Masheikh, a fact that may yet destroy you.

"The two Honored Matres I send with you will make an inspection of everything Tleilaxu and return to me with their report," she said.

He sighed as though in resignation. "Are the two younger women comely?"

"Honored Matres!" she corrected him.

"Is that the only name you use?"

"If they choose to give you names, that is their privilege, not yours." She leaned sideways and rapped a bony knuckle against the floor. Metal gleamed in her hand. She had a way of penetrating this room's shielding!

The hatch opened and two women dressed much like his Honored Matre entered. Their dark capes carried less decoration and both women were younger. Waff stared at them. Were they both . . . He tried not to show elation but knew he failed. No matter. The older one would think he admired the beauty of these two. By signs known only to the Masters, he saw that one of the two newcomers was a new Face Dancer. A successful exchange had been made and these Scattered Ones could not detect it! The Tleilaxu had successfully passed a hurdle! Would the Bene Gesserit be as blind to these new gholas?

"You are being sensibly agreeable about this, for which you will be rewarded," the old Honored Matre said.

"I recognize your powers, Honored Matre," he said. That was true. He bowed his head to conceal the resolution that he knew he could not keep from his eyes.

She gestured to the newcomers. "These two will accompany you. Their slightest whim is your command. They will be treated with all honor and respect."

"Of course, Honored Matre." Keeping his head bowed, he lifted both arms as though in salutation and submission. A dart hissed from each sleeve. As he released the darts, Waff jerked himself sideways in his chair. The motion was not quite rapid enough. The old Honored Matre's right foot shot out, catching him in the left thigh and hurling him backward on his chair.

It was the old Honored Matre's last living act. The dart from his left sleeve caught her in the back of her throat, entering through her opened mouth, a mouth left gaping in surprise. Narcotic poison cut off any outcry. The other dart hit the non-Face Dancer of the newcomers in the right eye. His Face Dancer accomplice cut off any warning shout by a blurred chop to the throat.

Two bodies slumped in death.

Painfully, Waff disentangled himself from the chair and righted it as he got to his feet. His thigh throbbed. A fraction of a meter more and she would have broken his thigh! He realized that her reaction had not been mediated by her central nervous system. As with some insects, attack could be initiated by the required muscle system. That development would have to be investigated!

His Face Dancer accomplice was listening at the open hatch. She stepped aside to allow the entry of another Face Dancer in the guise of an Ixian guard.

Waff massaged his injured thigh while his Face Dancers disrobed the dead women. The one who copied the Ixian put her head to that of the dead old Honored Matre. Things moved swiftly after that. Presently, there was no Ixian guard, only a faithful copy of the old Honored Matre and a younger Honored Matre attendant. Another pseudo-Ixian entered and copied the younger Honored Matre. Soon, there were only ashes where dead flesh had been. A new Honored Matre scooped the ashes into a bag and concealed it beneath her robe.

Waff made a careful examination of the room. The consequences of discovery made him shudder. Such arrogance as he had seen here came from obviously awesome powers. Those powers must be probed. He detained the Face Dancer who had copied the old one.

"You have printed her?"

"Yes, Master. Her waking memories were still alive when I copied."

"Transfer to her." He gestured to the one who had been an Ixian guard. They touched foreheads for a few heartbeats then parted.

"It is done," said the older one.

"How many other copies of these Honored Matres have we made?"

"Four, Master."

"None of them detected?"

"None, Master."

"Those four must return to the heartland of these Honored Matres and learn all there is to know about them. One of those four must get back to us with what is learned."

"That is impossible, Master."

"Impossible?"

"They have cut themselves off from their source. This is their way, Master. They are a new cell and have established themselves on Gammu."

"But surely we could . . ."

"Your pardon, Master. The coordinates of their place in the Scattering were contained only in a no-ship's workings and have been erased."

"Their tracks are completely covered?" There was dismay in his voice.

"Completely, Master."

Disaster! He was forced to rein in his thoughts from a sudden frenzied darting. "They must not learn what we have done here," he muttered.

"They will not learn from us, Master."

"What talents have they developed? What powers? Quickly!"

"They are what you would expect from a Reverend Mother of the Bene Gesserit but without the melange memories."

"You're sure?"

"There is no hint of it. As you know, Master, we—"

"Yes, yes. I know." He waved her to silence. "But the old one was so arrogant, so . . ."

"Your pardon, Master, but time presses. These Honored Matres have perfected the pleasures of sex far beyond that developed by any others."

"So it's true what our informants said."

"They went back to the primitive Tantric and developed their own ways of sexual stimulation, Master. Through this, they accept the worship of their followers."

"Worship." He breathed the word. "Are they superior to the Breeding Mistresses of the Sisterhood?"

"The Honored Matres believe so, Master. Shall we demon—"

"No!" Waff dropped his elfin mask at this discovery and assumed the expression of a dominant Master. The Face Dancers nodded their heads in submission. A look of glee came over Waff's face. The returned Tleilaxu of the Scattering reported truthfully! By a simple mind-print he had confirmed this new weapon of his people!

"What are your orders, Master?" the old one asked.

Waff resumed his elfin mask. "We will explore these matters only when we have returned to the Tleilaxu core at Bandalong. Meanwhile, even a Master does not give orders to an Honored Matre. You are *my* masters until we are free of prying eyes."

"Of course, Master. Shall I now convey your orders to the others outside?"

"Yes, and these are my orders: This no-ship must never return to Gammu. It must vanish without a trace. No survivors."

"It will be done, Master."

Technology, in common with many other activities, tends toward avoidance of risks by investors. Uncertainty is ruled out if possible. Capital investment follows this rule, since people generally prefer the predictable. Few recognize how destructive this can be, how it imposes severe limits on variability and thus makes whole populations fatally vulnerable to the shocking ways our universe can throw the dice.

—ASSESSMENT OF IX,

BENE GESSERIT ARCHIVES

On the morning after that initial test in the desert, Sheeana awoke in the priestly complex to find her bed surrounded by white-robed people.

Priests and priestesses!

"She's awake," a priestess said.

Fear gripped Sheeana. She clutched the bed covers close to her chin while she stared out at those intent faces. Were they going to abandon her in the desert again? She had slept the sleep of exhaustion in the softest bed with the cleanest linen she had experienced in her eight years but she knew everything the priests did could have a double meaning. They were not to be trusted!

"Did you sleep well?" It was the priestess who had spoken first. She was a gray-haired older woman, her face framed in a white cowl with purple trim. The old eyes were watery but alert. Pale blue. The nose was an up-turned stub above a narrow mouth and outjutting chin.

"Will you speak to us?" the woman persisted. "I am Cania, your night attendant. Remember? I helped you into your bed."

At least, the tone of voice was reassuring. Sheeana sat up and took a better look at these people. They were afraid! A desert child's nose could detect the telltale pheromones. To Sheeana, it was a simple, straightfor-ward observation: *That smell equals fear.*

"You thought you would hurt me," she said. "Why did you do that?"

The people around her exchanged looks of con-sternation.

Sheeana's fear dissipated. She had sensed the new or-der of things and yesterday's trial in the desert meant more change. She recalled how subservient the older woman . . . Cania? She had been almost groveling the previous night. Sheeana would learn in time that any person who lived through the decision to die evolved a new emotional balance. Fears were transitory. This new condition was interesting.

Cania's voice trembled when she responded: "Truly, Child of God, we did not intend harm."

Sheeana straightened the bedcovers on her lap. "My name is Sheeana." That was desert politeness. Cania al-ready had produced a name. "Who are these others?"

"They will be sent away if you don't want them . . . Shee-ana." Cania indicated a florid-faced woman at her left dressed in a robe similar to her own. "All except Alhosa, of course. She is your day attendant."

Alhosa curtsied at the introduction.

Sheeana stared up at a face puffy with waterfat, heavy features in a nimbus of fluffy blond hair. Shifting her attention abruptly, Sheeana looked at the men in the group. They watched her with heavy-lidded intentness, some with looks of trembling suspicion. The fear smell was strong.

Priests!

"Send them away." Sheeana waved a hand at the priests. "They are haram!" It was the gutter word, the lowest term of all for that which was most evil.

The priests recoiled in shock.

"Begone!" Cania commanded. There was no mistaking the look of malevolent glee on her face. Cania had not been included among the vile ones. But these priests clearly stood among those labeled as haram! They must have done something hideous for God to send a child-priestess to chastise them. Cania could believe it of priests. They had seldom treated her the way she deserved.

Like chastened bedogs, the priests bowed themselves backward and left Sheeana's chamber. Among those who went out into the hallway was a historian-locutor named Dromind, a dark man with a busy mind that tended to fasten onto ideas like the beak of a carrion bird onto a morsel of meat. When the chamber door closed behind them, Dromind told his trembling companions that the name Sheeana was a modern form of the ancient name, Siona.

"You all know Siona's place in the histories," he said. "She served Shai-hulud in His transformation from human shape into the Divided God."

Stiros, a wrinkled older priest with dark lips and pale, glistening eyes, looked wonderingly at Dromind. "That is extremely curious," Stiros said. "The Oral Histories claim that Siona was instrumental in His translation from the One into the Many. Sheeana. Do you think . . ."

"Let us not forget the Hadi Benotto translation of God's own holy words," another priest interrupted. "Shai-hulud referred many times to Siona."

"Not always with favor," Stiros reminded them. "Remember her full name: Siona Ibn Fuad al-Seyefa Atreides."

"Atreides," another priest whispered.

"We must study her with care," Dromind said.

A young acolyte-messenger hurried up the hallway to the group and sought among them until he spied Stiros. "Stiros," the messenger said, "you must clear this hallway immediately."

"Why?" It was an indignant voice from the press of the rejected priests.

"She is to be moved into the High Priest's quarters," the messenger said.

"By whose orders?" Stiros demanded.

"High Priest Tuek himself says this," the messenger said. "They have been listening." He waved a hand vaguely toward the direction from which he had come.

All of the group in the hall understood. Rooms could be shaped to send voices from them into other places. There were always listeners.

"What have they heard?" Stiros demanded. His old voice quavered.

"She asked if her quarters were the best. They are about to move her and she must not find any of you out here."

"But what are we to do?" Stiros asked.

"Study her," Dromind said.

The hall was cleared immediately and all of them began the process of studying Sheeana. The pattern born here would print itself on all of their lives over the subsequent years. The routine that took shape around Sheeana produced changes felt in the farthest reaches of the Divided God's influence. Two words ignited the change: "Study her."

How naive she was, the priests thought. How curiously naive. But she could read and she displayed an intense interest in the Holy Books she found in Tuek's quarters. Her quarters now.

All was propitiation from the highest to the lowest. Tuek moved into the quarters of his chief assistant and the bumping process moved downward. Fabricators waited upon Sheeana and measured her. The finest stillsuit was fashioned for her. She acquired new robes of priestly gold and white with purple trim.

People began avoiding historian-locutor Dromind. He took to buttonholing his fellows and expounding the history of the original Siona as though this said something important about the present bearer of the ancient name.

"Siona was the mate of the Holy Duncan Idaho," Dromind reminded anyone who would listen. "Their descendants are everywhere."

"Indeed? Pardon me for not listening further but I am really on an urgent errand."

At first, Tuek was more patient with Dromind. The history was interesting and its lessons obvious. "God has sent us a new Siona," Tuek said. "All should be clear."

Dromind went away and returned with more tidbits from the past. "The accounts from Dar-es-Balat take on a new meaning now," Dromind told his High Priest. "Should we not make further tests and comparisons of this child?"

Dromind had braced the High Priest immediately after breakfast. The remains of Tuek's meal still occupied the serving table on the balcony. Through the open window, they could hear stirrings overhead in Sheeana's quarters.

Tuek put a cautioning finger to his lips and spoke in a hushed voice. "The Holy Child goes of her own choice to the desert." He went to a wall map and pointed to an area southwest of Keen. "Apparently this is an area that interests her or . . . I should say, calls her."

"I am told she makes frequent use of dictionaries," Dromind said. "Surely, that cannot be a—"

"She is testing *us*," Tuek said. "Do not be fooled."

"But Lord Tuek, she asks the most childish questions of Cania and Alhosa."

"Do you question my judgment, Dromind?"

Belatedly, Dromind realized he had overstepped the proper bounds. He fell silent but his expression said many more words were compressed within him.

"God has sent her to weed out some evil that has crept into the ranks of the anointed," Tuek said. "Go! Pray and ask yourself if that evil has lodged itself within you."

When Dromind had gone, Tuek summoned a trusted aide. "Where is the Holy Child?"

"She has gone out into the desert, Lord, to commune with her Father."

"To the southwest?"

"Yes, Lord."

"Dromind must be taken far out to the east and left on the sand. Plant several thumpers to make sure he never returns."

"Dromind, Lord?"

"Dromind."

Even after Dromind was translated into the Mouth of God, the priests continued to follow his original injunction. They studied Sheeana.

Sheeana also studied.

Gradually, so gradually that she could not identify the point of transition, she recognized her great power over those around her. At first, it was a game, a continual Children's Day with adults jumping to obey each childish whim. But it appeared that no whim was too difficult.

Did she require a rare fruit for her table?

The fruit was served to her on a golden dish.

Did she glimpse a child far below on the teeming streets and require that child as a playmate?

That child was hustled up to Sheeana's temple quarters. When fear and shock passed, the child might even join in some game, which the priests and priestesses observed intently. Innocent skipping about on the rooftop garden, giggling whispers—all were subjected to intense analysis. Sheeana found the awe of such children a burden. She seldom called the same child back to her, preferring to learn new things from new playmates.

The priests achieved no consensus about the innocence of such encounters. The playmates were put through fearful interrogation until Sheeana discovered this and raged at her guardians.

Inevitably, word of Sheeana spread throughout Rakis and off-planet. The Sisterhood's reports accumulated.

The years passed in a kind of sublimely autocratic routine—feeding Sheeana's curiosity. It was a curiosity that appeared to have no limits. None of those among the immediate attendants thought of this as education: Sheeana teaching the priests of Rakis and they teaching her. The Bene Gesserit, however, observed this aspect of Sheeana's life at once and watched it closely.

"She is in good hands. Leave her there until she is ready for us," Taraza ordered. "Keep a defense force on constant alert and see that I get regular reports."

Not once did Sheeana reveal her true origins nor what Shaitan had done to her family and neighbors. That was a private thing between Shaitan and herself. She thought of her silence as payment for having been spared.

Some things paled for Sheeana. She made fewer trips into the desert. Curiosity continued but it became obvious that an explanation of Shaitan's behavior toward her might not be found on the open sand. And although she knew there were embassies of other powers on Rakis, the Bene Gesserit spies among her attendants made sure that Sheeana did not express too much interest in the Sisterhood. Soothing answers to dampen such interest were provided and metered out to Sheeana as required.

The message from Taraza to her observers on Rakis was direct and pointed: "The generations of preparation have become the years of refinement. We will move only at the proper moment. There is no longer any doubt that this child is the one."

In my estimation, more misery has been created by re-
formers than by any other force in human history.
Show me someone who says, "Something must be
done!" and I will show you a head full of vicious intentions that have no other outlet. What we must strive for
always! is to find the natural flow and go with it.

—THE REVEREND MOTHER TARAZA,
CONVERSATIONAL RECORD,
BG FILE GSXXMAT9

The overcast sky lifted as the sun of Gammu climbed,
picking up the scents of grass and surrounding forest extracted and condensed by the morning dampness.

Duncan Idaho stood at a Forbidden Window inhaling
the smells. This morning Patrin had told him: "You are
fifteen years of age. You must consider yourself a young
man. You no longer are a child."

"Is it my birthday?"

They were in Duncan's sleeping chamber where Patrin
had just aroused him with a glass of citrus juice.

"I do not know your birthday."

"Do gholas have birthdays?"

Patrin remained silent. It was forbidden to speak of
gholas with the ghola.

"Schwangyu says you can't answer that question,"
Duncan said.

Patrin spoke with obvious embarrassment. "The Bashar wishes me to tell you that your training class will be delayed this morning. He wishes you to do the leg and knee exercises until you are called."

"I did those yesterday!"

"I merely convey the Bashar's orders." Patrin took the empty glass and left Duncan alone.

Duncan dressed quickly. They would expect him for breakfast in the Commissary. *Damn them!* He did not need their breakfast. What was the Bashar doing? Why couldn't he start the classes on time? *Leg and knee exercises!* That was just make-work because Teg had some other unexpected duty. Angrily, Duncan took a Forbidden Route to a Forbidden Window. *Let the damned guards be punished!*

He found the odors coming through the open window evocative but could not place the memories that lurked at the edges of his awareness. He knew there were memories. Duncan found this frightening but magnetic—like walking along the edge of a cliff or openly confronting Schwangyu with his defiance. He had never walked along the edge of a cliff nor openly confronted Schwangyu with defiance, but he could imagine such things. Just seeing a filmbook holophoto of a cliff-edge path was enough to make his stomach tighten. As for Schwangyu, he often imagined angry disobedience and suffered the same physical reaction.

Someone else is in my mind, he thought.

Not just in his mind—*in his body.* He could sense other experiences as though he had just awakened, knowing he had dreamed but unable to recall the dream. This dream-stuff called up knowledge that he knew he could not possess.

Yet he did possess it.

He could name some of the trees he smelled out there but those names were not in the library's records.

This Forbidden Window was forbidden because it pierced an outer wall of the Keep and could be opened. It was often open, as now, for ventilation. The window was reached from his room by climbing over a balcony rail and slipping through a storeroom air shaft. He had learned to do this without the slightest disturbance of rail or storeroom or shaft. Quite early, it had been made clear to him that those trained by the Bene Gesserit could read extremely small signs. He could read some of those signs himself, thanks to the teachings of Teg and Lucilla.

Standing well back in the shadows of the upper hallway, Duncan focused on rolling slopes of forest climbing to rocky pinnacles. He found the forest compelling. The pinnacles beyond it possessed a magical quality. It was easy to imagine that no human had ever touched that land. How good it would be to lose himself there, to be only his own person without worrying that another person dwelled within him. A stranger there.

With a sigh, Duncan turned away and returned to his room along his secret route. Only when he was back in the safety of his room did he allow himself to say that he had done it once more. No one would be punished for this venture.

Punishments and pain, which hung like an aura around the places forbidden to him, only made Duncan exercise extreme caution when he broke the rules.

He did not like to think of the pain Schwangyu would cause him if she discovered him at a Forbidden Window. Even the worst pain, though, would not cause him to cry out, he told himself. He had never cried out even at her nastier tricks. He merely stared back at her, hating her but absorbing her lesson. To him, Schwangyu's lesson was direct: Refine his ability to move unobserved, unseen and unheard, leaving no spoor to betray his passage.

In his room, Duncan sat on the edge of his cot and contemplated the blank wall in front of him. Once, when he had stared at that wall, an image had formed there—a young woman with light amber hair and sweetly rounded features. She looked out of the wall at him and smiled. Her lips moved without sound. Duncan already had learned lip reading, though, and he read the words clearly.

"Duncan, my sweet Duncan."

Was that his mother? he wondered. His real mother?

Even gholas had real mothers somewhere back there. Lost in the time behind the axlotl tanks there had been a living woman who bore him and . . . and loved him. Yes, loved him because he was her child. If that face on the wall was his mother, how had her image found its way there? He could not identify the face but he wanted it to be his mother.

The experience frightened him but fear did not prevent him from wanting to repeat it. Whoever that young woman was, her fleeting presence tantalized him. The stranger within him knew that young woman. He felt sure of this. Sometimes, he wanted to be that stranger only for an instant—long enough to gather up all of those hidden memories—but he feared this desire. He would lose his real self, he thought, if the stranger entered his awareness.

Would that be like death? he wondered.

Duncan had seen death before he was six. His guards had repelled intruders and one of the guards was killed. Four intruders died as well. Duncan had watched the five bodies brought into the Keep—flaccid muscles, arms dragging. Some essential thing was gone from them. Nothing remained to call up memories—self-memories or stranger-memories.

The five were taken somewhere deep within the Keep. He heard a guard say later that the four intruders were loaded with "shere." That was his first encounter with the idea of an Ixian Probe.

"An Ixian Probe can raid the mind even of a dead person," Geasa explained. "Shere is a drug that protects you from the probe. Your cells will be totally dead before the drug effect is gone."

Adroit listening told Duncan the four intruders were being probed in other ways as well. These other ways were not explained to him but he suspected this must be something secret to the Bene Gesserit. He thought of it as another hellish trick of the Reverend Mothers. They must animate the dead and extract information from the unwilling flesh. Duncan visualized depersonalized muscles performing at the will of a diabolical observer.

The observer was always Schwangyu.

Such images filled Duncan's mind despite every effort by his teachers to dispel "foolishness invented by the ignorant." His teachers said these wild stories were valuable only to create fear of the Bene Gesserit among the *un*initiated. Duncan refused to believe that he was of the initiated. Looking at a Reverend Mother he always thought: *I'm not one of* them!

Lucilla was most persistent lately. "Religion is a source

of energy," she said. "You must recognize this energy. It can be directed for your own purposes."

Their purposes, not mine, he thought.

He imagined his own purposes and projected his own images of himself triumphant over the Sisterhood, especially over Schwangyu. Duncan felt that his imaginative projections were a subterranean reality that worked on him from that place where the stranger dwelled. But he learned to nod and give the appearance that he, too, found such religious credulity amusing.

Lucilla recognized the dichotomy in him. She told Schwangyu: "He thinks mystical forces are to be feared and, if possible, avoided. As long as he persists in this belief he cannot learn to use our most essential knowledge."

They met for what Schwangyu called "a regular assessment session," just the two of them in Schwangyu's study. The time was shortly after their light supper. The sounds of the Keep around them were those of transition—night patrols beginning, off-duty personnel enjoying one of their brief free-time periods. Schwangyu's study had not been completely insulated from such things, a deliberate contrivance of the Sisterhood's renovators. The trained senses of a Reverend Mother could detect many things from the sounds around her.

Schwangyu felt more and more at a loss in these "assessment sessions." It was increasingly obvious that Lucilla could not be won over to those opposing Taraza. Lucilla also was immune to a Reverend Mother's manipulative subterfuges. Most damnable of all, Lucilla and Teg between them were imparting highly volatile abilities to the ghola. Dangerous in the extreme. Added to all of her other problems, Schwangyu nurtured a growing respect for Lucilla.

"He thinks we use occult powers to practice our arts," Lucilla said. "How did he arrive at such a peculiar idea?"

Schwangyu felt the disadvantage imposed by this question. Lucilla already knew this had been done to weaken the ghola. Lucilla was saying: *"Disobedience is a crime against our Sisterhood!"*

"If he wants our knowledge, he will surely get it from you," Schwangyu said. No matter how dangerous, in Schwangyu's view, this was certainly a truth.

"His desire for knowledge is my best lever," Lucilla said, "but we both know that is not enough." There was no reproof in Lucilla's tone but Schwangyu felt it nevertheless.

Damn her! She's trying to win me over! Schwangyu thought.

Several responses entered Schwangyu's mind: *"I have not disobeyed my orders."* Pah! A disgusting excuse! *"The ghola has been treated according to standard Bene Gesserit training practices."* Inadequate and untrue. And this ghola was not a standard object of education. There were depths in him that could only be matched by a potential Reverend Mother. And that was the problem!

"I have made mistakes," Schwangyu said.

There! That was a double-pronged answer that another Reverend Mother could appreciate.

"You made no mistake when you damaged him," Lucilla said.

"But I failed to anticipate that another Reverend Mother might expose the flaws in him," Schwangyu said.

"He wants our powers only to escape us," Lucilla said.

"He's thinking: *Someday I'll know as much as they do and then I'll run away.*"

When Schwangyu did not respond, Lucilla said: "That was clever. If he runs, we will have to hunt him down and destroy him ourselves."

Schwangyu smiled.

"I will not make your mistake," Lucilla said. "I tell you openly what I know you would see anyway. I now understand why Taraza sent an Imprinter to one so young."

Schwangyu's smile vanished. "What are you doing?"

"I am bonding him to me the way we bond all of our acolytes to their teachers. I am treating him with candor and loyalty as one of our own."

"But he's male!"

"So the spice agony will be denied him, but nothing else. He is, I think, responding."

"And when the time comes for the ultimate stage of imprinting?" Schwangyu asked.

"Yes, that will be delicate. You think it will destroy him. That, of course, was your plan."

"Lucilla, the Sisterhood is not unanimous in following Taraza's designs for this ghola. Certainly, you know this."

It was Schwangyu's most powerful argument and the fact that it had been reserved for this moment said much. The fears that they might produce another Kwisatz Haderach were deep-seated and the dissension in the Bene Gesserit comparably powerful.

"He is primitive genetic stock and not bred to be a Kwisatz Haderach," Lucilla said.

"But the Tleilaxu have interfered with his genetic inheritance!"

"Yes; at our orders. They have sped up his nerve and muscle responses."

"Is that all they have done?" Schwangyu asked.

"You've seen the cell studies," Lucilla said.

"If we could do as much as the Tleilaxu we would not need them," Schwangyu said. "We would have our own axlotl tanks."

"You think they have hidden something from us," Lucilla said.

"They had him completely outside our observation for nine months!"

"I have heard all of these arguments," Lucilla said.

Schwangyu threw up her hands in a gesture of capitulation. "He's all yours, then, *Reverend Mother*. And the consequences are on your head. But you will not remove me from this post no matter what you report to Chapter House."

"Remove you? Certainly not. I don't want your faction sending someone unknown to us."

"There is a limit to the insults I will take from you," Schwangyu said.

"And there's a limit to how much treachery Taraza will accept," Lucilla said.

"If we get another Paul Atreides or, the Gods forbid, another Tyrant, it will be Taraza's doing," Schwangyu said. "Tell her I said so."

Lucilla stood. "You may as well know that Taraza left entirely at my discretion how much melange I feed this ghola. I have already begun increasing his intake of the spice."

Schwangyu pounded both fists on her desk. "Damn you all! You will destroy us yet!"

The Tleilaxu secret must be in their sperm. Our tests prove that their sperm does not carry forward in a straight genetic fashion. Gaps occur. Every Tleilaxu we have examined has hidden his inner self from us. They are naturally immune to an Ixian Probe! Secrecy at the deepest levels, that is their ultimate armor and their ultimate weapon.

—BENE GESSERIT ANALYSIS,

ARCHIVES CODE:

BTXX441WOR

On a morning of Sheeana's fourth year in priestly sanctuary, the reports of their spies brought a gleam of special interest to the Bene Gesserit watchers on Rakis.

"She was on the roof, you say?" the Mother Commander of the Rakian Keep asked.

Tamalane, the commander, had served previously on Gammu and knew more than most about what the Sisterhood hoped to conjoin here. The spies' report had interrupted Tamalane's breakfast of cifruit confit laced with melange. The messenger stood at ease beside the table while Tamalane resumed eating as she reread the report.

"On the roof, yes, Reverend Mother," the messenger said.

Tamalane glanced up at the messenger, Kipuna, a Rakian native acolyte being groomed for sensitive local duties. Swallowing a mouthful of her confit, Tamalane said: " *'Bring them back!'* Those were her exact words?"

Kipuna nodded curtly. She understood the question. Had Sheeana spoken with preemptory command?

Tamalane resumed scanning the report, looking for the sensitive signals. She was glad they had sent Kipuna herself. Tamalane respected the abilities of this Rakian woman. Kipuna had the soft round features and fuzzy hair common among much of the Rakian priestly class, but there was no fuzzy brain under that hair.

"Sheeana was displeased," Kipuna said. "The 'thopter passed nearby the rooftop and she saw the two manacled prisoners in it quite clearly. She knew they were being taken to death in the desert."

Tamalane put down the report and smiled. "So she ordered the prisoners brought back to her. I find her choice of words fascinating."

"Bring them back?" Kipuna asked. "That seems a simple enough order. How is it fascinating?"

Tamalane admired the directness of the acolyte's interest. Kipuna was not about to pass up a chance at learning how a real Reverend Mother's mind worked.

"It was not that part of her performance that interested me," Tamalane said. She bent to the report, reading aloud: "'You are servants unto Shaitan, not servants unto servants.'" Tamalane looked up at Kipuna. "You saw and heard all of this yourself?"

"Yes, Reverend Mother. It was judged important that I report to you personally should you have other questions."

"She still calls him Shaitan," Tamalane said. "How that must gall them! Of course, the Tyrant himself said it: 'They will call me Shaitan.'"

"I have seen the reports out of the hoard found at Dar-es-Balat," Kipuna said.

"There was no delay in bringing back the two prisoners?" Tamalane asked.

"As quickly as a message could be transmitted to the 'thopter, Reverend Mother. They were returned within minutes."

"So they are watching her and listening all the time. Good. Did Sheeana give any sign that she knew the two prisoners? Did any message pass between them?"

"I am sure they were strangers to her, Reverend Mother. Two ordinary people of the lower orders, rather dirty and poorly clothed. They smelled of the unwashed from the perimeter hovels."

"Sheeana ordered the manacles removed and then she spoke to this unwashed pair. Her exact words now: What did she say?"

"'You are my people.'"

"Lovely, lovely," Tamalane said. "Sheeana then ordered that these two be taken away, bathed and given new clothes before being released. Tell me in your own words what happened next."

"She summoned Tuek who came with three of his councillor-attendants. It was . . . almost an argument."

"Memory-trance, please," Tamalane said. "Replay the exchange for me."

Kipuna closed her eyes, breathed deeply and fell into memory-trance. Then: "Sheeana says, 'I do not like it when you feed my people to Shaitan.' Councillor Stiros says, 'They are sacrificed to Shai-hulud!' Sheeana says, 'To Shaitan!' Sheeana stamps her foot in anger. Tuek says, 'Enough, Stiros. I will not hear more of this dissension.' Sheeana says, 'When will you learn?' Stiros starts to speak but Tuek silences him with a glare and says, 'We have learned, Holy Child.' Sheeana says, 'I want—'"

"Enough," Tamalane said.

The acolyte opened her eyes and waited silently.

Presently, Tamalane said, "Return to your post, Kipuna. You have done very well, indeed."

"Thank you, Reverend Mother."

"There will be consternation among the priests," Tamalane said.

"Sheeana's wish is their command because Tuek believes in her. They will stop using the worms as instruments of punishment."

"The two prisoners," Kipuna said.

"Yes, very observant of you. The two prisoners will tell what happened to them. The story will be distorted. People will say that Sheeana protects them from the priests."

"Isn't that exactly what she's doing, Reverend Mother?"

"Ahhhh, but consider the options open to the priests. They will increase their alternative forms of punishment—whippings and certain deprivations. While fear of Shaitan eases because of Sheeana, fear of the priests will increase."

Within two months, Tamalane's reports to Chapter House contained confirmation of her own words.

"Short rations, especially short water rations, have become the dominant form of punishment," Tamalane reported. "Wild rumors have penetrated the farthest reaches of Rakis and soon will find lodging on many other planets as well."

Tamalane considered the implications of her report with care. Many eyes would see it, including some not in sympathy with Taraza. Any Reverend Mother would be able to call up an image of what must be happening on Rakis. Many on Rakis had seen Sheeana's arrival atop a wild worm from the desert. The priestly response of secrecy had been flawed from the beginning. Curiosity unsatisfied tended to create its own answers. Guesses were often more dangerous than facts.

Previous reports had told of the children brought to play with Sheeana. The much-garbled stories of such children were repeated with increasing distortions and those distortions had been dutifully sent on to Chapter House. The two prisoners, returned to the streets in their new finery, only compounded the growing mythology. The Sisterhood, artists in mythology, possessed on Rakis a ready-made energy to be subtly amplified and directed.

"We have fed a wish-fulfillment belief into the populace," Tamalane reported. She thought of the Bene Gesserit–originated phrases as she reread her latest report.

"Sheeana is the one we have long awaited."

It was a simple enough statement that its meaning could be spread without unacceptable distortion.

"The Child of Shai-hulud comes to chastise the priests!"

That one had been a bit more complicated. A few priests died in dark alleys as a result of popular fervency. This had fed a new alertness into the corps of priestly enforcers with predictable injustices inflicted upon the populace.

Tamalane thought of the priestly delegation that had

waited upon Sheeana as a result of turmoil among Tuek's councillors. Seven of them led by Stiros had intruded upon Sheeana's luncheon with a child from the streets. Knowing that this would happen, Tamalane had been prepared and a secret recording of the incident had been brought to her, the words audible, every expression visible, the thoughts quite apparent to a Reverend Mother's trained eye.

"We were sacrificing to Shai-hulud!" Stiros protested.

"Tuek told you not to argue with me about that," Sheeana said.

How the priestesses smiled at the discomfiture of Stiros and the other priests!

"But Shai-hulud—" Stiros began.

"Shaitan!" Sheeana corrected him and her expression was easily read: *Did these stupid priests know nothing?*

"But we have always thought—"

"You were wrong!" Sheeana stamped a foot.

Stiros feigned the need for instruction. "Are we to believe that Shai-hulud, the Divided God, is also Shaitan?"

What a complete fool he was, Tamalane thought. Even a pubescent girl could confound him, as Sheeana proceeded to do.

"Any child of the streets knows this almost as soon as she can walk!" Sheeana ranted.

Stiros spoke slyly: "How do you know what is in the minds of street children?"

"You are evil to doubt me!" Sheeana accused. It was an answer she had learned to use often, knowing it would get back to Tuek and cause trouble.

Stiros knew this only too well. He waited with downcast eyes while Sheeana, speaking with heavy patience as one telling an old fable to a child, explained to him that either god or devil or both could inhabit the worm of the desert. Humans had only to accept this. It was not left to humans to decide such things.

Stiros had sent people into the desert for speaking such heresy. His expression (so carefully recorded for Bene Gesserit analysis) said such wild concepts were always springing up from the muck at the bottom of the Rakian heap. But now! He had to contend with Tuek's insistence that Sheeana spoke gospel truth!

As she looked at the recording, Tamalane thought the pot was boiling nicely. This she reported to Chapter House. Doubts flogged Stiros; doubts everywhere except among the populace in their devotion to Sheeana. Spies close to Tuek said he was even beginning to doubt the wisdom of his decision to translate the historian-locutor, Dromind.

"Was Dromind right to doubt her?" Tuek demanded of those around him.

"Impossible!" the sycophants said.

What else could they say? The High Priest could make no mistake in such decisions. God would not allow it. Sheeana clearly confounded him, though. She put the decisions of many previous High Priests into a terrible limbo. Reinterpretation was being demanded on all sides.

Stiros kept pounding at Tuek: "What do we really know about her?"

Tamalane had a full account of the most recent such confrontation. Stiros and Tuek alone, debating far into the night, just the two of them (they thought) in Tuek's quarters, comfortably ensconced in rare blue chairdogs, melange-laced confits close at hand. Tamalane's holo-photo record of the meeting showed a single yellow glowglobe drifting on its suspensors close above the pair, the light dimmed to ease the strain on tired eyes.

"Perhaps that first time, leaving her in the desert with a thumper, was not a good test," Stiros said.

It was a sly statement. Tuek was noted for not having an excessively complicated mind. "Not a good test? Whatever do you mean?"

"God might wish us to perform other tests."

"You have seen her yourself! Many times in the desert talking to God!"

"Yes!" Stiros almost pounced. Clearly, it was the response he wanted. "If she can stand unharmed in the presence of God, perhaps she can teach others how this is accomplished."

"You know this angers her when we suggest it."

"Perhaps we have not approached the problem in quite the right way."

"Stiros! What if the child is right? We serve the *Divided* God. I have been thinking long and earnestly upon this. Why would God divide? Is this not God's ultimate test?"

The expression on Stiros' face said this was exactly the kind of mental gymnastics his faction feared. He tried to divert the High Priest but Tuek was not to be shifted from a single-track plunge into metaphysics.

"The ultimate test," Tuek insisted. "To see the good in evil and the evil in good."

Stiros' expression could only be described as consternation. Tuek was God's Supreme Anointed. No priest was allowed to doubt *that*! The thing that might now arise if Tuek went public with such a concept would shake the foundations of priestly authority! Clearly,

Stiros was asking himself if the time had not come to *translate* his High Priest.

"I would never suggest that I might debate such profound ideas with my High Priest," Stiros said. "But perhaps I can offer a proposal that might resolve many doubts."

"Propose then," Tuek said.

"Subtle instruments could be introduced in her clothing. We might listen when she talks to—"

"Do you think God would not know what we did?"

"Such a thought never crossed my mind!"

"I will not order her taken into the desert," Tuek said.

"But if it is her own idea to go?" Stiros assumed his most ingratiating expression. "She has done this many times."

"But not recently. She appears to have lost her need to consult with God."

"Could we not offer suggestions to her?" Stiros asked.

"Such as?"

"Sheeana, when will you speak again with your Father? Do you not long to stand once more in His presence?"

"That has more the sound of prodding than suggestion."

"I am only proposing that—"

"This Holy Child is no simpleton! She talks to God, Stiros. God might punish us sorely for such presumption."

"Did God not put her here for us to study?" Stiros asked.

This was too close to the Dromind heresy for Tuek's liking. He sent a baleful stare at Stiros.

"What I mean," Stiros said, "is that surely God means us to learn from her."

Tuek himself had said this many times, never hearing in his own words a curious echo of Dromind's words.

"She is not to be prodded and tested," Tuek said.

"Heaven forbid!" Stiros said. "I will be the soul of holy caution. And everything I learn from the Holy Child will be reported to you immediately."

Tuek merely nodded. He had his own ways to be sure Stiros spoke the truth.

The subsequent sly proddings and testings were reported immediately to Chapter House by Tamalane and her subordinates.

"Sheeana has a thoughtful look," Tamalane reported.

Among the Reverend Mothers on Rakis and those to whom they reported, this thoughtful look had an obvious interpretation. Sheeana's antecedents had been deduced long ago. Stiros' intrusions were making the child homesick. Sheeana kept a wise silence but she clearly thought much about her life in a pioneer village. Despite all of the fears and perils, those obviously had been happy times for her. She would remember the laughter, poling the sand for its weather, hunting scorpions in the crannies of the village hovels, smelling out spice fragments in the dunes. From Sheeana's repeated trips to the area, the Sisterhood had made a reasonably accurate guess as to the location of the lost village and what had happened to it. Sheeana often stared at one of Tuek's old maps on the wall of her quarters.

As Tamalane expected, one morning Sheeana stabbed a finger at the place on the wall map where she had gone many times. "Take me there," Sheeana commanded her attendants.

A 'thopter was summoned.

While priests listened avidly in a 'thopter hovering far overhead, Sheeana once more confronted her nemesis in the sand. Tamalane and her advisors, tuned into the priestly circuits, observed just as avidly.

Nothing even remotely suggesting a village remained on the duneswept waste where Sheeana ordered herself deposited. She used a thumper this time, however. Another of Stiros' sly suggestions accompanied by careful instructions on use of the ancient means to summon the Divided God.

A worm came.

Tamalane watched on her own relay projector, thinking the worm only a middling monster. Its length she estimated at about fifty meters. Sheeana stood only about three meters in front of the gaping mouth. The huffing of the worm's interior fires was clearly audible to the observers.

"Will you tell me why you did it?" Sheeana demanded.

She did not flinch from the worm's hot breath. Sand crackled beneath the monster but she gave no sign that she heard.

"Answer me!" Sheeana commanded.

No voice came from the worm but Sheeana appeared to be listening, her head cocked to one side.

"Then go back where you came from," Sheeana said. She waved the worm away.

Obediently, the worm backed off and returned beneath the sands.

For days, while the Sisterhood spied upon them with glee, the priests debated that sparse encounter. Sheeana could not be questioned lest she learn that she had been overheard. As before, she refused to discuss anything about her visits to the desert.

Stiros continued his sly prodding. The result was precisely what the Sisterhood expected. Without any warning, Sheeana would awaken some days and say: "Today, I will go into the desert."

Sometimes she used a thumper, sometimes she danced her summons. Far out on the sands beyond the sight of Keen or any other inhabited place, the worms came to her. Sheeana alone in front of a worm talked to it while others listened. Tamalane found the accumulated recordings fascinating as they passed through her hands on their way to Chapter House.

"I should hate you!"

What a turmoil that caused among the priests! Tuek wanted an open debate: "Should all of us hate the Divided God at the same time we love Him?"

Stiros barely shut off this suggestion with the argument that God's wishes had not been made clear.

Sheeana asked one of her gigantic visitors: "Will you let me ride you again?"

When she approached, the worm retreated and would not let her mount.

On another occasion, she asked: "Must I stay with the priests?"

This particular worm proved to be the target of many questions, and among them:

"Where do people go when you eat them?"

"Why are people false to me?"

"Should I punish the bad priests?"

Tamalane laughed at that final question, thinking of the turmoil it would cause among Tuek's people. Her spies duly reported the dismay of the priests.

"How does He answer her?" Tuek asked. "Has anyone heard God respond?"

"Perhaps He speaks directly into her soul," a councillor ventured.

"That's it!" Tuek leaped at this offering. "We must ask her what God tells her to do."

Sheeana refused to be drawn into such discussions.

"She has a pretty fair assessment of her powers," Tamalane reported. "She's not going into the desert very much now despite Stiros' proddings. As we might expect, the attraction has waned. Fear and elation will carry her just so far before paling. She has, however, learned an effective command:

"Go away!"

The Sisterhood marked this as an important development. When even the Divided God obeyed, no priest or priestess was about to question her authority to issue such a command.

"The priests are building towers in the desert," Tamalane reported. "They want more secure places from which to observe Sheeana when she does go out there."

The Sisterhood had anticipated this development and had even done some of its own prodding to speed up the projects. Each tower had its own windtrap, its own maintenance staff, its own water barrier, gardens and other elements of civilization. Each was a small community spreading the established areas of Rakis farther and farther into the domain of the worms.

Pioneer villages no longer were necessary and Sheeana got the credit for this development.

"She is *our* priestess," the populace said.

Tuek and his councillors spun on the point of a pin: *Shaitan and Shai-hulud in one body?* Stiros lived in daily fear that Tuek would announce the fact. Stiros' advisors finally rejected the suggestion that Tuek be translated. Another suggestion that Priestess Sheeana have a fatal accident was greeted with horror by all, even Stiros finding it too great a venture.

"Even if we remove this thorn, God may visit us with an even more terrible intrusion," he said. And he warned: "The oldest books say that a little child shall lead us."

Stiros was only the most recent among those who looked upon Sheeana as something not quite mortal. It was observable that those around her, Cania included, had come to love Sheeana. She was so ingenuous, so bright and responsive.

Many observed that this growing affection for Sheeana extended even to Tuek.

For the people touched by this power, the Sisterhood had an immediate recognition. The Bene Gesserit knew a label for this ancient effect: *expanding worship.* Tamalane reported profound changes moving through Rakis as people everywhere on the planet began praying to Sheeana instead of to Shaitan or even to Shai-hulud.

"They see that Sheeana intercedes for the weakest people," Tamalane reported. "It is a familiar pattern. All goes as ordered. When do you send the ghola?"

One of the Sisterhood's swifter lighters took Miles Teg up to the Guild Transport circling Gammu. He did not like leaving the Keep at this moment but the priorities were obvious. He also had a gut reaction about this venture. In his three centuries of experience, Teg had learned to trust his gut reactions. Matters were not going well on Gammu. Every patrol, every report of remote sensors, the accounts of Patrin's spies in the cities—everything fueled Teg's disquiet.

Mentat fashion, Teg felt the movement of forces around the Keep and within it. His ghola charge was threatened. The order for him to report aboard the Guild Transport prepared for violence, however, came from Taraza herself with an unmistakable crypto-identifier on it.

On the lighter taking him upward, Teg set himself for battle. Those preparations he could make had been made. Lucilla was warned. He felt confident about Lucilla. Schwangyu was another matter. He fully intended to discuss with Taraza a few essential changes in the

Gammu Keep. First, though, he had another battle to win. Teg had not the slightest doubt that he was entering combat.

As his lighter moved in to dock, Teg looked out a port and saw the gigantic Ixian symbol within the Guild cartouche on the Transport's dark side. This was a ship the Guild had converted to Ixian mechanism, substituting machines for the traditional navigator. There would be Ixian technicians aboard to service the equipment. A genuine Guild navigator would be there, too. The Guild had never quite learned to trust a machine even while they paraded these converted Transports as a message to Tleilaxu and Rakians.

"You see: we do not absolutely require your melange!"

This was the announcement contained in that giant symbol of Ix on the spaceship's side.

Teg felt the slight lurch of the docking grapples and took a deep, quieting breath. He felt as he always did just before battle: Empty of all false dreams. This was a failure. The talking had failed and now came the contest of blood . . . unless he could prevail in some other way. Combat these days was seldom a massive thing but death was there nonetheless. That represented a more permanent kind of failure. *If we cannot adjust our differences peacefully we are less than human.*

An attendant with the unmistakable signs of Ix in his speech guided Teg to the room where Taraza waited. All along the corridors and in the pneumotubes carrying him to Taraza, Teg looked for signs to confirm the secret warning in the Mother Superior's message. All seemed serene and ordinary—the attendant properly deferential toward the Bashar. "I was a Tireg commander at

Andioyu," the attendant said, naming one of the almost-battles where Teg had prevailed.

They came to an ordinary oval hatch in the wall of an ordinary corridor. The hatch opened and Teg entered a white-walled room of comfortable dimensions—sling chairs, low side tables, glowglobes tuned to yellow. The hatch slid into its seals behind him with a solid thump, leaving his guide behind him in the corridor.

A Bene Gesserit acolyte parted the gossamer hangings that concealed a passage on Teg's right. She nodded to him. He had been seen. Taraza would be notified.

Teg suppressed a trembling in his calf muscles.

Violence?

He had not misinterpreted Taraza's secret warning. Were his preparations adequate? There was a black sling chair at his left, a long table in front of it and another chair at the end of the table. Teg went to this side of the room and waited with his back to the wall. The brown dust of Gammu still clung to his boot toes, he noted.

Peculiar smell in the room. He sniffed. *Shere!* Had Taraza and her people armed themselves against an Ixian Probe? Teg had taken his usual shere capsule before embarking on the lighter. Too much knowledge in his head that might be useful to an enemy. The fact that Taraza left the smell of shere around her quarters had another implication: It was a statement to some observer whose presence she could not prevent.

Taraza entered through the gossamer hangings. She appeared tired, he thought. He found this remarkable because the Sisters were capable of concealing fatigue until almost ready to drop. Was she actually low in energy or was this another gesture for hidden observers?

Pausing just into the room, Taraza studied Teg. The Bashar appeared much older than when she had last seen him, Taraza thought. Duty on Gammu was having its effect, but she found this reassuring. Teg was doing his job.

"Your quick response is appreciated, Miles," she said.

Appreciated! Their agreed word for *"We are being watched secretly by a dangerous foe."*

Teg nodded while his gaze went to the hangings where Taraza had entered.

Taraza smiled and moved farther into the room. No signs of the melange cycle in Teg, she observed. Teg's advanced years always raised the suspicion that he might resort to the leavening effect of the spice. Nothing about him revealed even the faintest hint of the melange addiction that even the strongest sometimes turned to when they felt their end approaching. Teg wore his old uniform jacket of Supreme Bashar but without the gold starbursts at shoulder and collar. This was a signal she recognized. He said: "Remember how I earned this in your service. I have not failed you this time, either."

The eyes that studied her were level; no hint of judgment escaped them. His entire appearance spoke of quiet within, everything at variance with what she knew must be occurring in him at this moment. He awaited her signal.

"Our ghola must be awakened at the first opportunity," she said. She waved a hand to silence him as he started to respond. "I have seen Lucilla's reports and I know he is too young. But we are required to act."

She spoke for the watchers, he realized. Were her words to be believed?

"I now give you the order to awaken him," she said and she flexed her left wrist in the confirmation gesture of their secret language.

It was true! Teg glanced at the hangings that concealed the passage where Taraza had entered. Who was it listening there?

He put his Mentat talents to the problem. There were missing pieces but that did not stop him. A Mentat could work without certain pieces if he had enough to create a pattern. Sometimes, the sketchiest outline was enough. It supplied the hidden shape and then he could fit the missing pieces to complete a whole. Mentats seldom had all the data they might desire, but he was trained to sense patterns, to recognize systems and wholeness. Teg reminded himself now that he also had been trained in the ultimate military sense: You trained a recruit to *train* a weapon, *to aim the weapon correctly*.

Taraza was aiming him. His assessment of their situation had been confirmed.

"Desperate attempts will be made to kill or capture our ghola before you can awaken him," she said.

He recognized her tone: the coldly analytic offering of data to a Mentat. She saw that he was in Mentat mode, then.

The Mentat pattern-search rolled through his mind. First, there was the Sisterhood's design for the ghola, largely unknown to him, but ranging somehow around the presence of a young female on Rakis who (so they said) could command worms. Idaho gholas: charming persona and with something else that had made the Tyrant and the Tleilaxu repeat him countless times. Duncans by the shipload! What service did this ghola provide that the Tyrant had not let him remain among the dead? And the Tleilaxu: They had decanted Duncan Idaho gholas from their ax- lotl tanks for millennia, even after the death of the Ty- rant. The Tleilaxu had sold this ghola to the Sisterhood twelve times and the Sisterhood had paid in the hardest currency: melange from their own precious stores. Why did the Tleilaxu accept in payment something they pro- duced so copiously? Obvious: to deplete the Sisterhood's supplies. A special form of greed there. The Tleilaxu were buying supremacy—a *power game*!

Teg focused on the quietly waiting Mother Superior. "The Tleilaxu have been killing our gholas to control our timing," he said.

Taraza nodded but did not speak. So there was more. Once again, he fell into Mentat mode.

The Bene Gesserit were a valuable market for the Tleilaxu melange, not the only source because there was always the trickle from Rakis, but valuable, yes; very valuable. It was not reasonable that the Tleilaxu would alienate a valuable market unless they had a more valu- able market standing ready.

Who else had an interest in Bene Gesserit activities? The Ixians without a doubt. But Ixians were not a good market for melange. The Ixian presence on this ship spoke of their independence. Since Ixians and Fish Speak- ers made common cause, the Fish Speakers could be set aside from this pattern quest.

What great power or assemblage of powers in this uni- verse possessed . . .

Teg froze that thought as though he had applied the dive brakes in a 'thopter, letting his mind float free while he sorted other considerations.

Not in this universe.

The pattern took shape. *Wealth.* Gammu assumed a new role in his Mentat computations. Gammu had been gutted long ago by the Harkonnens, abandoned as a festering carcass, which the Danians had restored. There was a time, though, when even Gammu's hopes were gone. Without hopes there had not even been dreams. Climbing from that cesspool, the population had employed only the basest pragmatism. *If it works, it is good.*

Wealth.

In his first survey of Gammu he had noted the numbers of banking houses. They were even marked, some of them, as Bene Gesserit–safe. Gammu served as the fulcrum for manipulation of enormous wealth. The bank he had visited to study its use as an emergency contact came back fully into his Mentat awareness. He had realized at once that the place did not confine itself to purely planetary business. It was a bankers' bank.

Not just wealth but WEALTH.

A Prime Pattern development did not come into Teg's mind but he had enough for a Testing Projection. Wealth not of this universe. People from the Scattering.

All of this Mentat sorting had taken only a few seconds. Having reached a testing point, Teg set himself loose-of-muscle and nerve, glanced once at Taraza and strode across to the concealed entry. He noted that Taraza gave no sign of alarm at his movements. Whipping aside the hangings, Teg confronted a man almost as tall as himself: military-style clothing with crossed spears at the collar tabs. The face was heavy, the jaws wide; green eyes. A look of surprised alertness, one hand poised above a pocket that bulged obviously with a weapon.

Teg smiled at the man, let the hangings fall and returned to Taraza.

"We are being observed by people from the Scattering," he said.

Taraza relaxed. Teg's performance had been memorable.

The hangings swished aside. The tall stranger entered and stopped about two paces from Teg. A glacial expression of anger gripped his features.

"I warned you not to tell him!" The voice was a grating baritone with an accent new to Teg.

"And I warned you about the powers of this Mentat Bashar," Taraza said. A look of loathing flashed across her features.

The man subsided and a subtle look of fear came over his face. "Honored Matre, I—"

"Don't you dare call me that!" Taraza's body tensed in a fighting posture that Teg had never before seen her display.

The man inclined his head slightly. "Dear lady, you do not control the situation here. I must remind you that my orders—"

Teg had heard enough. "Through me, she does control here," he said. "Before coming here I set certain protective measures in motion. This . . ." he glanced around him and returned his attention to the intruder, whose face now bore a wary expression ". . . is not a no-ship. Two of our no-ship monitors have you in their sights at this moment."

"You would not survive!" the man barked.

Teg smiled amiably. "No one on this ship would survive." He clenched his jaw to key the nerve signal and activate the tiny pulsetimer in his skull. It played its graphic signals against his visual centers. "And you don't have much time in which to make a decision."

"Tell him how you knew to do this," Taraza said.

"The Mother Superior and I have our own private means of communication," Teg said. "But further than that, there was no need for her to warn me. Her summons was enough. The Mother Superior on a Guild Transport at a time like this? Impossible!"

"Impasse," the man growled.

"Perhaps," Teg said. "But neither Guild nor Ix will risk a total and all-out attack by Bene Gesserit forces under the command of a leader trained by me. I refer to the Bashar Burzmali. Your support has just dissolved and vanished."

"I told him nothing of this," Taraza said. "You have just witnessed the performance of a Mentat Bashar, which I doubt could be equaled in your universe. Think of that if you consider going against Burzmali, a man trained by this Mentat."

The intruder looked from Taraza to Teg and back to Taraza.

"This is the way out of our seeming impasse," Teg said. "The Mother Superior Taraza and her entourage leave with me. You must decide immediately. Time is running out."

"You're bluffing." There was no force in the words.

Teg faced Taraza and bowed. "It has been a great honor to serve you, Reverend Mother Superior. I bid you farewell."

"Perhaps death will not part us," Taraza said. It was the traditional farewell of a Reverend Mother to a Sister-equal.

"Go!" The heavy-featured man dashed to the corridor hatchway and flung it open, revealing two Ixian guards, looks of surprise on their faces. His voice hoarse, the man ordered: "Take them to their lighter."

Still relaxed and calm, Teg said: "Summon your people, Mother Superior." To the man standing at the hatchway, Teg said: "You value your own skin too much to be a good soldier. None of my people would have made such an error."

"There are true Honored Matres aboard this ship," the man grated. "I am sworn to protect them."

Teg grimaced and turned to where Taraza was leading her people from the adjoining room: two Reverend Mothers and four acolytes. Teg recognized one of the Reverend Mothers: Darwi Odrade. He had seen her before only at a distance but the oval face and lovely eyes were arresting: so like Lucilla.

"Do we have time for introductions?" Taraza asked.

"Of course, Mother Superior."

Teg nodded and grasped the hand of each woman as Taraza presented them.

As they left, Teg turned to the uniformed stranger. "One must always observe the niceties," Teg said. "Otherwise we are less than human."

Not until they were on the lighter, Taraza seated beside him and her entourage nearby, did Teg ask the overriding question.

"How did they take you?"

The lighter was plunging planetward. The screen in front of Teg showed that the Ix-branded Guildship obeyed his command to remain in orbit until his party was safely behind its planetary defenses.

Before Taraza could respond, Odrade leaned across the aisle separating them and said: "I have countermanded the Bashar's orders to destroy that Guildship, Mother."

Teg swiveled his head sharply and glared at Odrade. "But they took you captive and . . ." He scowled. "How did you know I—"

"Miles!"

Taraza's voice conveyed overwhelming reproof. He grinned ruefully. Yes, she knew him almost as well as he knew himself . . . better in some respects.

"They did not just capture us, Miles," Taraza said. "We allowed ourselves to be taken. Ostensibly, I was escorting Dar to Rakis. We left our no-ship at Junction and asked for the fastest Guild Transport. All of my Council, including Burzmali, agreed that these intruders from the Scattering would subvert the Transport and take us to you, aiming to pick up all the pieces of the ghola project."

Teg was aghast. *The risk!*

"We knew you would rescue us," Taraza said. "Burzmali was standing by in case you failed."

"That Guildship you've spared," Teg said, "will summon assistance and attack our—"

"They will not attack Gammu," Taraza said. "Too many diverse forces from the Scattering are assembled on Gammu. They would not dare alienate so many."

"I wish I were as certain of that as you appear to be," Teg said.

"Be certain, Miles. Besides, there are other reasons for not destroying the Guildship. Ix and the Guild have been caught taking sides. That's bad for business and they need all of the business they can get."

"Unless they have more important customers offering greater profits!"

"Ahhhhh, Miles." She spoke in a musing voice. "What we latter-day Bene Gesserit really do is try to let matters achieve a calmer tone, a balance. You know this."

Teg found this true but he locked on one phrase: ". . . latter-day . . ." The words conveyed a sense of summation-at-death. Before he could question this, Taraza continued:

"We like to settle the most passionate situations off the battlefield. I must admit we have the Tyrant to thank for that attitude. I don't suppose you've ever thought of yourself as a product of the Tyrant's conditioning, Miles, but you are."

Teg accepted this without comment. It was a factor in the entire spread of human society. No Mentat could avoid it as a datum.

"That quality in you, Miles, drew us to you in the first place," Taraza said. "You can be damnably frustrating at times but we wouldn't have you any other way."

By subtle revelations in tone and manner, Teg realized that Taraza was not speaking solely for his benefit, but was also directing her words at her entourage.

"Have you any idea, Miles, how maddening it is to hear you argue both sides of an issue with equal force? But your simpatico is a powerful weapon. How terrified some of our foes have been to find you confronting them where they had not the slightest suspicion you might appear!"

Teg allowed himself a tight smile. He glanced at the women seated across the aisle from them. Why was Taraza directing such words at this group? Darwi Odrade appeared to be resting, head back, eyes closed. Several of the others were chatting among themselves. None of this was conclusive to Teg. Even Bene Gesserit acolytes could follow several trains of thought simultaneously. He returned his attention to Taraza.

"You really feel things the way the enemy feels them," Taraza said. "That is what I mean. And, of course, when you're in that mental frame there is no enemy for you."

"Yes, there is!"

"Don't mistake my words, Miles. We have never doubted your loyalty. But it's uncanny how you make us see things we have no other way of seeing. There are times when you are our eyes."

Darwi Odrade, Teg saw, had opened her eyes and was looking at him. She was a lovely woman. Something disturbing about her appearance. As with Lucilla, she reminded him of someone in his past. Before Teg could follow this thought, Taraza spoke.

"Has the ghola this ability to balance between opposing forces?" she asked.

"He could be a Mentat," Teg said.

"He *was* a Mentat in one incarnation, Miles."

"Do you really want him awakened so young?"

"It is necessary, Miles. Deadly necessary."

The failure of CHOAM? Quite simple: They ignore the
fact that larger commercial powers wait at the edges of
their activities, powers that could swallow them the
way a slig swallows garbage. This is the true threat of
the Scattering—to them and to us all.

—BENE GESSERIT COUNCIL NOTES,
ARCHIVES #SXX9OCH

Odrade spared only part of her awareness to the conversation between Teg and Taraza. Their lighter was
a small one, its passenger quarters cramped. It would use
atmospherics to dampen its descent, she knew, and she prepared herself for the buffeting. The pilot would be sparing
of their suspensors on such a craft, saving energy.

She used these moments as she used all such time now
to gird herself for the coming necessities. Time pressed; a
special calendar drove her. She had looked at a calendar
before leaving Chapter House, caught as often happened
to her by the persistence of time and its language: seconds, minutes, hours, days, weeks, months, years . . . Standard Years, to be precise. Persistence was an inadequate
word for the phenomenon. Inviolability was more like it.
Tradition. Never disturb tradition. She held the comparisons firmly in mind, the ancient flow of time imposed on
planets that did not tick to the primitive human clock. A
week was seven days. Seven! How powerful that number

remained. Mystical. It was enshrined in the Orange Catholic Bible. The Lord made a world in six days "and on the seventh day He rested."

Good for Him! Odrade thought. *We all should rest after great labors.*

Odrade turned her head slightly and looked across the aisle at Teg. He had no idea how many memories of him she possessed. She could mark how the years had treated that strong face. Teaching the ghola had drained his energies, she saw. That child in the Gammu Keep must be a sponge absorbing anything and everything around him.

Miles Teg, do you know how we use you? she wondered.

It was a thought that weakened her but she allowed it to persist in her awareness almost with a feeling of defiance. How easy it would be to love that old man! Not as a mate, of course . . . but love, nonetheless. She could feel the bond tugging at her and recognized it with the fine edge of her Bene Gesserit abilities. Love, damnable love, weakening love.

Odrade had felt this tugging with the first mate she had been sent to seduce. Curious sensation. Her years of Bene Gesserit conditioning had made her wary of it. None of her proctors had allowed her the luxury of that unquestioning warmth, and she had learned in time the reasons behind such isolating care. But there she was, sent by the breeding mistresses, ordered to get that close to a single individual, to let him enter her. All of the clinical data lay there in her awareness and she could read the sexual excitement in her partner even as she allowed it in herself. She had, after all, been carefully prepared for this role by men the Breeding Mistresses selected and conditioned with exquisite nicety for just such training.

Odrade sighed and looked away from Teg, closing her eyes in remembrance. Training Males never let their emotions reflect a bonding abandonment to their students. It was a necessary flaw in the sexual education.

That first seduction upon which she had been sent: She had been quite unprepared for the melting ecstasy of a simultaneous orgasm, a mutuality and sharing as old as humankind . . . older! And with powers capable of overwhelming the reason. The look on her male companion's face, the sweet kiss, his total abandonment of all self-protective reserves, unguarded and supremely vulnerable. No Training Male had ever done that! Desperately, she grasped for the Bene Gesserit lessons. Through those lessons, she saw the essence of this man on his face, felt that essence in her deepest fibers. For just an instant, she permitted an equal response, experiencing a new height of ecstasy that none of her teachers had hinted might be attainable. For that instant, she understood what had happened to the Lady Jessica and the other Bene Gesserit *failures*.

This feeling was love!

Its power frightened her (as the Breeding Mistresses had known it would) and she fell back into the careful Bene Gesserit conditioning, allowing a mask of pleasure to take over the brief natural expression on her face, employing calculated caresses where natural caresses would have been easier (but less effective).

The male responded as expected, stupidly. It helped to think of him as stupid.

Her second seduction had been easier. She could still call up the features of that first one, though, doing it sometimes with a calloused sense of wonder. Sometimes, his face came to her of itself and for no reason she could identify immediately.

With the other males she had been sent to breed, the memory markers were different. She had to hunt her past for the look of them. The sensory recordings of those experiences did not go as deep. Not so with that first one!

Such was the dangerous power of love.

And look at the troubles this hidden force had caused the Bene Gesserit over the millennia. The Lady Jessica and her love for her Duke had been only one example among countless others. Love clouded reason. It diverted the Sisters from their duties. Love could be tolerated only where it caused no immediate and obvious disruptions or where it served the larger purposes of the Bene Gesserit. Otherwise it was to be avoided.

Always, though, it remained an object of disquieting watchfulness.

Odrade opened her eyes and glanced again at Teg and Taraza. The Mother Superior had taken up a new subject. How irritating Taraza's voice could be at times! Odrade closed her eyes and listened to the conversation, tied to those two voices by some link in her awareness that she could not avoid.

"Very few people realize how much of the infrastructure in a civilization is dependency infrastructure," Taraza said. "We have made quite a study of this."

Love is a dependency infrastructure, Odrade thought. Why had Taraza hit on this subject at this time? The Mother Superior seldom did anything without deep motives. "Dependency infrastructure is a term that includes all things necessary for a human population to survive at existing or increased numbers," Taraza said.

"Melange?" Teg asked.

"Of course, but most people look at the spice and say, 'How nice it is that we can have it and it can give us so much longer lives than were enjoyed by our ancestors.'"

"Providing they can afford it." Teg's voice had a bite in it, Odrade noted.

"As long as no single power controls all of the market, most people have enough," Taraza said.

"I learned economics at my mother's knee," Teg said. "Food, water, breathable air, living space not contaminated by poisons—there are many kinds of *money* and the value changes according to the dependency."

As she listened to him, Odrade almost nodded in agreement. His response was her own. *Don't belabor the obvious, Taraza! Get to your point.*

"I want you to remember your mother's teachings very clearly," Taraza said. *How mild her voice was suddenly!* Taraza's voice changed abruptly then and she snapped: "Hydraulic despotism!"

She does that shift of emphasis well, Odrade thought. Memory spewed up the data like a spigot suddenly opened full force. *Hydraulic despotism:* central control of an essential energy such as water, electricity, fuel, medicines, melange . . . Obey the central controlling power or the energy is shut off and you die!

Taraza was talking once more: "There's another useful concept that I'm sure your mother taught you—the key log."

Odrade was very curious now. Taraza was headed somewhere important with this conversation. *Key log:* a truly ancient concept from the days before suspensors when lumbermen sent their fallen timber rushing down rivers to central mill sites. Sometimes the logs jammed up in the river and an expert was brought in to find the one log, the key log, which would free the jam when removed. Teg, she knew, would have an intellectual understanding of the term but she and Taraza could call up actual witnesses from Other Memories, see the explosion of broken bits of wood and water as a jam was released.

"The Tyrant was a key log," Taraza said. "He created the jam and he released it."

The lighter began trembling sharply as it took its first bite of Gammu's atmosphere. Odrade felt the tightness of her restraining harness for a few seconds, then the craft's passage became steadier. Conversation stopped for this interval, then Taraza continued:

"Beyond the so-called natural dependencies are some religions that have been created psychologically. Even physical necessities can have such an underground component."

"A fact the Missionaria Protectiva understands quite well," Teg said. Again, Odrade heard that undercurrent of deep resentment in his voice. Taraza certainly must hear it, too. What was she doing? She could weaken Teg!

"Ahhh, yes," Taraza said. "Our Missionaria Protectiva. Humans have such a powerful need that their own belief structure be the 'true belief.' If it gives you pleasure or a sense of security *and* if it is incorporated into your belief structure, what a powerful dependency that creates!"

Again, Taraza fell silent while their lighter went through another atmospheric buffeting.

"I wish he would use his suspensors!" Taraza complained.

"It saves fuel," Teg said. "Less dependency."

Taraza chuckled. "Oh, yes, Miles. You know the lesson well. I see your mother's hand in it. Damn the dam when the child strikes out in a dangerous direction."

"You think of me as a child?" he asked.

"I think of you as someone who has just had his first direct encounter with the machinations of the so-called Honored Matres."

So that's it, Odrade thought. And with a feeling of shock, Odrade realized that Taraza was aiming her words at a broader target than just Teg.

She's talking to me!

"These Honored Matres, as they call themselves," Taraza said, "have combined sexual ecstasy and worship. I doubt that they have even guessed at the dangers."

Odrade opened her eyes and looked across the aisle at the Mother Superior. Taraza's gaze was fixed intently on Teg, an unreadable expression except for the eyes, which burned with the necessity for him to understand.

"Dangers," Taraza repeated. "The great mass of humankind possesses an unmistakable unit-identity. It can be one thing. It can act as a single organism."

"So the Tyrant said," Teg countered.

"So the Tyrant demonstrated! The Group Soul was his to manipulate. There are times, Miles, when survival demands that we commune with the soul. Souls, you know, are always seeking outlet."

"Hasn't communing with souls gone out of style in our time?" Teg asked. Odrade did not like the bantering tone in his voice and noted that it aroused a matching anger in Taraza.

"You think I talk about fashions in religion?" Taraza demanded, her high-pitched voice insistently harsh. "We both know religions can be created! I'm talking about these Honored Matres who ape some of our ways but have none of our deeper awareness. They dare place themselves at the center of worship!"

"A thing the Bene Gesserit always avoids," he said. "My mother said that worshipers and the worshiped are united by the faith."

"And they can be divided!"

Odrade saw Teg suddenly fall into Mentat mode, an unfocused stare in his eyes, his features placid. She saw now part of what Taraza was doing. *The Mentat rides Roman, one foot on each steed. Each foot is based on a different reality as the pattern-search hurtles him forward. He must ride different realities to a single goal.*

Teg spoke in a Mentat's musing, unaccented voice: "Divided forces will battle for supremacy."

Taraza gave a sigh of pleasure almost sensual in its natural venting.

"Dependency infrastructure," Taraza said. "These women from the Scattering would control dividing forces, all of those forces trying mightily to take the lead. That military officer on the Guildship, when he spoke of his Honored Matres, spoke with both awe and hatred. I'm sure you heard it in his voice, Miles. I know how well your mother taught you."

"I heard." Teg was once more focused on Taraza, hanging on her every word as was Odrade.

"Dependencies," Taraza said. "How simple they can be and how complex. Take, for example, tooth decay."

"Tooth decay?" Teg was shocked off his Mentat track and Odrade, observing this, saw that his reaction was precisely what Taraza wanted. Taraza was playing her Mentat Bashar with a fine hand.

And I am supposed to see this and learn from it, Odrade thought.

"Tooth decay," Taraza repeated. "A simple implant at birth prevents this bane for most of humankind. Still, we must brush the teeth and otherwise care for them. It is so natural to us that we seldom think about it. The devices we use are assumed to be wholly ordinary parts of our environment. Yet the devices, the materials in them, the instructors in tooth care and the Suk monitors, all have their interlocked relationships."

"A Mentat does not need interdependencies explained to him," Teg said. There was still curiosity in his voice but with a definite undertone of resentment.

"Quite," Taraza said. "That is the natural environment of a Mentat's thinking process."

"Then why do you belabor this?"

"Mentat, look at what you now know of these Honored Matres and tell me: What is their flaw?"

Teg spoke without hesitation: "They can only survive if they continue to increase the dependency of those who support them. It's an addict's dead-end street."

"Precisely. And the danger?"

"They could take much of humankind down with them."

"That was the Tyrant's problem, Miles. I'm sure he knew it. Now, pay attention to me with great care. And you, too, Dar." Taraza looked across the aisle and met Odrade's gaze. "Both of you listen to me. We of the Bene Gesserit are setting very powerful . . . *elements* adrift in the human current. They may jam up. They are sure to cause damage. And we . . ."

Once more, the lighter entered a period of severe buffeting. Conversation was impossible while they clung to their seats and listened to the roaring, creaking around them. When this interruption eased, Taraza raised her voice.

"If we survive this damnable machine and get down to Gammu, you must go aside with Dar there, Miles. You have seen the Atreides Manifesto. She will tell you about it and prepare you. That is all."

Teg turned and looked at Odrade. Once more, her features tugged at his memories: a remarkable likeness to Lucilla, but there was something else. He put this aside. *The Atreides Manifesto?* He had read it because it came to him from Taraza with instructions that he do so. *Prepare me? For what?*

Odrade saw the questioning look on Teg's face. Now, she understood Taraza's motive. The Mother Superior's orders took on a new meaning as did words from the Manifesto itself.

"Just as the universe is created by the participation of consciousness, the prescient human carries that creative faculty to its ultimate extreme. This was the profoundly misunderstood power of the Atreides bastard, the power that he transmitted to his son, the Tyrant."

Odrade knew those words with an author's intimacy but they came back to her now as though she had never before encountered them.

Damn you, Tar! Odrade thought. *What if you're wrong?*

At the quantum level our universe can be seen as an indeterminate place, predictable in a statistical way only when you employ large enough numbers. Between that universe and a relatively predictable one where the passage of a single planet can be timed to a picosecond, other forces come into play. For the in-between universe where we find our daily lives, *that which you believe* is a dominant force. Your beliefs order the unfolding of daily events. If enough of us believe, a new thing can be made to exist. Belief structure creates a filter through which chaos is sifted into order.

—ANALYSIS OF THE TYRANT,

THE TARAZA FILE:

BG ARCHIVES

Teg's thoughts were in turmoil as he returned to Gammu from the Guildship. He stepped from the lighter at the black-charred edge of the Keep's private landing field and looked around him as though for the first time. Almost noon. So little time had passed and so much had changed.

To what extent would the Bene Gesserit go in imparting an essential lesson? he wondered. Taraza had dislodged him from his familiar Mentat processes. He felt that the whole incident on the Guildship had been staged just for him. He had been shaken from a predictable course. How strange Gammu appeared as he crossed the guarded strip to the entry pits.

Teg had seen many planets, learned their ways and how they printed themselves on their inhabitants. Some planets had a big yellow sun that sat in close and kept living things warm, evolving, growing. Some planets had little shimmer-suns that hung far away in a dark sky, and their light touched very little. Variations existed within and even outside this range. Gammu was a yellow-green variation with a day of 31.27 standard hours and a 2.6 SY. Teg had thought he knew Gammu.

When the Harkonnens were forced to abandon it, colonists left behind by the Scattering came from the Danian group, calling it by the Halleck name given to it in the great remapping. The colonists had been known as Caladanian in those days but millennia tended to shorten some labels.

Teg paused at the entryway to the protective revetments that led from the field down beneath the Keep. Taraza and her party lagged behind him. He saw Taraza was talking intently to Odrade.

Atreides Manifesto, he thought.

Even on Gammu, few admitted to either Harkonnen or Atreides ancestry, although the genotypes were visible here—especially the dominant Atreides: those long, sharp noses, the high foreheads and sensual mouths. Often, the pieces were scattered—the mouth on one face, those piercing eyes on another and countless mixtures. Sometimes, though, one person carried it all and then you saw the pride, that inner knowledge:

"I am one of them!"

Gammu's natives recognized it and gave it walkway room but few labeled it.

Underlying all of this was what the Harkonnens had left behind—genetic lines tracing far away into the dawn times of Greek and Pathan and Mameluke, shadows of ancient history that few outside of professional historians or those trained by the Bene Gesserit could even name.

Taraza and her party caught up with Teg. He heard her say to Odrade: "You must tell Miles all of it."

Very well, she would tell him, he thought. He turned and led the way past the inner guards to the long passage under the pillboxes into the Keep proper.

Damn the Bene Gesserit! he thought. *What were they really doing here on Gammu?*

Plenty of Bene Gesserit signs could be seen on this planet: the back-breeding to fix selected traits, and here and there a visible emphasis on seductive eyes for women.

Teg returned a guard captain's salute without changing focus. *Seductive eyes, yes.* He had seen this soon after his arrival at the ghola's Keep and especially during his first inspection tour of the planet. He had seen himself in many faces, too, and recalled the thing old Patrin had mentioned so many times.

"You have the Gammu look, Bashar."

Seductive eyes! That guard captain back there had them. She and Odrade and Lucilla were alike in this. Few people paid much attention to the importance of eyes when it came to seduction, he thought. It took a Bene Gesserit upbringing to make that point. Big breasts in a woman and hard loins in a man (that tightly muscular look to the buttocks)—these were naturally important in sexual matchings. But without the eyes, the rest of it could go for nothing. Eyes were essential. You could drown in the right kind of eyes, he had learned, sink right into them and be unaware of what was being done to you until penis was firmly clasped in vagina.

He had noted Lucilla's eyes immediately after his arrival on Gammu and had walked cautiously. No doubts about how the Sisterhood used her talents!

There was Lucilla now, waiting at the central inspection and decontamination chamber. She gave him the flickering handsign that all was well with the ghola. Teg relaxed and watched as Lucilla and Odrade confronted each other. The two women had remarkably similar features despite the age difference. Their bodies were quite different, though, Lucilla more solid against Odrade's willowy form.

The guard captain of the seductive eyes came up beside Teg and leaned close to him. "Schwangyu has just learned who you brought back with you," she said, nodding toward Taraza. "Ahhh, there she is now."

Schwangyu stepped from a lift tube and crossed to Taraza, giving only an angry glare to Teg.

Taraza wanted to surprise you, he thought. *We all know why.*

"You don't appear happy to see me," Taraza said, addressing Schwangyu.

"I *am* surprised, Mother Superior," Schwangyu said. "I had no idea." She glanced once more at Teg, a look of venom in her eyes.

Odrade and Lucilla broke off their mutual examination. "I had heard about it, of course," Odrade said, "but it is a stopper to confront yourself in the face of another person."

"I warned you," Taraza said.

"What are your orders, Mother Superior?" Schwangyu

asked. It was as close as she could come to asking the purpose of Taraza's visit.

"I would like a private word with Lucilla," Taraza said.

"I'll have quarters prepared for you," Schwangyu said.

"Don't bother," Taraza said. "I'm not staying. Miles has already arranged for my transport. Duty requires my presence at Chapter House. Lucilla and I will talk outside in the courtyard." Taraza put a finger to her cheek. "Oh, and I'd like to watch the ghola unobserved for a few minutes. I'm sure Lucilla can arrange it."

"He's taking the more intense training quite well," Lucilla said as the two moved off toward a lift tube.

Teg turned his attention to Odrade, noting as his gaze passed across Schwangyu's face the intensity of her anger. She was not trying to conceal it.

Was Lucilla a sister or a daughter of Odrade? Teg wondered. It occurred to him suddenly that there must be a Bene Gesserit purpose behind the resemblance. Yes, of course—Lucilla was an Imprinter!

Schwangyu overcame her anger. She looked with curiosity at Odrade. "I was just about to take lunch, Sister," Schwangyu said. "Would you care to join me?"

"I must have a word alone with the Bashar," Odrade said. "If it is all right, perhaps we could remain here for our talk? I must not be seen by the ghola."

Schwangyu scowled, not trying to hide her upset from Odrade. They knew at Chapter House where loyalties lay! But no one . . . no one! would remove her from this post of observational command. Opposition had its rights!

Her thoughts were clear even to Teg. He noted the stiffness of Schwangyu's back as she left them.

"It is bad when Sister is turned against Sister," Odrade said.

Teg gave a handsign to his guard captain, ordering her to clear the area. *Alone*, Odrade said. *Alone it would be*. To Odrade, he said: "This is one of my areas. No spies or other means of observing us here."

"I thought as much," Odrade said.

"We have a service room over there." Teg nodded to his left. "Furniture, even chairdogs if you prefer."

"I hate it when they try to cuddle me," she said. "Could we talk here?" She put a hand under Teg's arm. "Perhaps we could walk a bit. I got so stiff sitting in that lighter."

"What is it you're supposed to tell me?" he asked as they strolled.

"My memories are no longer selectively filtered," she said. "I have them all, only on the female side, naturally."

"So?" Teg pursed his lips. This was not the overture he had expected. Odrade appeared more like one who would take off on a direct approach.

"Taraza says you have read the Atreides Manifesto. Good. You know it will cause upset in many quarters."

"Schwangyu already has made it the subject of a diatribe against 'you Atreides.'"

Odrade stared at him solemnly. As the reports all said, Teg remained an imposing figure, but she had known that without the reports.

"We are both Atreides, you and I," Odrade said.

Teg came to full alert.

"Your mother explained that to you in detail," Odrade

said, "when you took your first school leave back to Lernaeus."

Teg stopped and stared down at her. How could she know this? To his knowledge, he had never before met and conversed with this remote Darwi Odrade. Was he the subject of special discussions at Chapter House? He held his silence, forcing her to carry the conversation.

"I will recount a conversation between a man and my birth-mother," Odrade said. "They are in bed and the man says: 'I fathered a few children when I first escaped from the close bondage of the Bene Gesserit, back when I thought myself an independent agent, free to enlist and fight anywhere I chose.'"

Teg did not try to conceal his surprise. Those were his own words! Mentat memory told him Odrade had them down as accurately as a mechanical recorder. Even the tone!

"More?" she asked as he continued to stare at her. "Very well. The man says: 'That was before they sent me to Mentat training, of course. What an eye-opener that was! I had never been out of the Sisterhood's sight for an instant! I was never a free agent.'"

"Not even when I spoke *those* words," Teg said.

"True." She urged him by pressure on his arm as they continued their stroll across the chamber. "The children you fathered all belonged to the Bene Gesserit. The Sisterhood takes no chances that our genotype will be sent into the wild gene pool."

"Let my body go to Shaitan, their precious genotype remains in Sisterhood care," he said.

"My care," Odrade said. "I am one of your daughters."

Again, he forced her to stop.

"I think you know who my mother was," she said. She held up a hand for silence as he started to respond. "Names are not necessary."

Teg studied Odrade's features, seeing the recognizable signs there. Mother and daughter were matched. But what of Lucilla?

As though she heard his question, Odrade said: "Lucilla is from a parallel breeding line. Quite remarkable, isn't it, what careful breed-matching can achieve?"

Teg cleared his throat. He felt no emotional attachment to this newly revealed daughter. Her words and other important signals of her performance demanded his primary attention.

"This is no casual conversation," he said. "Is this all of what you were to reveal to me? I thought the Mother Superior said . . ."

"There is more," Odrade agreed. "The Manifesto—I am its author. I wrote it at Taraza's orders and following her detailed instructions."

Teg glanced around the large chamber as though to make sure no one overheard. He spoke in a lowered voice: "The Tleilaxu are spreading it far and wide!"

"Just as we hoped."

"Why are you telling me this? Taraza said you were to prepare me for . . ."

"There will come a time when you must know our purpose. It is Taraza's wish that you make your own decisions then, that you really become a free agent."

Even as she spoke, Odrade saw the Mentat glaze in his eyes.

Teg breathed deeply. *Dependencies and key logs!* He felt the Mentat sense of an enormous pattern just beyond the reach of his accumulated data. He did not even consider for an instant that some form of filial devotion had prompted these revelations. There was a fundamentalist, dogmatic, and ritualistic essence apparent in all Bene Gesserit training despite every effort to prevent this. Odrade, this daughter out of his past, was a full Reverend Mother with extraordinary powers of muscle and nerve control—full memories on the female side! She was one of the special ones! She knew tricks of violence that few humans ever suspected. Still, that similarity, that essence remained and a Mentat always saw it.

What does she want?

Affirmation of his paternity? She already had all of the confirmation she could need.

Observing her now, the way she waited so patiently for his thoughts to resolve, Teg reflected that it often was said with truth that Reverend Mothers no longer were completely members of the human race. They moved somehow outside the main flow, perhaps parallel to it, perhaps diving into it occasionally for their own purposes, but always removed from humankind. They removed themselves. It was an identifying mark of the Reverend Mother, a sense of extra identity that made them closer to the long-dead Tyrant than to the human stock from which they sprang.

Manipulation. That was their mark. They manipulated everyone and everything.

"I am to be the Bene Gesserit eyes," Teg said. "Taraza wants me to make a *human* decision for all of you."

Obviously pleased, Odrade squeezed his arm. "What a father I have!"

"Do you really have a father?" he asked and he

recounted for her what he had been thinking about the Bene Gesserit removing themselves from humanity.

"Outside humanity," she said. "What a curious idea. Are Guild navigators also outside their original humanity?"

He thought about this. Guild navigators diverged widely from humankind's more common shape. Born in space and living out their lives in tanks of melange gas, they distorted the original form, elongated and repositioned limbs and organs. But a young navigator in estrus and before entering the tank could breed with a norm. It had been demonstrated. They became non-human but not in the way of the Bene Gesserit.

"Navigators are not your mental kin," he said. "They think human. Guiding a ship through space, even with prescience to find the safe way, has a pattern a human can accept."

"You don't accept our pattern?"

"As far as I can, but somewhere in your development you shift outside the original pattern. I think you may perform a conscious act even to appear human. This way you hold my arm right now, as though you really were my daughter."

"I am your daughter but I'm surprised you think so little of us."

"Quite the contrary: I stand in awe of you."

"Of your own daughter?"

"Of any Reverend Mother."

"You think I exist only to manipulate lesser creatures?"

"I think you no longer really feel human. There's a gap in you, something missing, something you've removed. You no longer are one of us."

"Thank you," Odrade said. "Taraza told me you

would not hesitate to answer truthfully, but I knew that for myself."

"For what have you prepared me?"

"You will know it when it occurs, that is all I can say . . . all I am permitted to say."

Manipulating again! he thought. *Damn them!*

Odrade cleared her throat. She appeared about to say something more but she remained silent as she guided Teg around and strolled with him back across the chamber.

Even though she had known what Teg must say, his words pained her. She wanted to tell him that she was one of those who still felt human, but his judgment of the Sisterhood could not be denied.

We are taught to reject love. We can simulate it but each of us is capable of cutting it off in an instant.

There were sounds behind them. They stopped and turned. Lucilla and Taraza emerged from a lift tube speaking idly about their observations of the ghola.

"You are absolutely right to treat him as one of us," Taraza said.

Teg heard but made no comment as they awaited the approach of the two women.

He knows, Odrade thought. *He will not ask me about my birth-mother. There was no bonding, no real imprint. Yes, he knows.*

Odrade closed her eyes and memory startled her by producing of itself an image of a painting. The thing occupied a space on the wall of Taraza's morning room. Ixian artifice had preserved the painting in the finest hermetically sealed frame behind a cover of invisible plaz. Odrade often stopped in front of the painting, feeling each time that her hand might reach out and actually touch the ancient canvas so cunningly preserved by the Ixians.

Cottages at Cordeville.

The artist's name for his work and his own name were preserved on a burnished plate beneath the painting: *Vincent Van Gogh.*

The thing dated from a time so ancient that only rare remnants such as this painting remained to send a physical impression down the ages. She had tried to imagine the journeys that painting had taken, the serial chance that had brought it intact to Taraza's room.

The Ixians had been at their best in the preservation and restoration. An observer could touch a dark spot on the lower left corner of the frame. Immediately, you were engulfed in the true genius, not only of the artist, but of the Ixian who had restored and preserved the work. His name was there on the frame: Martin Buro. When touched by the human finger, the dot became a sense projector, a benign spin-off of the technology that had produced the Ixian Probe. Buro had restored not only the painting but the painter—Van Gogh's feeling—accompaniment to each brush stroke. All had been captured in the brush strokes, recorded there by human movements.

Odrade had stood there engrossed through the whole performance so many times she felt she could re-create the painting independently.

Recalling this experience so near to Teg's accusation, she knew at once why her memory had reproduced the image for her, why that painting still fascinated her. For the brief space of that replay she always felt totally human, aware of the cottages as places where real people dwelled, aware in some complete way of the living chain that had paused there in the person of the mad Vincent Van Gogh, paused to record itself.

Taraza and Lucilla stopped about two paces from Teg and Odrade. There was a smell of garlic on Taraza's breath.

"We stopped for a small bite to eat," Taraza said. "Would you like anything?"

It was exactly the wrong question. Odrade freed her hand from Teg's arm. She turned quickly and wiped her eyes on her cuff. Looking up once more at Teg, she saw surprise on his face. *Yes*, she thought, *those were real tears!*

"I think we've done everything here that we can," Taraza said.

"It's time you were on your way to Rakis, Dar."

"Past time," Odrade said.

Life cannot find reasons to sustain it, cannot be a source of decent mutual regard, unless each of us resolves to breathe such qualities into it.

—CHENOEH: "CONVERSATIONS WITH LETO II"

Hedley Tuek, High Priest of the Divided God, had grown increasingly angry with Stiros. Although too old himself ever to hope for the High Priest's bench, Stiros had sons, grandsons, and numerous nephews. Stiros had transferred his personal ambitions to his family. A cynical man, Stiros. He represented a powerful faction in the priesthood, the so-called scientific community, whose influence was insidious and pervasive. They veered dangerously close to heresy.

Tuek reminded himself that more than one High Priest had been *lost* in the desert, regrettable accidents. Stiros and his faction were capable of creating such an accident.

It was afternoon in Keen and Stiros had just departed, obviously frustrated. Stiros wanted Tuek to go into the desert and personally observe Sheeana's next venture there. Suspicious of the invitation, Tuek declined.

A strange argument ensued, full of innuendo and vague references to Sheeana's behavior plus wordy attacks on the Bene Gesserit. Stiros, always suspicious of the

Sisterhood, had taken an immediate dislike to the new commander of the Bene Gesserit Keep on Rakis, this . . . what was her name? Oh, yes, Odrade. Odd name but then the Sisters often took odd names. That was their privilege. God Himself had never spoken against the basic goodness of the Bene Gesserit. Against individual Sisters, yes, but the Sisterhood itself had shared God's Holy Vision.

Tuek did not like the way Stiros spoke of Sheeana. Cynical. Tuek had finally silenced Stiros with pronouncements delivered here in the Sanctus with its high altar and images of the Divided God. Prismatic beam relays cast thin wedges of brilliance through drifting incense from burning melange onto the double line of tall pillars that led up to the altar. Tuek knew his words went directly to God from this setting.

"God works through our latter-day Siona," Tuek had told Stiros, noting the confusion on the old councillor's face. "Sheeana is the living reminder of Siona, that human instrument who translated Him into His present Divisions."

Stiros raged, saying things he would not dare repeat before the full Council. He presumed too much on his long association with Tuek.

"I tell you she is sitting here surrounded by adults intent upon justifying themselves to her and—"

"And to God!" Tuek could not let such words pass.

Leaning close to the High Priest, Stiros grated: "She is at the center of an educational system geared to anything her imagination demands. We deny her nothing!"

"Nor should we."

It was as though Tuek had not spoken. Stiros said,

"Cania has provided her with recordings from Dar-es-Balat!"

"I am the Book of Fate," Tuek intoned, quoting God's own words from the hoard at Dar-es-Balat.

"Exactly! And she listens to every word!"

"Why does this disturb you?" Tuek asked in his calmest tone.

"We don't test *her* knowledge. She tests *ours*!"

"God must want it so."

No mistaking the bitter anger on Stiros' face. Tuek observed this and waited while the old councillor marshaled new arguments. Resources for such arguments were, of course, enormous. Tuek did not deny this. It was the interpretations that mattered. Which was why a High Priest must be the final interpreter. Despite (or perhaps because of) their way of viewing history, the priesthood knew a great deal of how God had come to reside on Rakis. They had Dar-es-Balat itself and all of its contents—the earliest known no-chamber in the universe. For millennia, while Shai-hulud translated the verdant planet of Arrakis into desert-Rakis, Dar-es-Balat waited under the sands. From that Holy Hoard, the priesthood possessed God's own voice, His printed words and even holophotos. Everything was explained and they knew that the desert surface of Rakis reproduced the original form of the planet, the way it looked in the beginning when it was the only known source of the Holy Spice.

"She asks about God's family," Stiros said. "Why should she have to ask about—"

"She tests us. Do we give Them Their proper places? The Reverend Mother Jessica to her son, Muad'Dib, to his son, Leto II—the Holy Triumvirate of Heaven."

"Leto III," Stiros muttered. "What of the other Leto who died at Sardaukar hands? What of him?"

"Careful, Stiros," Tuek intoned. "You know my great-grandfather pronounced upon that question from this very bench. Our Divided God was reincarnated with part of Him remaining in heaven to mediate the Ascendancy. That part of Him became nameless then, as the True Essence of God should always be!"

"Oh?"

Tuek heard the terrible cynicism in the old man's voice. Stiros' words seemed to tremble in the incense-laden air, inviting terrible retribution.

"Then why does she ask how our Leto was transformed into the Divided God?" Stiros demanded.

Did Stiros question the Holy Metamorphosis? Tuek was aghast. He said: "In time, she will enlighten us."

"Our feeble explanations must fill her with dismay," Stiros sneered.

"You go too far, Stiros!"

"Indeed? You do not think it enlightening that she asks how the sandtrout encapsulate most of Rakis' water and re-create the desert?"

Tuek tried to conceal his growing anger. Stiros *did* represent a powerful faction in the priesthood, but his tone and his words raised questions that had been answered by High Priests long ago. The Metamorphosis of Leto II had given birth to uncounted sandtrout, each carrying a Bit of Himself. Sandtrout to Divided God: The sequence was known and worshiped. To question this denied God.

"You sit here and do nothing!" Stiros accused. "We are pawns of—"

"Enough!" Tuek had heard all he wanted to hear of this old man's cynicism. Drawing his dignity around him, Tuek spoke the words of God:

"Your Lord knows very well what is in your heart. Your soul suffices this day as a reckoner against you. I need no witnesses. You do not listen to your soul, but listen instead to your anger and your rage."

Stiros retired in frustration.

After considerable thought, Tuek enrobed himself in his most suitable finery of white, gold, and purple. He went to visit Sheeana.

Sheeana was in the roof garden atop the central priestly complex, there with Cania and two others—a young priest named Baldik, who was in Tuek's private service, and an acolyte priestess named Kipuna, who behaved too much like a Reverend Mother for Tuek's liking. The Sisterhood had its spies here, of course, but Tuek did not like to be aware of it. Kipuna had taken over much of Sheeana's physical training and there had grown a rapport between child and acolyte priestess that aroused Cania's jealousy. Even Cania, however, could not stand in the way of Sheeana's commands.

The four of them stood beside a stone bench almost in the shadow of a ventilator tower. Kipuna held Sheeana's right hand, manipulating the child's fingers. Sheeana was growing tall, Tuek noted. Six years she had been his charge. He could see the first beginnings of breasts poking out her robe. There was not a breath of wind on the rooftop and the air felt heavy in Tuek's lungs.

Tuek glanced around the garden to assure himself that his security arrangements were not being ignored. One never knew from what quarter danger might appear. Four of Tuek's own personal guards, well armed but concealing it, shared the rooftop at a distance—one at each corner. The parapet enclosing the garden was a high one, just the guards' heads standing above the rim. The only building higher than this priestly tower was Keen's primary windtrap about a thousand meters to the west.

Despite the visible evidence that his security orders were being carried out, Tuek sensed danger. Was God warning him? Tuek still felt disturbed by Stiros' cynicism. Was it wrong to allow Stiros that much latitude?

Sheeana saw Tuek approaching and stopped the odd finger-flexing exercises she was performing at Kipuna's instructions. Giving every appearance of knowledgeable patience, the child stood silently with her gaze fixed on the High Priest, forcing her companions to turn and watch with her.

Sheeana did not find Tuek a fearsome figure. She rather liked the old man although some of his questions were so bumbling. And his answers! Quite by accident, she had discovered the question that most disturbed Tuek.

"Why?"

Some of the attendant priests interpreted her question aloud as: "Why do you believe this?" Sheeana immediately picked up on this and thereafter her probings of Tuek and the others took the unvarying form:

"Why do you believe this?"

Tuek stopped about two paces from Sheeana and bowed. "Good afternoon, Sheeana." He twisted his neck nervously against the collar of his robe. The sun felt hot on his shoulders and he wondered why the child chose to be out here so often.

Sheeana maintained her probing stare at Tuek. She knew this gaze disturbed him.

Tuek cleared his throat. When Sheeana looked at him that way, he always wondered: *Is it God looking at me through her eyes?*

Cania spoke. "Sheeana has been asking today about the Fish Speakers."

In his most unctuous tones, Tuek said: "God's own Holy Army."

"All of them women?" Sheeana asked. She spoke as though she could not believe it. To those at the base of Rakian society, Fish Speakers were a name from ancient history, people cast out in the Famine Times.

She is testing me, Tuek thought. Fish Speakers. The modern carriers of the name had only a small trading-spying delegation on Rakis, composed of both men and women. Their ancient origins no longer were significant to their current activities, mostly working as an arm of Ix.

"Men always served the Fish Speakers in an advisory capacity," Tuek said. He watched carefully to see how Sheeana would respond.

"Then there were always the Duncan Idahos," Cania said.

"Yes, yes, of course: the Duncans." Tuek tried not to scowl. That woman was always interrupting! Tuek did not like being reminded of this aspect to God's historical presence on Rakis. The recurrent ghola and his position in the Holy Army carried overtones of Bene Tleilax indulgence. But there was no avoiding the fact that Fish Speakers had guarded the Duncans from harm, acting of course at the behest of God. The Duncans were holy, no doubt of it, but in a special category. By God's own account, He had killed some of the Duncans himself, obviously *translating* them immediately into heaven.

"Kipuna had been telling me about the Bene Gesserit," Sheeana said.

How the child's mind darted around!

Tuek cleared his throat, recognizing his own ambivalent attitude toward the Reverend Mothers. Reverence was demanded for those who were "Beloved of God," such as the Saintly Chenoeh. And the first High Priest had constructed a logical account of how the Holy Hwi Noree, Bride of God, had been a secret Reverend Mother. Honoring these special circumstances, the priesthood felt an irritating responsibility toward the Bene Gesserit, which was carried out chiefly by selling melange to the Sisterhood at a price ridiculously below that charged by the Tleilaxu.

In her most ingenuous tones, Sheeana said: "Tell me about the Bene Gesserit, Hedley."

Tuek glanced sharply at the adults around Sheeana, trying to catch a smile on their faces. He did not know how to deal with Sheeana calling him by his first name that way. In one sense, it was demeaning. In another sense, she honored him by such intimacy.

God tests me sorely, he thought.

"Are the Reverend Mothers good people?" Sheeana asked.

Tuek sighed. The records all confirmed that God harbored reservations about the Sisterhood. God's words had been examined carefully and submitted finally to a High Priest's interpretation. God did not let the Sisterhood threaten his Golden Path. That much was clear.

"Many of them are good," Tuek said.

"Where is the nearest Reverend Mother?" Sheeana asked.

"At the Sisterhood's Embassy here in Keen," Tuek said.

"Do you know her?"

"There are many Reverend Mothers in the Bene Gesserit Keep," he said.

"What's a Keep?"

"That's what they call their home here."

"One Reverend Mother must be in charge. Do you know that one?"

"I knew her predecessor, Tamalane, but this one is new. She has only just arrived. Her name is Odrade."

"That's a funny name."

Tuek's own thought, but he said: "One of our historians tells me it is a form of the name Atreides."

Sheeana reflected upon this. *Atreides.* That was the family that had brought Shaitan into being. Before the Atreides there had been only the Fremen and Shai-hulud. The Oral History, which her people preserved against all priestly prohibition, chanted the begats of the most important people on Rakis. Sheeana had heard these names many nights in her village.

"Muad'Dib begat the Tyrant."

"The Tyrant begat Shaitan."

Sheeana did not feel like arguing truth with Tuek. Anyway, he looked tired today. She said merely: "Bring me this Reverend Mother Odrade."

Kipuna hid a gloating smile behind her hand.

Tuek stepped back, aghast. How could he comply with such a demand? Even the Rakian priesthood did not command the Bene Gesserit! What if the Sisterhood refused him? Could he offer a gift of melange in exchange?

That might be a sign of weakness. The Reverend Mothers might bargain! No harder bargainers lived than the Sisterhood's cold-eyed Reverend Mothers. This new one, this Odrade, looked to be one of the worst.

All of these thoughts fled through Tuek's mind in an instant.

Cania intruded, giving Tuek the needed approach. "Perhaps Kipuna could convey Sheeana's invitation," Cania said.

Tuek darted a glance at the young acolyte priestess. Yes! Many suspected (Cania among them, obviously) that Kipuna spied for the Bene Gesserit. Of course, everyone on Rakis spied for someone. Tuek put on his most gracious smile as he nodded to Kipuna.

"Do you know any of the Reverend Mothers, Kipuna?"

"Some of them are known to me, My Lord High Priest," Kipuna said.

At least she still shows the proper deference!

"Excellent," Tuek said. "Would you be so kind as to start this gracious invitation from Sheeana moving up through the Sisterhood's embassy."

"I will do my poor best, My Lord High Priest."

"I'm sure you will!"

Kipuna began a prideful turn toward Sheeana, the knowledge of success growing within her. Sheeana's request had been ridiculously easy to ignite, given the techniques provided by the Sisterhood. Kipuna smiled and opened her mouth to speak. A movement at the parapet about forty meters behind Sheeana caught Kipuna's attention. Something glinted in the sunlight there. Something small and . . .

With a strangled cry, Kipuna grabbed up Sheeana, hurled

her at the startled Tuek and shouted: "Run!" With that, Kipuna dashed toward the swiftly advancing brightness—a tiny seeker trailing a long length of shigawire.

In his younger days, Tuek had played batball. He caught Sheeana instinctively, hesitated for an instant and then recognized the danger. Whirling with the squirming, protesting girl in his arms, Tuek dashed through the open door of the stair tower. He heard the door slam behind him and Cania's rapid footsteps close on his heels.

"What is it? What is it?" Sheeana pounded her fists against Tuek's chest as she shouted.

"Hush, Sheeana! Hush!" Tuek paused on the first landing. Both a chute and suspensor-drop led from this landing into the building's core. Cania stopped beside Tuek, her panting loud in the narrow space.

"It killed Kipuna and two of your guards," Cania gasped. "Cut them up! I saw it. God preserve us!"

Tuek's mind was a maelstrom. Both the chute and the suspensor-drop system were enclosed wormholes through the tower. They could be sabotaged. The attack on the roof might be only one element in a far more complex plot.

"Put me down!" Sheeana insisted. "What's happening?"

Tuek eased her to the floor but kept one of her hands clutched in his hand. He bent over her, "Sheeana, dear, someone is trying to harm us."

Sheeana's mouth formed a silent "O," then: "They hurt Kipuna?"

Tuek looked up at the roof door. Was that an ornithopter he heard up there? *Stiros!* Conspirators could take three vulnerable people into the desert so easily!

Cania had regained her breath. "I hear a 'thopter," she said. "Shouldn't we be getting away from here?"

"We will go down by the stairs," Tuck said.

"But the—"

"Do as I say!"

Keeping a firm hold on Sheeana's hand, Tuek led the way down to the next landing. In addition to the chute and suspensor access, this landing had a door into a wide curving hall. Only a few short steps beyond the door lay the entrance to Sheeana's quarters, once Tuek's own quarters. Again, he hesitated.

"Something's happening on the roof," Cania whispered.

Tuek looked down at the fearfully silent child beside him. Her hand felt sweaty.

Yes, there was some sort of uproar on the roof— shouts, the hiss of burners, much running about. The roof door, now out of sight above them, crashed open. This decided Tuek. He flung open the door into the hallway and dashed out into the arms of a tightly grouped wedge of black-robed women. With an empty sense of defeat, Tuek recognized the woman at the point of the wedge: *Odrade!*

Someone plucked Sheeana away from him and hustled her back into the press of robed figures. Before Tuek or Cania could protest, hands were clapped over their mouths. Other hands pinioned them against a wall of the hallway. Some of the robed figures went through the doorway and up the stairs.

"The child is safe and that's all that's important for the moment," Odrade whispered. She looked into Tuek's eyes. "Make no outcry." The hand was removed from his mouth. Using Voice, she said: "Tell me about the roof!"

Tuek found himself complying without reservation. "A seeker towing a long shigawire. It came over the parapet. Kipuna saw it and—"

"Where is Kipuna?"

"Dead. Cania saw it." Tuek described Kipuna's brave dash toward the threat.

Kipuna dead! Odrade thought. She concealed a fiercely angry sense of loss. What a waste. There must be admiration for such a brave death, but the loss! The Sisterhood always needed such courage and devotion, but it also required the genetic wealth Kipuna had represented. *It was gone, taken by these stumbling fools!*

At a gesture from Odrade, the hand was removed from Cania's mouth. "Tell me what you saw," Odrade said.

"The seeker whipped the shigawire around Kipuna's neck and . . ." Cania shuddered.

The dull thump of an explosion reverberated above them, then silence. Odrade waved a hand. Robed women spread along the hallway, moving silently out of sight beyond the curve. Only Odrade and two others, both chill-eyed younger women with intense expressions, remained beside Tuek and Cania. Sheeana was nowhere to be seen.

"The Ixians are in this somewhere," Odrade said.

Tuek agreed. *That much shigawire* . . . "Where have you taken the child?" he asked.

"We are protecting her," Odrade said. "Be still." She tipped her head, listening.

A robed woman sped back around the curve of the hallway and whispered something in Odrade's ear. Odrade produced a tight smile.

"It is over," Odrade said. "We will go to Sheeana."

Sheeana occupied a softly cushioned blue chair in the main room of her quarters. Black-robed women stood in a protective arc behind her. The child appeared to Tuek quite recovered from the shock of the attack and escape but her eyes glittered with excitement and unasked questions. Sheeana's attention was directed at something off to Tuek's right. He stopped and looked there, gasping at what he saw.

A naked male body lay against the wall in an oddly crumpled position, the head twisted until the chin lay back over the left shoulder. Open eyes stared out with the emptiness of death.

Stiros!

The shredded rags of Stiros' robe, obviously torn from him violently, lay in an untidy heap near the body's feet.

Tuek looked at Odrade.

"He was in on it," she said. "There were Face Dancers with the Ixians."

Tuek tried to swallow in a dry throat.

Cania shuffled past him toward the body. Tuek could not see her face but Cania's presence reminded him that there had been something between Stiros and Cania in their younger days. Tuek moved instinctively to place himself between Cania and the seated child.

Cania stopped at the body and nudged it with a foot.

She turned a gloating expression on Tuek. "I had to make sure he was really dead," she said.

Odrade glanced at a companion. "Get rid of the body." She looked at Sheeana. It was Odrade's first chance for a more careful study of the child since leading the assault force here to deal with the attack on the temple complex.

Tuek spoke behind Odrade. "Reverend Mother, could you explain please what—"

Odrade interrupted without turning. "Later."

Sheeana's expression quickened at Tuek's words. "I *thought* you were a Reverend Mother!"

Odrade merely nodded. What a fascinating child. Odrade experienced the sensations she felt while standing in front of the ancient painting in Taraza's quarters. Some of the fire that had gone into the work of art inspired Odrade now. Wild inspiration! That was the message from the mad Van Gogh. Chaos brought into magnificent order. Was that not part of the Sisterhood's coda?

This child is my canvas, Odrade thought. She felt her hand tingle to the feeling of that ancient brush. Her nostrils flared to the smells of oils and pigments.

"Leave me alone with Sheeana," Odrade ordered. "Everybody out."

Tuek started to protest but stopped when one of Odrade's robed companions gripped his arm. Odrade glared at him.

"The Bene Gesserit have served you before," she said. "This time, we saved your life."

The woman holding Tuek's arm tugged at him.

"Answer his questions," Odrade said. "But do it somewhere else."

Cania took a step toward Sheeana. "That child is my—"

"Leave!" Odrade barked, all the powers of Voice in the command.

Cania froze.

"You almost lost her to a bumbling lot of conspirators!" Odrade said, glaring at Cania. "We will consider whether you get any further opportunity to associate with Sheeana."

Tears started in Cania's eyes but Odrade's condemnation could not be denied. Turning, Cania fled with the others.

Odrade returned her attention to the watchful child.

"We've been a long time waiting for you," Odrade said. "We will not give those fools another opportunity to lose you."

Law always chooses sides on the basis of enforcement power. Morality and legal niceties have little to do with it when the real question is: Who has the clout?

—BENE GESSERIT COUNCIL PROCEEDINGS:
ARCHIVES #X0X232

Immediately after Taraza and her party left Gammu, Teg threw himself into his work. New in-Keep procedures had to be laid out, holding Schwangyu at arm's length from the ghola. Taraza's orders.

"She can observe all she wants. She can't touch."

In spite of the work pressures, Teg found himself staring into space at odd moments, prey to free-floating anxiety. The experience of rescuing Taraza's party from the Guildship and Odrade's odd revelations did not fit into any data classification he constructed.

Dependencies . . . key logs . . .

Teg found himself seated in his own workroom, an assignment schedule projected in front of him with shift changes to approve and, for a moment, he had no idea of the time or even the date. It took a moment to relocate himself.

Midmorning. Taraza and her party had been gone two days. He was alone. Yes, Patrin had taken over this day's training schedule with Duncan, freeing Teg for the command decisions.

The workroom around Teg felt alien. Yet, when he looked at each element in it, he found each thing familiar. Here was his own personal data console. His uniform jacket had been draped neatly across a chair-back beside him. He tried to fall into Mentat mode and found his own mind resisting. He had not encountered that phenomenon since training days.

Training days.

Taraza and Odrade between them had thrown him back into some form of training.

Self-training.

In a detached way, he felt his memory offering up a long-ago conversation with Taraza. How familiar it was. He was right there, caught in the moments of his own memory-snare.

Both he and Taraza had been quite tired after making the decisions and taking the actions to prevent a bloody confrontation—the Barandiko incident. Nothing but a hiccough in history now but at the time it had demanded all of their combined energies.

Taraza invited him into the small parlor of her quarters on her no ship after the agreement was signed. She spoke casually, admiring his sagacity, the way he had seen through to the weaknesses that would force a compromise.

They had been awake and active for almost thirty hours and Teg was glad for the opportunity to sit while Taraza dialed her foodrink installation. It dutifully produced two tall glasses of creamy brown liquid.

Teg recognized the smell as she handed him his glass. It was a quick source of energy, a pick-me-up that the Bene Gesserit seldom shared with outsiders. But Taraza no longer considered him an outsider.

His head tipped back, Teg took a long swallow of the drink, his gaze on the ornate ceiling of Taraza's small parlor. This no-ship was an old-fashioned model, built in the days when more care had been taken with decoration—heavily incised cornices, baroque figures carved in every surface.

The taste of the drink pushed his memory back into childhood, the heavy infusion of melange . . .

"My mother made this for me whenever I was overly strenuous," he said, looking at the glass in his hand. He already could feel the calming energy flow through his body.

Taraza took her own drink to a chairdog opposite him, a fluffy white bit of animate furniture that fitted itself to her with the ease of long familiarity. For Teg, she had provided a traditional green upholstered chair, but she saw his glance flick across the chairdog and grinned at him.

"Tastes differ, Miles." She sipped her drink and sighed. "My, that was strenuous but it was good work. There were moments when it was right on the edge of getting very nasty."

Teg found himself touched by her relaxation. No pose, no ready-made mask to set them apart and define their separate roles in the Bene Gesserit hierarchy. She was being obviously friendly and not even a hint of seductiveness. So this was just what it seemed to be—as much as that could be said about any encounter with a Reverend Mother.

With quick elation, Teg realized that he had become quite adept at reading Alma Mavis Taraza, even when she adopted one of her masks.

"Your mother taught you more than she was told to

teach you," Taraza said. "A wise woman but another heretic. That's all we seem to be breeding nowadays."

"Heretic?" He was caught by resentment.

"That's a private joke in the Sisterhood," Taraza said. "We're supposed to follow a Mother Superior's orders with absolute devotion. And we do, except when we disagree."

Teg smiled and took a deep draught of his drink.

"It's odd," Taraza said, "but while we were in that tight little confrontation I found myself reacting to you as I would to one of my Sisters."

Teg felt the drink warming his stomach. It left a tingling in his nostrils. He placed the empty glass on a side table and spoke while looking at it. "My eldest daughter . . ."

"That would be Dimela. You should have let us have her, Miles."

"It was not my decision."

"But one word from you . . ." Taraza shrugged. "Well, that's past. What about Dimela?"

"She thinks I'm often too much like one of you."

"Too much?"

"She is fiercely loyal to me, Mother Superior. She doesn't really understand our relationship and—"

"What is our relationship?"

"You command and I obey."

Taraza looked at him over the lip of her glass. When she put down the glass, she said: "Yes, you've never really been a heretic, Miles. Perhaps . . . someday . . ."

He spoke quickly, wanting to divert Taraza from such ideas. "Dimela thinks the long use of melange makes many people become like you."

"Is that so? Isn't it odd, Miles, that a geriatric potion should have so many side effects?"

"I don't find that odd."

"No, of course you wouldn't." She drained her glass and put it aside. "I was addressing the way a significant life extension has produced in some people, you especially, a profound knowledge of human nature."

"We live longer and observe more," he said.

"I don't think it's quite that simple. Some people never observe anything. Life just happens to them. They get by on little more than a kind of dumb persistence, and they resist with anger and resentment anything that might lift them out of that false serenity."

"I've never been able to strike an acceptable balance sheet for the spice," he said, referring to a common Mentat process of data sorting.

Taraza nodded. Obviously, she found the same difficulty. "We of the Sisterhood tend to be more single-track than Mentats," she said. "We have routines to shake ourselves out of it but the condition persists."

"Our ancestors have had this problem for a long time," he said.

"It was different before the spice," she said.

"But they lived such short lives."

"Fifty, one hundred years; that doesn't seem very long to us, but still . . ."

"Did they compress more into the available time?"

"Oh, they were frenetic at times."

She was giving him observations from her Other Memories, he realized. Not the first time he had shared in such ancient lore. His mother had produced such memories on occasion, but always as a lesson. Was Taraza doing that now? Teaching him something?

"Melange is a many-handed monster," she said.

"Do you sometimes wish we had never found it?"

"The Bene Gesserit would not exist without it."

"Nor the Guild."

"But there would have been no Tyrant, no Muad'Dib. The spice gives with one hand and takes with all of its others."

"Which hand contains that which we desire?" he asked. "Isn't that always the question?"

"You're an oddity, you know that, Miles? Mentats so seldom dip into philosophy. I think it's one of your strengths. You are supremely able to doubt."

He shrugged. This turn in the conversation disturbed him.

"You are not amused," she said. "But cling to your doubts anyway. Doubt is necessary to a philosopher."

"So the Zensunni assure us."

"All mystics agree on it, Miles. Never underestimate the power of doubts. Very persuasive. S'tori holds up doubt and surety in a single hand."

Really quite surprised, he asked: "Do Reverend Mothers practice Zensunni rituals?" He had never even suspected this before.

"Just once," she said. "We achieve an exalted form of s'tori, total. It involves every cell."

"The spice agony," he said.

"I was sure your mother told you. Obviously, she never explained the affinity with the Zensunni."

Teg swallowed past a lump in his throat. Fascinating!

She gave him a new insight into the Bene Gesserit. This changed his entire concept, including his image of his own mother. They were removed from him into an unattainable place where he could never follow. They might think of him as a comrade on occasion but he could never enter the intimate circle. He could simulate, no more. He would never be like Muad'Dib or the Tyrant.

"Prescience," Taraza said.

The word shifted his attention. She had changed the subject but not changed it.

"I *was* thinking about Muad'Dib," he said.

"You think he predicted the future," she said.

"That is the Mentat teaching."

"I hear the doubt in your voice, Miles. Did he predict or did he create? Prescience can be deadly. The people who demand that the oracle predict for them really want to know next year's price on whalefur or something equally mundane. None of them wants an instant-by-instant prediction of his personal life."

"No surprises," Teg said.

"Exactly. If you possessed such fore-knowledge, your life would become an unutterable bore."

"You think Muad'Dib's life was a bore?"

"And the Tyrant's, too. We think their entire lives were devoted to trying to break out of chains they them-selves created."

"But they believed . . ."

"Remember your philosopher's doubts, Miles. Be-ware! The mind of the believer stagnates. It fails to grow outward into an unlimited, infinite universe."

Teg sat silently for a moment. He sensed the fatigue that had been driven beyond his immediate awareness by

the drink, sensed also the way his thoughts were roiled
by the intrusion of new concepts. These were things that
he had been taught would weaken a Mentat, yet he felt
strengthened by them.

She is teaching me, he thought. *There is a lesson here.*

As though projected into his mind and outlined there
in fire, he found his entire Mentat-attention fixated on
the Zensunni admonition that was taught to every beginning student in the Mentat School:

*By your belief in granular singularities, you deny all
movement—evolutionary or devolutionary. Belief fixes a
granular universe and causes that universe to persist. Nothing
can be allowed to change because that way your non-moving
universe vanishes. But it moves of itself when you do not move.
It evolves beyond you and is no longer accessible to you.*

"The oddest thing of all," Taraza said, sinking into
tune with this mood she had created, "is that the scien-
tists of Ix cannot see how much their own beliefs dominate their universe."

Teg stared at her, silent and receptive.

"Ixian beliefs are perfectly submissive to the choices
they make on how they will look at their universe," Taraza
said. "Their universe does not act of itself but performs
according to the kinds of experiments they choose."

With a start, Teg came out of the memories and awoke
to find himself in the Gammu Keep. He still sat in the
familiar chair in his workroom. A glance around the
room showed nothing moved from where he had put it.
Only a few minutes had passed but the room and its contents no longer were alien. He dipped into and out of
Mentat mode. *Restored.*

The smell and taste of the drink Taraza had given him

so long ago still tingled on his tongue and in his nostrils. A Mentat blink and he knew he could call up the scene entire once more—the low light of shaded glowglobes, the feeling of the chair beneath him, the sounds of their voices. It was all there for replay, frozen into a time-capsule of isolated memory.

Calling up that old memory created a magical universe where his abilities were amplified beyond his wildest expectations. No atoms existed in that magical universe, only waves and awesome movements all around. He was forced there to discard all barriers built of belief and understanding. This universe was transparent. He could see through it without any interfering screens upon which to project its forms. The magical universe reduced him to a core of active imagination where his own image-making abilities were the only screen upon which any projection might be sensed.

There, I am both the performer and the performed!

The workroom around Teg wavered into and out of his sensory reality. He felt his awareness constricted to its tightest purpose and yet that purpose filled his universe. He was open to infinity.

Taraza did this deliberately! he thought. *She has amplified me!*

A feeling of awe threatened him. He recognized how his daughter, Odrade, had drawn upon such powers to create the Atreides Manifesto for Taraza. His own Mentat powers were submerged in that greater pattern.

Taraza was demanding a fearful performance from him. The need for such a thing both challenged and terrified him. It could very well mean the end of the Sisterhood.

The basic rule is this: Never support weakness; always support strength.

—THE BENE GESSERIT CODA

"How is it that you can order the priests around?" Sheeana asked. "This is their place."

Odrade answered casually but picked her words to fit the knowledge she knew Sheeana already possessed: "The priests have Fremen roots. They've always had Reverend Mothers somewhere near. Besides, child, you order them around, too."

"That's different."

Odrade suppressed a smile.

Little more than three hours had passed since her assault force had broken the attack on the temple complex. In that time, Odrade had set up a command center in Sheeana's quarters, carried on the necessary business of assessment and preliminary retaliation, all the while prompting and observing Sheeana.

Simulflow.

Odrade glanced around the room she had chosen as command center. A scrap of Stiros' ripped garments still lay near the wall in front of her. *Casualties.* The room was an oddly shaped place. No two walls parallel. She sniffed. Still a residual smell of ozone from the snoopers with which her people had assured the privacy of these quarters.

Why the odd shape? The building was ancient, remodeled and added to many times, but that did not explain this room. A pleasantly rough texture of creamy stucco on walls and ceiling. Elaborate spice-fiber hangings flanked the two doors. It was early evening and sunlight filtered by lattice shades stippled the wall opposite the windows. Silver-yellow glowglobes hovered near the ceiling, all tuned to match the sunlight. Muted street sounds came through the ventilators beneath the windows. The soft pattern of orange rugs and gray tiles on the floor spoke of wealth and security but Odrade suddenly did not feel secure.

A tall Reverend Mother came from the adjoining communications room. "Mother Commander," she said, "the messages have been sent to Guild, Ix, and Tleilaxu."

Odrade spoke absently. "Acknowledged."

The messenger returned to her duties.

"What are you doing?" Sheeana asked.

"Studying something."

Odrade pursed her lips in thought. Their guides through the temple complex had brought them along a maze of hallways and stairs, glimpses of courtyards through arches, then into a splendid Ixian suspensor-tube system, which carried them silently to another hallway, more stairs, another curved hallway . . . finally, into this room.

Once more, Odrade swept her gaze around the room.

"Why are you studying this room?" Sheeana asked.

"Hush, child!"

The room was an irregular polyhedron with the smaller side to the left. About thirty-five meters long, half that at the widest. Many low divans and chairs in various degrees of comfort. Sheeana sat in queenly splendor on a bright yellow chair with wide soft arms. Not a chairdog in the place. Much brown and blue and yellow fabric. Odrade stared at the white lattice of a ventilator above a painting of mountains on the wider end wall. A cool breeze came through the ventilators below the windows and wafted toward the ventilator above the painting.

"This was Hedley's room," Sheeana said.

"Why do you annoy him by using his first name, child?"

"Does that annoy him?"

"Don't play word games with me, child! You know it annoys him and that's why you do it."

"Then why did you ask?"

Odrade ignored this while continuing her careful study of the room. The wall opposite the painting stood at an oblique angle to the outer wall. She had it now. *Clever!* This room had been constructed so that even a whisper here could be heard by someone beyond the high ventilator. No doubt the painting concealed another airway to carry sounds from this room. No snooper, sniffer, or other instrument would detect such an arrangement. Nothing would "beep" at a spying eye or ear. Only the wary senses of someone trained in deception had winkled it out.

A hand signal summoned a waiting acolyte. Odrade's fingers flickered in silent communication: *"Find out who is listening beyond that ventilator."* She nodded toward the ventilator above the painting. *"Let them continue. We must know to whom they report."*

"How did you know to come and save me?" Sheeana asked.

The child had a lovely voice but it needed training, Odrade thought. There was a steadiness to it, though, that could be shaped into a powerful instrument.

"Answer me!" Sheeana ordered.

The imperious tone startled Odrade, arousing quick anger, which she was forced to suppress. Corrections would have to be made immediately!

"Calm yourself, child," Odrade said. She pitched the command in a precise tenor and saw it take effect.

Again, Sheeana startled her: "That's another kind of Voice. You're trying to calm me. Kipuna told me all about Voice."

Odrade turned squarely facing Sheeana and looked down at her. Sheeana's first grief had passed but there was still anger when she spoke of Kipuna.

"I am busy shaping our response to that attack," Odrade said. "Why do you distract me? I should think you would want them punished."

"What will you do to them? Tell me! What will you do?"

A surprisingly vindictive child, Odrade thought. That would have to be curbed. Hatred was as dangerous an emotion as love. The capacity for hatred was the capacity for its opposite.

Odrade said: "I have sent Guild, Ix, and Tleilaxu the message we always dispatch when we have been annoyed. Three words: 'You will pay.'"

"How will they pay?"

"A proper Bene Gesserit punishment is being fashioned. They will feel the consequences of their behavior."

"But *what* will you do?"

"In time, you may learn. You may even learn how we design our punishment. For now, there is no need that you know."

A sullen look came over Sheeana's face. She said: "You're not even angry. Annoyed. That's what you said."

"Curb your impatience, child! There are things you do not understand."

The Reverend Mother from the communications room returned, glanced once at Sheeana and spoke to Odrade. "Chapter House acknowledges receipt of your report. They approve your response."

When the Reverend Mother from communications remained standing there, Odrade said: "There is more?"

A flickering glance to Sheeana spoke of the woman's reservations. Odrade held up her right palm, the signal for silent communication.

The Reverend Mother responded, her fingers dancing with unleashed excitement: *Taraza's message—The Tleilaxu are the pivotal element. Guild must be made to pay dearly for its melange. Shut down Rakian supply to them. Throw Guild and Ix together. They will overextend selves in face of crushing competition from the Scattering. Ignore Fish Speakers for now. They fall with Ix. Master of Musters responds to us from Tleilaxu. He goes to Rakis. Trap him.*

Odrade smiled softly to acknowledge that she understood. She watched the other woman leave the room. Not only did Chapter House agree with actions taken on Rakis, a suitable Bene Gesserit punishment had been fashioned with fascinating speed. Obviously Taraza and her advisors had anticipated this moment.

Odrade allowed herself a sigh of relief. The message to

Chapter House had been terse: an outline account of the attack, the list of the Sisterhood's casualties, identification of the attackers and a confirming note to Taraza that Odrade already had transmitted the required warning to the guilty: "You will pay."

Yes, those fool attackers now knew the hornet's nest had been aroused. That would create fear—an essential part of the punishment.

Sheeana squirmed in her chair. Her attitude said she would now try a new approach. "One of your people said there were Face Dancers." She gestured with her chin toward the roof.

What a vast reservoir of ignorance this child was, Odrade thought. That emptiness would have to be filled. *Face Dancers!* Odrade thought about the bodies they had examined. The Tleilaxu had finally sent their Face Dancers into action. It was a test of the Bene Gesserit, of course. These new ones were extremely difficult to detect. They still gave off the characteristic smell of their unique pheromones, though. Odrade had sent that datum in her message to Chapter House.

The problem now was to keep the Bene Gesserit knowledge secret. Odrade summoned an acolyte messenger. Indicating the ventilator with a flick of her eyes, Odrade spoke silently with her fingers: *"Kill those who listen!"*

"You are too interested in Voice, child," Odrade said, speaking down to Sheeana in the chair. "Silence is a most valuable tool for learning."

"But could I learn Voice? I want to learn it."

"I am telling you to be silent and to learn by your silence."

"I command you to teach me Voice!"

Odrade reflected on Kipuna's reports. Sheeana had established effective Voice control over most of those around her. The child had learned it on her own. An intermediate level Voice for a limited audience. She was a natural. Tuek and Cania and the others were frightened by Sheeana. Religious fantasies contributed to that fear, of course, but Sheeana's mastery of Voice pitch and tone displayed an admirable unconscious selectivity.

The indicated response to Sheeana was obvious, Odrade knew. Honesty. It was a most powerful lure and it served more than one purpose.

"I am here to teach you many things," Odrade said, "but I do not do this at your command."

"Everyone obeys me!" Sheeana said.

She's barely into puberty and already at Aristocrat level, Odrade thought. *Gods of our own making! What can she become?*

Sheeana slipped out of her chair and stood looking up at Odrade with a questioning expression. The child's eyes were on a level with Odrade's shoulders. Sheeana was going to be tall, a commanding presence. If she survived.

"You answer some of my questions but you won't answer others," Sheeana said. "You said you'd been waiting for me but you won't explain. Why won't you obey me?"

"A foolish question, child."

"Why do you keep calling me child?"

"Are you not a child?"

"I menstruate."

"But you're still a child."

"The priests obey me."

"They're afraid of you."

"You aren't?"

"No, I'm not."

"Good! It gets tiresome when people only fear you."

"The priests think you come from God."

"Don't you think that?"

"Why should I? We—" Odrade broke off as an acolyte messenger entered. The acolyte's fingers danced in silent communication: *"Four priests listened. They have been killed. All were minions of Tuek."*

Odrade waved the messenger away.

"She talks with her fingers," Sheeana said. "How does she do that?"

"You ask too many of the wrong questions, child. And you haven't told me why I should consider you an instrument of God."

"Shaitan spares me. I walk on the desert and when Shaitan comes, I talk to him."

"Why do you call him Shaitan instead of Shai-hulud?"

"Everybody asks that same stupid question!"

"Then give me your stupid answer."

The sullen expression returned to Sheeana's face. "It's because of how we met."

"And how did you meet?"

Sheeana tipped her head to one side and looked up at Odrade for a moment, then: "That's a secret."

"And you know how to keep secrets?"

Sheeana straightened and nodded but Odrade saw uncertainty in the movement. The child knew when she was being led into an impossible position!

"Excellent!" Odrade said. "The keeping of secrets is

one of a Reverend Mother's most essential teachings. I'm glad we won't have to bother with that one."

"But I want to learn everything!"

Such petulance in her voice. Very poor emotional control.

"You must teach me everything!" Sheeana insisted.

Time for the whip, Odrade thought. Sheeana had spoken and postured sufficiently that even a fifth-grade acolyte could feel confident of controlling her now.

Using the full power of Voice, Odrade said: "Don't take that tone with me, child! Not if you wish to learn anything!"

Sheeana went rigid. She was more than a minute absorbing what had happened to her and then relaxing. Presently, she smiled, a warm and open expression. "Oh, I'm so glad you came! It's been so boring lately."

Nothing surpasses the complexity of the human mind.

—LETO II: DAR-ES-BALAT RECORDS

The Gammu night, often quickly foreboding in this latitude, was almost two hours away. Gathering clouds shadowed the Keep. At Lucilla's command, Duncan had returned to the courtyard for an intense session of self-directed practice.

Lucilla observed from the parapet where she had first watched him.

Duncan moved in the tumbling twists of the Bene Gesserit eightfold combat, hurling his body across the grass, rolling, flipping himself from side to side, darting up and then down.

It was a fine display of random dodging, Lucilla thought. She could see no predictable pattern in his movements and the speed was dazzling. He was almost sixteen SY and already coming onto the platform potential of his prana-bindu endowment.

The carefully controlled movements of his training exercises revealed so much! He had responded quickly when she first ordered these evening sessions. The initial step of her instructions from Taraza had been accomplished. The ghola loved her. No doubt of it. She was mother-fixed to him. And it had been accomplished without seriously weakening him, although Teg's anxieties had been aroused.

My shadow is on this ghola but he is not a supplicant nor a dependent follower, she reassured herself. *Teg worries about it for no reason.*

Just that morning, she had told Teg, "Wherever his strengths dictate, he continues to express himself freely."

Teg should see him right now, she thought. These new practice movements were largely Duncan's own creation.

Lucilla suppressed a gasp of appreciation at a particularly nimble leap, which took Duncan almost to the center of the courtyard. The ghola was developing a nerve-muscle equilibrium that, given time, might be matched to a psychological equilibrium at least equal to Teg's. The cultural impact of such an achievement would be awesome. Look at all those who gave instinctive allegiance to Teg and, through Teg, to the Sisterhood.

We have the Tyrant to thank for much of that, she thought.

Before Leto II, no widespread system of cultural adjustments had ever endured long enough to approach the balance that the Bene Gesserit held as an ideal. It was this equilibrium—*"flowing along the blade of a sword"*—that fascinated Lucilla. It was why she lent herself so unreservedly to a project whose total design she did not know, but which demanded of her a performance that instinct labeled repugnant.

Duncan is so young!

What the Sisterhood required of her next had been

spelled out explicitly by Taraza: *the Sexual Imprint*. Only that morning, Lucilla had posed naked before her mirror, forming the attitudes and motions of face and body that she knew she would use to obey Taraza's orders. In artificial repose, Lucilla had seen her own face appear like that of a prehistoric love goddess—opulent with flesh and the promise of softness into which an aroused male might hurl himself.

In her education, Lucilla had seen ancient statues from the First Times, little stone figures of human females with wide hips and sagging breasts that assured abundance for a suckling infant. At will, Lucilla could produce a youthful simulation of that ancient form.

In the courtyard below Lucilla, Duncan paused a moment and appeared to be thinking out his next movements. Presently, he nodded to himself, leaped high and twisted in the air, landing like a springbok on one leg, which kicked him sideways into gyrations more akin to dance than to combat.

Lucilla drew her mouth into a tight line of resolution. *Sexual Imprint*.

The secret of sex was no secret at all, she thought. The roots were attached to life itself. This explained, of course, why her first command-seduction for the Sisterhood had planted a male face in her memory. The Breeding Mistress had told her to expect this and not be alarmed by it. But Lucilla had realized then that the Sexual Imprint was a two-edged sword. You might learn to flow along the edge of the blade but you could be cut by it. Sometimes, when that male face of her first command-seduction returned unbidden into her mind, Lucilla felt confounded by it. The memory came so frequently at the peak of an

intimate moment, forcing her to great efforts of concealment.

"You are strengthened thus," the Breeding Mistresses
reassured her.

Still, there were times when she felt that she had trivi-
alized something better left a mystery.

A feeling of sourness at what she must do swept over
Lucilla. These evenings when she observed Duncan's
training sessions had been her favorite times each day.
The lad's muscular development showed such definite
progress—moving in the growth of sensitive muscle and
nerve links—all of the prana-bindu marvels for which the
Sisterhood was so famous. The next step was almost
upon her, though, and she no longer could sink into
watchful appreciation of her charge.

Miles Teg would come out presently, she knew. Duncan's training would move again into the practice room
with its more deadly weapons.

Teg.

Once more, Lucilla wondered about him. She had felt
herself more than once attracted to him in a particular
way that she recognized immediately. An Imprinter enjoyed some latitude in selecting her own breeding partners, provided she had no prior commitments nor
contrary orders. Teg was old but his records suggested he
might still be virile. She would not be able to keep the
child, of course, but she had learned to deal with that.

Why not? she had asked herself.

Her plan had been simple in the extreme. Complete
the Imprint on the ghola and then, registering her intent
with Taraza, conceive a child by the redoubtable Miles
Teg. Practical introductory seduction had been indicated,

but Teg had not succumbed. His Mentat cynicism stopped her one afternoon in the dressing chamber off the Weapons Room.

"My breeding days are over, Lucilla. The Sisterhood should be satisfied with what I already have given."

Teg, clad only in black exercise leotards, finished wiping his sweaty face with a towel and dropped the towel into a hamper. He spoke without looking at her: "Would you please leave me now?"

So he saw through her overtures!

She should have anticipated that, Teg being who he was. Lucilla knew she might still seduce him. No Reverend Mother of her training should fail, not even with a Mentat of Teg's obvious powers.

Lucilla stood there a moment undecided, her mind automatically planning how to circumvent this preliminary rejection. Something stopped her. Not anger at the rejection, not the remote possibility that he might indeed be proof against her wiles. Pride and its possible fall (there was always that possibility) had little to do with it.

Dignity.

There was a quiet dignity in Teg and she had the certain knowledge of what his courage and prowess had already given to the Sisterhood. Not quite sure of her motives, Lucilla turned away from him. Possibly it was the underlying gratitude that the Sisterhood felt toward him. To seduce Teg now would be demeaning, not only of him but of herself. She could not bring herself to such an action, not without a direct order from a superior.

As she stood on the parapet, some of these memories clouded her senses. There was movement in the shadows at the doorway from the Weapons Wing. Teg could be glimpsed there. Lucilla took a firmer grip on her responses and focused on Duncan. The ghola had stopped his controlled tumbling across the lawn. He stood quietly, breathing deeply, his attention aimed upward at Lucilla. She saw perspiration on his face and in dark blotchings on his light blue singlesuit.

Leaning over the parapet, Lucilla called down to him: "That was very good, Duncan. Tomorrow, I will begin teaching you more of the foot-fist combinations."

The words came out of her without censoring and she knew their source at once. They were for Teg standing in the shadowed doorway down there, not for the ghola. She was saying to Teg: "See! You aren't the only one who teaches him deadly abilities."

Lucilla realized then that Teg had insinuated himself further into her psyche than she should permit. Grimly, she swung her gaze to the tall figure emerging from the doorway's shadows. Duncan already was running toward the Bashar.

As Lucilla focused on Teg, reaction flashed through her ignited by the most elemental Bene Gesserit responses. The steps of this reaction could be defined later: *Something wrong! Danger! Teg is not Teg!* In the reactive flash, however, none of this took separate form. She responded, hurling all the volume of Voice she could muster:

"*Duncan! Down!*"

Duncan dropped flat on the grass, his attention riveted to the Teg-figure emerging from the Weapons Wing. There was a field-model lasgun in the man's hands.

Face Dancer! Lucilla thought. Only hyperalertness revealed him to her. *One of the new ones!*

"Face Dancer!" Lucilla shouted.

Duncan kicked himself sideways and leaped up, twisting flat in the air at least a meter off the ground. The speed of his reaction shocked Lucilla. She had not known any human could move that fast! The lasgun's first bolt cut beneath Duncan as he seemed to float in the air.

Lucilla jumped to the parapet and dropped to a hand-hold on the window ledge of the next lower level. Before she was stopped, her right hand shot out and found the protruding rainspout that memory told her was there. Her body arched sideways and she dropped to a window ledge at the next level. Desperation drove her even though she knew she would be too late.

Something crackled on the wall above her. She saw a molten line cut toward her as she flung herself to the left, twisting and dropping onto the lawn. Her gaze captured the scene around her in a flashing deit-grasp as she landed.

Duncan moved toward the attacker, dodging and twisting in a terrifying replay of his practice session. The speed of his movements!

Lucilla saw indecision in the face of the false Teg.

She darted toward the Face Dancer, *feeling* the creature's thoughts: *Two of them after me!*

Failure was inevitable, though, and Lucilla knew it even as she ran. The Face Dancer had only to shift his weapon into full burn at close range. He could lace the air in front of him. Nothing could penetrate such a defense. As she cast about in her mind, desperately seeking some way to defeat the attacker, she saw red smoke appear on the false Teg's breast. A line of red darted upward at an oblique angle through the muscles of the arm holding the lasgun. The arm fell away like a piece dropping from a statue. The shoulder tipped away from the torso in a spout of blood. The figure toppled, dissolving into more red smoke and blood spray, crumbling into pieces on the steps, all dark tans and blue-tinged reds.

Lucilla smelled the distinctive Face Dancer pheromones as she stopped. Duncan came up beside her. He peered past the dead Face Dancer at movement in the hallway.

Another Teg emerged behind the dead one. Lucilla identified the reality: Teg himself.

"That's the Bashar," Duncan said.

Lucilla experienced a small surge of pleasure that Duncan had learned this identity-lesson so well: how to recognize your friends even if you only saw bits of them. She pointed to the dead Face Dancer. "Smell him."

Duncan inhaled. "Yes, I have it. But he wasn't a very good copy. I saw what he was as soon as you did."

Teg emerged into the courtyard carrying a heavy lasgun cradled across his left arm. His right hand held a firm grip on the stock and trigger. He swept his gaze around the courtyard, then focused on Duncan and finally on Lucilla.

"Bring Duncan inside," Teg said.

It was the order of a battlefield commander, depending only on superior knowledge of what should be done in the emergency. Lucilla obeyed without question.

Duncan did not speak as she led him by the hand past the bloody meat that had been the Face Dancer, then into the Weapons Wing. Once inside, he glanced back at the sodden heap and asked: "Who let him in?"

Not: "How did he get in?" she observed. Duncan

already had seen past the inconsequentials to the heart of their problem.

Teg strode ahead of them toward his own quarters. He stopped at the door, glanced inside and motioned for Lucilla and Duncan to follow.

In Teg's bedroom there was the thick smell of burned flesh and wisps of smoke dominated by the charred barbecue odor that Lucilla so detested: cooked human meat! A figure in one of Teg's uniforms lay face down on the floor where it had fallen off his bed.

Teg rolled the figure over with one boot toe, exposing the face: staring eyes, a rictus grin. Lucilla recognized one of the perimeter guards, one of those who had come to the Keep with Schwangyu, so the Keep's records said.

"Their point man," Teg said. "Patrin took care of him and we put one of my uniforms on him. It was enough to fool the Face Dancers because we didn't let them see the face before we attacked. They didn't have time to make a memory print."

"You know about that?" Lucilla was startled.

"Bellonda briefed me thoroughly!"

Abruptly, Lucilla saw the further significance of what Teg said. She suppressed a swift flare of anger. "How did you let one of them get into the courtyard?"

His voice mild, Teg said: "There was rather urgent activity in here. I had to make a choice, which turned out to be the right one."

She did not try to hide her anger. "The choice to let Duncan fend for himself?"

"To leave him in your care or let other attackers get themselves firmly entrenched inside. Patrin and I had a bad time clearing this wing. We had our hands full." Teg glanced at Duncan. "He came through very well, thanks to our training."

"That . . . that *thing* almost got him!"

"Lucilla!" Teg shook his head. "I had it timed. You two could last at least a minute out there. I knew you would throw yourself in that *thing*'s path and sacrifice yourself to save Duncan. Another twenty seconds."

At Teg's words, Duncan turned a shiny-eyed look on Lucilla. "Would you have done that?"

When Lucilla did not respond, Teg said: "She would have done that."

Lucilla did not deny it. She remembered now, though, the incredible speed with which Duncan had moved, the dazzling shifts of his attack.

"Battle decisions," Teg said, looking at Lucilla.

She accepted this. As usual, Teg had made the correct choice. She knew, though, that she would have to communicate with Taraza. The prana-bindu accelerations in this ghola went beyond anything she had expected. She stiffened as Teg straightened to full alert, his gaze on the doorway behind her. Lucilla whirled.

Schwangyu stood there, Patrin behind her, another heavy lasgun over his arm. Its muzzle, Lucilla noted, was aimed at Schwangyu.

"She insisted," Patrin said. There was an angry set to the old aide's face. The deep lines beside his mouth pointed downward.

"There's a trail of bodies clear out to the south pillbox," Schwangyu said. "Your people won't let me out there to inspect. I command you to countermand those orders immediately."

"Not until my clean-up crews are finished," Teg said.

"They're still killing people out there! I can hear it!" A venomous edge had entered Schwangyu's voice. She glared at Lucilla.

"We're also questioning people out there," Teg said.

Schwangyu shifted her glare to Teg. "If it's too dangerous here then we will take the . . . the child to my quarters. Now!"

"We will not do that," Teg said. His tone was low-key but positive.

Schwangyu stiffened with displeasure. Patrin's knuckles went white on the stock of his lasgun. Schwangyu swung her gaze past the gun and up to Lucilla's appraising stare. The two women looked into each other's eyes.

Teg allowed the moment to hold for a beat, then said: "Lucilla, take Duncan into my sitting room." He nodded toward a door behind him.

Lucilla obeyed, pointedly keeping her body between Schwangyu and Duncan the whole time.

Once behind the closed door, Duncan said: "She almost called me 'the ghola.' She's really upset."

"Schwangyu has let several things slip past her guard," Lucilla said.

She glanced around Teg's sitting room, her first view of this part of his quarters: the Bashar's inner sanctum. It reminded her of her own quarters—that same mixture of orderliness and casual disarray. Reading spools lay in a clutter on a small table beside an old-fashioned chair upholstered in soft gray. The spool reader had been swung aside as though its user had just stepped out for a moment, intending to return soon. A Bashar's black uniform jacket lay across a nearby hard chair with sewing material in a small open box atop it. The jacket's cuff showed a carefully patched hole.

So he does his own mending.

This was an aspect of the famous Miles Teg she had not expected. If she had thought about it, she would have said Patrin would absorb such chores.

"Schwangyu let the attackers in, didn't she?" Duncan asked.

"Her people did." Lucilla did not hide her anger. "She has gone too far. A pact with the Tleilaxu!"

"Will Patrin kill her?"

"I don't know nor do I care!"

Outside the door, Schwangyu spoke with anger, her voice loud and quite clear: "Are we just going to wait here, Bashar?"

"You can leave anytime you wish." That was Teg.

"But I can't enter the south tunnel!"

Schwangyu sounded petulant. Lucilla knew it for something the old woman did deliberately. What was she planning? Teg must be very cautious now. He had been clever out there, revealing for Lucilla the gaps in Schwangyu's control, but they had not plumbed Schwangyu's resources. Lucilla wondered if she should leave Duncan here and return to Teg's side.

Teg said: "You can go now but I advise you not to return to your quarters."

"And why not?" Schwangyu sounded surprised, really surprised and not covering it well.

"One moment," Teg said.

Lucilla became aware of shouting at a distance. A heavy thumping explosion sounded from nearby and then another one more distant. Dust sifted from the cornice above the door to Teg's sitting room.

"What was that?" Schwangyu again, her voice overly loud.

Lucilla moved to place herself between Duncan and the wall to the hallway.

Duncan stared at the door, his body poised for defense.

"That first blast was what I expected them to do." Teg again. "The second, I fear, was what *they* did not expect."

A whistle piped nearby loud enough to cover something Schwangyu said.

"That's it, Bashar!" Patrin.

"What is happening?" Schwangyu demanded.

"The first explosion, dear Reverend Mother, was your quarters being destroyed by our attackers. The second explosion was us destroying the attackers."

"I just got the signal, Bashar!" Patrin again. "We got them all. They came down by floater from the no-ship just as you expected."

"The ship?" Teg's voice was full of angry demand.

"Destroyed the instant it came through the space fold. No survivors."

"You fools!" Schwangyu screamed. "Do you know what you've done?"

"I carried out my orders to protect that boy from any attack," Teg said. "By the way, weren't you supposed to be in your quarters at this hour?"

"What?"

"They were after you when they blasted your quarters. The Tleilaxu are very dangerous, Reverend Mother."

"I don't believe you!"

"I suggest you go look. Patrin, let her pass."

As she listened, Lucilla heard the unspoken argument. The Mentat Bashar had been trusted here more than a Reverend Mother and Schwangyu knew it. She would be desperate. That was clever, suggesting her quarters had been destroyed. She might not believe it, though. Foremost in Schwangyu's mind now would be the realization that both Teg and Lucilla recognized her complicity in the attack. There was no telling how many others were aware of this. Patrin knew, of course.

Duncan stared at the closed door, his head tipped slightly to the right. There was a curious expression on his face, as though he saw through the door and actually watched the people out there.

Schwangyu spoke, the most careful control in her voice. "I don't believe my quarters were destroyed." She knew Lucilla was listening.

"There is only one way to make sure," Teg said.

Clever! Lucilla thought. Schwangyu could not make a decision until she was certain whether the Tleilaxu had acted treacherously.

"You will wait here for me, then! That's an order!" Lucilla heard the swish of Schwangyu's robes as the Reverend Mother departed.

Very bad emotional control, Lucilla thought. What this revealed about Teg, though, was equally disturbing. *He did it to her!* Teg had kept a Reverend Mother off balance.

The door in front of Duncan swung open. Teg stood there, one hand on the latch. "Quick!" Teg said. "We must be out of the Keep before she returns."

"Out of the Keep?" Lucilla did not hide her shock.

"Quick, I say! Patrin has prepared a way for us."

"But I must—"

"You must nothing! Come as you are. Follow me or we will be forced to take you."

"Do you really think you could take a . . ." Lucilla broke off. This was a new Teg in front of her and she knew he would not have made such a threat unless he was prepared to carry it out.

"Very well," she said. She took Duncan's hand and followed Teg out of his quarters.

Patrin stood in the hallway looking to his right. "She's gone," the old man said. He looked at Teg. "You know what to do, Bashar?"

"Pat!"

Lucilla had never before heard Teg use the batman's diminutive name.

Patrin grinned, a gleaming full-toothed smile. "Sorry, Bashar. The excitement, you know. I'll leave you to it, then. I have my part to play."

Teg waved Lucilla and Duncan down the hallway to the right. She obeyed and heard Teg close on her heels. Duncan's hand was sweaty in her hand. He pulled free and strode beside her without looking back.

The suspensor-drop at the end of the hallway was guarded by two of Teg's own people. He nodded to them. "Nobody follows."

They spoke in unison: "Right, Bashar."

Lucilla realized as she entered the drop with Duncan and Teg that she had chosen sides in a dispute whose workings she did not fully understand. She could feel the movements of the Sisterhood's politics like a swift current of water pouring all around her. Usually, the movement remained mostly a gentle wave washing the strand, but now she sensed a great destructive surge preparing to thunder its surf upon her.

Duncan spoke as they emerged into the sorting chamber for the south pillbox.

"We should all be armed," he said.

"We will be very soon," Teg said. "And I hope you're prepared to kill anyone who tries to stop us."

The significant fact is this: No Bene Tleilax female has ever been seen away from the protection of their core planets. (Face Dancer mules who simulate females do not count in this analysis. They cannot be breeders.) The Tleilaxu sequester their females to keep them from our hands. This is our primary deduction. It must also be in the eggs that the Tleilaxu Masters conceal their most essential secrets.

—BENE GESSERIT ANALYSIS,

ARCHIVES #XOXTM99 041

"So we meet at last," Taraza said.

She stared across the two meters of open space between their chairs at Tylwyth Waff. Her analysts assured her that this man was Tleilaxu Master of Masters. What an elfin little figure he was to hold so much power. The prejudices of appearance must be discarded here, she warned herself.

"Some would not believe this possible," Waff said.

He had a piping little voice, Taraza noted; something else to be measured by different standards.

They sat in the neutrality of a Guild no-ship with Bene Gesserit and Tleilaxu monitors clinging to the Guildship's hull like predatory birds on a carcass. (The Guild had been cravenly anxious to placate the Bene Gesserit. *"You will pay."* The Guild knew. Payment had been exacted from them before.) The small oval room in which they met was conventionally copper-walled and "spy-proof." Taraza did not believe this for an instant. She presumed also that the bonds between Guild and Tleilaxu, forged of melange, still existed in full force.

Waff did not try to delude himself about Taraza. This woman was far more dangerous than any Honored Matre. If he killed Taraza, she would be replaced immediately by someone just as dangerous, someone with every essential piece of information possessed by the present Mother Superior.

"We find your new Face Dancers very interesting," Taraza said.

Waff grimaced involuntarily. Yes, *far* more dangerous than the Honored Matres, who were not yet even blaming the Tleilaxu for the loss of an entire no-ship.

Taraza glanced at the small double-faced digital clock on the low side table at her right, a position where the clock could be read easily by either of them. The Waff-side face had been matched to his internal clock. She noted that the two internal-time readings stood within ten seconds of synchronization at an arbitrary midafternoon. It was one of the niceties of this confrontation where even the positioning and spacing between their chairs had been specified in the arrangements.

The two of them were alone in the room. The oval space around them was about six meters in its long dimension, half that in width. They occupied identical sling chairs of peg-fastened wood, which supported orange fabric; not a bit of metal or other foreign material in either of them. The only other furnishing of the room was the side table with its clock. The table was a thin black surface of plaz on three spindly wooden legs. Each of the principals in this meeting had been snooped with care. Each had three personal guards outside the room's one hatch. Taraza did not think the Tleilaxu would try a Face Dancer exchange, not under the present circumstances!

"*You will pay.*"

The Tleilaxu, too, were extremely aware of their vulnerability, especially now that they knew a Reverend Mother could expose the new Face Dancers.

Waff cleared his throat. "I do not expect us to reach an agreement," he said.

"Then why did you come?"

"I seek an explanation of this odd message we have received from your Keep on Rakis. For what are we supposed to pay?"

"I beg of you, Ser Waff, drop these foolish pretenses in this room. There are facts known to both of us that cannot be avoided."

"Such as?"

"No female of the Bene Tleilax has ever been provided to us for breeding." And she thought: *Let him sweat that one!* It was damnably frustrating not to have a line of Tleilaxu Other Memories for Bene Gesserit investigation and Waff would know it.

Waff scowled. "Surely you don't think I would bargain with the life of—" He broke off and shook his head. "I cannot believe this is the payment you would ask."

When Taraza did not respond, Waff said: "The stupid attack on the Rakian temple was undertaken independently by people on the scene. They have been punished."

Expected gambit number three, Taraza thought.

She had participated in numerous analysis-briefings before this meeting, if one could call them briefings. Analyses there had been in excess. Very little was known about this Tleilaxu Master, this Tylwyth Waff. Some extremely important optional projections had been arrived at by inference (if these proved to be true). The trouble was that some of the most interesting data came from unreliable sources. One salient fact could be depended upon, however: The elfin figure seated across from her was deadly dangerous.

Waff's *gambit number three* engaged her attention. It was time to respond. Taraza produced a knowing smile.

"That is precisely the kind of lie we expected from you," she said.

"Do we begin with insults?" He spoke without heat.

"You set the pattern. Let me warn you that you will not be able to deal with us the way you dealt with those whores from the Scattering."

Waff's frozen stare invited Taraza to a daring gambit. The Sisterhood's deductions, based partly on the disappearance of an Ixian conference ship, were accurate! Maintaining her same smile, she now pursued the optional conjecture line as though it were known fact. "I think," she said, "the whores might like to learn that they have had Face Dancers among them."

Waff suppressed his anger. *These damnable witches! They knew! Somehow, they knew!* His councillors had been extremely doubtful about this meeting. A substantial minority had recommended against it. The witches were so . . . so devilish. And their retaliations!

Time to shift his attention to Gammu, Taraza thought.

Keep him off balance. She said: "Even when you subvert one of us, as you did with Schwangyu on Gammu, you learn nothing of value!"

Waff flared: "She thought to . . . to *hire* us like a band of assassins! We only taught her a lesson!"

Ahhhh, his pride shows itself, Taraza thought. *Interesting. The implications of a moral structure behind such pride must be explored.*

"You've never really penetrated our ranks," Taraza said.

"And you have never penetrated the Tleilaxu!" Waff managed to produce this boast with passable calm. *He needed time to think! To plan!*

"Perhaps you would like to know the price of our silence," Taraza suggested. She took Waff's stony glare for agreement and added: "For one thing, you will share with us everything you learn about those Scattering-spawned whores who call themselves Honored Matres."

Waff shuddered. Much had been confirmed by killing the Honored Matres. The sexual intricacies! Only the strongest psyche could resist entanglement in such ecstasies. The potential of this tool was enormous! Must that be shared with these witches?

"*Everything* you learn from them," Taraza insisted.

"Why do you call them whores?"

"They try to copy us, yet they sell themselves for power and make a mockery of everything we represent. Honored Matres!"

"They outnumber you at least ten thousand to one! We have seen the evidence."

"One of us could defeat them all," Taraza said.

Waff sat in silence, studying her. Was that merely a boast? You could never be sure when it came to the Bene

Gesserit witches. They *did* things. The dark side of the magic universe belonged to them. On more than one occasion the witches had blunted the Shariat. Was it God's will that the true believers pass through another trial?

Taraza allowed the silence to continue building its own tensions. She sensed Waff's turmoil. It reminded her of the Sisterhood's preliminary conference in preparation for this meeting with him. Bellonda had asked the question of deceptive simplicity:

"What do we *really* know about the Tleilaxu?"

Taraza had felt the answer surge into every mind around the Chapter House conference table: *We may know for sure only what they want us to know.*

None of her analysts could avoid the suspicion that the Tleilaxu had deliberately created a masking-image of themselves. Tleilaxu intelligence had to be measured against the fact that they alone controlled the secret of the axlotl tanks. Was that a lucky accident as some suggested? Then why had others been unable to duplicate this accomplishment in all of these millennia?

Gholas.

Were the Tleilaxu using the ghola process for their own kind of immortality? She could see suggestive hints in Waff's actions . . . nothing definite, but highly suspicious.

At the Chapter House conferences, Bellonda had returned repeatedly to their basic suspicions, hammering at them: "All of it . . . all of it, I say! Everything in our archives could be garbage fit only for slig fodder!"

This allusion had caused some of the more relaxed Reverend Mothers around the table to shudder.

Sligs!

Those slowly creeping crosses between giant slugs and pigs might provide meat for some of the most expensive meals in their universe but the creatures themselves embodied everything the Sisterhood held repugnant about the Tleilaxu. Sligs had been one of the earliest Bene Tleilax barter items, a product grown in their tanks and formed with the helical core from which all life took its shapes. That the Bene Tleilax made them added to the aura of obscenity around a creature whose multi-mouths ground incessantly on almost any garbage, passing that garbage swiftly into excrement that not only smelled of the sty but was slimy.

"The sweetest meat this side of heaven," Bellonda had quoted from a CHOAM promotion.

"And it comes from obscenity," Taraza had added.

Obscenity.

Taraza thought of this as she stared at Waff. For what possible reason might people build around themselves a mask of obscenity? Waff's flare of pride could not be fitted neatly into that image.

Waff coughed lightly into his hand. He felt the pressure of the seams where he had concealed two of his potent dart-throwers. The minority among his councillors had advised: "As with the Honored Matres, the winner in this encounter with the Bene Gesserit will be the one who emerges carrying the most secret information about the other. Death of the opponent guarantees success."

I might kill her but what then?

Three more full Reverend Mothers waited outside that hatch. Doubtless Taraza had a signal prepared for the instant the hatch was opened. Without that signal, violence and disaster were sure to ensue. He did not believe for an instant that even his new Face Dancers could overcome those Reverend Mothers out there. The witches would be on full alert. They would have recognized the nature of Waff's guards.

"We will share," Waff said. The admissions implicit in this hurt him but he knew he had no alternatives. Taraza's brag about relative abilities might be inaccurate because of its extreme claim, but he sensed truth in it nonetheless. He had no illusions, however, about what would ensue if the Honored Matres learned what had actually happened to their envoys. The missing no-ship could not yet be laid at the Tleilaxu door. Ships did vanish. Deliberate assassination was another matter altogether. The Honored Matres surely would try to exterminate such a brash opponent. If only as an example. Tleilaxu returned from the Scattering said as much. Having seen Honored Matres, Waff now believed those stories.

Taraza said: "My second agenda item for this meeting is our ghola."

Waff squirmed in the sling chair.

Taraza felt repelled by Waff's tiny eyes, the round face with its snub nose and too-sharp teeth.

"You have been killing our gholas to control the movement of a project in which you have no part other than to provide a single element," Taraza accused.

Waff once more wondered if he must kill her. Was nothing hidden from these damnable witches? The implication that the Bene Gesserit had a traitor in the Tleilaxu core could not be ignored. How else could they know?

He said: "I assure you, Reverend Mother Superior, that the ghola—"

"Assure me of nothing! We assure ourselves." A look of sadness on her face, Taraza shook her head slowly from side to side. "And you think we don't know that you sold us damaged goods."

Waff spoke quickly: "He meets every requirement imposed by your contract!"

Again, Taraza shook her head from side to side. This diminutive Tleilaxu Master had no idea what he was revealing here. "You have buried your own scheme in his psyche," Taraza said. "I warn you, Ser Waff, that if your *alterations* obstruct our design, we will wound you deeper than you think possible."

Waff passed a hand across his face, feeling the perspiration on his forehead. Damnable witches! But she did not know everything. The Tleilaxu returned from the Scattering and the Honored Matres she maligned so bitterly had provided the Tleilaxu with a sexually loaded weapon that would *not* be shared, no matter the promises made here!

Taraza digested Waff's reactions silently and decided on a bold lie. "When we captured your Ixian conference ship, your new Face Dancers did not die quite fast enough. We learned a great deal."

Waff poised himself on the edge of violence.

Bullseye! Taraza thought. The bold lie had opened an avenue of revelation into one of the more outrageous suggestions from her advisors. It did not seem outrageous now. *"The Tleilaxu ambition is to produce a complete prana-bindu mimic,"* her advisor had suggested.

"Complete?"

All of the Sisters at the conference had been astonished by the suggestion. It implied a form of mental copy going beyond the memory print about which they already knew.

The advisor, Sister Hesterion from Archives, had come armed with a tightly organized list of supporting material. *"We already know that what an Ixian Probe does mechanically, the Tleilaxu do with nerves and flesh. The next step is obvious."*

Seeing Waff's reaction to her bold lie, Taraza continued to watch him carefully. He was at his most dangerous right now.

A look of rage came over Waff's face. The things the witches knew were too dangerous! He did not doubt Taraza's claim in the slightest. *I must kill her no matter the consequences to me! We must kill them all. Abominations! It's their word and it describes them perfectly.*

Taraza correctly interpreted his expression. She spoke quickly: "You are in absolutely no danger from us as long as you do not injure our designs. Your religion, your way of life, those are your business."

Waff hesitated, not so much from what Taraza said as from the reminder of her powers. What else did they know? To continue in a subservient position, though! After rejecting such an alliance with the Honored Matres. And with ascendancy so near after all of those millennia. Dismay filled him. The minority among his councillors had been right after all: *"There can be no bond between our peoples. Any accord with powindah forces is a union based upon evil."*

Taraza still sensed the potential violence in him. Had she pushed him too far? She held herself in defensive readiness. An involuntary jerking of his arms alerted her. *Weapons in his sleeves!* Tleilaxu resources were not to be underestimated. Her snoopers had detected nothing.

"We know about the weapons you carry," she said. Another bold lie suggested itself. "If you make a mistake now, the whores will also learn how you use those weapons."

Waff took three shallow breaths. When he spoke, he had himself under control: "We will not be Bene Gesserit satellites!"

Taraza responded in an even-toned, soothing voice: "I have not by word or action suggested such a role for you."

She waited. There was no change in Waff's expression, no slightest shift in the unfocused glare he directed at her.

"You threaten us," he muttered. "You demand that we share everything we—"

"Share!" she snapped. "One does not *share* with un-equal partners."

"And what would you share with us?" he demanded.

She spoke with the chiding tone she would use to a child: "Ser Waff, ask yourself why you, a ruling member of your oligarchy, came to this meeting?"

His voice still firmly controlled, Waff countered: "And why did you, Mother Superior of the Bene Gesserit, come here?"

She spoke mildly: "To strengthen us."

"You did not say what you would share," he accused. "You still hope for advantage."

Taraza continued to watch him carefully. She had seldom sensed such suppressed rage in a human. "Ask me openly what you want," she said.

"And you will give it out of your great generosity!"

"I will negotiate."

"Where was the negotiation when you ordered me . . . ORDERED ME! to—"

"You came here firmly resolved to break any agreement we made," she said. "Not once have you tried to negotiate! You sit in front of someone willing to bargain with you and you can only—"

"Bargain?" Waff's memory was hurled back to the Honored Matre's anger at that word.

"I said it," Taraza said. "Bargain."

Something like a smile twitched the corners of Waff's mouth. "You think I have authority to *bargain* with you?"

"Have a care, Ser Waff," she said. "You have the ultimate authority. It resides in that final ability to destroy an opponent utterly. I have not threatened that, but you have." She glanced at his sleeves.

Waff sighed. What a quandary. She was powindah! How could one bargain with a powindah?

"We have a problem that cannot be resolved by rational means," Taraza said.

Waff hid his surprise. Those were the very words the Honored Matre had used! He cringed inwardly at what that might signify. Could Bene Gesserit and Honored Matres make common cause? Taraza's bitterness argued otherwise, but when were the witches to be trusted?

Once more, Waff wondered if he dared sacrifice himself to eliminate this witch. What would it serve? Others among them surely knew what she knew. It would only precipitate the disaster. There was that internal dispute among the witches, but, again, that might just be another ruse.

"You ask us to share something," Taraza said. "What

if I were to offer you some of our prize human blood-lines?"

There was no mistaking how Waff's interest quick-ened.

He said: "Why should we come to you for such things? We have our tanks and we can pick up genetic examples almost anywhere."

"Examples of what?" she asked.

Waff sighed. You could never escape that Bene Gesserit incisiveness. It was like a sword thrust. He guessed that he had revealed things to her that led naturally to this subject. The damage already had been done. She correctly deduced (or spies had told her!) that the wild pool of human genes held little interest for the Tleilaxu with their more sophisticated knowledge of life's inner-most language. It never paid to underestimate either the Bene Gesserit or the products of their breeding pro-grams. God Himself knew they had produced Muad'Dib and the Prophet!

"What more would you demand in exchange for this?" he asked.

"Bargaining at last!" Taraza said. "We both know, of course, that I am offering breeding mothers of the Atre-ides line." And she thought: *Let him hope for that! They will look like Atreides but they will not be Atreides!*

Waff felt his pulse quicken. Was this possible? Did she have the slightest idea what the Tleilaxu might learn from an examination of such source material?

"We would want first selection of their offspring," Taraza said.

"No!"

"Alternate first selection, then?"

"Perhaps."

"What do you mean, perhaps?" She leaned forward. Waff's intensity told her she was on a hot trail.

"What else would you ask of us?"

"Our breeding mothers must have unfettered access to your genetic laboratories."

"Are you mad?" Waff shook his head in exasperation. Did she think the Tleilaxu would give away their strongest weapon just like that?

"Then we will accept a fully operational axlotl tank."

Waff merely stared at her.

Taraza shrugged. "I had to try."

"I suppose you did."

Taraza sat back and reviewed what she had learned here. Waff's reaction to that Zensunni probe had been interesting. *A problem that cannot be resolved by rational means.* The words had produced a subtle effect on him. He had seemed to rise out of some place within himself, a questioning look in his eyes. *Gods preserve us all! Is Waff a secret Zensunni?*

No matter the dangers, this had to be explored. Odrade must be armed with every possible advantage on Rakis.

"Perhaps we have done all we can for now," Taraza said. "There is time to complete our bargain. God alone in His infinite mercy has given us infinite universes where anything may happen."

Waff clapped his hands once without thinking. "The gift of surprises is the greatest gift of all!" he said.

Not just Zensunni, Taraza thought. *Sufi also. Sufi!* She began to readjust her perspective on the Tleilaxu. *How long have they been holding this close to their breasts?*

"Time does not count itself," Taraza said, probing. "One has only to look at any circle."

"Suns are circles," Waff said. "Each universe is a circle." He held his breath waiting for her response.

"Circles are enclosures," Taraza said, picking the proper response out of her Other Memories. "Whatever encloses and limits must expose itself to the infinite."

Waff raised his hands to show her his palms then dropped his arms into his lap. His shoulders lost some of their tense upward thrust. "Why did you not say these things at the beginning?" he asked.

I must exercise great care, Taraza cautioned herself. The admissions in Waff's words and manner required careful review.

"What has passed between us reveals nothing unless we speak more openly," she said. "Even then, we would only be using words."

Waff studied her face, trying to read in that Bene Gesserit mask some confirmation of the things implied by her words and manner. She was powindah, he reminded himself. The powindah could never be trusted . . . but if she shared the Great Belief . . .

"Did God not send His Prophet to Rakis, there to test us and teach us?" he asked.

Taraza delved deep into her Other Memories. *A Prophet on Rakis? Muad'Dib? No . . . that did not square with either Sufi or Zensunni beliefs in . . .*

The Tyrant! She closed her mouth into a grim line. "What one cannot control one must accept," she said.

"For surely that is God's doing," Waff replied.

Taraza had seen and heard enough. The Missionaria Protectiva had immersed her in every known religion.

Other Memories reinforced this knowledge and filled it out. She felt a great need to get herself safely away from this room. Odrade must be alerted!

"May I make a suggestion?" Taraza asked.

Waff nodded politely.

"Perhaps there is here the substance of a greater bond between us than we imagined," she said. "I offer you the hospitality of our Keep on Rakis and the services of our commander there."

"An Atreides?" he asked.

"No," Taraza lied. "But I will, of course, alert our Breeding Mistresses to your needs."

"And I will assemble the things you require in payment," he said. "Why will the bargain be completed on Rakis?"

"Is that not the proper place?" she asked. "Who could be false in the home of the Prophet?"

Waff sat back in his chair, his arms relaxed in his lap. Taraza certainly knew the proper responses. It was a revelation he had never expected.

Taraza stood. "Each of us listens to God personally," she said.

And together in the kehl, he thought. He looked up at her, reminding himself that she was powindah. None of them could be trusted. *Caution!* This woman was, after all, a Bene Gesserit witch. They were known to create religions for their own ends. *Powindah!*

Taraza went to the hatch, opened it and gave her security signal. She turned once more toward Waff who still sat in his chair. *He has not penetrated our true design,* she thought. *The ones we send to him must be chosen with extreme care. He must never suspect that he is part of our bait.*

His elfin features composed, Waff stared back at her.

How bland he looked, Taraza thought. But he could be trapped! An alliance between Sisterhood and Tleilaxu offered new attractions. *But on our terms!*

"Until Rakis," she said.

What social inheritances went outward with the Scattering? We know those times intimately. We know both the mental and physical settings. The Lost Ones took with them a consciousness confined mostly to manpower and hardware. There was a desperate need for room to expand driven by the myth of Freedom. Most had not learned the deeper lesson of the Tyrant, that violence builds its own limits. The Scattering was wild and random movement interpreted as growth (expansion). It was goaded by a profound fear (often unconscious) of stagnation and death.

—THE SCATTERING: BENE GESSERIT ANALYSIS (ARCHIVES)

Odrade lay full length on her side along the ledge of the bow window, her cheek lightly touching the warm plaz through which she could see the Great Square of Keen. Her back was supported by a red cushion, which smelled of melange as did many things here on Rakis. Behind her lay three rooms, small but efficient and well removed from both Temple and Bene Gesserit Keep. This removal had been a requirement of the Sisterhood's agreement with the priests.

"Sheeana must be guarded more securely," Odrade had insisted.

"She cannot become the ward of only the Sisterhood!" Tuek had objected.

"Nor of the priests," Odrade countered.

Six stories below Odrade's bow window vantage, an enormous bazaar spread out in loosely organized confusion, almost filling the Great Square. The silvered yellow light of a lowering sun washed the scene with brilliance, picking out the bright colors of canopies, drawing long shadows across the uneven ground. There was a dusty radiance about the light where scattered clumps of people milled about patched umbrellas and the jumbled alignments of wares.

The Great Square was not actually square. It stretched out around the bazaar a full kilometer across from Odrade's window and easily twice that distance to the left and right—a giant rectangle of packed earth and old stones, which had been churned into bitter dust by daytime shoppers braving the heat in hopes of gaining a bargain then.

As evening advanced, a different sense of activity unfolded beneath Odrade—more people arriving, a quickening and more frenetic pulse to the movement.

Odrade tipped her head to peer down sharply at the ground near her building. Some of the merchants directly beneath her window had wandered off to their nearby quarters. They would return soon, after a meal and short siesta, ready to make full use of those more valuable hours when people in the open could breathe air that did not burn their throats.

Sheeana was overdue, Odrade noted. The priests dared not delay much longer. They would be working frantically now, firing questions at Sheeana, admonishing her to remember that she was God's own emissary to His Church. Reminding Sheeana of many contrived allegiances that

Odrade would have to ferret out and make humorous before dispatching such trivia into proper perspective.

Odrade arched her back and went through a silent minute of tiny exercises to relieve tensions. She admitted to a certain sympathy for Sheeana. The girl's thoughts would be chaos right now. Sheeana knew little or nothing about what to expect once she came fully under a Reverend Mother's tutelage. There was little doubt that the young mind was cluttered with myths and other misinformation.

As my mind was, Odrade thought.

She could not avoid remembrance at a moment such as this. Her immediate task was clear: exorcism, not only for Sheeana but for herself.

She thought the haunting thoughts of a Reverend Mother in her memories: *Odrade, age five, the comfortable house on Gammu. The road outside the house is lined with what pass for middle-echelon mansions in the planet's sea-coast cities—low one-story buildings on wide avenues. The houses reach far down to an outcurving sea frontage where they are much wider than along the avenues. Only on the sea side do they become more expansive and less jealous of every square meter.*

Odrade's Bene Gesserit-honed memory rolled through that faraway house, its occupants, the avenue, the playmates. She felt the tightness in her breast that told her such memories were attached to later events.

The Bene Gesserit crèche on Al Dhanab's artificial world, one of the original Sisterhood safe planets. (Later, she learned that the Bene Gesserit once considered making the entire planet into a no-chamber. Energy requirements defeated this plan.)

The crèche was a cascade of variety to a child from Gammu's comforts and friendships. Bene Gesserit education included intense physical training. There were regular admonishments that she could not hope to become a Reverend Mother without passage through much pain and frequent periods of seemingly hopeless muscular exercises.

Some of her companions failed at this stage. They left to become nurses, servants, laborers, casual breeders. They filled niches of necessity wherever the Sisterhood required them. There were times when Odrade felt longingly that this *failure* might not be a bad life—fewer responsibilities, lesser goals. That had been before she emerged from Primary Training.

I thought of it as emerging, coming through victorious. I came out the other side.

Only to find herself immersed in new and harsher demands.

Odrade sat up on her Rakian window ledge and pushed her cushion aside. She turned her back on the bazaar. It was becoming noisier out there. Damned priests! They were stretching delay to its absolute limits!

I must think about my own childhood because that will help me with Sheeana, she thought. Immediately, she sneered at her own weakness. *Another excuse!*

It took some postulants at least fifty years to become Reverend Mothers. This was ground into them during Secondary Training: a lesson of patience. Odrade showed an early penchant for deep study. There was consideration that she might become one of the Bene Gesserit Mentats and probably an Archivist. This idea was dropped on the discovery that her talents lay in a more profitable direction. She was aimed at more sensitive duties in Chapter House.

Security.

That wild talent among the Atreides often had this employment. Care with details, that was Odrade's hallmark. She knew her sisters could predict some of her actions simply from their deep knowledge of her. Taraza did it regularly. Odrade had overheard the explanation from Taraza's own lips:

"Odrade's persona is exquisitely reflected in her performance of duties."

There was a joke in Chapter House: "Where does Odrade go when she's off duty? She goes to work."

Chapter House imposed little need to adopt the covering masks that a Reverend Mother used automatically on the Outside. She might show emotions momentarily, deal openly with mistakes of her own and of others, feel sad or bitter or even, sometimes, happy. Men were available—not for breeding, but for occasional solace. All such Bene Gesserit Chapter House males were quite charming and a few were even sincere in their charm. These few, of course, were much in demand.

Emotions.

Recognition twisted through Odrade's mind.

So I come to it as I always do.

Odrade felt the warm evening sunlight of Rakis on her back. She knew where her body sat, but her mind opened itself to the coming encounter with Sheeana.

Love!

It would be so easy and so dangerous.

In this moment, she envied the Station Mothers, the ones allowed to live out a lifetime with a mated breeding partner. Miles Teg came from such a union. Other Memories told her how it had been for the Lady Jessica and her Duke. Even Muad'Dib had chosen that form of mating.

It is not for me.

Odrade admitted to a bitter jealousy that she had not been permitted such a life. What were the compensations of the life into which she had been guided?

"A life without love can be devoted more intensely to the Sisterhood. We provide our own forms of support to the initiated. Do not worry about sexual enjoyment. That is available whenever you feel the need."

With charming men!

Since the days of the Lady Jessica, through the Tyrant's times and beyond, many things had changed . . . including the Bene Gesserit. Every Reverend Mother knew it.

A deep sigh shuddered through Odrade. She glanced back over her shoulder at the bazaar. Still no sign of Sheeana.

I must not love this child!

It was done. Odrade knew she had played out the mnemonic game in its required Bene Gesserit form. She swiveled her body and sat cross-legged on the ledge. It was a commanding view of the bazaar and over the rooftops of the city and its basin. Those few remnant hills out there south of here were, she knew, the last of what had been the Shield Wall of Dune, the high ramparts of basement rock breached by Muad'Dib and his sandworm-mounted legions.

Heat danced from the ground beyond the qanat and canal that protected Keen from intrusions by the new worms. Odrade smiled softly. The priests found nothing strange in moating their communities to keep their Divided God from intruding upon them.

We will worship you, God, but don't bother us. This is our religion, our city. You see, we no longer call this place Arrakeen. Now, it's Keen. The planet no longer is Dune or Arrakis. Now, it's Rakis. Keep your distance, God. You are the past and the past is an embarrassment.

Odrade stared at those distant hills dancing in the heat shimmer. Other Memories could superimpose the ancient landscape. She knew that past.

If the priests delay bringing Sheeana much longer I will punish them.

Heat still filled the bazaar below her, held there by storage in the ground and the thick walls surrounding the Great Square. Temperature diffusion was amplified by the smoke of many small fires lighted in the surrounding buildings and among the tent-sheltered congeries of life scattered through the bazaar. It had been a hot day, well above thirty-eight degrees. This building, though, had been a Fish Speaker Center in the old days and was cooled by Ixian machinery with evaporation pools on the roof.

We will be comfortable here.

And they would be as secure as Bene Gesserit protective measures could make them. Reverend Mothers walked those halls out there. The priests had their representatives in the building but none of those would intrude where Odrade did not want them. Sheeana would meet with them here on occasion but the occasions would be only as Odrade permitted.

It is happening, Odrade thought. *Taraza's plan moves ahead.*

Fresh in Odrade's mind was the latest communication from Chapter House. What that revealed about the Tleilaxu filled Odrade with excitement that she carefully dampened. This Waff, this Tleilaxu Master, would be a fascinating study.

Zensunni! And Sufi!

"A ritual pattern frozen for millennia," Taraza said.

Unspoken in Taraza's report was another message. *Taraza is placing her complete confidence in me.* Odrade felt strength flow into her from this awareness.

Sheeana is the fulcrum. We are the lever. Our strength will come from many sources.

Odrade relaxed. She knew that Sheeana would not permit the priests to delay much longer. Odrade's own patience had suffered the assaults of anticipation. It would be worse for Sheeana.

They had become conspirators, Odrade and Sheeana. The first step. It was a marvelous game to Sheeana. She had been born and bred to distrust priests. What fun to have an ally at last!

Some form of activity stirred the people directly below Odrade's window. She peered downward, curious. Five naked men there had linked arms in a circle. Their robes and stillsuits lay in a pile at one side watched over by a dark-skinned young girl in a long brown dress of spice fiber. Her hair was bound by a red rag.

Dancers!

Odrade had seen many reports of this phenomenon but this was her first personal view of it since arriving. The onlookers included a trio of tall Priest Guardians in yellow helmets with high crests. The Guardians wore short robes that freed their legs for action, and each carried a metal-clad staff.

As the dancers circled, the watchful crowd grew predictably restive. Odrade knew the pattern. Soon, there would be a chanting outcry and a great melee. Heads would be cracked. Blood would flow. People would scream and run about. Eventually, it would all subside without official intervention. Some would go away weeping. Some would depart laughing. And the Priest Guardians would not interfere.

The pointless insanity of this dance and its consequences had fascinated the Bene Gesserit for centuries. Now it held Odrade's rapt attention. The devolution of this ritual had been followed by the Missionaria Protectiva. Rakians called it "Dance Diversion." They had other names for it, as well, and the most significant was "Siaynoq." This dance was what had become of the Tyrant's greatest ritual, his moment of sharing with his Fish Speakers.

Odrade recognized and respected the energy in this phenomenon. No Reverend Mother could fail to see that. The waste of it, however, disturbed her. Such things should be channeled and focused. This ritual needed some useful employment. All it did now was drain away forces that might prove destructive to the priests if left untapped.

A sweet fruit odor wafted into Odrade's nostrils. She sniffed and looked at the vents beside her window; heat from the mob and the warmed earth created an updraft. This carried odors from below through the Ixian vents. She pressed her forehead and nose against the plaz to peer directly downward. Ahhh, the dancers or the mob had tipped over a merchant's stall. The dancers were stomping in the fruit. Yellow pulp spurted up to their thighs.

Odrade recognized the fruit merchant among the on-lookers, a familiar wizened face she had seen several times at his stall beside her building's entrance. He appeared unconcerned by his loss. Like all the others around him, he concentrated his attention on the dancers. The five naked men moved with a disjointed high lift of their feet, an unrhythmic and seemingly uncoordinated display, which came around periodically to a repeated pattern—three of the dancers with both feet on the ground and the other two held aloft by their partners.

Odrade recognized it. This was related to the ancient Fremen way of sandwalking. This curious dance was a fossil with roots in the need to move without signaling your presence to a worm.

People began to crowd nearer the dancers out of the bazaar's great rectangle, hopping upward like children's toys to raise their eyes above the throng for a glimpse of the five naked men.

Odrade saw Sheeana's escort then, movement far off to the right where a wide avenue entered the square. Animal-track symbols on a building there said the wide avenue was God's Way. Historical awareness said the avenue had been Leto II's route into the city from his high-walled Sareer far off to the south. With a care for details, one could still discern some of the forms and patterns that had been the Tyrant's city of Onn, the festival center built around the more ancient city of Arrakeen. Onn had obliterated many marks of Arrakeen but some avenues persisted: some buildings were too useful to replace. Buildings inevitably defined streets.

Sheeana's escort came to a stop where the avenue debouched into the bazaar. Yellow-helmeted Guardians probed ahead, clearing a path with their staves. The guards were tall: When grounded, the thick, two-meter staff would come only to the shoulders of the shortest among them. Even in the most disordered crowd you could not miss a Priest Guardian, but Sheeana's protectors were the tallest of the tall.

They were in motion once more leading their party toward Odrade. Their robes swung open at each stride revealing the slick gray of the best stillsuits. They walked straight ahead, fifteen of them in a shallow vee which skirted the thicker clusters of stalls.

A loose band of priestesses with Sheeana at their center marched behind the guards. Odrade caught glimpses of Sheeana's distinctive figure, that sun-streaked hair and proudly upthrust face, within her escort. It was the yellow-helmeted Priest Guardians, though, who attracted Odrade's attention. They moved with an arrogance conditioned into them from infancy. These guards knew they were better than the ordinary folk. And the ordinary folk reacted predictably by opening a way for Sheeana's party.

It was all done so naturally that Odrade could see the ancient pattern of it as though she watched another ritual dance, which had not changed in millennia.

As she had often done, Odrade thought of herself now as an archeologist, not one who sifted the dusty detritus of the ages but rather a person who focused where the

Sisterhood frequently concentrated its awareness: on the ways people carried their past within them. The Tyrant's own design was apparent here. Sheeana's approach was a thing laid down by the God Emperor himself.

Beneath Odrade's window the five naked men continued to dance. Among the onlookers, however, Odrade saw a new awareness. Without any concerted turning of heads toward the approaching phalanx of Priest Guardians, the watchers below Odrade *knew*.

Animals always know when the herders arrive.

Now, the crowd's restiveness produced a quicker pulse. They would not be denied their chaos! A clod of dirt flew from the throng's outskirts and struck the ground near the dancers. The five men did not miss a step in their extended pattern but their speed increased. The length of the series between repetitions spoke of remarkable memories.

Another clod of dirt flew from the crowd and struck a dancer's shoulder. None of the five men faltered.

The crowd began to scream and chant. Some shouted curses. The chanting became a hand-clapping intrusion onto the dancers' movements.

Still, the pattern did not change.

The mob's chanting became a harsh rhythm, repeated shouts that echoed against the Great Square's wails. They were trying to break the dancers' pattern. Odrade sensed a profound importance in the scene below her.

Sheeana's party had come more than halfway across the bazaar. They moved through the wider lanes between stalls and turned now directly toward Odrade. The crowd was at its densest about fifty meters ahead of the Priest Guardians. The Guardians moved at a steady pace, disdainful of those who scurried aside. Under the yellow helmets, eyes were fixed straight ahead, staring over the mob. Not one of the advancing Guardians gave any outward sign that he saw mob or dancers or any other barrier that might impede him.

The mob stopped its chanting abruptly as though an invisible conductor had waved his hand for silence. The five men continued to dance. The silence below Odrade was charged with a power that made her neck hairs stand up. Directly below Odrade, the three Priest Guardians among the onlookers turned as one man and moved out of view into her building.

Deep within the crowd, a woman shouted a curse.

The dancers gave no sign that they heard.

The mob crowded forward, diminishing the space around the dancers by at least half. The girl who guarded the dancers' stillsuits and robes no longer was visible.

Onward, Sheeana's phalanx marched, the priestesses and their young charge directly behind.

Violence erupted off to Odrade's right. People there began striking each other. More missiles arced toward the five dancing men. The mob resumed its chant in a quicker beat.

At the same time, the rear of the crowd parted for the Guardians. Watchers there did not take their attention from the dancers, did not pause in their contributions to the growing chaos, but a way was opened through them.

Absolutely captivated, Odrade stared downward. Many things occurred simultaneously: the melee, the people cursing and striking each other, the continuing chant, the implacable advance of the Guardians.

Within the shield of priestesses, Sheeana could be seen

darting her gaze from side to side, trying to see the excitement around her.

Some within the crowd produced clubs and struck out at the people around them, but nobody threatened the Guardians or any other member of Sheeana's party.

The dancers continued to prance within a tightening circle of watchers. Everyone crowded close against Odrade's building, forcing her to press her head against the plaz and peer at a sharp angle downward.

The Guardians leading Sheeana's party advanced through a widening lane amidst this chaos. The priestesses looked neither left nor right. Yellow-helmeted Guardians stared straight ahead.

Disdain was too feeble a word for this performance, Odrade decided. And it was not correct to say that the swirling mob ignored the incoming party. Each was aware of the other but they existed in separate worlds, observing the strict rules of that separation. Only Sheeana ignored the secret protocol, hopping upward to try for a glimpse past the bodies shielding her.

Directly beneath Odrade, the mob surged forward. The dancers were overwhelmed by the crush, swept aside like ships caught in a gigantic wave. Odrade saw spots of naked flesh being pummeled and thrust from hand to hand through the screaming chaos. Only by the most intense concentration could Odrade separate the sounds being carried up to her.

It was madness!

None of the dancers resisted. Were they being killed? Was it a sacrifice? The Sisterhood's analyses did not even begin to touch this actuality.

Yellow helmets moved aside beneath Odrade, opening

HERETICS OF DUNE 267

a way for Sheeana and her priestesses to pass into the
building, then the Guardians closed ranks. They turned
and formed a protective arc around the building's entrance. They held their staves horizontally and over-
lapped at waist height.

The chaos beyond them began to subside. None of
the dancers was visible but there were casualties, people
sprawled on the ground, others staggering. Bloody heads
could be seen.

Sheeana and the priestesses were out of Odrade's view
in the building. Odrade sat back and tried to sort out
what she had just witnessed.

Incredible.

Absolutely none of the Sisterhood's accounts or holophoto records captured this thing! Part of it was the
smells—dust, sweat, an intense concentration of human
pheromones. Odrade took a deep breath. She felt herself
trembling inside. The mob had become individuals who
moved out into the bazaar. She saw weepers. Some
cursed. Some laughed.

The door behind Odrade burst open. Sheeana entered
laughing. Odrade whirled and glimpsed her own guards
and some of the priestesses in the hallway before Sheeana
closed the door.

The girl's dark brown eyes glittered with excitement.
Her narrow face, already beginning to soften with the
curves she would display as an adult, was tense with suppressed emotion. The tension dissolved as she focused on
Odrade.

Very good, Odrade thought, as she observed this. *Lesson one of the bonding already has begun.*

"You saw the dancers?" Sheeana demanded, whirling

and skipping across the floor to stop in front of Odrade. "Weren't they beautiful? I think they're so beautiful! Cania didn't want me to look. She says it's dangerous for me to take part in Siaynoq. But I don't care! Shaitan would never eat those dancers!"

With a sudden outflowing awareness, which she had experienced before only during the spice agony, Odrade saw through to the total pattern of what she had just witnessed in the Great Square. It had needed only Sheeana's words and presence to make the thing clear.

A language!

Deep within the collective awareness of these people they carried, all unconsciously, a language that could say things to them they did not want to hear. The dancers spoke it. Sheeana spoke it. The thing was composed of voice tones and movements and pheromones, a complex and subtle combination that had evolved the way all languages evolved.

Out of necessity.

Odrade grinned at the happy girl standing in front of her. Now, Odrade knew how to trap the Tleilaxu. Now, she knew more of Taraza's design.

I must accompany Sheeana into the desert at the first opportunity. We will wait only for the arrival of this Tleilaxu Master, this Waff. We will take him with us!

Liberty and Freedom are complex concepts. They go
back to religious ideas of Free Will and are related to
the Ruler Mystique implicit in absolute monarchs.
Without absolute monarchs patterned after the Old
Gods and ruling by the grace of a belief in religious
indulgence, Liberty and Freedom would never have
gained their present meaning. These ideals owe their
very existence to past examples of oppression. And the
forces that maintain such ideas will erode unless renewed by dramatic teaching or new oppressions. This
is the most basic key to my life.

—LETO II, GOD EMPEROR OF DUNE:
DAR ES-BALAT RECORDS

Some thirty kilometers into the thick forest northeast
of the Gammu Keep, Teg kept them waiting under
the cover of a life-shield blanket until the sun dipped
behind the high ground to the west.

"Tonight, we go a new direction," he said.

For three nights now, he had led them through tree-
enclosed darkness with a masterful demonstration of
Mentat Memory, each step directed precisely along the
track that Patrin had laid out for him.

"I'm stiff from too much sitting," Lucilla complained.
"And it's going to be another cold night."

Teg folded the life-shield blanket and put it in the top

of his pack. "You two can start moving around a bit," he said. "But we won't leave here until full dark."

Teg sat up with his back against the bole of a thickly branched conifer, looking out from the deeper shadows as Lucilla and Duncan moved into the glade. The two of them stood there a moment, shivering as the last of the day's warmth fled into the night's chill. Yes, it would be cold again tonight, Teg thought, but they would have little chance to think about that.

The unexpected.

Schwangyu would never expect them still to be this close to the Keep and on foot.

Taraza should have been more emphatic in her warnings about Schwangyu, Teg thought. Schwangyu's violent and open disobedience of a Mother Superior defied tradition. Mentat logic would not accept the situation without more data.

His memory brought up a saying from school days, one of those warning aphorisms by which a Mentat was supposed to rein in his logic.

"Given a trail of logic, occam's razor laid out with impeccable detail, the Mentat may follow such logic to personal disaster."

So logic was known to fail.

He thought back to Taraza's behavior on the Guildship and immediately afterward. *She wanted me to know I would be completely on my own. I must see the problem in my own way, not in her way.*

So the threat from Schwangyu had to be a real threat that he discovered and faced and solved on his own.

Taraza had not known what would happen to Patrin because of all this.

Taraza did not really care what happened to Patrin. Or to me. Or to Lucilla.

But what about the ghola?

Taraza must care!

It was not logical that she would . . . Teg dumped this line of reasoning. Taraza did not want him to act logically. She wanted him to do exactly what he was doing, what he had always done in the tight spots.

The unexpected.

So there was a species of logic to all of this but it kicked the performers out of the nest into chaos.

From which we must make our own order.

Grief welled up in his consciousness. *Patrin! Damn you, Patrin! You knew and I didn't! What will I do without you?*

Teg could almost hear the old aide's response, that stiffly formal voice Patrin always used when he was chiding his commander.

"You will do your best, Bashar."

The most coldly progressive reasoning said Teg would never again see Patrin in the flesh nor hear the old man's actual voice. Still . . . the voice remained. The person persisted in memory.

"Shouldn't we be going?"

It was Lucilla, standing close in front of his position beneath the tree. Duncan waited beside her. Both of them had shouldered their packs.

While he sat thinking, night had fallen. Rich starlight created vague shadows in the glade. Teg lifted himself to his feet, took his pack and, bending to avoid the low branches, emerged into the glade. Duncan helped Teg shoulder his pack.

"Schwangyu will consider this eventually," Lucilla said. "Her searchers will come after us here. You know it."

"Not until they have followed out the false trail and found the end of it," Teg said. "Come."

He led the way westward through an opening in the trees.

Three nights he had led them along what he called "Patrin's memory-path." As he walked on this fourth night, Teg berated himself for not projecting the logical consequences of Patrin's behavior.

I understood the depths of his loyalty but I did not project that loyalty into a most obvious result. We were together so many years I thought I knew his mind as I knew my own. Patrin, damn you! There was no need for you to die!

Teg admitted to himself then that there *had* been a need. Patrin had seen it. The Mentat had not permitted himself to see it. Logic could move just as blindly as any other faculty.

As the Bene Gesserit often said *and demonstrated.*

So we walk. Schwangyu does not expect this.

Teg was forced to admit that walking the wild places of Gammu created a whole new perspective for him. This entire region had been allowed to overgrow with plant life during the Famine Times and the Scattering. It had been replanted later but mostly as a random wilderness. Secret trails and private landmarks guided today's access. Teg imagined Patrin as a youth learning this region—that rocky butte visible in starlight through a gap in the trees, that spiked promontory, these lanes through giant trees.

"They will expect us to make a run for a no-ship," he and Patrin had agreed, fleshing out their plan. *"The decoy must take the searchers in that direction."*

Patrin had not said that *he* would be the decoy.

Teg swallowed past a lump in his throat.

Duncan could not be protected in the Keep, he justified himself.

That was true.

Lucilla had jittered through their first day under the life-shield that protected them from discovery by the instruments of aerial searchers.

"We must get word to Taraza!"

"When we can."

"What if something happens to you? I must know all of your escape plan."

"If something happens to me, you will not be able to follow Patrin's path. There isn't time to put it in your memory."

Duncan took little part in the conversation that day. He watched them silently or dozed, awakening fitful and with an angry look in his eyes.

On the second day under the shielding blanket, Duncan suddenly demanded of Teg: "Why do they want to kill me?"

"To frustrate the Sisterhood's plan for you," Teg said.

Duncan glared at Lucilla. "What is that plan?"

When Lucilla did not answer, Duncan said: "She knows. She knows because I'm supposed to depend on her. I'm supposed to love her!"

Teg thought Lucilla concealed her dismay quite well. Obviously, her plans for the ghola had fallen into disarray, all of the sequencing thrown out of joint by this flight.

Duncan's behavior revealed another possibility: Was the ghola a latent Truthsayer? What additional powers had been bred into this ghola by the sly Tleilaxu?

At their second nightfall in the wilderness, Lucilla was full of accusations. "Taraza ordered you to restore his original memories! How can you do that out here?"

"When we reach sanctuary."

A silent and acutely alert Duncan accompanied them that night. There was a new vitality in him. He had heard!

Nothing must harm Teg, Duncan thought. Wherever and whatever sanctuary might be, Teg must reach it safely. *Then, I will know!*

Duncan was not sure *what* he would know but now he fully accepted the prize in it. This wilderness must lead to that goal. He recalled staring out at the wild places from the Keep and how he had thought to be free here. That sense of untouched freedom had vanished. The wilderness was only a path to something more important.

Lucilla, bringing up the rear of this march, forced herself to remain calm, alert, and to accept what she could not change. Part of her awareness held firmly to Taraza's orders:

"Stay close to the ghola and, when the moment comes, complete your assignment."

One pace at a time, Teg's body measured out the kilometers. This was the fourth night. Patrin had estimated four nights to reach their goal.

And what a goal!

The emergency escape plan centered on a discovery Patrin had made here as a teenager of one of Gammu's many mysteries. Patrin's words came back to Teg: "On the excuse of a personal reconnaissance, I returned to the place two days ago. It is untouched. I am still the only person who has ever been there."

"How can you be sure?"

"I took my own precautions when I left Gammu years ago, little things that would be disturbed by another person. Nothing has been moved."

"A Harkonnen no-globe?"

"Very ancient but the chambers are still intact and functioning."

"What about food, water . . ."

"Everything you could want or need is there, laid down in the nullentropy bins at the core."

Teg and Patrin made their plans, hoping they would never have to use this emergency bolt hole, holding the secret of it close while Patrin replayed for Teg the hidden way to this childhood discovery.

Behind Teg, Lucilla let out a small gasp as she tripped over a root.

I should have warned her, Teg thought. Duncan obviously was following Teg's lead by sound. Lucilla, just as obviously, had much of her attention on her own private thoughts.

Her facial resemblance to Darwi Odrade was remarkable, Teg told himself. Back there at the Keep, the two women side by side, he had marked the differences dictated by their differing ages. Lucilla's youth showed itself in more subcutaneous fat, a rounding of the facial flesh. But the voices! Timbre, accent, tricks of atonal inflection, the common stamp of Bene Gesserit speech mannerisms. They would be almost impossible to tell apart in the dark.

Knowing the Bene Gesserit as he did, Teg knew this was no accident. Given the Sisterhood's propensity for doubling and redoubling its prized genetic lines to protect the investment, there had to be a common ancestral source.

Atreides, all of us, he thought.

Taraza had not revealed her design for the ghola, but just being within that design gave Teg access to the growing shape of it. No complete pattern, but he could already sense a wholeness there.

Generation after generation, the Sisterhood dealing with the Tleilaxu, buying Idaho gholas, training them here on Gammu, only to have them assassinated. All of that time waiting for the right moment. It was like a terrible game, which had come into frenetic prominence because a girl capable of commanding the worms had appeared on Rakis.

Gammu itself had to be part of the design. Caladanian marks all over the place. Danian subtleties piled atop the more brutal ancient ways. Something other than population had come out of the Danian Sanctuary where the Tyrant's grandmother, the Lady Jessica, had lived out her days.

Teg had seen the overt and covert marks when he made his first reconnaissance tour of Gammu.

Wealth!

The signs were here to be read. It flowed around their universe, moving amoebalike to insinuate itself into any place where it could lodge. There was wealth from the Scattering on Gammu, Teg knew. Wealth so great that few suspected (or could imagine) its size and power.

He stopped walking abruptly. Physical patterns in the immediate landscape demanded his full attention. Ahead of them lay an exposed ledge of barren rock, its identifying markers planted in his memory by Patrin. This passage would be one of the more dangerous.

"No caves or heavy growth to conceal you. Have the blanket ready."

Teg removed the life-shield from his pack and carried it over his arm. Once more he indicated that they should continue. The dark weave of the shield fabric hissed against his body as he moved.

Lucilla was becoming less of a cipher, he thought. She aspired to a *Lady* in front of her name. *The Lady Lucilla*. No doubt that had a pleasing sound to her. A few such titled Reverend Mothers were appearing now that Major Houses were emerging from the long obscurity imposed by the Tyrant's Golden Path.

Lucilla, the Seductress-Imprinter.

All such women of the Sisterhood were sexual adepts. Teg's own mother had educated him in the workings of that system, sending him to well-selected local women when he was quite young, sensitizing him to the signs he must observe within himself as well as in the women. It was a forbidden training outside of Chapter House surveillance, but Teg's mother had been one of the Sisterhood's *heretics*.

"You will have a need for this, Miles."

No doubt there had been some prescience in her. She had armed him against the Imprinters who were trained in orgasmic amplification to fix the unconscious ties—male to female.

Lucilla and Duncan. An imprint on her would be an imprint on Odrade.

Teg almost heard the pieces go *snick* as they locked together in his mind. Then what of the young woman on Rakis? Would Lucilla teach the techniques of seduction to her imprinted pupil, arm him to ensnare the one who commanded worms?

Not enough data yet for a Prime Computation.

Teg paused at the end of the dangerous open rock passage. He put away the blanket and sealed his pack while Duncan and Lucilla waited close behind. Teg heaved a sigh. The blanket always worried him. It did not have the deflective powers of a full battle shield but if a lasgun's beam hit the thing the consequent quick-fire could be fatal.

Dangerous toys!

This was how Teg always classified such weapons and mechanical devices. Better to rely on your wits, your own flesh, and the Five Attitudes of the Bene Gesserit Way as his mother had taught him.

Use the instruments only when they are absolutely required to amplify the flesh: that was the Bene Gesserit teaching.

"Why are we stopping?" Lucilla whispered.

"I am listening to the night," Teg said.

Duncan, his face a ghostly blur in the tree-filtered starlight, stared at Teg. Teg's features reassured him. They were lodged somewhere in an unavailable memory, Duncan thought. *I can trust this man.*

Lucilla suspected that they were stopping here because Teg's old body demanded respite but she could not bring herself to say this. Teg said his escape plan included a way of getting Duncan to Rakis. Very well. That was all that mattered for the moment.

She already had figured out that this sanctuary somewhere ahead of them must involve a no-ship or a no-chamber. Nothing else would suffice. Somehow, Patrin had been the key to it. Teg's few hints had revealed that Patrin was the source of their escape route.

Lucilla had been the first to realize how Patrin would have to pay for their escape. Patrin was the weakest link.

He remained behind where Schwangyu could capture him. Capture of the decoy was inevitable. Only a fool would suppose that a Reverend Mother of Schwangyu's powers would be incapable of wresting secrets from a mere male. Schwangyu would not even require the heavy persuasion. The subtleties of Voice and those painful forms of interrogation that remained a Sisterhood monopoly—the agony box and nerve node pressures—those were all she would require.

The form Patrin's loyalty would take had been clear to Lucilla then. How could Teg have been so blind?

Love!

That long, trusting bond between the two men. Schwangyu would act swiftly and brutally. Patrin knew it Teg had not examined his own certain knowledge.

Duncan's voice shocked her from these thoughts.

"'Thopter! Behind us!"

"Quick!" Teg whipped the blanket from his pack and threw it over them. They huddled in earth-smelling darkness, listening to the ornithopter pass above them. It did not pause or return.

When they felt certain they had not been detected, Teg once more led them up Patrin's *memory-track*.

"That was a searcher," Lucilla said. "They are beginning to suspect . . . or Patrin . . ."

"Save your energy for walking," Teg snapped.

She did not press him. They both knew Patrin was dead. Argument over this had been exhausted.

This Mentat goes deep, Lucilla told herself.

Teg was the child of a Reverend Mother and that mother had trained him beyond the permitted limits before the Sisterhood took him into their manipulative hands. The ghola was not the only one here with unknown resources.

Their trail turned back and forth upon itself, a game track climbing a steep hill through thick forest. Starlight did not penetrate the trees. Only the Mentat's marvelous memory kept them on the path.

Lucilla felt duff underfoot. She listened to Teg's movements, reading them to guide her feet.

How silent Duncan is, she thought. *How closed in upon himself.* He obeyed orders. He followed where Teg led them. She sensed the quality of Duncan's obedience. He kept his own counsel. Duncan obeyed because it suited him to do so—for now. Schwangyu's rebellion had planted something wildly independent in the ghola. And what things of their own had the Tleilaxu planted in him?

Teg stopped at a level spot beneath tall trees to regain his wind. Lucilla could hear him breathing deeply. This reminded her once more that the Mentat was a very old man, far too old for these exertions. She spoke quietly:

"Are you all right, Miles?"

"I'll tell you when I'm not."

"How much farther?" Duncan asked.

"Only a short way now."

Presently, he resumed his course through the night. "We must hurry," he said. "This saddle-back ridge is the last bit."

Now that he had accepted the fact of Patrin's death, Teg's thoughts swung like a compass needle to Schwangyu and what she must be experiencing. Schwangyu would feel her world falling in around her. The fugitives had been gone four nights! People who could elude a Reverend Mother this way might do anything! Of course, the fugitives probably were off-planet by now. A no-ship. But what if . . .

Schwangyu's thoughts would be full of what-ifs.

Patrin had been the fragile link but Patrin had been well trained in the removal of fragile links, trained by a master—Miles Teg.

Teg dashed dampness from his eyes with a quick shake of his head. Immediate necessity required that core of internal honesty which he could not avoid. Teg had never been a good liar, not even to himself. Quite early in his training, he had realized that his mother and the others involved in his upbringing had conditioned him to a deep sense of personal honesty.

Adherence to a code of honor.

The code itself, as he recognized its shape in him, attracted Teg's fascinated attention. It began with recognition that humans were not created equal, that they possessed different inherited abilities and experienced different events in their lives. This produced people of different accomplishments and different worth.

To obey this code, Teg realized early that he must place himself accurately into the flow of observable hierarchies accepting that a moment might come when he could evolve no further.

The code's conditioning went deep. He could never find its ultimate roots. It obviously was attached to something intrinsic to his humanity. It dictated with enormous power the limits of behavior permitted to those above as well as to those below him in the hierarchical pyramid.

The key token of exchange: loyalty.

Loyalty went upward and downward, lodging wherever

it found a deserving attachment. Such loyalties, Teg knew, were securely locked into him. He felt no doubts that Taraza would support him in everything except a situation demanding that he be sacrificed to the survival of the Sisterhood. And that was right in itself. That was where the loyalties of all of them eventually lodged.

I am Taraza's Bashar. That is what the code says.

And this was the code that had killed Patrin.

I hope you suffered no pain, old friend.

Once more, Teg paused under the trees. Taking his fighting knife from its boot sheath, he scratched a small mark in a tree beside him.

"What are you doing?" Lucilla demanded.

"This is a secret mark," Teg said. "Only the people I have trained know about it. And Taraza, of course."

"But why are you . . ."

"I will explain later."

Teg moved forward, stopping at another tree where he made the tiny mark, a thing which an animal might make with a claw, something to blend into the natural forms of this wilderness.

As he worked his way ahead, Teg realized he had come to a decision about Lucilla. Her plans for Duncan must be deflected. Every Mentat projection Teg could make about Duncan's safety and sanity required this. The awakening of Duncan's pre-ghola memories must come ahead of any Imprint by Lucilla. It would not be easy to block her, Teg knew. It required a better liar than he had ever been to dissemble for a Reverend Mother.

It must be made to appear accidental, the normal outcome of the circumstances. Lucilla must never suspect opposition. Teg held few illusions about succeeding against an aroused Reverend Mother in close quarters. Better to kill her. That, he thought he could do. But the consequences! Taraza could never be made to see such a bloody act as obedience to her orders.

No, he would have to bide his time, wait and watch and listen.

They emerged into a small open area with a high barrier of volcanic rock close ahead of them. Scrubby bushes and low thorn trees grew close against the rock, visible as dark blotches in the starlight.

Teg saw the blacker outline of a crawl space under the bushes.

"It's belly crawling from here in," Teg said

"I smell ashes," Lucilla said. "Something's been burned here."

"This is where the decoy came," Teg said. "He left a charred area just down to our left—simulating the marks of a no-ship's take-off burn."

Lucilla's quickly indrawn breath was audible. *The audacity!* Should Schwangyu dare bring in a prescient searcher to follow Duncan's tracks (because Duncan alone among them had no Siona blood in his ancestry to shield him) all of the marks would agree that they had come this way and fled off-planet in a no ship . . . provided . . .

"But where are you taking us?" she asked.

"It's a Harkonnen no-globe," Teg said. "It has been here for millennia and now it's ours."

Quite naturally, holders of power wish to suppress wild research. Unrestricted questing after knowledge has a long history of producing unwanted competition. The powerful want a "safe line of investigations," which will develop only those products and ideas that can be controlled and, most important, that will allow the larger part of the benefits to be captured by inside investors. Unfortunately, a random universe full of relative variables does not insure such a "safe line of investigations."

—ASSESSMENT OF IX, BENE GESSERIT ARCHIVES

Hedley Tuek, High Priest and titular ruler of Rakis, felt himself inadequate to the demands just imposed upon him.

Dust-fogged night enveloped the city of Keen, but here in his private audience chamber the brilliance of many glowglobes dispelled shadows. Even here, in the heart of the Temple, though, the wind could be heard, a distant moan, this planet's periodic torment.

The audience chamber was an irregular room seven meters long and four meters at its widest end. The opposite end was almost imperceptibly narrower. The ceiling, too, made a gentle slope in that direction. Spice fiber hangings and clever shadings in light yellows and grays concealed these irregularities. One of the hangings covered a focusing horn that carried even the smallest sounds to listeners outside the room.

Only Darwi Odrade, the new commander of the Bene Gesserit Keep on Rakis, sat with Tuek in the audience chamber. The two of them faced each other across a narrow space defined by their soft green cushions.

Tuek tried to conceal a grimace. The effort twisted his normally imposing features into a revealing mask. He had taken great care in preparing himself for this night's confrontations. Dressers had smoothed his robe over his tall, rather stout figure. Golden sandals covered his long feet. The stillsuit under his robe was only for display: no pumps or catchpockets, no uncomfortable and time-consuming adjustments required. His silky gray hair was combed long to his shoulders, a suitable frame for his square face with its wide thick mouth and heavy chin. His eyes fell abruptly into a look of benevolence, an expression he had copied from his grandfather. This was how he had looked on entering the audience chamber to meet Odrade. He had felt himself altogether imposing, but, now, he suddenly felt naked and disheveled.

He's really a rather empty-headed fellow, Odrade thought.

Tuek was thinking: *I cannot discuss that terrible Manifesto with her! Not with a Tleilaxu Master and those Face Dancers listening in the other room. What ever possessed me to allow that?*

"It is heresy, pure and simple," Tuek said.

"But you are only one religion among many," Odrade countered. "And with people returning from the Scattering, the proliferation of schisms and variant beliefs . . ."

"We are the only true belief!" Tuek said.

Odrade hid a smile. *He said it right on cue. And Waff surely heard him.* Tuek was remarkably easy to lead. If the Sisterhood was right about Waff, Tuek's words would enrage the Tleilaxu Master.

In a deep and portentous tone, Odrade said: "The Manifesto raises questions that all must address, believers and non-believers alike."

"What has all this to do with the Holy Child?" Tuek demanded. "You told me we must meet on matters concerning—"

"Indeed! Don't try to deny that you know there are many people who are beginning to worship Sheeana. The Manifesto implicates—"

"Manifesto! Manifesto! It is a heretical document, which will be obliterated. As for Sheeana, she must be returned to our exclusive care!"

"No." Odrade spoke softly.

How agitated Tuek was, she thought. His stiff neck moved minimally as he turned his head from side to side. The movements pointed to a wall hanging on Odrade's right, defining the place as though Tuek's head carried an illuminating beam to reveal that particular hanging. What a transparent man, this High Priest. He might just as well announce that Waff listened to them somewhere behind that hanging.

"Next, you will spirit her away from Rakis," Tuek said.

"She stays here," Odrade said. "Just as we promised you."

"But why can't she . . ."

"Come now! Sheeana has made her wishes clear and

I'm sure her words have been reported to you. She wishes to be a Reverend Mother."

"She already is the—"

"M'Lord Tuek! Don't try to dissemble with me. She has stated her wishes and we are happy to comply. Why should you object? Reverend Mothers served the Divided God in the Fremen times. Why not now?"

"You Bene Gesserit have ways of making people say things they do not want to say," Tuek accused. "We should not be discussing this privately. My councillors—"

"Your councillors would only muddy our discussion. The implications of the Atreides Manifesto —"

"I will discuss only Sheeana!" Tuek drew himself up in what he thought of as his posture of adamant High Priest.

"We *are* discussing her," Odrade said.

"Then let me make it clear that we require more of our people in her entourage. She must be guarded at all—"

"The way she was guarded on that rooftop?" Odrade asked.

"Reverend Mother Odrade, this is Holy Rakis! You have no rights here that we do not grant!"

"Rights? Sheeana has become the target, yes the target! of many ambitions and you wish to discuss rights?"

"My duties as High Priest are clear. The Holy Church of the Divided God will—"

"M'Lord Tuek! I am trying very hard to maintain the necessary courtesies. What I do is for your benefit as well as our own. The actions we have taken—"

"Actions? What actions?" The words were pressed

from Tuek with a hoarse grunting. These terrible Bene Gesserit witches! Tleilaxu behind him and a Reverend Mother in front! Tuek felt like a ball in a fearsome game, bounced back and forth between terrifying energies. Peaceful Rakis, the secure place of his daily routines, had vanished and he had been projected into an arena whose rules he did not fully understand.

"I have sent for the Bashar Miles Teg," Odrade said. "That is all. His advance party should arrive soon. We are going to reinforce your planetary defenses."

"You dare to take over—"

"We take over nothing. At your own father's request, Teg's people redesigned your defenses. The agreement under which this was done contains, at your father's insistence, a clause requiring our periodic review."

Tuek sat in dazed silence. Waff, that ominous little Tleilaxu, had heard all of this. There would be conflict! The Tleilaxu wanted a secret agreement setting melange prices. They would not permit Bene Gesserit interference.

Odrade had spoken of Tuek's father and now Tuek wished only that his long-dead father sat here. A hard man. He would have known how to deal with these opposing forces. *He* had always handled the Tleilaxu quite well. Tuek recalled listening (just as Waff listened now!) to a Tleilaxu envoy named Wose . . . and another one named Pook. Ledden Pook. What odd names they had.

Tuek's confused thoughts abruptly offered up another name. Odrade had just mentioned it: *Teg!* Was that old monster still active?

Odrade was speaking once more. Tuek tried to swallow in a dry throat as he leaned forward, forcing himself to pay attention.

"Teg will also look into your on-planet defenses. After that rooftop fiasco—"

"I officially forbid this interference with our internal affairs," Tuek said. "There is no need. Our Priest Guardians are adequate to—"

"Adequate?" Odrade shook her head sadly. "What an inadequate word, given the new circumstances on Rakis."

"What new circumstances?" There was terror in Tuek's voice.

Odrade merely sat there staring at him.

Tuek tried to force some order into his thoughts. Could she know about the Tleilaxu listening back there? Impossible! He inhaled a trembling breath. What was this about the defenses of Rakis? The defenses were excellent, he reassured himself. They had the best Ixian monitors and no-ships. More than that, it was to the advantage of all independent powers that Rakis remain equally independent as another source of the spice.

To the advantage of everyone except the Tleilaxu with the damnable melange overproduction from their axlotl tanks!

This was a shattering thought. A Tleilaxu Master had heard every word spoken in this audience chamber!

Tuek called on Shai-hulud, the Divided God, to protect him. That terrible little man back there said he spoke also for Ixians and Fish Speakers. He produced documents. Was that the "new circumstances" of which Odrade spoke? Nothing remained long hidden from the witches!

The High Priest could not repress a shudder at the thought of Waff: that round little head, those glittering eyes; that pug nose and those sharp teeth in that brittle smile. Waff looked like a slightly enlarged child until you met those eyes and heard him speak in his squeaky voice. Tuek recalled that his own father had complained of those voices: "The Tleilaxu say such terrible things in their childish voices!"

Odrade shifted on her cushions. She thought of Waff listening out there. Had he heard enough? Her own secret listeners certainly would be asking themselves that question now. Reverend Mothers always replayed these verbal contests, seeking improvements and new advantages for the Sisterhood.

Waff has heard enough, Odrade told herself. *Time to shift the play.*

In her most matter-of-fact tones, Odrade said: "M'Lord Tuek, someone important is listening to what we say here. Is it polite that such a person listen secretly?"

Tuek closed his eyes. *She knows!*

He opened his eyes and met Odrade's unrevealing stare. She looked like someone who might wait through eternity for his response.

"Polite? I . . . I . . ."

"Invite the secret listener to come sit with us," Odrade said.

Tuek passed a hand across his damp forehead. His father and grandfather, High Priests before him, had laid down ritual responses for most occasions, but nothing for a moment such as this. Invite the Tleilaxu to sit here? In this chamber with . . . Tuek was reminded suddenly that he did not like the smell of Tleilaxu Masters. His father had complained of that: "They smell of disgusting food!"

Odrade got to her feet. "I would much rather look

upon those who hear my words," she said. "Shall I go myself and invite the hidden listener to—"

"Please!" Tuek remained seated but lifted a hand to stop her. "I had little choice. He comes with documents from Fish Speakers and Ixians. He said he would help us to return Sheeana to our—"

"Help you?" Odrade looked down at the sweating priest with something akin to pity. This one thought he ruled Rakis?

"He is of the Bene Tleilax," Tuek said. "He is called Waff and—"

"I know what he is called and I know why he is here, M'Lord Tuek. What astonishes me is that you would allow him to spy on—"

"It is not spying! We were negotiating. I mean, there are new forces to which we must adjust our—"

"New forces? Oh, yes: the whores from the Scattering. Does this Waff bring some of them with him?"

Before Tuek could respond, the audience chamber's side door opened. Waff entered right on cue, two Face Dancers behind him.

He was told not to bring Face Dancers! Odrade thought.

"Just you!" Odrade said, pointing. "Those others were not invited, were they, M'Lord Tuek?"

Tuek lifted himself heavily to his feet, noting the nearness of Odrade, remembering all of the terrible stories about the Reverend Mothers' physical prowess. The presence of Face Dancers added to his confusion. They always filled him with such terrible misgivings.

Turning toward the door and trying to compose his features into a look of invitation, Tuek said: "Only . . . only Ambassador Waff, please."

Speech hurt Tuek's throat. This was worse than terrible! He felt naked before these people.

Odrade gestured to a cushion near her. "Waff is it? Please come and sit down."

Waff nodded to her as though he had never seen her before. *How polite!* With a gesture to his Face Dancers that they remain outside, he crossed to the indicated cushion but stood waiting beside it.

Odrade saw a flux of tensions move through the little Tleilaxu. Something like a snarl flickered across his lips. He still had those weapons in his sleeves. Was he about to break their agreement?

It was time, Odrade knew, for Waff's suspicions to regain all of their original strength and more. He would be feeling trapped by Taraza's maneuverings. Waff wanted his breeding mothers! The reek of his pheromones announced his deepest fears. He carried in his mind, then, his part of their agreement—or at least a *form* of that sharing. Taraza did not expect Waff really to share all of the knowledge he had gained from the Honored Matres.

"M'Lord Tuek tells me you have been . . . ahhh, negotiating," Odrade said. *Let him remember that word!* Waff knew where the real negotiation must be concluded. As she spoke, Odrade sank to her knees, then back onto her cushion, but her feet remained positioned to throw her out of any line of attack from Waff.

Waff glanced down at her and at the cushion she had indicated for him. Slowly, he sank onto his cushion but his arms remained on his knees, the sleeves directed at Tuek.

What is he doing? Odrade wondered. Waff's movements said he was embarked on a plan of his own.

Odrade said: "I have been trying to impress upon the High Priest the importance of the Atreides Manifesto to our mutual—"

"Atreides!" Tuek blurted. He almost collapsed onto his cushion. "It cannot be Atreides."

"A very persuasive manifesto," Waff said, reinforcing Tuek's obvious fears.

At least *that* was according to plan, Odrade thought. She said: "The promise of s'tori cannot be ignored. Many people equate s'tori with the presence of their god."

Waff sent a surprised and angry stare at her.

Tuek said: "Ambassador Waff tells me that Ixians and Fish Speakers are alarmed by that document, but I have reassured him that—"

"I think we may ignore the Fish Speakers," Odrade said. "They hear the noise of god everywhere."

Waff recognized the cant in her words. Was she jibing at him? She was right about the Fish Speakers, of course. They had been so far weaned from their old devotions that they influenced very little and whatever they *did* influence could be guided by the new Face Dancers who now led them.

Tuek tried to smile at Waff. "You spoke of helping us to . . ."

"Time for that later," Odrade interrupted. She had to keep Tuek's attention on the document that disturbed him so much. She paraphrased from the Manifesto: "Your will and your faith—your belief system—dominate your universe."

Tuek recognized the words. He had read the terrible document. This *Manifesto* said God and all of His works were no more than human creations. He wondered how he should respond. No High Priest could let such a thing go unchallenged.

Before Tuek could find words, Waff locked eyes with Odrade and responded in a way he knew she would interpret correctly. Odrade could do no less, being who she was.

"The error of prescience," Waff said. "Isn't that what this document calls it? Isn't that where it says the mind of the believer stagnates?"

"Exactly!" Tuek said. He felt thankful for the Tleilaxu intervention. That was precisely the core of this dangerous heresy!

Waff did not look at him, but continued to stare at Odrade. Did the Bene Gesserit think their design inscrutable? Let her meet a greater power. She thought herself so strong! But the Bene Gesserit could not really know how the Almighty guarded the future of the Shariat!

Tuek was not to be stopped. "It assaults everything we hold sacred! And it's being spread everywhere!"

"By the Tleilaxu," Odrade said.

Waff lifted his sleeves, directing his weapons at Tuek. He hesitated only because he saw that Odrade had recognized part of his intentions.

Tuek stared from one to the other. Was Odrade's accusation true? Or was that just another Bene Gesserit trick?

Odrade saw Waff's hesitation and guessed its reason. She cast through her mind, seeking an answer to his motivations. What advantage could the Tleilaxu gain by killing Tuek? Obviously, Waff aimed to substitute one of his Face Dancers for the High Priest. But what would that gain him?

Sparring for time, Odrade said: "You should be very cautious, *Ambassador* Waff."

"When has caution ever governed great necessities?" Waff asked.

Tuek lifted himself to his feet and moved heavily to one side, wringing his hands. "Please! These are holy precincts. It is wrong to discuss heresies here unless we plan to destroy them." He looked down on Waff. "It's not true, is it? You are not the authors of that terrible document?"

"It is not ours," Waff agreed. *Damn that fop of a priest!* Tuek had moved well to one side and once more presented a moving target.

"I knew it!" Tuek said, striding around behind Waff and Odrade.

Odrade kept her gaze on Waff. He planned murder! She was sure of it.

Tuek spoke from behind her. "You do not know how you wrong us, Reverend Mother. Ser Waff has asked that we form a melange cartel. I explained that our price to you must remain unchanged because one of you was the grandmother of God."

Waff bowed his head, waiting. The priest would come back into range. God would not permit a failure.

Tuek stood behind Odrade looking down at Waff. A shudder passed through the priest. Tleilaxu were so . . . so repellent and amoral. They could not be trusted. How could Waff's denial be accepted?

Not wavering from her contemplation of Waff, Odrade said: "But, M'Lord Tuek, was not the prospect of increased income attractive to you?" She saw Waff's right arm come around slightly, almost aimed at her. His intentions became clear.

"M'Lord Tuek," Odrade said, "this Tleilaxu intends to murder us both."

At her words, Waff jerked both arms up, trying to aim at the two separated and difficult targets. Before his muscles responded, Odrade was under his guard. She heard the faint hiss of dart throwers but felt no sting. Her left arm came up in a slashing blow to break Waff's right arm. Her right foot broke his left arm.

Waff screamed.

He had never suspected such speed in the Bene Gesserit. It was almost a match for what he had seen in the Honored Matre on the Ixian conference ship. Even through his pain he realized that he must report this. Reverend Mothers command synaptic bypasses under duress!

The door behind Odrade burst open. Waff's Face Dancers rushed into the chamber. But Odrade already was behind Waff, both hands on his throat. "Stop or he dies!" she shouted.

The two froze.

Waff squirmed under her hands.

"Be still!" she commanded. Odrade glanced at Tuek sprawled on the floor to her right. One dart had hit its target.

"Waff has killed the High Priest," Odrade said, speaking for her own secret listeners.

The two Face Dancers continued to stare at her. Their indecision was easy to see. None of them, she saw, had realized how this played into Bene Gesserit hands. Trap the Tleilaxu indeed!

Odrade spoke to the Face Dancers. "Remove yourselves and that body to the corridor and close the door.

Your Master has done a foolish thing. He will have need of you later." To Waff, she said: "For the moment, you need me more than you need your Face Dancers. Send them away."

"Go," Waff squeaked.

When the Face Dancers continued to stare at her, Odrade said: "If you do not leave immediately, I will kill him and then I will dispatch both of you."

"Do it!" Waff screamed.

The Face Dancers took this as the command to obey their Master. Odrade heard something else in Waff's voice. He obviously would have to be talked out of suicidal hysteria.

Once she was alone with him, Odrade removed the exhausted weapons from his sleeves and pocketed them. They could be examined in detail later. There was little she could do for his broken bones except render him briefly unconscious and set them. She improvised splints from cushions and torn strips of green fabric from the High Priest's furnishings.

Waff reawakened quickly. He groaned when he looked at Odrade.

"You and I are now allies," Odrade said. "The things that have transpired in this chamber have been heard by some of my people and by representatives from a faction that wants to replace Tuek with one of their own number."

It was too fast for Waff. He was a moment grasping what she had said. His mind fastened, though, on the most important thing.

"Allies?"

"I imagine Tuek was difficult to deal with," she said.

"Offer him obvious benefits and he invariably waffled. You have done some of the priests a favor by killing him."

"They are listening now?" Waff squeaked.

"Of course. Let us discuss your proposed spice monopoly. The late lamented High Priest said you mentioned this. Let me see if I can deduce the extent of your offer."

"My arms," Waff moaned.

"You're still alive," she said. "Be thankful for my wisdom. I could have killed you."

He turned his head away from her. "That would have been better."

"Not for the Bene Tleilax and certainly not for my Sisterhood," she said. "Let me see. Yes, you promised to provide Rakis with many new spice harvesters, the new airborne ones, which only touch the desert with their sweeper heads."

"You listened!" Waff accused.

"Not at all. A very attractive proposal, since I'm sure the Ixians are providing them free for their own reasons. Shall I continue?"

"You said we are allies."

"A monopoly would force the Guild to buy more Ixian navigation machines," she said. "You would have the Guild in the jaws of your crusher."

Waff lifted his head to glare at her. The movement sent agony through his broken arms and he groaned. Despite the pain, he studied Odrade through almost lidded eyes. Did the witches really believe that was the extent of the Tleilaxu plan? He hardly dared hope the Bene Gesserit were so misled.

"Of course that was not your basic plan," Odrade said.

Waff's eyes snapped wide open. She was reading his mind! "I am dishonored," he said. "When you saved my life you saved a useless thing." He sank back.

Odrade inhaled a deep breath. *Time to use the results of the Chapter House analyses.* She leaned close to Waff and whispered in his ear: "The Shariat needs you yet."

Waff gasped.

Odrade sat back. That gasp said it all. Analysis confirmed.

"You thought you had better allies in the people from the Scattering," she said. "Those Honored Matres and other hetairas of that ilk. I ask you: does the slig make alliance with its garbage?"

Waff had heard that question uttered only in khel. His face pale, he breathed in shallow gasps. The implications in her words! He forced himself to ignore the pain in his arms. *Allies*, she said. She knew about the Shariat! How could she possibly know?

"How can either of us be unmindful of the many advantages in an alliance between Bene Tleilax and Bene Gesserit?" Odrade asked.

Alliance with the powindah witches? Waff's mind was filled with turmoil. The agony of his arms was held so tentatively at bay. This moment felt so fragile! He tasted acid bile on the back of his tongue.

"Ahhhh," Odrade said. "Do you hear that? The priest, Krutansik, and his faction have arrived outside our door. They will propose that one of your Face Dancers assume the guise of the late Hedley Tuek. Any other course would cause too much turmoil. Krutansik is a fairly wise man who has held himself in the background until now. His Uncle Stiros groomed him well."

"What does your Sisterhood gain from alliance with us?" Waff managed.

Odrade smiled. Now she could speak the truth. That was always much easier and often the most powerful argument.

"Our survival in the face of the storm that is brewing among the Scattered Ones," she said. "Tleilaxu survival, too. The farthest thing from our desires is an end to those who preserve the *Great Belief.*"

Waff cringed. She spoke it openly! Then he understood. What matter if others heard? They could not see through to the secrets beneath her words.

"Our breeding mothers are ready for you," Odrade said. She stared hard into his eyes and made the handsign of a Zensunni priest.

Waff felt a tight band release itself from his breast. The unexpected, the unthinkable, the *unbelievable* thing was true! The Bene Gesserit were not powindah! All the universe would yet follow the Bene Tleilax into the True Faith! God would not permit otherwise. Especially not here on the planet of the Prophet!

The reports, the summations and scattered tidbits lay
in rows across the long table where Taraza sat. Except
for the night watch and essential services, Chapter House
Core slumbered around her. Only the familiar sounds of
maintenance activities penetrated her private chambers.
Two glowglobes hovered over her table, bathing the dark
wood surface and rows of ridulian paper in yellow light.
The window beyond her table was a dark mirror reflecting
the room.

Archives!

The holoprojector flickered with its continuing pro-
duction above the tabletop—more bits and pieces that
she had summoned.

Taraza rather distrusted Archivists, which she knew
was an ambivalent attitude because she recognized the
underlying necessity for data. But Chapter House Records could only be viewed as a jungle of abbreviations,
special notations, coded insertions, and footnotes. Such

material often required a Mentat for translation or, what was worse, in times of extreme fatigue demanded that she delve into Other Memories. All Archivists were Mentats, of course, but this did not reassure Taraza. You could never consult Archival Records in a straightforward manner. Much of the interpretation that emerged from that source had to be accepted on the word of the ones who brought it or (hateful!) you had to rely on the mechanical search by the holosystem. This, in its turn, required a dependency on those who maintained the system. It gave functionaries more power than Taraza cared to delegate.

Dependencies!

Taraza hated dependency. This was a rueful admission, reminding her that few developing situations were ever precisely what you imagined they would be. Even the best of Mentat projections accumulated errors . . . given enough time.

Still, every move the Sisterhood made required the consultation of Archives and seemingly endless analyses. Even ordinary commerce demanded it. She found this a frequent irritation. Should they form this group? Sign that agreement?

There always came the moment during a conference when she was forced to introduce a note of decision:

"Analysis by Archivist Hesterion accepted."

Or, as was often the case: "Archivists' report rejected; not pertinent."

Taraza leaned forward to study the holoprojection: "Possible breeding plan for Subject Waff."

She scanned the numbers, gene plans from the cell sample forwarded by Odrade. Fingernail scrapings seldom produced enough material for a secure analysis but Odrade had done quite well under the cover of setting the man's broken bones. Taraza shook her head at the data. Offspring would surely be like all the previous ones the Bene Gesserit had attempted with Tleilaxu: The females would be immune to memory probing: males, of course, would be an impenetrable and repellent chaos.

Taraza sat back and sighed. When it came to breeding records, the monumental cross-referencing assumed staggering proportions. Officially, it was the "College of Ancestral Pertinence," CAP to the Archivists. Among the Sisters at large, it was known as the "Stud Record," which, although accurate, failed to convey the sense of detail listed under the proper Archival headings. She had asked for Waff's projections to be carried out into three hundred generations, an easy and rather rapid task, sufficient for all practical purposes. Three-hundred-Gen mainlines (such as Teg, his collaterals and siblings) had proved themselves dependable for millennia. Instinct told her it would be bootless to waste more time on the Waff projections.

Fatigue welled up in Taraza. She put her head in her hands and rested them for a moment on the table, feeling the coolness of the wood.

What if I am wrong about Rakis?

Opposition arguments could not be shuffled away into Archival dust. *Damn this dependency on computers!* The Sisterhood had carried its main lines in computers even back in the Forbidden Days after the Butlerian Jihad's wild smashing of "the thinking machines." In these "more enlightened" days, one tended not to question the unconscious motives behind that ancient orgy of destruction.

Sometimes, we make very responsible decisions for un-conscious reasons. A conscious search of Archives or Other Memories carries no guarantees.

Taraza released one of her hands and slapped it against the tabletop. She did not like dealing with the Archivists who came trotting in with *answers* to her questions. A disdainful lot they were, full of secret jokes. She had heard them comparing their CAP work to stock breeding, to Farm Forms and Animal Racing Authority. Damn their jokes! The right decision now was far more important than they could possibly imagine. Those serving sisters who only obeyed orders did not have Taraza's responsibilities.

She lifted her head and looked across the room at the niche with its bust of Sister Chenoeh, the ancient one who had met and conversed with the Tyrant.

You knew, Taraza thought. *You were never a Reverend Mother but still you knew. Your reports show it. How did you know to make the right decision?*

Odrade's request for military assistance required an immediate answer. The time limits were too tight. But with Teg, Lucilla, and the ghola missing, the contingency plan had to be brought into play.

Damn Teg!

More of his unexpected behavior. He could not leave the ghola in jeopardy, of course. Schwangyu's actions had been predictable.

What had Teg done? Had he gone to ground in Ysai or one of the other major cities on Gammu? No. If that were the case, Teg would have reported by now through one of the secret contacts they had prepared. He possessed a complete list of those contacts and had investigated some of them personally.

Obviously, Teg did not place full trust in the contacts. He had seen something during his inspection tour that he had not passed along through Bellonda.

Burzmali would have to be called in and briefed, of course. Burzmali was the best, trained by Teg himself; prime candidate for Supreme Bashar. Burzmali must be sent to Gammu.

I'm playing a hunch, Taraza thought.

But if Teg had gone to ground, the trail started on Gammu. The trail could have ended there as well. Yes, Burzmali to Gammu. Rakis must wait. There were certain obvious attractions in this move. It would not alert the Guild. The Tleilaxu and the ones from the Scattering, however, would certainly rise to the bait. If Odrade failed to trap the Tleilaxu . . . no, Odrade would not fail. That one had become almost a certainty.

The unexpected.

You see, Milles? I have learned from you.

None of this deflected the opposition within the Sisterhood, though.

Taraza put both palms flat on her table and pressed hard, as though trying to sense the people out there in Chapter House, the ones who shared Schwangyu's opinions. Vocal opposition had subsided but that always meant the violence was being readied.

What shall I do?

The Mother Superior was supposed to be immune to indecision in a crisis. But the Tleilaxu connection had unbalanced their data. Some of the recommendations for

Odrade appeared obvious and already had been transmitted. That much of the plan was plausible and simple.

Take Waff into the desert far beyond unwanted eyes. Contrive a situation-in-extremis and the consequent religious experience in the old and reliable pattern dictated by the Missionaria Protectiva. Test whether the Tleilaxu were using the ghola process for their own kind of immortality. Odrade was perfectly capable of carrying out that much of the revised plan. It depended heavily on this young woman, Sheeana, though.

The worm itself is the unknown.

Taraza reminded herself that today's worm was not the original worm of Rakis. Despite Sheeana's demonstrated command over them, they were unpredictable. As Archives would say, they had no track record. Taraza held little doubt that Odrade had made an accurate deduction about the Rakians and their dances. That was a plus.

A language.

But we do not yet speak it. That was a negative.

I must make a decision tonight!

Taraza sent her surface awareness roaming backward along that unbroken line of Mothers Superior, all of those female memories encapsulated within the fragile awareness of herself and two others—Bellonda and Hesterion. It was a tortuous track through Other Memories, which she felt too tired to follow. Right at the edge of the track would be observations of Muad'Dib, the Atreides bastard who had shaken the universe twice—once by dominating the Imperium with his Fremen hordes, and then by spawning the Tyrant.

If we are defeated this time it could be the end of us, she thought. *We could be swallowed whole by these hell-spawned females from the Scattering.*

Alternatives presented themselves: The female child on Rakis could be passed into the Sisterhood's core to live out her life somewhere at the end of a no-ship's flight. An ignominious retreat.

So much depended on Teg. Had he failed the Sisterhood at last or had he found an unexpected way to conceal the ghola?

I must find a way to delay, Taraza thought. *We must give Teg time to communicate with us. Odrade will have to drag out the plan on Rakis.*

It was dangerous but it had to be done.

Stiffly, Taraza lifted herself from her chairdog and went to the darkened window across from her. Chapter House Planet lay in star-shadowed darkness. A refuge: Chapter House Planet. Such planets were not even recipients of names anymore; only numbers somewhere in Archives. This planet had seen fourteen hundred years of Bene Gesserit occupancy but even that must be considered temporary. She thought of the guardian no-ships orbiting overhead: Teg's own defense system in depth. Still, Chapter House remained vulnerable.

The problem had a name: "accidental discovery."

It was an eternal flaw. Out there in the Scattering, humankind expanded exponentially, swarming across unlimited space. The Tyrant's Golden Path secure at last. Or was it? Surely, the Atreides worm had planned more than the simple survival of the species.

He did something to us that we have not yet unearthed— even after all of these millennia. I think I know what he did. My opposition says otherwise.

It was never easy for a Reverend Mother to contemplate the bondage they had suffered under Leto II as he whipped his Imperium for thirty-five hundred years along his Golden Path.

We stumble when we review those times.

Seeing her own reflection in the window's dark plaz, Taraza glared at herself. It was a grim face and the fatigue easily visible.

I have every right to be tired and grim!

She knew that her training had channeled her deliberately into negative patterns. These were her defenses and her strengths. She remained distant in all human relationships, even in the seductions she had performed for the Breeding Mistresses. Taraza was the perpetual devil's advocate and this had become a dominant force in the entire Sisterhood, a natural consequence of her elevation to Mother Superior. Opposition developed easily in that environment.

As the Sufis said: *Rot at the core always spreads outward.*

What they did not say was that some rots were noble and valuable.

She reassured herself now with her more dependable data: The Scattering took the Tyrant's lessons outward in the human migrations, changed in unknown ways but ultimately submissive to recognition. And in time, a way would be found to nullify a no-ship's invisibility. Taraza did not think the people of the Scattering had found this—at least not the ones skulking back into the places that had spawned them.

There was absolutely no safe course through the conflicting forces, but she thought the Sisterhood had armed itself as well as it could. The problem was akin to that of a Guild navigator threading his ship through the folds of space in a way that avoided collisions and entrapments.

Entrapments, they were the key, and there was Odrade springing the Sisterhood's traps on the Tleilaxu.

When Taraza thought about Odrade, which was often in these crisis times, their long association reasserted itself. It was as though she looked at a faded tapestry in which some figures remained bright. Brightest of all, assuring Odrade's position close to the seats of Sisterhood command, was her capacity for cutting across details and getting at the surprising meat of a conflict. It was a form of that dangerous Atreides prescience working secretly within her. Using this hidden talent was the one thing that had aroused the most opposition, and it was the one argument that Taraza admitted had the most validity. That thing working far below the surface, its hidden movements indicated only by occasional turbulence, *that* was the problem!

"Use her but stand ready to eliminate her," Taraza had argued. "We will still have most of her offspring."

Taraza knew she could depend on Lucilla . . . provided Lucilla had found sanctuary somewhere with Teg and the ghola. Alternate assassins existed at the Keep on Rakis, of course. That weapon might have to be armed soon.

Taraza experienced a sudden turmoil within herself. Other Memories advised caution in the utmost. Never again lose control of the breeding lines! Yes, if Odrade escaped an elimination attempt, she would be alienated forever. Odrade was a full Reverend Mother and some of those must still remain out there in the Scattering—not among the Honored Matres the Sisterhood had observed . . . but still . . .

Never Again! That was the operational motto. Never another Kwisatz Haderach or another Tyrant.

Control the breeders: Control their offspring.

Reverend Mothers did not die when their flesh died. They sank farther and farther into the Bene Gesserit living core until their casual instructions and even their unconscious observations became a part of the continuing Sisterhood.

Make no mistakes about Odrade!

The response to Odrade required specific tailoring and exquisite care. Odrade, who allowed certain limited affections, "a mild warmth," she called them, argued that emotions provided valuable insights if you did not let them govern you. Taraza saw this *mild warmth* as a way into the heart of Odrade, a vulnerable opening.

I know what you think of me, Dar, with your mild warmth toward an old companion from school days. You think I am a potential danger to the Sisterhood but that I can be saved from myself by watchful "friends."

Taraza knew that some of her advisors shared Odrade's opinion, listened quietly and reserved judgment. Most of them still followed the Mother Superior's lead but many knew of Odrade's wild talent and had recognized Odrade's doubts. Only one thing kept most of the Sisters in line and Taraza did not try to delude herself about it.

Every Mother Superior acted out of a profound loyalty to her Sisterhood. Nothing must endanger Bene Gesserit continuity, not even herself. In her precise and harshly self-judgmental way, Taraza examined her relationship to the Sisterhood's continuing life.

Obviously, there was no immediate necessity to eliminate Odrade. Yet, Odrade was now so close to the center of the ghola design that little occurring there could escape her sensitive observation. Much that had not been revealed to her would become known. The Atreides Manifesto had been almost a gamble. Odrade, the obvious person to produce the Manifesto, could only achieve a deeper insight as she wrote the document, but the words themselves were the ultimate barrier to revelation.

Waff would appreciate that, Taraza knew.

Turning from the dark window, Taraza went back to her chairdog. The moment of crucial decision—go or no-go—could be delayed but intermediate steps must be taken. She composed a sample message in her mind and examined it while sending a summons to Burzmali. The Bashar's favorite student would have to be sent into action but not as Odrade wanted.

The message to Odrade was essentially simple:

"Help is on the way. You are on the scene, Dar. Where safety of girl Sheeana is concerned, use own judgment. In all other matters that do not conflict with my orders, carry out the plan."

There. That was it. Odrade had her instructions, the essentials that she would accept as "the plan" even while she would recognize an incomplete pattern. Odrade would obey. The "Dar" was a nice touch, Taraza thought. Dar and Tar. That opening into Odrade's *mild warmth* would not be well shielded from the Dar-and-Tar direction.

The long table on the right is set for a banquet of roast desert hare in sauce cepeda. The other dishes, clockwise to the right from the far end of the table, are aplomage sirian, chukka under glass, coffee with melange (note the hawk crest of the Atreides on the urn), pot-a-oie and, in the Balut crystal bottle, sparkling Caladan wine. Note the ancient poison detector concealed in the chandelier.

Teg found Duncan in the tiny dining alcove off the no-globe's gleaming kitchen. Pausing in the passage to the alcove, Teg studied Duncan carefully: eight days here and the lad appeared finally to have recovered from the peculiar rage that had seized him as they entered the globe's access tube.

They had come through a shallow cave musky with the odors of a native bear. The rocks at the back of the lair were not rocks, although they would have deceived even the most sophisticated examination. A slight protrusion in the *rocks* would shift if you knew or stumbled upon the secret code. That circular and twisting movement opened the entire rear wall of the cave.

The access tube, brilliantly lighted automatically once they sealed the portal behind them, was decorated with Harkonnen griffins on walls and ceiling. Teg was struck by the image of a young Patrin stumbling into this place for the first time (*The shock! The awe! The elation!*) and he failed to observe Duncan's reaction until a low growl swelled in the enclosed space.

Duncan stood growling (almost a moan), fists clenched, gaze fixed on a Harkonnen griffin along the right-hand wall. Rage and confusion warred for supremacy on his face. He lifted both fists and crashed them against the raised figure, drawing blood from his hands.

"Damn them to the deepest pits of hell!" he shouted.

It was an oddly mature curse issuing from the youthful mouth.

The instant the words were out Duncan relapsed into uncontrolled shudders. Lucilla put an arm around him and stroked his neck in a soothing, almost sensual way, until the shuddering subsided.

"Why did I do that?" Duncan whispered.

"You will know when your original memories are restored," she said.

"Harkonnens," Duncan whispered and blood suffused his face. He looked up at Lucilla. "Why do I hate them so much?"

"Words cannot explain it," she said. "You will have to wait for the memories."

"I don't want the memories!" Duncan shot a startled look at Teg. "Yes! Yes, I do want them."

Later as he looked up at Teg in the no-globe's dining alcove, Duncan's memory obviously returned to that moment.

"When, Bashar?"

"Soon."

Teg glanced around the area. Duncan sat alone at the

auto-scrubbed table, a cup of brown liquid in front of him. Teg recognized the smell: one of the many melange-laced items from the nullentropy bins. The bins were a treasure house of exotic foods, clothing, weapons, and other artifacts—a museum whose value could not be calculated. There was a thin layer of dust all through the globe but no deterioration of the things stored here. Every bit of the food was laced with melange, not at an addict level unless you were a glutton, but always notice-able. Even the preserved fruit had been dusted with the spice.

The brown liquid in Duncan's cup was one of the things Lucilla had tasted and pronounced capable of sustaining life. Teg did not know precisely how Reverend Mothers did this, but his own mother had been capable of it. One taste and they knew the contents of food or drink.

A glance at the ornate clock set into the wall at the closed end of the alcove told Teg it was later than he thought, well into the third hour of their arbitrary afternoon. Duncan should still be up on the elaborate practice floor but they both had seen Lucilla take off into the globe's upper reaches and Teg saw this as a chance for them to talk unobserved.

Pulling up a chair, Teg seated himself on the opposite side of the table.

Duncan said, "I hate those clocks!"

"You hate everything here," Teg said, but he took a second look at the clock. It was another antique, a round face with two analog hands and a digital second counter. The two hands were priapean—naked human figures: a large male with enormous phallus and a smaller female with legs spread wide. Each time the two clock hands met, the male appeared to enter the female.

"Gross," Teg agreed. He pointed to Duncan's drink: "You like that?"

"It's all right, sir. Lucilla says I should have it after exercise."

"My mother used to make me a similar drink for after heavy exertions," Teg said. He leaned forward and inhaled, remembering the aftertaste, the cloying melange in his nostrils.

"Sir, how long must we stay here?" Duncan asked.

"Until we are found by the right people or until we're sure we will not be found."

"But . . . cut off in here, how will we know?"

"When I judge it's time, I'll take the life-shield blanket and start keeping watch outside."

"I *hate* this place!"

"Obviously. But have you learned nothing about patience?"

Duncan grimaced. "Sir, why are you keeping me from being alone with Lucilla?"

Teg, exhaling as Duncan spoke, locked on the partial exhalation and then resumed breathing. He knew, though, that the lad had observed. If Duncan knew, then Lucilla must know!

"I don't think Lucilla knows what you're doing, sir," Duncan said, "but it's getting pretty obvious." He glanced around him. "If this place didn't take so much of her attention . . . Where does she dash off to like that?"

"I think she's up in the library."

"Library!"

"I agree it's primitive but it's also fascinating." Teg lifted his gaze to the scrollwork on the nearby kitchen ceiling. The moment of decision had arrived. Lucilla could not be depended upon to remain distracted much longer. Teg shared her fascination, though. It was easy to lose yourself in these marvels. The whole no-globe complex, some two hundred meters in diameter, was a fossil preserved intact from the time of the Tyrant.

When she spoke about it, Lucilla's voice took on a husky, whispering quality. "Surely, the Tyrant must have known about this place."

Teg's Mentat awareness had been immersed immediately in this suggestion. *Why did the Tyrant permit Family Harkonnen to squander so much of their last remaining wealth on such an enterprise?*

Perhaps for that very reason—to drain them.

The cost in bribes and Guild shipping from the Ixian factories must have been astronomical.

"Did the Tyrant know that one day we would need this place?" Lucilla asked.

No avoiding the prescient powers that Leto II had so often demonstrated, Teg agreed.

Looking at Duncan seated across from him, Teg felt his neck hairs rising. There was something eerie about this Harkonnen hideaway, as though the Tyrant himself might have been here. What had happened to the Harkonnens who built it? Teg and Lucilla had found absolutely no clues to why the globe had been abandoned.

Neither of them could wander through the no-globe without experiencing an acute sense of history. Teg was constantly confounded by unanswered questions.

Lucilla, too, commented on this.

"Where did they go? There's nothing in my Other Memories to give the slightest clue."

"Did the Tyrant lure them out and kill them?"

"I'm going back to the library. Perhaps today I'll find something."

For the first two days of their occupation, the globe had received a careful examination by Lucilla and Teg. A silent and sullen Duncan tagged along as though he feared to be left alone. Each new discovery awed them or shocked them.

Twenty-one skeletons preserved in transparent plaz along a wall near the core! Macabre observers of everyone who passed through there to the machinery chambers and the nullentropy bins.

Patrin had warned Teg about the skeletons. On one of his first youthful examinations of the globe, Patrin had found records that said the dead ones were the artisans who had built the place, all slain by the Harkonnens to preserve the secret.

Altogether, the globe was a remarkable achievement, an enclosure cut out of Time, sealed away from everything external. After all of these millennia, its frictionless machinery still created a mimetic projection that even the most modern instruments could not distinguish from the background of dirt and rock.

"The Sisterhood must acquire this place intact!" Lucilla kept saying. "It's a treasure house! They even kept their family's breeding records!"

That wasn't all the Harkonnens had preserved here. Teg kept finding himself repelled by subtle and gross touches on almost everything in the globe. Like that clock! Clothing, instruments for maintaining the environment, for education and pleasure—everything had been marked by that Harkonnen compulsion to flaunt their uncaring sense of superiority to all other people and all other standards.

Once more, Teg thought of Patrin as a youth in this place, probably no older than the ghola. What had prompted Patrin to keep it a secret even from his wife of so many years? Patrin had never touched on the reasons for secrecy, but Teg made his own deductions. An unhappy childhood. The need for his own secret place. Friends who were not friends but only people waiting to sneer at him. None of those companions could be permitted to share such a wonder. It was his! This was more than a place of lonely security. It had been Patrin's private token of victory.

"I spent many happy hours there, Bashar. Everything still works. The records are ancient but excellent once you grasp the dialect. There is much knowledge in the place. But you will understand when you get there. You will understand many things I have never told you."

The antique practice floor showed signs of Patrin's frequent usage. He had changed the weapons coding on some of the automata in a way Teg recognized. The time-counters told of muscle-torturing hours at the complicated exercises. This globe explained those abilities which Teg had always found so remarkable in Patrin. Natural talents had been honed here.

The automata of the no-globe were another matter.

Most of them represented defiance of the ancient proscriptions against such devices. More than that, some had been designed for pleasure functions that confirmed the more revolting stories Teg had heard about the Harkonnens. Pain as pleasure! In its own way, these things explained the primly unbending morality that Patrin had taken away from Gammu.

Revulsion created its own patterns.

Duncan took a deep swallow of his drink and looked at Teg over the lip of the cup.

"Why did you come down here alone when I asked you to complete that last round of exercises?" Teg asked.

"The exercises made no sense." Duncan put down his cup.

Well, Taraza, you were wrong, Teg thought. *He has struck out for complete independence sooner than you predicted.*

Also, Duncan had stopped addressing his Bashar as "sir."

"You disobey me?"

"Not exactly."

"Then *exactly* what is it you're doing?"

"I have to *know!*"

"You won't like me very much when you do know."

Duncan looked startled. "Sir?"

Ahhhh, the "sir" is back!

"I have been preparing you for certain kinds of very intense pain," Teg said. "It is necessary before we can restore your original memories."

"Pain, sir?"

"We know of no other way to bring back the original Duncan Idaho—the one who died."

"Sir, if you can do that, I will be nothing but grateful."

"So you say. But you may very well see me then as just one more whip in the hands of those who have recalled you to life."

"Isn't it better to know, sir?"

Teg passed the back of a hand across his mouth. "If you hate me . . . can't say I'd blame you."

"Sir, if you were in my place, is that how you would feel?" Duncan's posture, tone of voice, facial expression—all showed trembling confusion.

So far so good, Teg thought. The procedural steps were laid out with a precision that demanded that every response from the ghola be interpreted with care. Duncan was now filled with uncertainty. He wanted something and he feared that thing.

"I'm only your teacher, not your father!" Teg said.

Duncan recoiled at the harsh tone. "Aren't you my friend?"

"That's a two-way street. The original Duncan Idaho will have to answer that for himself."

A veiled look entered Duncan's eyes. "Will I remember this place, the Keep, Schwangyu and . . ."

"Everything. You'll undergo a kind of double-vision memory for a time, but you'll remember it all."

A cynical look came over the young face and, when he spoke, it was with bitterness. "So you and I will become comrades."

All of a Bashar's command and presence in his voice, Teg followed the reawakening instructions precisely.

"I'm not particularly interested in becoming your comrade." He fixed a searching glare on Duncan's face. "You might make Bashar someday. I think it possible you have the right stuff. But I'll be long dead by then."

"You're only comrades with Bashars?"

"Patrin was my comrade and he never rose above squad leader."

Duncan looked into his empty cup and then at Teg.

"Why didn't you order something to drink? You worked hard up there, too."

Perceptive question. It did not do to underestimate this youth. He knew that food sharing was one of the most ancient rituals of association.

"The smell of yours was enough," Teg said. "Old memories. I don't need them right now."

"Then why did you come down here?"

There it was, revealed in the young voice—hope and fear. He wanted Teg to say a particular thing.

"I wanted to take a careful measurement of how far those exercises have carried you," Teg said. "I needed to come down here and look at you."

"Why so careful?"

Hope and fear! It was time for the precise shift of focus.

"I've never trained a ghola before."

Ghola. The word lay suspended between them, hanging on the cooking smells that the globe's filters had not scrubbed from the air. *Ghola!* It was laced with spice pungency from Duncan's empty cup.

Duncan leaned forward without speaking, his expression eager. Lucilla's observation came into Teg's mind: *"He knows how to use silence."*

When it became obvious that Teg would not expand on that simple statement, Duncan sank back with a disappointed look. The left corner of his mouth turned downward, a sullen, festering expression. Everything focused inward the way it had to be.

"You did not come down here to be alone," Teg said. "You came here to hide. You're still hiding in there and you think no one will ever find you."

Duncan put a hand in front of his mouth. It was a

signal gesture for which Teg had been waiting. The instructions for this moment were clear: *"The ghola wants the original memories wakened and fears this utterly. That is the major barrier you must sunder."*

"Take your hand away from your mouth!" Teg ordered.

Duncan dropped his hand as though it had been burned. He stared at Teg like a trapped animal.

"Speak the truth," Teg's instructions warned. *"At this moment, every sense afire, the ghola will see into your heart."*

"I want you to know," Teg said, "that what the Sisterhood has ordered me to do to you, that this is distasteful to me."

Duncan appeared to crouch into himself. "What did they order you to do?"

"The skills I was ordered to give you are flawed."

"F-flawed?"

"Part of it was comprehensive training, the intellectual part. In that respect, you have been brought to the level of regimental commander."

"Better than Patrin?"

"Why must you be better than Patrin?"

"Wasn't he your comrade?"

"Yes."

"You said he never rose above squad leader!"

"Patrin was fully capable of taking over command of an entire multi-planet force. He was a tactical magician whose wisdom I employed on many occasions."

"But you said he never—"

"It was his choice. The low rank gave him the common touch that we both found useful many times."

"Regimental commander?" Duncan's voice was little more than a whisper. He stared at the tabletop.

"You have an intellectual grasp of the functions, a bit impetuous but experience usually smooths that out. Your weapons skills are superior for your age."

Still not looking at Teg, Duncan asked: "What is my age . . . sir?"

Just as the instructions cautioned: *"The ghola will dance all around the central issue. 'What is my age?' How old is a ghola?"*

His voice coldly accusing, Teg said: "If you want to know your ghola-age, why don't you ask that?"

"Wha . . . what is that age, sir?"

There was such a weight of misery in the youthful voice that Teg felt tears start in the corners of his eyes. He had been warned about this, too. *"Do not reveal too much compassion!"* Teg covered the moment by clearing his throat. He said: "That's a question only you can answer."

The instructions were explicit: *"Turn it back on him! Keep him focused inward. Emotional pain is as important to this process as the physical pain."*

A deep sigh shuddered through Duncan. He closed his eyes tightly. When Teg had first seated himself at the table, Duncan had thought: *Is this the moment? Will he do it now?* But Teg's accusing tone, the verbal attacks, were completely unexpected. And now Teg sounded patronizing.

He's patronizing me!

Cynical anger surged into Duncan. Did Teg think him such a fool that he could be taken in by the most common ploy of a commander? *Tone of voice and attitude alone can subjugate another's will.* Duncan sensed something else in the patronizing, though: a core of plasteel that would not be penetrated. Integrity . . . purpose. And Duncan had seen the tears start, the covering gesture.

Opening his eyes and looking directly at Teg, Duncan said: "I don't mean to be disrespectful or ungrateful or rude, sir. But I can't go on without answers."

Teg's instructions were clear: *"You will know when the ghola reaches the point of desperation. No ghola will try to hide this. It is intrinsic to their psyche. You will recognize it in voice and posture."*

Duncan had almost reached the critical point. Silence was mandatory for Teg now. Force Duncan to ask his questions, to take his own course.

Duncan said: "Did you know that I once thought of killing Schwangyu?"

Teg opened his mouth and closed it without a sound. *Silence!* But the lad was serious!

"I was afraid of her," Duncan said. "I don't like being afraid." He lowered his gaze. "You once told me that we only hate what's really dangerous to us."

"He will approach it and retreat, approach and retreat. Wait until he plunges."

"I don't hate you," Duncan said, looking once more at Teg. "I resented it when you said *ghola* to my face. But Lucilla's right: We should never resent the truth even when it hurts."

Teg rubbed his own lips. The desire to speak filled him but it was not yet plunge time.

"Doesn't it surprise you that I considered killing Schwangyu?" Duncan asked.

Teg held himself rigid. Even the shaking of his head would be taken as a response.

"I thought of slipping something into her drink," Duncan said. "But that's a coward's way and I'm not a coward. Whatever else, I'm not that."

Teg remained silently immobile.

"I think you really care what happens to me, Bashar," Duncan said. "But you're right: we will never be comrades. If I survive, I will surpass you. Then . . . it will be too late for us to be comrades. You spoke the truth."

Teg was unable to prevent himself from inhaling a deep breath of Mentat realization: no avoiding the signs of strength in the ghola. Somewhere recently, perhaps in this very alcove just now, the youth had ceased being a youth and had become a man. The realization saddened Teg. It went so fast! No normal growing-up in between.

"Lucilla does not really care what happens to me the way you do," Duncan said. "She's just following her orders from that Mother Superior, Taraza."

Not yet! Teg cautioned himself. He wet his lips with his tongue.

"You have been obstructing Lucilla's orders," Duncan said. "What is it she's supposed to do to me?"

The moment had come. "What do you think she's supposed to do?" Teg demanded.

"I don't know!"

"The original Duncan Idaho would know."

"You know! Why won't you tell me?"

"I'm only supposed to help restore your original memories."

"Then do it!"

"Only you can really do it."

"I don't know how!"

Teg sat forward on the edge of his chair, but did not speak. *Plunge point?* He sensed something lacking in Duncan's desperation.

"You know I can read lips, sir," Duncan said. "Once I went up to the tower observatory. I saw Lucilla and Schwangyu down below talking. Schwangyu said: 'Never mind that he's so young! You've had your orders.'"

Once more cautiously silent, Teg stared back at Duncan. It was like Duncan to move around secretly in the Keep, spying, seeking knowledge. And he had seated himself in that memory-mode now, not realizing that he still was spying and seeking . . . but in a different way.

"I didn't think she was supposed to kill me," Duncan said. "But you know what she was supposed to do because you've been obstructing her." Duncan pounded a fist on the table. "Answer me, damn you!"

Ahhhh, full desperation!

"I can only tell you that what she intends conflicts with my orders. I was commanded by Taraza herself to strengthen you and guard you from harm."

"But you said my training was . . . was flawed!"

"Necessary. It was done to prepare you for your original memories."

"What am I supposed to do?"

"You already know."

"I don't, I tell you! Please teach me!"

"You do many things without having been taught them. Did we teach you disobedience?"

"Please help me!" It was a desperate wail.

Teg forced himself to chilly remoteness. "What in the nether hell do you think I'm doing?"

Duncan clenched both fists and pounded them on the table, making his cup dance. He glared at Teg. Abruptly, an odd expression came over Duncan's face—something grasping in his eyes.

"Who are you?" Duncan whispered.

The key question!

Teg's voice was a lash striking out at a suddenly defenseless victim: "Who do you think I am?"

A look of utter desperation twisted Duncan's features. He managed only a gasping stutter: "You're . . . you're . . ."

"Duncan! Stop this nonsense!" Teg jumped to his feet and stared down with assumed rage.

"You're . . ."

Teg's right hand shot out in a swift arc. The open palm cracked against Duncan's cheek. "How dare you disobey me?" Left hand out, another rocking slap. "How *dare* you?"

Duncan reacted so swiftly that Teg experienced an electric instant of absolute shock. *Such speed!* Although there were separate elements in Duncan's attack, it occurred in one fluid blur: a leap upward, both feet on the chair, rocking the chair, using that motion to slash the right arm down at Teg's vulnerable shoulder nerves.

Responding out of trained instincts, Teg dodged sideways and flailed his left leg over the table into Duncan's groin. Teg still did not completely escape. The heel of Duncan's hand continued downward to strike beside the knee of Teg's flailing leg. It numbed the whole leg.

Duncan sprawled across the tabletop, trying to slide

backward in spite of the disabling kick. Teg supported himself, left hand on table, and chopped with the other hand to the base of Duncan's spine, into the nexus deliberately weakened by the exercises of the past few days.

Duncan groaned as paralyzing agony shot through his body. Another person would have been immobilized, screaming, but Duncan merely groaned as he clawed toward Teg, continuing the attack.

Relentless in the necessities of the moment, Teg proceeded to create greater pain in his victim, making sure each time that Duncan saw the attacker's face at the instant of greatest agony.

"Watch his eyes!" the instructions warned. And Bellonda, reinforcing the procedure, had cautioned: *"His eyes will seem to look through you but he will call you Leto."*

Much later. Teg found difficulty in recalling each detail of his obedience to the reawakening procedure. He knew that he continued to function as commanded but his memory went elsewhere, leaving the flesh free to carry out his orders. Oddly, his trick memory fastened onto another act of disobedience: the Cerbol Revolt, himself at middle age but already a Bashar with a formidable reputation. He had donned his best uniform without its medals (a subtle touch, that) and had presented himself in the scorching noon heat of Cerbol's battle-plowed fields. Completely unarmed in the path of the advancing rebels!

Many among the attackers owed him their lives. Most of them had once given him their deepest allegiance. Now, they were in violent disobedience. And Teg's presence in their path said to those advancing soldiers:

"I will not wear the medals that tell what I did for you

when we were comrades. I will not be anything that says I am one of you. I wear only the uniform that announces that I am still the Bashar. Kill me if that is how far you will carry your disobedience."

When most of the attacking force threw down their arms and came forward, some of their commanders bent the knee to their old Bashar and he remonstrated: "You never needed to bow to me or get on your knees! Your new leaders have taught you bad habits."

Later, he told the rebels he shared some of their grievances. Cerbol had been badly misused. But he also warned them:

"One of the most dangerous things in the universe is an ignorant people with real grievances. That is nowhere near as dangerous, however, as an informed and intelligent society with grievances. The damage that vengeful intelligence can wreak, you cannot even imagine. The Tyrant would seem a benevolent father figure by comparison with what you were about to create!"

It was all true, of course, but in a Bene Gesserit context, and it helped little with what he was commanded to do to the Duncan Idaho ghola—creating mental and physical agony in an almost helpless victim.

Easiest to recall was the look in Duncan's eyes. They did not change focus, but glared directly up into Teg's face, even at the instant of the final screaming shout:

"Damn you, Leto! What are you doing?"

He called me Leto.

Teg limped backward two steps. His left leg tingled and ached where Duncan had struck it. Teg realized that he was panting and at the end of his reserves. He was much too old for such exertions and the things he had just done made him feel dirty. The reawakening procedure was thoroughly fixed in his awareness, though. He knew that gholas once had been awakened by conditioning them unconsciously to attempt murder on someone they loved. The ghola psyche, shattered and forced to reassemble, was always psychologically scarred. This new technique left the scars in the one who managed the process.

Slowly, moving against the outcry of muscles and nerves that had been stunned by agony, Duncan slid backward off the table and stood leaning against his chair, trembling and glaring at Teg.

Teg's instructions said: *"You must stand very quietly. Do not move. Let him look at you as he will."*

Teg stood unmoving as he had been instructed. Memory of the Cerbol Revolt left his mind: He knew what he had done then and now. In a way, the two times were similar. He had told the rebels no ultimate truths (if such existed); only enough to lure them back into the fold. Pain and its predictable consequences. *"This is for your own good."*

Was it really good, what they did to this Duncan Idaho ghola?

Teg wondered what was occurring in Duncan's consciousness. Teg had been told as much as was known about these moments, but he could see that the words were inadequate. Duncan's eyes and face gave abundant evidence of internal turmoil—a hideous twisting of mouth and cheeks, the gaze darting this way and that.

Slowly, exquisite in its slowness, Duncan's face relaxed. His body continued to tremble. He felt the throbbing of his body as a distant thing, aches and darting pains that had happened to someone else. He was here, though, in this immediate moment—whatever and wherever this was. His memories would not mesh. He felt suddenly out of place in flesh too young, not fitted to his pre-ghola existence. The darting and twisting of awareness was all internal now.

Teg's instructors had said: *"He will have ghola-imposed filters on his pre-ghola memories. Some of the original memories will come flooding back. Other recollections will return more slowly. There will be no meshing, though, until he recalls that original moment of death."* Bellonda had then given Teg the known details of that fatal moment.

"Sardaukar," Duncan whispered. He looked around him at the Harkonnen symbols that permeated the no-globe. "The Emperor's crack troops wearing Harkonnen uniforms!" A wolfish grin twisted his mouth. "How they must have hated that!"

Teg remained silently watchful.

"They killed me," Duncan said. It was a flatly unemotional statement, all the more chilling for its positive delivery. A violent shudder passed through him and the trembling subsided. "At least a dozen of them in that little room." He looked directly at Teg. "One of them got through at me like a meat cleaver right down on my head." He hesitated, his throat working convulsively. His gaze remained on Teg. "Did I buy Paul enough time to escape?"

"Answer all of his questions truthfully."

"He escaped."

Now, they came to a testing moment. Where had the Tleilaxu acquired the Idaho cells? The Sisterhood's tests said they were original, but suspicions remained. The

Tleilaxu had done something of their own to this ghola. His memories could be a valuable clue to that thing.

"But the Harkonnens . . ." Duncan said. His memories from the Keep meshed. "Oh, yes. Oh, *yes*!" A fierce laugh shook him. He sent a roaring victory shout at the long-dead Baron Vladimir Harkonnen: "I paid you back, Baron! Oh, I did it to you for all of the ones you destroyed!"

"You remember the Keep and the things we taught you?" Teg asked.

A puzzled frown drew deep crease lines across Duncan's forehead. Emotional pain warred with his physical pains. He nodded in response to Teg's question. There were two lives, one that had been walled off behind the axlotl tanks and another . . . another . . . Duncan felt incomplete. Something remained suppressed within him. The reawakening was not finished. He stared angrily at Teg. Was there more? Teg had been brutal. Necessary brutality? Was this how you had to restore a ghola?

"I . . ." Duncan shook his head from side to side like a great wounded animal in front of the hunter.

"Do you have all of your memories?" Teg insisted.

"All? Oh, yes. I remember Gammu when it was Giedi Prime—the oil-soaked, blood-soaked hell hole of the Imperium! Yes, indeed, Bashar. I was your dutiful student. Regimental commander!" Again, he laughed, throwing his head back in an oddly adult gesture for that young body.

Teg experienced the sudden release of a deep satisfaction, far deeper than relief. It had worked as they said it would.

"Do you hate me?" he asked.

"Hate you? Didn't I tell you I would be grateful?"

Abruptly, Duncan lifted his hands and peered at them. He shifted his gaze downward at his youthful body. "What a temptation!" he muttered. He dropped his hands and focused on Teg's face, tracing the lines of identity. "Atreides," he said. "You're all so damned alike!"

"Not all," Teg said.

"I'm not talking about appearance, Bashar." His eyes went out of focus. "I asked my age." There was a long silence, then: "Gods of the deep! So much time has passed!"

Teg said what he had been instructed to say: "The Sisterhood has need of you."

"In this immature body? What am I supposed to do?"

"Truly, I don't know, Duncan. The body will mature and I presume a Reverend Mother will explain matters to you."

"Lucilla?"

Abruptly, Duncan looked up at the ornate ceiling, then at the alcove and its baroque clock. He remembered coming here with Teg and Lucilla. This place was the same but it was different. "Harkonnens," he whispered. He sent a glowering look at Teg. "Do you know how many of my family the Harkonnens tortured and killed?"

"One of Taraza's Archivists gave me a report."

"A report? You think words can tell it?"

"No. But that was the only answer I had to your question."

"Damn you, Bashar! Why do you Atreides always have to be so truthful and honorable?"

"I think it's bred into us."

"That's quite right." The voice was Lucilla's and came from behind Teg.

Teg did not turn. How much had she heard? How long had she been there?

Lucilla came up to stand beside Teg but her attention was on Duncan. "I see that you've done it, Miles."

"Taraza's orders to the letter," Teg said.

"You have been very clever, Miles," she said. "Much more clever than I suspected you could be. That mother of yours should have been severely punished for what she taught you."

"Ahhhh, Lucilla the seductress," Duncan said. He glanced at Teg and returned his attention to Lucilla. "Yes, now I can answer my other question—what she's supposed to do."

"They're called Imprinters," Teg said.

"Miles," Lucilla said, "if you have complicated my task in ways that prevent me from carrying out my orders, I will have you roasted on a skewer."

The emotionless quality of her voice sent a shudder through Teg. He knew her threat was a metaphor, but the implications in the threat were real.

"A punishment banquet!" Duncan said. "How nice."

Teg addressed himself to Duncan: "There's nothing romantic about what we've done to you, Duncan. I've assisted the Bene Gesserit in more than one assignment that left me feeling dirty, but never dirtier than this one."

"Silence!" Lucilla ordered. The full force of Voice was in the command.

Teg let it flow through him and past him as his mother had taught, then: "Those of us who give our true loyalty to the Sisterhood have only one concern: survival of the Bene Gesserit. Not survival of any individual but of the

Sisterhood itself. Deceptions, dishonesties—those are empty words when the question is the Sisterhood's survival."

"Damn that mother of yours, Miles!" Lucilla paid him the compliment of not hiding her rage.

Duncan stared at Lucilla. Who was she? Lucilla? He felt his memories stirring of themselves. Lucilla was not the same person . . . not the same at all, and yet . . . bits and pieces were the same. Her voice. Her features. Abruptly, he saw again the face of the woman he had glimpsed on the wall of his room at the Keep.

"Duncan, my sweet Duncan."

Tears fell from Duncan's eyes. His own mother— another Harkonnen victim. Tortured . . . who knew what else? Never seen again by her "sweet Duncan."

"Gods, I wish I had one of them to kill right now," Duncan moaned.

Once more, he focused on Lucilla. Tears blurred her features and made the comparisons easier. Lucilla's face blended with that of the Lady Jessica, beloved of Leto Atreides. Duncan glanced at Teg, back to Lucilla, shaking the tears from his eyes as he moved. The memory faces dissolved into that of the real Lucilla standing in front of him. Similarities . . . but never the same. Never again the same.

Imprinter.

He could guess the meaning. A pure Duncan Idaho wildness arose in him. "Is it my child you want in your womb, Imprinter? I know you're not called mothers for nothing."

Her voice cold, Lucilla said: "We'll discuss it another time."

"Let us discuss it in a congenial place," Duncan said, "Perhaps I'll sing you a song. Not as good as old Gurney Halleck would do it but good enough to prepare for a little bedsport."

"You find this amusing?" she asked.

"Amusing? No, but I *am* reminded of Gurney. Tell me, Bashar, have you brought him back from the dead, too?"

"Not to my knowledge," Teg said.

"Ahhhh, there was a singing man!" Duncan said. "He could be killing you while he sang and never miss a note."

Her manner still icy, Lucilla said: "We of the Bene Gesserit have learned to avoid music. It evokes too many confusing emotions. Memory-emotions, of course."

It was meant to awe him with a reminder of all those Other Memories and the Bene Gesserit powers these implied but Duncan only laughed louder.

"What a shame that is," he said. "You miss so much of life." And he began humming an old Halleck refrain:

"Review friends, troops long past review . . ."

But his mind whirled elsewhere with the rich new flavor of these reborn moments and once more he felt the eager touch of something powerful that remained buried within him. Whatever it was, it was violent and it concerned Lucilla, the Imprinter. In imagination, he saw her dead and her body awash in blood.

People always want something more than immediate joy or that deeper sense called happiness. This is one of the secrets by which we shape the fulfillment of our designs. The something more assumes amplified power with people who cannot give it a name or who (most often the case) do not even suspect its existence. Most people only react unconsciously to such hidden forces. Thus, we have only to call a calculated *something more* into existence, define it and give it shape, then people will follow.

—LEADERSHIP SECRETS OF THE BENE GESSERIT

With a silent Waff about twenty paces ahead of them, Odrade and Sheeana walked down a weed-fringed road beside a spice-storage yard. All of them wore new desert robes and glistening stillsuits. The gray nulplaz fence that defined the yard beside them held bits of grass and cottony seedpods in its meshes. Looking at the seedpods, Odrade thought of them as life trying to break through a human intervention.

Behind them, the blocky buildings that had arisen around Dar-es-Balat baked in the sunlight of early afternoon. Hot dry air burned her throat when she inhaled too quickly. Odrade felt dizzy and at war within herself. Thirst nagged at her. She walked as though balanced on

the edge of a precipice. The situation she had created at
Taraza's command might explode momentarily.

How fragile it is!

Three forces balanced, not really supporting each
other but joined by motives that could shift in an instant
and topple the whole alliance. The military people sent
by Taraza did not reassure Odrade. Where was Teg?
Where was Burzmali? For that matter, where was the
ghola? He should be here by now. Why had she been
ordered to delay matters?

Today's venture would certainly delay matters! Although it had Taraza's blessing, Odrade thought this
excursion into the desert of the worms might be a permanent delay. And there was Waff. If he survived, would
there be any pieces for him to pick up?

Despite the healing applications of the Sisterhood's best
quicknit amplifiers, Waff said his arms still ached where
Odrade had broken them. He was not complaining, merely
providing information. He appeared to accept their fragile
alliance, even the modifications that incorporated the Rakian priestly cabal. No doubt he was reassured that one of
his own Face Dancers occupied the High Priest's bench in
the guise of Tuek. Waff spoke forcefully when he demanded his "breeding mothers" from the Bene Gesserit
and, consequently, withheld his part of their bargain.

"Only a small delay while the Sisterhood reviews the
new agreement," Odrade explained. "Meanwhile . . ."

Today was "meanwhile."

Odrade put aside her misgivings and began to enter
the mood of this venture. Waff's behavior fascinated her,
especially his reaction on meeting Sheeana: quite plainly
fearful and more than a little in awe.

The minion of his Prophet.

Odrade glanced sideways at the girl walking dutifully beside her. There was the real leverage for shaping these events into the Bene Gesserit design.

The Sisterhood's breakthrough into the reality behind Tleilaxu behavior excited Odrade. Waff's fanatic "true faith" gained shape with each new response from him. She felt fortunate just to be here studying a Tleilaxu Master in a religious setting. The very grit under Waff's feet ignited behavior that she had been trained to identify.

We should have guessed, Odrade thought. *The manipulations of our own Missionaria Protectiva should have told us how the Tleilaxu did it: keeping themselves to themselves, blocking off every intrusion for all of those plodding millennia.*

They did not appear to have copied the Bene Gesserit structure. And what other force could do such a thing? It was a religion. The Great Belief!

Unless the Tleilaxu are using their ghola system as a kind of immortality.

Taraza could be right. Reincarnated Tleilaxu Masters would not be like Reverend Mothers—no Other Memories, only personal memories. But prolonged!

Fascinating!

Odrade looked ahead at Waff's back. *Plodding.* It appeared to come naturally to him. She recalled that he called Sheeana "Alyama." Another confirming linguistic insight into Waff's Great Belief. It meant "Blessed One." The Tleilaxu had kept an ancient language not only alive but unchanged.

Did Waff not know that only powerful forces such as religions did that?

We have the roots of your obsession in our grasp, Waff! It is not unlike some that we have created. We know how to manipulate such things for our own purposes.

Taraza's communication burned in Odrade's awareness: "The Tleilaxu plan is transparent: Ascendancy. The human universe must be made into a Tleilaxu universe. They could not hope to achieve such a goal without help from the Scattering. Ergo."

The Mother Superior's reasoning could not be denied. Even the opposition within that deep schism that threatened to shatter the Sisterhood agreed. But the thought of those human masses in the Scattering, their numbers exploding exponentially, produced a lonely sense of desperation in Odrade.

We are so few compared to them.

Sheeana stooped and picked up a pebble. She looked at it a moment and then threw it at the fence beside them. The pebble sailed through the meshes without touching them.

Odrade took a firmer grip on herself. The sounds of their footsteps on the blown sand that drifted across this little-used roadway seemed suddenly over-loud. The spindly causeway leading out over the Dar-es-Balat ring-qanat and moat lay no more than two hundred paces ahead at the end of this narrow road.

Sheeana spoke: "I am doing this because you ordered it, Mother. But I still don't know why."

Because this is the crucible where we test Waff and, through him, reshape the Tleilaxu!

"It is a demonstration," Odrade said.

That was true. It was not the whole truth, but it served.

Sheeana walked head down, gaze intent on where she placed each step. Was this how she always approached her Shaitan? Odrade wondered. Thoughtful and remote?

Odrade heard a faint *thwocking* sound high up behind her. The watchful ornithopters were arriving. They would keep their distance, but many eyes would observe this *demonstration*.

"I will dance," Sheeana said. "That usually calls a big one."

Odrade felt her heartbeat quicken. Would the "big one" continue to obey Sheeana despite the presence of two companions?

This is suicidal madness!

But it had to be done: Taraza's orders.

Odrade glanced at the fenced spice yard beside them. The place appeared oddly familiar. More than déjà vu. Inner certainty informed by Other Memories told her this place remained virtually unchanged from ancient times. The design of the spice silos in the yard was as old as Rakis: oval tanks on tall legs, metal and plaz insects waiting stilt-legged to leap upon their prey. She suspected an unconscious message from the original designers: *Melange is both boon and bane.*

Beneath the silos, a sandy wasteland where no growth was permitted spread out beside mud-walled buildings, an amoeba arm of Dar-es-Balat reaching almost to the qanat edge. The Tyrant's long-hidden no-globe had produced a teeming religious community that hid most of its activities behind windowless walls and underground.

The secret working of our unconscious desires!

Once more, Sheeana spoke: "Tuek is different."

Odrade saw Waff's head lift sharply. He had heard. He

would be thinking: *Can we conceal things from the Prophet's messenger?*

Too many people already knew that a Face Dancer masqueraded as Tuek, Odrade thought. The priestly cabal, of course, believed they were giving the Tleilaxu enough netting in which to snare not only the Bene Tleilax but the Sisterhood as well.

Odrade smelled the biting odors of chemicals that had been used to kill wild growth in the spice storage yard. The odors forced her attention back to necessities. She did not dare indulge in mental wanderings out here! It would be so easy for the Sisterhood to become caught in its own trap.

Sheeana stumbled and emitted a small cry, more irritation than pain. Waff turned his head sharply and looked at Sheeana before returning his attention to the roadway. The child had merely stumbled on a break in the road surface, he saw. Drifted sand concealed places where the roadway had been cracked. The faery structure of the causeway ahead of him appeared sound, however. Not substantial enough to support one of the Prophet's descendants, but more than enough for a supplicant human to cross it into the desert.

Waff thought of himself chiefly as a supplicant.

I come as a beggar into the land of thy messenger, God.

He had his suspicions about Odrade. The Reverend Mother had brought him here to drain him of his knowledge before killing him. *With God's help, I may surprise her yet.* He knew his body was proof against an Ixian Probe, although she obviously did not have such a cumbersome device on her person. But it was the strength of his own will and confidence in God's grace that reassured Waff.

And what if the hand they hold out to us is held out in sincerity?

That, too, would be God's doing.

Alliance with the Bene Gesserit, firm control of Rakis: What a dream that was! The Shariat ascendant at last and the Bene Gesserit as missionaries.

When Sheeana again missed her footing and uttered another small sound of complaint, Odrade said: "Don't favor yourself, child!"

Odrade saw Waff's shoulders stiffen. He did not like that peremptory manner with his "Blessed One." There was backbone in the little man. Odrade recognized it as the strength of fanaticism. Even if the worm came to kill him, Waff would not flee. Faith in God's will would carry him directly into his own death—unless he were shaken out of his religious security.

Odrade suppressed a smile. She could follow his thinking process: *God will soon reveal His Purpose.*

But Waff was thinking about his cells growing in the slow renewal at Bandalong. No matter what happened here, his cells would carry on for the Bene Tleilax . . . and for God—a serial-Waff always serving the Great Belief.

"I can smell Shaitan, you know," Sheeana said.

"Right now?" Odrade looked up at the causeway ahead of them. Waff already was a few steps onto that arching surface.

"No, only when he comes," Sheeana said.

"Of course you can, child. Anyone could."

"I can smell him a long way off."

Odrade inhaled deeply through her nose, sorting the smells from the background of burnt flint: faint whiffs of melange . . . ozone, something distinctly acid. She motioned for Sheeana to precede her single-file onto the causeway. Waff was holding his steady twenty paces ahead. The causeway dipped down to the desert some sixty meters ahead of him.

I will taste the sand at the first opportunity, Odrade thought. *That will tell me many things.*

As she mounted the causeway over the water moat, she looked off to the southwest at a low barrier along the horizon. Abruptly, Odrade was confronted by a compelling Other Memory. There was none of the crispness in it of actual vision, but she recognized it—a mingling of images from the deepest sources within her.

Damn! she thought. *Not now!*

There was no escape. Such intrusions came with purpose, an unavoidable demand upon her awareness.

Warning!

She squinted at the horizon, allowing the Other Memory to superimpose itself: a long-ago high barrier far away out there . . . people moving along the top of it. There was a faery bridge in that memory-distance, insubstantial and beautiful. It linked one part of that vanished barrier to another part and she knew without seeing it that a river ran beneath that long-gone bridge. The Idaho River! Now, the superimposed image provided movement: objects falling from the bridge. They were too far away to identify but she had the labels for this image projection now. With a sense of horror and elation, she identified that scene.

The faery bridge was collapsing! Tumbling into the river below it.

This vision was not some random destruction. This was classical violence carried in many memories, which had come down to her in the moments of spice agony.

Odrade could classify the finely tuned components of the image: Thousands of her ancestors had watched that scene in imaginative reconstruction. Not a real visual memory but an assemblage of accurate reports.

That is where it happened!

Odrade stopped and let the image projections have their way with her awareness. *Warning!* Something dangerous had been identified. She did not try to dig out the warning's substance. If she did that, she knew it could fall apart in skeins, any one of which might be relevant, but the original certainty would vanish.

This thing out there was fixed in the Atreides history. Leto II, the Tyrant, had fallen to his dissolution from that faery bridge. The great worm of Rakis, the Tyrant God Emperor himself, had been tumbled from that bridge on his wedding peregrination.

There! Right there in the Idaho River beneath his destroyed bridge, the Tyrant had been submerged in his own agony. Right there, the transubstantiation from which the Divided God was born— it all began there.

Why is that a warning?

Bridge and river had vanished from this land. The high wall that had enclosed the Tyrant's dryland Sareer was eroded into a broken line on a heat-shimmering horizon.

If a worm came now with its encapsulated pearl of the Tyrant's forever-dreaming memory, would that memory be dangerous? So Taraza's opposition in the Sisterhood argued.

"He will awaken!"

Taraza and her advisors denied even the possibility.

Still, this claxon from Odrade's Other Memories could not be shunted aside.

"Reverend Mother, why have we stopped?"

Odrade felt her awareness lurch back into an immediate present that demanded her attention. Out there in that warning vision was where the Tyrant's endless dream began but other dreams intruded. Sheeana stood in front of her with a puzzled expression.

"I was looking out there." Odrade pointed. "That was where Shai-hulud began, Sheeana."

Waff stopped at the end of the causeway, one step short of the encroaching sand and now about forty paces ahead of Odrade and Sheeana. Odrade's voice brought him to stiff alertness but he did not turn. Odrade could feel the displeasure in his posture. Waff would not like even a hint of cynicism directed at his Prophet. He always suspected cynicism from Reverend Mothers. Especially where religious matters were concerned. Waff was not yet ready to accept that the long-detested and feared Bene Gesserit might share his Great Belief. That ground would have to be filled in with care—as was always the way with the Missionaria Protectiva.

"They say there was a big river," Sheeana said.

Odrade heard the lilting note of derision in Sheeana's voice. The child learned quickly!

Waff turned and scowled at them. He heard it, too. What was he thinking about Sheeana now?

Odrade held Sheeana's shoulder with one hand and pointed with the other. "There was a bridge right there. The great wall of the Sareer was left open there to permit the passage of the Idaho River. The bridge spanned that break."

Sheeana sighed. "A real river," she whispered.

"Not a qanat and too big for a canal," Odrade said.

"I've never seen a river," Sheeana said.

"That was where they dumped Shai-hulud into the river," Odrade said. She gestured to her left. "Over on this side, many kilometers in that direction, he built his palace."

"There's nothing over there but sand," Sheeana said.

"The palace was torn down in the Famine Times," Odrade said. "People thought there was a hoard of spice in it. They were wrong, of course. He was much too clever for that."

Sheeana leaned close to Odrade and whispered: "There is a great treasure of the spice, though. The chantings tell about it. I've heard it many times. My . . . they say it's in a cave."

Odrade smiled. Sheeana referred to the Oral History, of course. And she had almost said: "My father . . ." meaning her real father who had died in this desert. Odrade already had lured that story from the girl.

Still whispering close to Odrade's ear, Sheeana said: "Why is that little man with us? I don't like him."

"It is necessary for the demonstration," Odrade said.

Waff took that moment to step off the causeway onto the first soft slope of open sand. He moved with care but no visible hesitation. Once on the sand, he turned, his eyes glistening in the hot sunlight, and stared first at Sheeana and then at Odrade.

Still that awe in him when he looks at Sheeana, Odrade thought. *What great things he believes he will discover here. He will be restored. And the prestige!*

Sheeana sheltered her eyes with one hand and studied the desert.

"Shaitan likes the heat," Sheeana said. "People hide inside when it's hot but that's when Shaitan comes."

Not Shai-hulud, Odrade thought. *Shaitan! You predicted it well, Tyrant. What else did you know about our times?*

Was it really the Tyrant out there dormant in all of his worm descendants?

None of the analyses Odrade had studied gave a sure explanation of what had driven one human being to make himself into a symbiote with that original worm of Arrakis. What went through his mind in the millennia of that awful transformation? Was any of that, even the smallest fragment, preserved in today's Rakian worms?

"He is near, Mother," Sheeana said. "Do you smell him?"

Waff peered apprehensively at Sheeana.

Odrade inhaled deeply: a rich swelling of cinnamon on the bitter flint undertones. Fire, brimstone—the crystal-banked inferno of the great worm. She stooped and brought up a pinch of blown sand to her tongue. All of the background was there: the Dune of Other Memory and the Rakis of this day.

Sheeana pointed at an angle to her left, directly into the light breeze from the desert. "Out there. We must hurry."

Without waiting for permission from Odrade, Sheeana ran lightly down the causeway, past Waff and out onto the first dune. She stopped there until Odrade and Waff caught up with her. Off the dune face she led them, up another with sand clogging their passage, out along a great curving barracan with wisps of dusty saltation blowing from its crest. Soon, they had put almost a kilometer between themselves and the water-girded security of Dar-es-Balat.

Again, Sheeana stopped.

Waff came to a panting halt behind her. Perspiration glistened where his stillsuit hood crossed his brow.

Odrade stopped a pace behind Waff. She took deep, calming breaths while she peered past Waff to where Sheeana's attention was fixed.

A furious tide of sand had poured across the desert beyond the dune where they stood, driven by a storm wind. Bedrock lay exposed in a long narrow avenue of giant boulders, which lay scattered and upturned like the broken building blocks of a mad promethean. Through this wild maze, the sand had poured like a river, leaving its signature in deep scratches and gouges, then plunging off a low escarpment to lose itself in more dunes.

"Down there," Sheeana said, pointing at the avenue of bedrock. Off their dune she went, sliding and scrambling in spilled sand. At the bottom, she stopped beside a boulder at least twice her height.

Waff and Odrade paused just behind her.

The slipface of another giant barracan, sinuous as the back of a sporting whale, lifted into the silver-blue sky beside them.

Odrade used the pause to recompose her oxygen balance. That mad run had made great demands on flesh. Waff, she noted, was red-faced and breathing deeply. The flinty cinnamon smell was oppressive in the confined passage. Waff sniffed and rubbed at his nose with the back of a hand. Sheeana lifted herself on one toe, pivoted and darted ten paces across the rocky avenue. She put one foot up on the sandy incline of the outer dune and lifted both arms to the sky. Slowly at first and then with increasing tempo, she began to dance, moving up onto the sand.

The 'thopter sounds grew louder overhead.

"Listen!" Sheeana called, not pausing in her dance.

It was not to the 'thopters that she called their attention. Odrade turned her head to present both ears to a new sound intruding on their rock-tumbled maze.

A sibilant hiss, subterranean and muted by sand—it became louder with shocking swiftness. There was heat in it, a noticeable warming of the breeze that twisted down their rocky avenue. The hissing swelled to a crescendo roar. Abruptly, the crystal-ringed gaping of a gigantic mouth lifted over the dune directly above Sheeana.

"Shaitan!" Sheeana screamed, not breaking the rhythm of her dance. "Here I am, Shaitan!"

As it crested the dune, the worm dipped its mouth downward toward Sheeana. Sand cascaded around her feet, forcing her to stop her dance. The smell of cinnamon filled the rocky defile. The worm stopped above them.

"Messenger of God," Waff breathed.

Heat dried the perspiration on Odrade's exposed face and made the automatic insulation of her stillsuit puff outward perceptibly. She inhaled deeply, sorting the components behind that cinnamon assault. The air around them was sharp with ozone and swiftly oxygen rich. Her senses at full alert, Odrade stored impressions.

If I survive, she thought.

Yes, this was valuable data. The day might come when others would use it.

Sheeana backed out of the spilled sand onto the exposed rock. She resumed her dance, moving more wildly, flinging her head at each turn. Hair whipped across her face and each time she whirled to confront the worm, she screamed "Shaitan!"

Daintily, like a child on unfamiliar ground, the worm once more moved forward. It slid across the dune crest, curled itself down onto the exposed rock and presented its burning mouth slightly above and about two paces from Sheeana.

As it stopped, Odrade became conscious of the deep furnace rumbling of the worm. She could not tear her gaze away from the reflections of lambent orange flames within the creature. It was a cave of mysterious fire.

Sheeana stopped her dance. She clenched both fists at her sides and stared back at the monster she had summoned.

Odrade took timed breaths, the controlled pacing of a Reverend Mother gathering all of her powers. If this was the end—well, she had obeyed Taraza's orders. Let the Mother Superior learn what she would from the watchers overhead.

"Hello, Shaitan," Sheeana said. "I have brought a Reverend Mother and a man of the Tleilaxu with me."

Waff slumped to his knees and bowed.

Odrade slipped past him to stand beside Sheeana.

Sheeana breathed deeply. Her face was flushed.

Odrade heard the click-ticking of their overworked stillsuits. The hot, cinnamon-drenched air around them was charged with the sounds of this meeting, all dominated by the murmurous burning within the quiescent worm.

Waff came up beside Odrade, his trancelike gaze fixed on the worm.

"I am here," he whispered.

Odrade silently cursed him. Any unwarranted noise could attract this beast onto them. She knew what Waff was thinking, though: No other Tleilaxu had ever stood this close to a descendant of his Prophet. Not even the Rakian priests had ever done this!

With her right hand, Sheeana made a sudden downward gesture. "Down to us, Shaitan!" she said.

The worm lowered its gaping mouth until the internal firepit filled the rocky defile in front of them.

Her voice little more than a whisper, Sheeana said: "See how Shaitan obeys me, Mother?"

Odrade could feel Sheeana's control over the worm, a pulse of hidden language between child and monster. It was uncanny.

Her voice rising in impudent arrogance, Sheeana said: "I will ask Shaitan to let us ride him!" She scrambled up the slipface of the dune beside the worm.

Immediately, the great mouth lifted to follow her movements. "Stay there!" Sheeana shouted. The worm stopped.

It's not her words that command it, Odrade thought. *Something else . . . something else . . .*

"Mother, come with me," Sheeana called.

Thrusting Waff ahead of her, Odrade obeyed. They scrambled up the sandy slope behind Sheeana. Dislodged sand spilled down beside the waiting worm, piling up in the defile. Ahead of them, the worm's tapering tail curved along the dune crest. Sheeana led them at a sand-clotted trot to the very tip of the thing. There, she gripped the leading edge of a ring in the corrugated surface and scrambled up onto her desert beast.

More slowly, Odrade and Waff followed. The worm's warm surface felt non-organic to Odrade, as though it were some Ixian artifact.

Sheeana skipped forward along the back and squatted just behind its mouth where the rings bulged thick and wide.

"Like this," Sheeana said. She leaned forward and clutched beneath the leading edge of a ring, lifting it slightly to expose pink softness underneath.

Waff obeyed her immediately but Odrade moved with more caution, storing impressions. The ring surface was as hard as plascrete and covered with tiny encrustations. Odrade's fingers probed the softness under the leading edge. It pulsed faintly. The surface around them lifted and fell with an almost imperceptible rhythm. Odrade heard a tiny rasping with each movement.

Sheeana kicked the worm surface behind her.

"Shaitan, go!" she said.

The worm did not respond.

"Please, Shaitan," Sheeana pleaded.

Odrade heard the desperation in Sheeana's voice. The child was so confident of her Shaitan but Odrade knew that the girl had been allowed to ride only that first time. Odrade had the full story from death-wish to priestly confusion but none of it told her what would happen next.

Abruptly, the worm lurched into motion. It lifted sharply, twisted to the left and made a tight curve out of the rocky defile, then moved directly away from Dar-es-Balat into the open desert.

"We go with God!" Waff shouted.

The sound of his voice shocked Odrade. Such wildness!

She sensed the power in his faith. The thwock-thwock of following ornithopters came from overhead. The wind of their passage whipped past Odrade full of ozone and the hot furnace odors stirred up by the friction of the rushing behemoth.

Odrade glanced over her shoulders at the 'thopters, thinking how easy it would be for enemies to rid this planet of a troublesome child, an equally troublesome Reverend Mother and a despised Tleilaxu—all in one violently vulnerable moment on the open desert. The priestly cabal might attempt it, she knew, hoping that Odrade's own watchers up there would be too late to prevent it.

Would curiosity and fear hold them back?

Odrade admitted to a mighty curiosity herself.

Where is this thing taking us?

Certainly, it was not headed toward Keen. She lifted her head and peered past Sheeana. On the horizon directly ahead lay that telltale indentation of fallen stones, that place where the Tyrant had been spilled from the surface of his faery bridge.

The place of Other Memory warning.

Abrupt revelation locked Odrade's mind. She understood the warning. The Tyrant had died at a place of his own choosing. Many deaths had left their imprint on that place but his the greatest. The Tyrant chose his peregrination route with purpose. Sheeana had not told her worm to go there. It moved that way of its own volition. The magnet of the Tyrant's endless dream drew it back to the place where the dream began.

There was this drylander who was asked which was more important, a literjon of water or a vast pool of water? The drylander thought a moment and then said: "The literjon is more important. No single person could own a great pool of water. But a literjon you could hide under your cloak and run away with it. No one would know."

—THE JOKES OF ANCIENT DUNE,
BENE GESSERIT ARCHIVES

It was a long session in the no-globe's practice hall, Duncan in a mobile cage driving the exercise, adamant that this particular training series would continue until his new body had adapted to the seven central attitudes of combat response against attack from eight directions. His green singlesuit was dark with perspiration. Twenty days they had been at this one lesson!

Teg knew the ancient lore that Duncan revived here but knew it by different names and sequencing. Before they had been into it five days, Teg doubted the superiority of modern methods. Now, he was convinced that Duncan did something completely new—mixing the old with what he had learned in the Keep.

Teg sat at his own control console, as much an observer as a participant. The consoles that guided the dangerous shadow forces in this practice had required mental adjustment by Teg, but he felt familiar with them now and moved the attack with facility and frequent inspiration.

A simmering Lucilla glanced into the hall occasionally. She watched and then left without comment. Teg did not know what Duncan was doing about the Imprinter but there was a feeling that the reawakened ghola played a delaying game with his *seductress*. She would not allow that to continue long, Teg knew, but it was out of his hands. Duncan no longer was "too young" for the Imprinter. That young body carried a mature male mind with experiences from which to make his own decisions.

Duncan and Teg had been on the floor with only one break all morning. Hunger pangs gnawed at Teg but he felt reluctant to halt the session. Duncan's abilities had climbed to a new level today and he was still improving.

Teg, seated in a fixed console's cage seat, twisted the attack forces into a complex maneuver, striking from left, right, and above.

The Harkonnen armory had produced an abundance of these exotic weapons and training instruments, some of which Teg had known only from historical accounts. Duncan knew them all, apparently, and with an intimacy that Teg admired. Hunter-seekers geared to penetrate a force shield were part of the shadow system they used now.

"They automatically slow down to go through the shield," Duncan explained in his young-old voice. "Too fast a strike, of course, and the shield repels."

"Shields of that type have almost gone out of fashion," Teg said. "A few societies maintain them as a kind of sport but otherwise . . ."

Duncan executed a riposte of blurred speed that dropped three hunter-seekers to the floor damaged enough to require the no-globe's maintenance services. He removed the cage and damped the system but left it idling while he came over to Teg, breathing deeply but easily. Looking past Teg, Duncan smiled and nodded. Teg whirled but there was only the flick of Lucilla's gown as she left them.

"It's like a duel," Duncan said. "She tries to thrust through my guard and I counterattack."

"Have a care," Teg said. "That's a full Reverend Mother."

"I've known a few of them in my time, Bashar."

Once more, Teg found himself confounded. He had been warned that he would have to readjust to this different Duncan Idaho but he had not fully anticipated the constant mental demands of that readjustment. The look in Duncan's eyes right now was disconcerting.

"Our roles are changed a bit, Bashar," Duncan said. He picked up a towel from the floor and mopped his face.

"I'm no longer sure of what I can teach you," Teg admitted. He wished, though, that Duncan would take his warning about Lucilla. Did Duncan imagine that the Reverend Mothers of those ancient days were identical with the women of today? Teg thought that highly unlikely. In the way of all other life, the Sisterhood evolved and changed.

It was obvious to Teg that Duncan had come to a decision about his place in Taraza's machinations. Duncan was not merely biding his time. He was training his body to a personally chosen peak and he had made a judgment about the Bene Gesserit.

He has made that judgment on insufficient data, Teg thought.

Duncan dropped the towel and looked at it for a moment. "Let me be the judge of what you can teach me, Bashar." He turned and stared narrowly at Teg seated in the cage.

Teg inhaled deeply. He smelled the faint ozone from all of this durable Harkonnen equipment ticking away in readiness for Duncan's return to action. The ghola's perspiration carried a bitter dominant.

Duncan sneezed.

Teg sniffed, recognizing the omnipresent dust of their activities. It could be more tasted than smelled at times. Alkaline. Over it all was the fragrance of the air scrubbers and oxy regenerators. There was a distinct floral aroma built into the system but Teg could not identify the flower. In the month of their occupation, the globe also had taken on human odors, slowly insinuated into the original composite— perspiration, cooking smells, the never-quite-suppressed acridity of waste reclamation. To Teg, these reminders of their presence were oddly offensive. And he found himself sniffing and listening for sounds of intrusion—something more than the echoing passage of their own footsteps and the subdued metallic clashings from the kitchen area.

Duncan's voice intruded: "You're an odd man, Bashar."

"What do you mean?"

"There's your resemblance to the Duke Leto. The facial identity is weird. He was a bit shorter than you but the identity . . ." He shook his head, thinking of the Bene Gesserit designs behind those genetic markers in Teg's face—that hawk look, the crease lines and that inner thing, that certainty of moral superiority.

How moral and how superior?

According to the records he had seen at the Keep (and Duncan was sure they had been placed there especially for him to discover) Teg's reputation was an almost universal thing throughout human society of this age. At the Battle of Markon, it had been enough for the enemy to know that Teg was there opposite them in person. They sued for terms. Was that true?

Duncan looked at Teg in the console cage and put this question to him.

"Reputation can be a beautiful weapon," Teg said. "It often spills less blood."

"At Arbelough, why did you go to the front with your troops?" Duncan asked.

Teg showed surprise. "Where did you learn that?"

"At the Keep. You might have been killed. What would that have served?"

Teg reminded himself that this young flesh standing over him held unknown knowledge, which must guide Duncan's quest for information. It was in that unknown area, Teg suspected, that Duncan was most valuable to the Sisterhood.

"We took severe losses at Arbelough on the preceding two days," Teg said. "I failed to make a correct assessment of the enemy's fear and fanaticism."

"But the risk of . . ."

"My presence at the front said to my own people: 'I share your risks.'"

"The Keep's records said Arbelough had been perverted by Face Dancers. Patrin told me you vetoed your aides when they urged you to sweep the planet clean, sterilize it and—"

"You were not there, Duncan."

"I am trying to be. So you spared your enemy against all advice."

"Except for the Face Dancers."

"But then you walked unarmed through the enemy ranks and before they had laid down their weapons."

"To assure them they would not be mistreated."

"That was very dangerous."

"Was it? Many of them came over to us for the final assault on Kroinin where we broke the anti-Sisterhood forces."

Duncan stared hard at Teg. Not only did this old Bashar resemble Duke Leto in appearance, but he also had that same Atreides charisma: a legendary figure even among his former enemies. Teg had said he was descended from Ghanima of the Atreides, but there had to be more in it than that. The ways of the Bene Gesserit breeding mastery awed him.

"We will go back to the practice now," Duncan said.

"Don't damage yourself."

"You forget, Bashar. I remember a body as young as this one and right here on Giedi Prime."

"Gammu!"

"It was properly renamed but my body still recalls the original. That is why they sent me here. I know it."

Of course he would know it, Teg thought.

Restored by the brief respite, Teg introduced a new element in the attack and sent a sudden burn-line against Duncan's left side.

How easily Duncan parried the attack!

He was using an oddly mixed variation on the five

attitudes, each response seemingly invented before it was required.

"Each attack is a feather floating on the infinite road," Duncan said. His voice gave no hint of exertion. "As the feather approaches, it is diverted and removed."

As he spoke, he parried the shifting attack and countered.

Teg's Mentat logic followed the movements into what he recognized as dangerous places. *Dependencies and key logs!*

Duncan shifted over to attack, moving ahead of it, pacing his movements rather than responding. Teg was forced to his utmost abilities as the shadow forces burned and flickered across the floor. Duncan's weaving figure in its mobile cage danced along the space between them. Not one of Teg's hunter-seekers or burn-line counters touched the moving figure. Duncan was over them, under them, seeming totally unafraid of the real pain that this equipment could bring him.

Once more, Duncan increased the speed of his attack.

A bolt of pain shot up Teg's left arm from his hand on the controls to his shoulder.

With a sharp exclamation, Duncan shut down the equipment. "Sorry, Bashar. That was superb defense on your part but I'm afraid age defeated you."

Once more, Duncan crossed the floor and stood over Teg.

"A little pain to remind me of the pain I caused you," Teg said. He rubbed his tingling arm.

"Blame the heat of the moment," Duncan said. "We have done enough for now."

"Not quite," Teg said. "It is not enough to strengthen only your muscles."

At Teg's words, Duncan felt an alerting sensation throughout his body. He sensed the disorganized touch of that uncompleted thing that the reawakening had failed to arouse. Something crouched within him, Duncan thought. It was like a coiled spring waiting for release.

"What more would you do?" Duncan asked. His voice sounded hoarse.

"Your survival is in the balance here," Teg said. "All of this is being done to save you and get you to Rakis."

"For Bene Gesserit reasons, which you say you do not know!"

"I don't know them, Duncan."

"But you're a Mentat."

"Mentats require data to make projections."

"Do you think Lucilla knows?"

"I'm not sure but let me warn you again about her. She has orders to get you to Rakis *prepared* for what you must do there."

"Must?" Duncan shook his head from side to side. "Am I not my own person with rights to make my own choices? What do you think you've reawakened here, a damned Face Dancer capable only of obeying orders?"

"Are you telling me you will not go to Rakis?"

"I'm telling you I will make my own decisions when I know what it is I'm to do. I'm not a hired assassin."

"You think I am, Duncan?"

"I think you're an honorable man, someone to be admired. Give me credit for having my own standards of duty and honor."

"You've been given another chance at life and—"

"But you are not my father and Lucilla is not my mother. Imprinter? For what does she hope to *prepare* me?"

"It may be that she does not know, Duncan. Like me, she may have only part of the design. Knowing how the Sisterhood works, that is highly likely."

"So the two of you just train me and deliver me to Arrakis. Here's the package you ordered!"

"This is a far different universe than the one where you were originally born," Teg said. "As it was in your day, we still have a Great Convention against atomics and the pseudo-atomics of lasgunshield interaction. We still say that sneak attacks are forbidden. There are pieces of paper scattered around to which we have put our names and we—"

"But the no-ships have changed the basis for all of those treaties," Duncan said. "I think I learned my history fairly well at the Keep. Tell me, Bashar, why did Paul's son have the Tleilaxu provide him with my gholaself, hundreds of me! for all those thousands of years?"

"Paul's son?"

"The Keep's records call him the God Emperor. You name him Tyrant."

"Oh. I don't think we know why he did it. Perhaps he was lonely for someone from—"

"You brought me back to confront the worm!" Duncan said.

Is that what we're doing? Teg wondered. He had considered this possibility more than once, but it was only a possibility, not a projection. Even so, there had to be something more in Taraza's design. Teg sensed this with every fiber of his Mentat training. Did Lucilla know? Teg did not delude himself that he could pry revelation from a full Reverend Mother. No . . . he would have to bide his time, wait and watch and listen. In his own way, this obviously was what Duncan had decided. It was a dangerous course if he thwarted Lucilla!

Teg shook his head. "Truly, Duncan, I do not know."

"But you follow orders."

"By my oath to the Sisterhood."

"Deceptions, dishonesties—those are empty words when the question is the Sisterhood's survival," Duncan quoted him.

"Yes, I said that," Teg agreed.

"I trust you now *because* you said it," Duncan said. "But I do not trust Lucilla."

Teg dropped his chin to his breast. *Dangerous . . . dangerous . . .*

Much more slowly than once he had done, Teg brought his attention out of such thoughts and went through the mental cleansing process, concentrating on the necessities laid upon him by Taraza.

"You are my Bashar."

Duncan studied the Bashar for a moment. Fatigue lines were obvious on the old man's face. Duncan was reminded suddenly of Teg's great age, wondering if it ever tempted men such as Teg to seek out the Tleilaxu and become gholas. Probably not. They knew they might become Tleilaxu puppets.

This thought flooded Duncan's awareness, holding him immobile so plainly that Teg, lifting his gaze, saw it at once.

"Is something wrong?"

"The Tleilaxu have done something to me, something that has not yet been exposed," Duncan husked.

"Exactly what we feared!" It was Lucilla speaking from the doorway behind Teg. She advanced to within two paces of Duncan. "I have been listening. You two are very informative."

Teg spoke quickly, hoping to blunt the anger he sensed in her. "He has mastered the seven attitudes today."

"He strikes like fire," Lucilla said, "but remember that we of the Sisterhood flow like water and fill in every place." She glanced down at Teg. "Do you not see that our ghola has gone beyond the attitudes?"

"No fixed position, no attitude," Duncan said.

Teg looked up sharply at Duncan, who stood with his head erect, his forehead smooth, his eyes clear as he returned Teg's gaze. Duncan had grown surprisingly in the short time since being awakened to his original memories.

"Damn you, Miles!" Lucilla muttered.

But Teg kept his attention on Duncan. The youth's entire body seemed wired to a new kind of vigor. There was a poise about him that had not been there before.

Duncan shifted his attention to Lucilla. "You think you will fail in your assignment?"

"Surely not," she said. "You're still a male."

And she thought: *Yes, that young body must flow hot with the juices of procreation. Indeed, the hormonal igniters are all intact and susceptible to arousing.* His present stance, though, and the way he looked at her, forced her to raise her awareness to new, energy-demanding levels.

"What have the Tleilaxu done to you?" she demanded.

Duncan spoke with a flippancy that he did not feel: "O Great Imprinter, if I knew I would tell you."

"You think it's a game we play?" she demanded.

"I do not know *what* it is we play at!"

"By now, many people know we are not on Rakis where we would have been expected to flee," she said.

"And Gammu swarms with people returned from the Scattering," Teg said. "They have the numbers to explore many possibilities here."

"Who would suspect the existence of a lost no-globe from the Harkonnen days?" Duncan asked.

"Anyone who made the association between Rakis and Dar-es-Balat," Teg said.

"If you think this is a game, consider the urgencies of the play," Lucilla said. She pivoted on one foot to concentrate on Teg. "And *you* have disobeyed Taraza!"

"You are wrong! I have done exactly what she ordered me to do. I am her Bashar and you forget how well she knows me."

With an abruptness that shocked her to silence, the subtleties of Taraza's maneuverings impressed themselves upon Lucilla . . .

We are pawns!

What a delicate touch Taraza always demonstrated in the way she moved her pawns about. Lucilla did not feel diminished by the realization that she was a pawn. That was knowledge bred and trained into every Reverend Mother of the Sisterhood. Even Teg knew it. *Not diminished, no.* The thing around them had escalated in Lucilla's awareness. She felt awed by Teg's words. How shallow had been her previous view of the forces within which they were enmeshed. It was as though she had seen only the surface of a turbulent river and, from that, had glimpsed the currents beneath. Now, however, she felt the flow all around her and a dismaying realization.

Pawns are expendable.

By your belief in singularities, in granular absolutes, you deny movement, even the movement of evolution! While you cause a granular universe to persist in your awareness, you are blind to movement. When things change, your absolute universe vanishes, no longer accessible to your self-limiting perceptions. The universe has moved beyond you.

—FIRST DRAFT, ATREIDES MANIFESTO,
BENE GESSERIT ARCHIVES

Taraza put her hands beside her temples, palms flat in front of her ears, and pressed inward. Even her fingers could feel the tiredness in there: right between the hands—fatigue. A brief flicker of eyelids and she fell into the relaxation trance. Hands against head were the sole focal points of fleshly awareness.

One hundred heartbeats.

She had practiced this regularly since learning it as a child, one of her first Bene Gesserit skills. Exactly one hundred heartbeats. After all of those years of practice, her body could pace them automatically by an unconscious metronome.

When she opened her eyes at the count of one hundred, her head felt better. She hoped she would have at least two more hours in which to work before fatigue overcame her once more. Those one hundred heartbeats had given her extra years of wakefulness in her lifetime.

Tonight, though, thinking of that old trick sent her memories spiraling backward. She found herself caught in her own childhood, the dormitory with the Sister Proctor pacing the aisle at night to make sure they all remained properly asleep in their beds.

Sister Baram, the Night Proctor.

Taraza had not thought of that name in years. Sister Baram had been short and fat, a failed Reverend Mother. Not for any immediately visible reason, but the Medical Sisters and their Suk doctors had found something. Baram had never been permitted to try the spice agony. She had been quite forthcoming about what she knew of her defect. It had been discovered while she was still in her teens: periodic nerve tremors, which manifested when she began to sink into sleep. A symptom of something deeper that had caused her to be sterilized. The tremors made Baram wakeful in the night. Aisle patrol was a logical assignment.

Baram had other weaknesses not detected by her superiors. A wakeful child toddling to the washroom could lure Baram into low-voiced conversation. Naive questions elicited mostly naive answers, but sometimes Baram imparted useful knowledge. She had taught Taraza the relaxation trick.

One of the older girls had found Sister Baram dead in the washroom one morning. The Night Proctor's tremors had been the symptom of a fatal defect, a fact important mostly to the Breeding Mistresses and their endless records.

Because the Bene Gesserit did not usually schedule the full "solo death education" until well into the acolyte stage, Sister Baram was the first dead person Taraza had seen. Sister Baram's body had been found partly beneath a washbasin, the right cheek pressed to the tile floor, her left hand caught in the plumbing under a sink. She had tried to pull her failing body upright and death had caught her in the attempt, exposing that last motion like an insect caught in amber.

When they rolled Sister Baram over to carry her away, Taraza saw the red mark where a cheek had been pressed to the floor. The Day Proctor explained this mark with a scientific practicality. Any experience could be turned into data for these potential Reverend Mothers to incorporate later into their acolyte "Conversations With Death."

Post Mortem lividity.

Seated at her Chapter House table, all of those years removed from the event, Taraza was forced to use her carefully focused powers of concentration to dispel that memory, leaving her free to deal with the work spread before her. So many lessons. So fearfully full, her memory. So many lifetimes stored there. It reaffirmed her sense of being alive to see the work in front of her. Things to do. She was needed. Eagerly, Taraza bent to her labors.

Damn the necessity to train the ghola on Gammu!

But this ghola required it. Familiarity with dirt underfoot preceded the required restoration of that original persona.

It had been wise to send Burzmali into the Gammu arena. If Miles had really found a hideaway . . . if he were to emerge now, he would need all the help he could get. Once more, she considered whether it was time to play the prescient game. So dangerous! And the Tleilaxu had been alerted that their replacement ghola might be required.

"Ready him for delivery."

Her mind swung to the Rakis problem. That fool Tuek should have been monitored more carefully. How long could a Face Dancer safely impersonate him? There was no faulting Odrade's on-scene decision, though. She had put the Tleilaxu into an untenable position. The impersonator could be exposed, plunging the Bene Tleilaxu into a sink of hatred.

The game within the Bene Gesserit design had become very delicate. For generations now, they had held out to the Rakian priesthood the bait of a Bene Gesserit alliance. But now! The Tleilaxu must consider that *they* had been chosen instead of the priests. Odrade's three-cornered alliance, let the priests think every Reverend Mother would take the Oath of Subservience to the Divided God. The Priestly Council would stutter with excitement at the prospect. The Tleilaxu, of course, saw the chance to monopolize melange, controlling at last the one source independent of them.

A rap at Taraza's door told her the acolyte had arrived with tea. It was a standing order when the Mother Superior worked late. Taraza glanced at the table chrono, an Ixian device so accurate it would gain or lose only one second in a century: 1:23:11 a.m.

She called to admit the acolyte. The girl, a pale blond with coldly observant eyes, entered and bent to arrange the contents of her tray beside Taraza.

Taraza ignored the girl and stared at the work remaining on the table. So much to do. Work was more important than sleep. But her head ached and she felt the telltale dazed sensation akin to a stunned brain that told her the tea would provide little relief. She had worked herself into mental starvation and it would have to be put right before she could even stand. Her shoulders and back throbbed.

The acolyte started to leave but Taraza motioned for her to wait. "Rub my back please, Sister."

The acolyte's educated hands slowly worked out the constrictions in Taraza's back. *Good girl.* Taraza smiled at this thought. Of course she was good. No lesser creature could be assigned to the Mother Superior.

When the girl had gone, Taraza sat silently in deep thought. *So little time.* She begrudged every minute of sleep. There was no escaping it, though. Eventually, the body made its unavoidable demands. She had pressed herself beyond easy recuperation for days now. Ignoring the tea laid out beside her, Taraza arose and went down the hall to her tiny sleeping cell. There, she left a call with the Night Guard for 11:00 a.m. and composed herself fully robed on the hard cot.

Quietly, she regulated her breathing, insulated her senses from distraction and fell into the between-state.

Sleep did not come.

She went through her full repertoire and still sleep evaded her.

Taraza lay there for a long time, recognizing at last the futility of willing herself to sleep with any of the techniques at her disposal. The between-state would have to do its slow mending first. Meanwhile, her mind continued to churn.

The Rakian priesthood she had never considered to be

a central problem. Already caught up in religion, the priests could be manipulated by religion. They saw the Bene Gesserit chiefly as a power that could enforce their dogma. Let them continue to think this. It was bait that would blind them.

Damn that Miles Teg! Three months of silence, and no favorable report from Burzmali, either. Charred ground, signs of a no-ship's lift-off. Where could Teg have gone? The ghola might be dead. Teg had never before done such a thing. Old Reliability. That was why she had chosen him. That and his military skills and his likeness to the old Duke Leto—all of the things they had prepared in him.

Teg and Lucilla. A perfect team.

If not dead, was the ghola beyond their reach? Did the Tleilaxu have him? Attackers from the Scattering? Many things were possible. Old Reliability. Silent. Was his silence a message? If so, what was he trying to say?

With both Schwangyu and Patrin dead, there was the smell of conspiracy around the Gammu events. Could Teg be someone planted long ago by the Sisterhood's enemies? Impossible! His own family was proof against such doubts. Teg's daughter at the family home was as mystified as anyone.

Three months now and not a word.

Caution. She had warned Teg to exercise the utmost caution in protecting the ghola. Teg had seen the great danger on Gammu. Schwangyu's last reports made that clear.

Where could Teg and Lucilla have taken the ghola?

Where had they acquired a no-ship? Conspiracy?

Taraza's mind kept circling around her deep suspicions. Was it Odrade's doing? Then who conspired with Odrade?

Lucilla? Odrade and Lucilla had never met before that brief encounter on Gammu. Or had they? Who bent close to Odrade and breathed a mutual air weighted with whispers? Odrade gave no sign, but what proof was that? Lucilla's loyalty had never been doubted. They both functioned perfectly as assigned. But so would conspirators.

Facts! Taraza hungered for facts. The bed rustled beneath her and her sense-insulation collapsed, shattered by worries as much as by the sound of her own movements. Resignedly, Taraza once more composed herself for relaxation.

Relaxation and *then* sleep.

Ships from the Scattering flitted through Taraza's fatigue-fogged imagination. Lost Ones returned in their uncounted no-ships. Was that where Teg found a ship? This possibility was being explored as quietly as they could on Gammu and elsewhere. She tried counting imaginary ships but they refused to proceed in the orderly fashion required for sleep induction. Taraza came alert without moving on her cot.

Her deepest mind was trying to reveal something. Fatigue had blocked that path of communication but now— she sat up fully awake.

The Tleilaxu had been dealing with people returned from the Scattering. With these whorish Honored Matres and with returned Bene Tleilax as well. Taraza sensed a single design behind events. The Lost Ones did not return out of simple curiosity about their roots. The gregarious desire to reunite all of humankind was not enough in itself to bring them back. The Honored Matres clearly came with dreams of conquest.

But what if the Tleilaxu sent out in the Scattering had

not carried with them the secret of the axlotl tanks? What then? Melange. The orange-eyed whores obviously used an inadequate substitute. The people of the Scattering might not have solved the mystery of the Tleilaxu tanks. They *would* know about axlotl tanks and try to re-create them. But if they failed—melange!

She began to explore this projection.

The Lost Ones ran out of the true melange their ancestors took into the Scattering. What sources did they have then? The worms of Rakis and the original Bene Tleilax. The whores would not dare reveal their true interest. Their ancestors believed that the worms could not be transplanted. Was it possible the Lost Ones had found a suitable planet for the worms? Of course it was possible. They might begin bargaining with the Tleilaxu as a diversion. Rakis would be their real target. Or the reverse could be true.

Transportable wealth.

She had seen Teg's reports on the wealth being accumulated on Gammu. Some among the ones returning had coinages and other negotiable chips. That much was plain from the banking activities.

What greater currency was there, though, than the spice?

Wealth. That was it, of course. And whatever the chips, the bargaining had begun.

Taraza grew aware of voices outside her door. The acolyte Sleep-Guard was arguing with someone. The voices were low but Taraza heard enough to bring her into full alert.

"She left a wake-up for late morning," the Sleep-Guard protested.

Someone else whispered: "She said she was to be told the moment I returned."

"I tell you she is very tired. She needs—"

"She needs to be obeyed! Tell her I'm back!"

Taraza sat up and swung her legs over the edge of the cot. Her feet found the floor. Gods! How her knees ached. It pained her, too, that she could not place the intruding whisper, the person arguing with her guard.

Whose return did I . . . Burzmali!

"I'm awake," Taraza called.

Her door opened and the Sleep-Guard leaned in. "Mother Superior, Burzmali has returned from Gammu."

"Send him in at once!" Taraza activated a single glow-globe at the head of her cot. Its yellow light washed away the room's darkness.

Burzmali entered and closed the door behind him. Without being told, he touched the sound-insulation switch on the door and all outside noises vanished.

Privacy? It was bad news then.

She looked up at Burzmali. He was a short, slender fellow with a sharply triangular face narrowing to a thin chin. Blond hair swept over a high forehead. His widely spaced green eyes were alert and watchful. He looked far too young for the responsibilities of a Bashar, but then Teg had looked even younger at Arbelough. *We are getting old, damn it.* She forced herself to relax and place her trust in the fact that Teg had trained this man and expressed full confidence in him.

"Tell me the bad news," Taraza said.

Burzmali cleared his throat. "Still no sign of the Bashar and his party on Gammu, Mother Superior." He had a heavy, masculine voice.

And that's not the worst of it, Taraza thought. She saw the clear signs of Burzmali's nervousness.

"Let's have it all," she ordered. "Obviously, you have completed your examination of the Keep's ruins."

"No survivors," he said. "The attackers were thorough."

"Tleilaxu?"

"Possible."

"You have doubts?"

"The attackers used that new Ixian explosive, 12-Uri. I . . . I think it may have been used to mislead us. There were mechanical brain-probe holes in Schwangyu's skull, too."

"What of Parrin?"

"Exactly as Schwangyu reported. He blew himself up in that decoy ship. They identified him from bits of two fingers and one intact eye. There was nothing left big enough to probe."

"But you have doubts! Get to them!"

"Schwangyu left a message that only we might read."

"In the wear marks on furniture?"

"Yes, Mother Superior, and—"

"Then she knew she would be attacked and had time to leave a message. I saw your earlier report on the devastation of the attack."

"It was quick and totally overpowering. The attackers did not try to take captives."

"What did she say?"

"Whores."

Taraza tried to contain her shock, although she had been expecting that word. The effort to remain calm almost drained her energies. This was very bad. Taraza permitted herself a deep sigh. Schwangyu's opposition had persisted to the end. But then, seeing disaster, she had made a proper decision. Knowing she would die without the opportunity to transfer her Memory Lives to another Reverend Mother, she had acted from the most basic loyalty. If you can do nothing else, arm your Sisters and frustrate the enemy.

So the Honored Matres have acted!

"Tell me about your search for the ghola," Taraza ordered.

"We were not the first searchers over that ground, Mother Superior. There was much additional burning of trees and rocks and underbrush."

"But it was a no-ship?"

"The *marks* of a no-ship."

Taraza nodded to herself. A silent message from Old Reliability?

"How closely did you examine the area?"

"I flew over it but on a routine trip from one place to another."

Taraza motioned Burzmali to a chair near the foot of her cot. "Sit down and relax. I want you to do some guessing for me."

Burzmali lowered himself carefully onto the chair. "Guessing?"

"You were his favorite student. I want you to imagine that you are Miles Teg. You know you must get the ghola out of the Keep. You do not place your full trust in anyone around you, not even in Lucilla. What will you do?"

"An unexpected thing, of course."

"Of course."

Burzmali rubbed his narrow chin. Presently, he said: "I trust Patrin. I trust him fully."

"All right, you and Patrin. What do you do?"

"Patrin is a native of Gammu."

"I have been wondering about that myself," she said.

Burzmali looked at the floor in front of him. "Patrin and I will make an emergency plan long before it is needed. I always prepare secondary ways of dealing with problems."

"Very good. Now —the plan. What do you do?"

"Why did Patrin kill himself?" Burzmali asked.

"You're sure that's what he did."

"You saw the reports. Schwangyu and several others were sure of it. I accept it. Patrin was loyal enough to do that for his Bashar."

"For you! You are Miles Teg now. What plan have you and Patrin concocted?"

"I would not deliberately send Patrin to certain death."

"Unless?"

"Patrin did that on his own. He might if the plan originated with him and not with . . . me. He might do it to protect me, to make sure no one discovered the plan."

"How could Patrin summon a no-ship without our learning of it?"

"Patrin was a Gammu native. His family goes back to the Giedi Prime days."

Taraza closed her eyes and turned her head away from Burzmali. So Burzmali followed the same suggestive tracks that she had been probing in her mind. *We knew Patrin's origins.* What was the significance of that Gammu association? Her mind refused to speculate. This was what came of allowing herself to become too tired! She looked once more at Burzmali.

"Did Patrin find a way to make secret contact with family and old friends?"

"We've explored every contact we could find."

"Depend on it; you haven't traced them all."

Burzmali shrugged. "Of course not. I have not acted on that assumption."

Taraza took a deep breath. "Go back to Gammu. Take with you as much help as our Security can spare. Tell Bellonda those are my orders. You must insinuate agents into every walk of life. Find out who Patrin knew. What of his surviving family? Friends? Winkle them out."

"That will cause a stir no matter how careful we are. Others will know."

"That cannot be helped. And Burzmali!"

He was on his feet. "Yes, Mother Superior?"

"The other searchers: You must stay ahead of them."

"May I use a Guild navigator?"

"No!"

"Then how—"

"Burzmali, what if Miles and Lucilla and our ghola are still on Gammu?"

"I've already told you that I do not accept the idea of their leaving in a no-ship!"

For a long silent period, Taraza studied the man standing at the foot of her cot. Trained by Miles Teg. The old Bashar's favorite student. What was Burzmali's trained instinct suggesting.

In a low voice, she prompted: "Yes?"

"Gammu was Giedi Prime, a Harkonnen place."

"What does that suggest to you?"

"They were rich, Mother Superior. Very rich."

"So?"

"Rich enough to accomplish the secret installation of a no-room . . . even of a large no-globe."

"There are no records! Ix has never even vaguely suggested such a thing. They have not probed on Gammu for . . ."

"Bribes, third-party purchases, many transshipments," Burzmali said. "The Famine Times were very disruptive and before that there were all those millennia of the Tyrant."

"When the Harkonnens kept their heads down or lost them. Still, I will admit the possibility."

"Records could have been lost," Burzmali said.

"Not by us or the other governments that survived. What prompts this line of speculation?"

"Patrin."

"Ahhhhh."

He spoke quickly: "If such a thing were discovered, a Gammu native might know about it."

"How many of them would know? Do you think they could have kept such a secret for . . . Yes! I see what you mean. If it were a secret of Patrin's family . . ."

"I have not dared question any of them about it."

"Of course not! But where would you look . . . without alerting . . ."

"That place on the mountain where the no-ship marks were left."

"It would require you to go there in person!"

"Very hard to conceal from spies," he agreed. "Unless I went with a very small force and seemingly on another purpose."

"What other purpose?"

"To place a funeral marker in memory of my old Bashar."

"Suggesting that we know he is dead? Yes!"

"You've already asked the Tleilaxu to replace our ghola."

"That was a simple precaution and does not bear on . . . Burzmali, this is extremely dangerous. I doubt we can mislead the kinds of people who will observe you on Gammu."

"The mourning of myself and the people I take with me will be dramatic and believable."

"The believable does not necessarily convince a wary observer."

"Do you not trust my loyalty and the loyalty of the people I will take with me?"

Taraza pursed her lips in thought. She reminded herself that fixed loyalty was a thing they had learned to improve upon from the Atreides pattern. How to produce people who command the utmost devotion. Burzmali and Teg both were fine examples.

"It might work," Taraza agreed. She stared speculatively at Burzmali. Teg's favorite student could be right!

"Then I'll go," Burzmali said. He turned to leave.

"One moment," Taraza said.

Burzmali turned. "You will saturate yourselves with shere, all of you. And if you're captured by Face Dancers— these new ones!—you must burn your own heads or shatter them completely. Take the necessary precautions."

The suddenly sobered expression on Burzmali's face reassured Taraza. He had been proud of himself for a moment there. Better to dampen his pride. No need for him to be reckless.

We have long known that the objects of our palpable sense experiences can be influenced by choice—both conscious choice and unconscious. This is a demonstrated fact that does not require that we believe some force within us reaches out and touches the universe. I address a pragmatic relationship between belief and what we identify as "real." All of our judgments carry a heavy burden of ancestral beliefs to which we of the Bene Gesserit tend to be more susceptible than most. It is not enough that we are aware of this and guard against it. Alternative interpretations must always receive our attention.

—MOTHER SUPERIOR TARAZA: ARGUMENT IN COUNCIL

"God will judge us here," Waff gloated.

He had been doing that at unpredictable moments all during this long ride across the desert. Sheeana appeared not to notice but Waff's voice and comments had begun to wear on Odrade.

The Rakian sun had moved far down to the west but the worm that carried them appeared untiring in its drive across the ancient Sareer toward the remnant mounds of the Tyrant's barrier wall.

Why this direction? Odrade wondered.

No answer satisfied. The fanaticism and renewed danger from Waff, though, demanded immediate response.

She called up the cant of the Shariat that she knew drove him.

"Let God do the judging and not men."

Waff scowled at the taunting note in her voice. He looked at the horizon ahead and then up at the 'thopters, which kept pace with them.

"Men must do God's work," he muttered.

Odrade did not answer. Waff had been deflected into his doubts and now would be asking himself: Did these Bene Gesserit witches really share the Great Belief?

Her thoughts dove back into the unanswered questions, tumbling through all she knew about the worms of Rakis. Personal memories and Other Memories wove a mad montage. She could visualize robed Fremen atop a worm even larger than this one, each rider leaning back against a long hooked pole that dug into a worm's rings as her hands now gripped this one. She felt the wind against her cheeks, the robe whipping against her shanks. This ride and others merged into a long familiarity.

It has been a long time since an Atreides rode this way.

Was there a clue to their destination back in Dar-es-Balat? How could there be? But it had been so hot and her mind had been questing forward to what might happen on this venture into the desert. She had not been as alert as she might have been.

In common with every other community on Rakis, Dar-es-Balat pulled inward from its edges during the heat of the early afternoon. Odrade recalled the chafing of her new stillsuit while she waited in a building's shadows near the western limits of Dar-es-Balat. She waited for the separate escorts to bring Sheeana and Waff from the safe houses where Odrade had installed them.

What a tempting target she had made. But they had to be certain of Rakian compliance. The Bene Gesserit escorts delayed deliberately.

"Shaitan likes the heat," Sheeana had said.

Rakians hid from the heat but the worms came out then. Was that a significant fact, revealing the reason for this worm to take them in a particular direction?

My mind is bouncing around like a child's ball!

What did it signify that Rakians hid from the sun while a little Tleilaxu, a Reverend Mother, and a wild young girl went coursing across the desert atop a worm? It was an ancient pattern on Rakis. Nothing surprising about it at all. The ancient Fremen had been mostly nocturnal, though. Their modern descendants depended more on shade to protect them from the hottest sunlight.

How safe the priests felt behind their guardian moats!

Every resident of a Rakian urban center knew the qanat was out there, water running slick in shadowed darkness, trickles diverted to feed the narrow canals whose evaporation was recaptured in the windtraps.

"Our prayers protect us," they said, but they knew very well what really protected them.

"His holy presence is seen in the desert."

The Holy Worm.

The Divided God.

Odrade looked down at the worm rings in front of her. *And here he is!*

She thought of the priests among the watchers in the 'thopters overhead. How they loved to spy on others! She had felt them watching her back in Dar-es-Balat while she awaited the arrival of Sheeana and Waff. Eyes behind the high grills of hidden balconies. Eyes peering through slits in thick walls. Eyes concealed behind mirror-plaz or staring out from shadowed places.

Odrade had forced herself to ignore the dangers while she marked the passage of time by the movement of the shadow line on a wall above her: a sure clock in this land where few kept other than suntime.

Tensions had built, amplified by the need to appear unconcerned. Would they attack? Would they dare, knowing that she had taken her own precautions? How angry were the priests at being forced to join the Tleilaxu in this secret triumvirate? Her Reverend Mother advisors from the Keep had not liked this dangerous baiting of the priests.

"Let one of *us* be the bait!"

Odrade had been adamant: "They would not believe it. Suspicions would keep them away. Besides, they are sure to send Albertus."

So Odrade had waited in the Dar-es-Balat courtyard, green-shadowed in the depths where she stood looking upward at the sunline six stories overhead—past lacy balustrades at each balconied level: green plants, brilliant red, orange, and blue flowers, a rectangle of silvery sky above the tiers.

And the hidden eyes.

Motion at the wide street door to her right! A single figure in priestly gold, purple, and white let himself into the courtyard. She studied him, looking for signs that the Tleilaxu might have extended their sway by another Face Dancer mimic. But this was a man, a priest she recognized: Albertus, the senior of Dar-es-Balat.

Just as we expected.

Albertus moved through the wide atrium and across

the courtyard toward her, walking with careful dignity. Were there dangerous portents in him? Would he signal his assassins? She glanced upward at the tiered balconies: little flickering motions at the higher levels. The approaching priest was not alone.

But neither am I!

Albertus came to a stop two paces from Odrade and looked up at her from where he had kept his attention— on the intricate gold and purple designs of the court- yard's tiled floor.

He has weak bones, Odrade thought.

She gave no sign of recognition. Albertus was one of those who knew that his High Priest had been replaced by a Face Dancer mimic.

Albertus cleared his throat and took a trembling breath.

Weak bones! Weak flesh!

While the thought amused Odrade, it did not reduce her wariness. Reverend Mothers always noted that sort of thing. You looked for the marks of the breeding. Such selectivity as existed in the ancestry of Albertus carried flaws, elementals that the Sisterhood would try to correct in his descendants if it ever appeared worthwhile to breed him. This would be considered, of course. Albertus had risen to a position of power, doing it quietly but defi- nitely, and it must be determined whether that implied valuable genetic material. Albertus had been poorly edu- cated, though. A first-year acolyte could have handled him. Conditioning among the Rakian priesthood had degenerated badly since the old Fish Speaker days.

"Why are you here?" Odrade demanded, making it as much an accusation as a question.

Albertus trembled. "I bring a message from your people, Reverend Mother."

"Then say it!"

"There has been a slight delay, something about the route here being known by too many."

That, at least, was the story they had agreed to tell the priests. But the other things on the face of Albertus were easy to read. Secrets shared with him were dangerously close to exposure.

"I almost wish I had ordered you killed," Odrade said.

Albertus recoiled two full paces. His eyes went vacant, as though he had died right there in front of her. She recognized the reaction. Albertus had entered that fully revelatory phase where fear gripped his scrotum. He knew that this terrible Reverend Mother Odrade might pass a death sentence upon him quite casually or kill him with her own hands. Nothing he said or did would escape her awful scrutiny.

"You have been considering whether to kill *me* and destroy our Keep at Keen," Odrade accused.

Albertus trembled violently. "Why do you say such things, Reverend Mother?" There was a revealing whine in his voice.

"Don't try to deny it," she said. "I wonder how many have found you as easy to read as I do? You are supposed to be a keeper of secrets. You are not supposed to be walking around with all of our secrets written on your face!"

Albertus fell to his knees. She thought he would grovel.

"But your own people sent me!"

"And you were only too happy to come and decide whether it might be possible to kill me."

"Why would we—"

"Silence! You do not like it that we control Sheeana. You are fearful of the Tleilaxu. Matters have been taken from your *priestly* hands and things have been set in motion that terrify you."

"Reverend Mother! What are we to do? What are we to do?"

"You will obey us! More than that, you will obey Sheeana! You fear what we venture this day? You have greater things to fear!"

She shook her head in mock dismay, knowing the effect all of this was having on poor Albertus. He cringed beneath the weight of her anger.

"On your feet!" she ordered. "And remember that you are a priest and the truth is demanded of you!"

Albertus stumbled to his feet and kept his head bowed. She could see his body responding to the decision that he abandon subterfuge. What a trial that must be for him! Dutiful to the Reverend Mother who so obviously read his heart, now he must be dutiful to his religion. He must confront the ultimate paradox of all religions:

God knows!

"You hide nothing from me, nothing from Sheeana, and nothing from God," Odrade said.

"Forgive me, Reverend Mother."

"Forgive you? It is not in my power to forgive you nor should you ask it of me. You are a priest!"

He lifted his gaze to Odrade's angry face.

The paradox was upon him completely now. God was surely here! But God was usually a long way away and confrontations could be put off. Tomorrow was another day of life. Surely it was. And it was acceptable if you permitted yourself a few small sins, perhaps a lie or two. For the time being only. And maybe a big sin if temptations were great. Gods were supposed to be more understanding of great sinners. There would be time to make amends.

Odrade stared at Albertus with the analyzing eye of the Missionaria Protectiva.

Ahhh, Albertus, she thought. *But now you stand in the presence of a fellow human who knows all of the things you believed were secrets between you and your god.*

For Albertus, his present situation could be little different from death and that ultimate submission to the final judgment of his god. That surely described the unconscious setting for the way Albertus let his will power crumble now. All of his religious fears had been called up and were focused on a *Reverend* Mother.

In her driest tones, not even compelling him with Voice, Odrade said: "I want this farce ended immediately."

Albertus tried to swallow. He knew he could not lie. He might know a remote capability of lying but that was useless. Submissively, he looked up at Odrade's forehead where the line of her stillsuit cap had been drawn tightly across her brow. He spoke in little more than a whisper:

"Reverend Mother, it is only that we feel deprived. You and the Tleilaxu go into the desert with *our* Sheeana. Both of you will learn from her and . . ." His shoulders sagged. "Why do you take the Tleilaxu?"

"Sheeana wishes it," Odrade lied.

Albertus opened his mouth and closed it without speaking. She could see acceptance flood through him.

"You will return to your fellows with my warning,"

Odrade said. "The survival of Rakis and of your priesthood depend utterly on how well you obey me. You will not hinder us in the slightest! And as to these puerile plots against us—Sheeana reveals to us your every evil thought!"

Albertus surprised her then. He shook his head and emitted a dry chuckle. Odrade already had noted that many of these priests enjoyed discomfiture but had not suspected that they might find amusement in their own failures.

"I find your laughter shallow," she said.

Albertus shrugged and restored some of his facial mask. Odrade had seen several such masks on him. Facades! He wore them in layers. And far down under all of that defensiveness lay the someone who cared, the one she had exposed here so briefly. These priests had a dangerous way of falling into florid explanations, though, when taxed too heavily with questions.

I must restore the one who cares, Odrade thought. She cut him off as he started to speak.

"No more! You will wait upon me when I return from the desert. For now, you are *my* messenger. Carry my message accurately and you will win a greater reward than you have ever imagined. Fail and you will suffer the agonies of Shaitan!"

Odrade watched Albertus scurry out of the courtyard, shoulders hunched, his head thrust forward as though he could not get his mouth within speaking distance of his peers soon enough.

On the whole, she thought, it had gone well. A calculated risk and very dangerous to her personally. She was sure there had been assassins on the balconies above her waiting for a signal from Albertus. And now, the fear he carried back with him was a thing the Bene Gesserit understood intimately through millennia of manipulations. As contagiously virulent as any plague. The teaching Sisters called it "a directed hysteria." It had been *directed* (aimed was more accurate) at the heart of the Rakian priesthood. It could be relied upon, especially with the reinforcement that now would be set in motion. The priests would submit. Only the few immune heretics were to be feared now.

This is the awe-inspiring universe of magic: There are no atoms, only waves and motions all around. Here, you discard all belief in barriers to understanding. You put aside understanding itself. This universe cannot be seen, cannot be heard, cannot be detected in any way by fixed perceptions. It is the ultimate void where no preordained screens occur upon which forms may be projected. You have only one awareness here—the screen of the magi: Imagination! Here, you learn what it is to be human. You are a creator of order, of beautiful shapes and systems, an organizer of chaos.

—THE ATREIDES MANIFESTO, BENE GESSERIT ARCHIVES

"What you are doing is too dangerous," Teg said. "My orders are to protect you and strengthen you. I cannot permit this to continue."

Teg and Duncan stood in the long, wood-paneled hallway just outside the no-globe's practice floor. It was late afternoon by the clock of their arbitrary routine and Lucilla had just swept away in anger after a vituperative confrontation.

Every meeting between Duncan and Lucilla lately had taken on the nature of a battle. Just now, she had stood in the doorway to the practice hall, a solid figure saved from being stolid by her softening curves, the seductive movements obvious to both males.

"Stop it, Lucilla!" Duncan had ordered.

Only her voice betrayed her anger: "How long do you think I will wait to carry out my orders?"

"Until you or someone else tells me that I—"

"Taraza requires things of you that none of us here knows!" Lucilla said.

Teg tried to soothe the mounting angers: "Please. Isn't it enough that Duncan continues to improve his performance? In a few days, I will start keeping regular watch outside. We can—"

"You can stop interfering with me, damn you!" Lucilla snapped. She whirled and stalked away.

As he saw the hard resolution on Duncan's face now, something furious began to work in Teg. He felt impelled by the necessities of their isolated situation. His intellect, that marvelously honed Mentat instrument, was shielded here from the mental uproar to which it adjusted on the outside. He thought that if he could only silence his mind, bring everything to stillness, all things would become clear to him.

"Why are you holding your breath, Bashar?"

Duncan's voice impaled Teg. It required a supreme act of will to resume normal breathing. He felt the emotions of his two companions in the no-globe as an ebb and flow temporarily removed from other forces.

Other forces.

Mentat awareness could be an idiot in the presence of other forces that swept through the universe. There might exist in the universe people whose lives were infused with powers he could not imagine. Before such forces he would be chaff moved on the froth of wild currents.

Who could plunge into such an uproar and emerge intact?

"What can Lucilla possibly do if I continue to resist her?" Duncan asked.

"Has she used Voice on you?" Teg asked. His own voice sounded remote to him.

"Once."

"You resisted?" Remote surprise lurked somewhere within Teg.

"I learned the way of that from Paul Muad'Dib himself."

"She is capable of paralyzing you and—"

"I think her orders prohibit violence."

"What is violence, Duncan?"

"I'm going to the showers, Bashar Are you coming?"

"In a few minutes." Teg took a deep breath, sensing how close he was to exhaustion. This afternoon on the practice floor and afterward had drained him. He watched Duncan leave. Where was Lucilla? What was she planning? How long could she wait? That was the central question and it put the no-globe's peculiar emphasis on their isolation from Time.

Again, he sensed that ebb and flow which their three lives influenced. *I must talk to Lucilla! Where has she gone? The library? No! There is something else I must do first.*

Lucilla sat in the room she had chosen for her personal quarters. It was a small space with an ornate bed filling an inset into one wall. Gross and subtle signs around her said this had been the room of a favorite Harkonnen hetaira. Pastel blues with darker blue accents shaded the fabrics.

Despite the baroque carvings on bed, alcove, ceiling, and every functioning appurtenance, the room itself could be swept out of her consciousness once she relaxed here. She lay back on the bed and closed her eyes against the sexually gross figures on the alcove ceiling.

Teg will have to be dealt with.

It would have to be done in such a way that it did not offend Taraza or weaken the ghola. Teg presented a special problem in many ways, especially in the way his mental processes could dip into and out of deeper sources akin to those of the Bene Gesserit.

The Reverend Mother who bore him, of course!

Something passed from such a mother to such a child. It began in the womb and probably did not end even when they were finally separated. He had never undergone the all-ravening transmutation that produced Abominations . . . no, not that. But he had subtle and real powers. Those born of Reverend Mothers learned things impossible to others.

Teg knew precisely how Lucilla viewed love in all of its manifestations. She had seen it on his face that once in his quarters at the Keep.

"Calculating witch!"

He might as well have spoken it aloud.

She recalled the way she had favored him with her benign smile and dominating expression. That had been a mistake, demeaning to both of them. She sensed in such thoughts a latent sympathy for Teg. Somewhere within her, despite all of the careful Bene Gesserit training, there were chinks in her armor. Her teachers had warned her about that many times.

"To be capable of inducing real love, you must feel it, but only temporarily. And once is enough!"

Teg's reactions to the Duncan Idaho ghola said much. Teg was both drawn to and repelled by their young charge.

As I am.

Perhaps it had been a mistake not to seduce Teg.

In her sex education, where she had been taught to gain strength from intercourse rather than lose herself in it, her teachers had emphasized analysis and historical comparisons, of which there were many in a Reverend Mother's Other Memories.

Lucilla focused her thoughts on Teg's male presence. Doing this, she could feel a female response, her flesh wanting Teg close to her and aroused to sexual peak—ready for the moment of mystery.

Faint amusement crept into Lucilla's awareness. Not orgasm. No scientific labels! It was purest Bene Gesserit cant: *moment of mystery,* the Imprinter's ultimate specialty. Immersion in the long Bene Gesserit continuity required this concept. She had been taught to believe deeply in a duality: the scientific knowledge by which the Breeding Mistresses guided them *but,* at the same time, the moment of mystery that confounded all knowledge. Bene Gesserit history and science said the procreative drive must remain irretrievably buried in the psyche. It could not be removed without destroying the species.

The safety net.

Lucilla gathered her sexual forces around her now as only a Bene Gesserit Imprinter could. She began to focus her thoughts on Duncan. By now, he would be in the showers and thinking about this evening's training session with his Reverend Mother–teacher.

I will go to my student presently, she thought. *The important lesson must be taught or he will not be fully prepared for Rakis.*

Those were Taraza's instructions.

Lucilla swung the focus of her thoughts fully onto Duncan. It was almost as though she saw him standing naked under the shower.

How little he understood of what there might be to learn!

Duncan sat alone in the dressing cubicle off the showers which adjoined the practice hall. He was immersed in a deep sadness. This brought remembered pains to old wounds that this young flesh had never experienced.

Some things never changed! The Sisterhood was at its old-old games again.

He looked up and around this dark-paneled Harkonnen place. Arabesques were carved into walls and ceiling, strange designs in the tesserae of the floor. Monsters and lovely human bodies intermingled across the same defining lines. Only a flicker of attention separated one from the other.

Duncan looked down at this body that the Tleilaxu and their axlotl tanks had produced for him. It still felt strange at moments. He had been a man of many adult experiences in the last instant he remembered from his pre-ghola life—fighting off a swarm of Sardaukar warriors, giving his young Duke a chance to escape.

His Duke! Paul had been no older than this flesh then. Conditioned, though, the way the Atreides always were: Loyalty and honor above all else.

The way they conditioned me after they saved me from the Harkonnens.

Something within him could not evade that ancient debt. He knew its source. He could outline the process by which it had been embedded in him.

There it remained.

Duncan glanced at the tiled floor. Words had been worked in the tile along the cubicle's splashboard. It was a script that one part of him identified as an ancient thing from the old Harkonnen times but that another part of him found to be an all-too-familiar Galach.

"CLEAN SWEET CLEAN BRIGHT CLEAN PURE CLEAN"

The ancient script repeated itself around the room's perimeter as though the words themselves might create something that Duncan knew was alien to the Harkonnens of his memories.

Over the door to the showers, more script:

"CONFESS THY HEART AND FIND PURITY"

A religious admonition in a Harkonnen stronghold? Had the Harkonnens changed in the centuries after his death? Duncan found this hard to believe. These words were things that the builders probably had thought appropriate.

He felt rather than heard Lucilla enter the room behind him. Duncan stood and fastened the clips of the tunic he had appropriated from the nullentropy bins (but only after removing all Harkonnen insignia!).

Without turning, he said: "What now, Lucilla?"

She stroked the fabric of the tunic along his left arm. "The Harkonnens had rich tastes."

Duncan spoke quietly: "Lucilla, if you touch me again

without my permission, I will *try* to kill you. I will try so hard that you very likely will have to kill me."

She recoiled.

He stared into her eyes. "I am not some damned stud for the witches!"

"Is that what you think we want of you?"

"Nobody has said what you want of me but your actions are obvious!"

He stood poised on the balls of his feet. The unawakened thing within him stirred and sent his pulse racing.

Lucilla studied him carefully. *Damn that Miles Teg!* She had not expected resistance to take this form. There was no doubting Duncan's sincerity. Words by themselves no longer would serve. He was immune to Voice. *Truth.*

It was the only weapon left to her.

"Duncan, I do not know precisely what it is Taraza expects you to do on Rakis. I can guess but my guess may be wrong."

"Guess, then."

"There is a young girl on Rakis, barely into her teens. Her name is Sheeana. The worms of Rakis obey her. Somehow, the Sisterhood must gather this talent into its own store of abilities."

"What could I possibly . . ."

"If I knew, I certainly would tell you now."

He heard her sincerity unmasked by her desperation.

"What does your *talent* have to do with this?" he demanded.

"Only Taraza and her councillors know."

"They want some hold on me, something from which I cannot escape!"

Lucilla already had arrived at this deduction but she had not expected him to see it that quickly. Duncan's youthful face concealed a mind that worked in ways she had not yet fathomed. Lucilla's thoughts raced.

"Control the worms and you could revive the old religion." It was Teg's voice from the doorway behind Lucilla.

I did not hear him arrive!

She whirled. Teg stood there with one of the antique Harkonnen lasguns held casually across his left arm, its muzzle directed at her.

"This is to insure that you listen to me," he said.

"How long have you been there listening?"

Her angry glare did not change his expression.

"From the moment you admitted you don't know what Taraza expects of Duncan," Teg said. "Nor do I. But I can make a few Mentat projections—nothing firm yet but all of them suggestive. Tell me if I am wrong."

"About what?"

He glanced at Duncan. "One of the things you were told to do was to make him irresistible to most women."

Lucilla tried to conceal her dismay. Taraza had warned her to conceal this from Teg as long as possible. She saw that concealment no longer was possible. Teg had read her reaction with those damnable abilities imparted to him by his damnable mother!

"A great deal of energy is being gathered and aimed at Rakis," Teg said. He looked steadily at Duncan. "No matter what the Tleilaxu have buried in him, he has the stamp of ancient humankind in his genes. Is that what the Breeding Mistresses need?"

"A damned Bene Gesserit stud!" Duncan said.

"What do you intend to do with that weapon?" Lucilla asked. She nodded at the antique lasgun in Teg's hands.

"This? I didn't even put a charge cartridge in it." He lowered the lasgun and leaned it into a corner beside him.

"Miles Teg, you will be punished!" Lucilla grated.

"That will have to wait," he said. "It's almost night outside. I've been out there under the life-shield. Burzmali has been here. He has left his sign to tell me he read the message I scratched with those animal marks on the trees."

A glittering alertness came into Duncan's eyes.

"What will you do?" Lucilla asked.

"I have left new marks arranging a rendezvous. Right now, we are all going up to the library. We are going to study the maps. We will commit them to memory. At the very least, we should know where we are when we run."

She gave him the benefit of a curt nod.

Duncan noted her movement with only part of his awareness. His mind already had leaped ahead to the ancient equipment in the Harkonnen library. He had been the one to show both Lucilla and Teg how to use it correctly, calling up an ancient map of Giedi Prime dating from the time when the no-globe had been built.

With Duncan's pre-ghola memory as guide and his own more modern knowledge of the planet, Teg had tried to bring the map up to date.

"Forest Guard Station" became "Bene Gesserit Keep."

"Part of it was a Harkonnen hunting lodge," Duncan had said. "They hunted human game raised and conditioned specifically for that purpose."

Towns vanished under Teg's updating. Some cities

remained but received new labels. "Ysai," the nearest metropolis, had been marked "Barony" on the original map.

Duncan's eyes went hard in memory. "That's where they tortured me."

When Teg exhausted his memory of the planet, much was marked *unknown* but there were frequent curly-ended Bene Gesserit symbols to identify the places where Taraza's people had told Teg he might find temporary sanctuary.

Those were the places Teg wanted committed to memory.

As he turned to lead them up to the library, Teg said: "I will erase the map when we have learned it. There's no telling who might find this place and study it."

Lucilla swept past him. "It's on your head, Miles!" she said.

Teg called after her retreating back: "A Mentat tells you that I did what was required of me."

She spoke without turning: "How logical!"

This room reconstructs a bit of the desert of Dune. The sandcrawler directly in front of you dates from the Atreides times. Grouped around it, moving clockwise from your left, are a small harvester, a carryall, a primitive spice factory and the other support equipment. All are explained at each station. Note the illuminated quotation above the display: "FOR THEY SHALL SUCK OF THE ABUNDANCE OF THE SEAS AND OF THE TREASURE IN THE SAND." This ancient religious quotation was oft repeated by the famous Gurney Halleck.

—GUIDE ANNOUNCEMENT, MUSEUM OF DAR-ES-BALAT

The worm did not slow its relentless progress until just before dusk. By then, Odrade had played out her questions and still had no answers. How did Sheeana control the worms? Sheeana said she was not steering her *Shaitan* in this direction. What was this hidden language to which the desert monster responded? Odrade knew that her Sister-guardians up there in the 'thopters that paced them would be exhausting the same questions plus one more.

Why did Odrade let this ride continue?

They might even hazard a few guesses: *She does not call us in because that might disturb the beast. She does not trust us to pluck her party from its back.*

The truth was far simpler: curiosity.

The hissing passage of the worm could have been a surging vessel breasting seas. The dry flinty odors of overheated sand, swept across them by a following wind, said otherwise. Only open desert stretched around them now, kilometer after kilometer of whaleback dunes as regular in their spacing as ocean waves.

Waff had been silent for a long period. He crouched in a miniature reproduction of Odrade's position, his attention directed ahead, a blank expression on his face. His most recent statement:

"God guard the faithful in the hour of our trial!"

Odrade thought of him as living proof that a strong enough fanaticism could endure for ages. Zensunni and the old Sufi survived in the Tleilaxu. It was like a deadly microbe that had lain dormant all of those millennia, waiting for the right host to feed its virulence.

What will happen to the thing I planted in the Rakian priesthood? she wondered. Saint Sheeana was a certainty.

Sheeana sat on a ring of her Shaitan, her robe pulled up to expose her thin shanks. She gripped the ring with both hands between her legs.

She had said that her first worm ride went directly to the city of Keen. Why there? Had the worm simply been taking her to her own kind?

This one beneath them now certainly had a different goal. Sheeana no longer questioned but then Odrade had ordered her to remain silent and practice the low trance. That, at least, would assure that every last detail of this experience could be recalled easily from her memory. If there were a hidden language between Sheeana and worm, they would find it later.

Odrade peered at the horizon. The remnant base of the ancient wall around the Sareer was only a few kilometers ahead. Long shadows from it lay across the dunes, telling Odrade that the remnant was higher than she had originally suspected. It was a shattered and broken outline now, with great boulders strewn along its base. The notch where the Tyrant had tumbled from his bridge into the Idaho River lay well to their right, at least three kilometers off their path. No river flowed there now.

Waff stirred beside her. "I heed Thy call, God," he said. "It is Waff of the Entio who prays in Thy Holy Place."

Odrade swiveled her gaze toward him without moving her head. *Entio?* Her Other Memories knew an Entio, a tribal leader in the great Zensunni Wandering, long before Dune. What was this? What ancient memories did these Tleilaxu keep alive?

Sheeana broke her silence. "Shaitan is slowing."

The remains of the ancient wall blocked their way. It loomed at least fifty meters over the highest dunes. The worm turned slightly to the right and moved between two giant boulders that towered above them. It came to a stop. The long ridged back lay parallel to a mostly intact section of the wall's base.

Sheeana stood and looked at the barrier.

"What is this place?" Waff asked. He raised his voice above the sound of the 'thopters circling overhead.

Odrade released her tiring grip and flexed her fingers. She continued to kneel while she studied their surroundings. Shadows from the tumbled boulders drew hard lines on sand spills and smaller rocks. Seen close up, not twenty meters away, the wall revealed cracks and fissures, dark openings into the ancient foundation.

Waff stood and massaged his hands.

"Why have we been brought here?" he asked. His voice was faintly plaintive.

The worm twitched.

"Shaitan wants us to get off," Sheeana said.

How does she know? Odrade wondered. The worm's movement had not been enough to make any of them stumble. It could have been some private reflex after the long journey.

But Sheeana faced the ancient wall's foundation, sat down on the curve of the worm and slid off. She dropped in a crouch on soft sand.

Odrade and Waff moved forward and watched with fascination as Sheeana slogged through the sand to the front of the creature. There, Sheeana placed both hands on her hips and faced the gaping mouth. Hidden flames played orange light across the young face.

"Shaitan, why are we here?" Sheeana demanded.

Again, the worm twitched.

"He wants all of you off him," Sheeana called.

Waff looked at Odrade. "If God wishes thee to die, He causes thy steps to lead thee to the place of thy death."

Odrade gave him back a paraphrase from the cant of the Shariat: "Obey God's messenger in all things."

Waff sighed. Doubt was plain on his face. But he turned and was first off the worm, dropping just ahead of Odrade. They followed Sheeana's example, moving to the front of the creature. Odrade, every sense alert, fixed her gaze on Sheeana.

It was much hotter in front of the gaping mouth. The familiar bite of melange filled the air around them.

"We are here, God," Waff said.

Odrade, getting more than a little tired of his religious awe, spared a glance for their surroundings—the shattered rocks, the eroded barrier reaching into the dusky sky, sand sloping against the time-scarred stones, and the slow scorching huff-huff of the worm's internal fires.

But where is here? Odrade wondered. *What is special about this place to make it the worm's destination?*

Four of the watching 'thopters passed in line overhead. The sound of their wing fans and the hissing jets momentarily drowned out the worm's background rumblings.

Shall I call them down? Odrade wondered. It would take only a hand signal. Instead, she lifted two hands in the signal for the watchers to remain aloft.

Evening's chill was on the sand now. Odrade shivered and adjusted her metabolism to the new demands. She felt confident that the worm would not engulf them with Sheeana beside them.

Sheeana turned her back on the worm. "He wants us to be here," she said.

As though her words were a command, the worm twisted its head away from them and slid off through the tall scattering of giant boulders. They could hear it speeding away back into the desert.

Odrade faced the base of the ancient wall. Darkness would be upon them soon but enough light remained in the high desert's long dusk that they might yet see some explanation of why the creature had brought them here. A tall fissure in the rock wall to her right seemed as good a place to investigate as any. Keeping part of her attention on the sounds from Waff, Odrade climbed a sandy incline toward the dark opening. Sheeana kept pace with her.

"Why are we here, Mother?"

Odrade shook her head. She heard Waff following.

The fissure directly in front of her was a shadowy hole into darkness. Odrade stopped and held Sheeana beside her. She judged the opening to be about a meter wide and some four times that in height. The rocky sides were curiously smooth, as though polished by human hands. Sand had drifted into the opening. Light from the setting sun reflected off the sand to bathe one side of the opening in a wash of gold.

Waff spoke from behind them: "What is this place?"

"There are many old caves," Sheeana said. "Fremen hid their spice in caves." She inhaled deeply through her nose. "Do you smell it, Mother?"

There was a definite melange odor to the place, Odrade agreed.

Waff moved past Odrade and into the fissure. He turned there, looking up at the walls where they met in a sharp angle above him. Facing Odrade and Sheeana, he backed farther into the opening, his attention on the walls. Odrade and Sheeana stepped closer to him. With an abrupt hissing of spilled sand, Waff vanished from their sight. In the same instant, the sand all around Odrade and Sheeana slipped forward into the fissure, dragging both of them with it. Odrade grabbed Sheeana's hand.

"Mother!" Sheeana cried.

The sound echoed from invisible rock walls as they slid down a long slope of spilling sand into concealing darkness. The sand drifted them to a stop in a final wash of gentle movement. Odrade, in sand up to her knees, extricated herself and pulled Sheeana with her onto a hard surface.

Sheeana started to speak but Odrade said: "Hush! Listen!"

There was a grating disturbance off to the left.

"Waff?"

"I'm in it up to my waist." There was terror in his voice.

Odrade spoke dryly. "God must want it that way. Pull yourself out gently. It feels like rock under our feet. Gently now! We don't need another avalanche."

As her eyes adjusted, Odrade looked up the sand slope down which they had tumbled. The opening where they had entered this place was a distant slit of dusky gold far away above them.

"Mother," Sheeana whispered. "I'm scared."

"Say the Litany Against Fear," Odrade ordered. "And be still. Our friends know we are here. They will help us get out."

"God has brought us to this place," Waff said.

Odrade did not respond. In the silence, she pursed her lips and gave a high-pitched whistle, listening for the echoes. Her ears told her they were in a large space with some sort of low obstruction behind them. She turned her back on the narrow fissure and gave another whistle.

The low barrier lay about a hundred meters away.

Odrade freed her hand from Sheeana's. "Stay right here, please. Waff?"

"I hear the 'thopters," he said.

"We all hear them," Odrade said. "They are landing.

We will have help presently. Meanwhile, please stay where you are and remain silent. I need the silence."

Whistling and listening for the echoes, placing each foot carefully, Odrade worked her way deeper into the darkness. An outstretched hand encountered a rough rock surface. She felt along it. Only about waist high. She could feel nothing beyond it. The echoes of her whistles said it was a smaller space there and partly enclosed.

A voice called from high behind her. "Reverend Mother! Are you there?"

Odrade turned, cupped her hands around her mouth and shouted: "Stay back! We've been spilled into a deep cave. Bring a light and a long rope."

A tiny dark figure moved back out of the distant opening. The light up there was growing dimmer. She lowered her cupped hands and spoke into the darkness.

"Sheeana? Waff? Come toward me about ten paces and wait there."

"Where are we, Mother?" Sheeana asked.

"Patience, child."

A low, muttering sound came from Waff. Odrade recognized the ancient words of the Islamiyat. He was praying. Waff had dropped all attempts to conceal his origins from her. Good. The believer was a receptacle for her to feed with the sweets of the Missionaria Protectiva.

Meanwhile, the possibilities of this place where the worm had brought them excited Odrade. Guided by one hand on the rock barrier, she explored along it to her left. The top was quite smooth in places. All of it sloped inward away from her. Other Memories offered a sudden projection:

Catchbasin!

This was a Fremen water storage basin. Odrade inhaled deeply, testing for moisture. The air was flint dry.

A bright light from the fissure stabbed downward, driving away the darkness. A voice called from the opening and Odrade recognized it as one of her Sisters.

"We can see you!"

Odrade stepped back from the low barrier and turned, peering all around. Waff and Sheeana stood about sixty meters away staring at their surroundings. The chamber was roughly circular, some two hundred meters in diameter. A rock dome arched high overhead. She examined the low barrier beside her: yes, a Fremen catchbasin. She could discern the small rock island in its center where a captive worm could be kept ready to spill into the water. Other Memories replayed that agonized, twisting death which produced the spice poison to ignite a Fremen orgy.

A low arch framed more darkness on the far side of the basin. She could see the spillway there where water had been brought down from a windtrap. There would be more catchbasins back there, an entire complex of them designed to hold a wealth of moisture for an ancient tribe. She knew the name of this place now.

"Sietch Tabr," Odrade whispered.

The words ignited a flood of useful memories. This had been Stilgar's place in the time of Muad'Dib. *Why did that worm bring us to Sietch Tabr?*

A worm took Sheeana to the City of Keen. That others might know of her? Then what was there to know here? Were there people back there in that darkness? Odrade sensed no indications of life in that direction.

Her Sister at the opening interrupted these thoughts. "We've had to ask for the rope to be brought from

Dar-es-Balat! The people at the museum say this is probably Sietch Tabr! They thought it had been destroyed!"

"Send down a light so I can explore it," Odrade called.

"The priests ask that we leave it undisturbed!"

"Send me a light!" Odrade insisted.

Presently, a dark object tumbled down the sandslope
in a small spill of sand. Odrade sent Sheeana scampering
for it. A touch on the switch and a bright beam went
lancing at the dark archway beyond the catchbasin. *Yes,
more basins there.* And beside this basin, a narrow stairway cut into the rock. The steps led upward, turning and
removing themselves from her view.

Odrade bent and whispered in Sheeana's ear. "Watch
Waff carefully. If he moves after us, call out."

"Yes, Mother. Where are we going?"

"I must look at this place. I am the one who has been
brought here for a purpose." She raised her voice and
addressed Waff: "Waff, please wait there for the rope."

"What have you been whispering?" he demanded.
"Why must I wait? What are you doing?"

"I have been praying," Odrade said. "Now, I must
continue this pilgrimage alone."

"Why alone?"

In the old language of the Islamiyat, she said: "It is
written."

That stopped him!

Odrade led the way at a fast walk toward the rock
stairs.

Sheeana, hurrying along beside Odrade, said: "We
must tell people about this place. The old Fremen caves
are safe from Shaitan."

"Be still, child," Odrade said. She aimed the light up

into the stairway. It curved through the rock, angling sharply to the right up there. Odrade hesitated. The warning sense of danger she had felt at the beginning of this venture came back intensified. It was an almost palpable thing within her.

What is up there?

"Wait here, Sheeana," Odrade said. "Don't let Waff follow me."

"How can I stop him?" Sheeana glanced fearfully back across the chamber where Waff stood.

"Tell him it is God's will that he remain. Say it this way . . ." Odrade bent close to Sheeana and repeated the words in Waff's ancient language, then: "Say nothing else. Stand in his way and repeat it if he tries to pass."

Sheeana mouthed the new words quietly. She had them, Odrade saw. The girl was quick.

"He's afraid of you," Odrade said. "He won't try to harm you."

"Yes, Mother." Sheeana turned, folded her arms across her breast and looked across the chamber at Waff.

Aiming the light ahead of her, Odrade went up the rock stairs. *Sietch Tabr! What surprise have you left for us here, old worm?*

In a long low hallway at the top of the stairs, Odrade came on the first desert-mummified bodies. There were five of them, two men and three women, no identifying marks or clothing on them. They had been completely stripped and left for the desert's dryness to preserve. Dehydration had pulled skin and flesh tightly around the bones. The bodies were propped in a row, their feet extended across the passage. Odrade was forced to step over each of these macabre obstructions.

She passed her handlight across each body as she went. They had been stabbed almost identically. A slashing blade had been thrust upward just below the arch of the sternum.

Ritual killings?

Dryly puckered flesh had been withdrawn from the wounds, leaving a dark spot to mark them. These bodies were not from Fremen times, Odrade knew. Fremen death stills made ashes of all flesh to recover a body's water.

Odrade probed ahead with her light and paused to consider her position. Discovery of the bodies intensified her sense of peril. *I should have brought a weapon.* But that would have aroused Waff's suspicions.

The persistence of that inner warning could not be evaded. This relic of Sietch Tabr was perilous.

The beam of her light revealed another stairway at the end of this hall. Cautiously, Odrade moved forward. At the first step, she sent the beam of her light probing upward. Shallow steps. Only a little way up, more rock—a wider space up there. Odrade turned and sent the light stabbing around this hallway. Chips and burn marks scarred the rock walls. Once more, she looked up the stairway.

What is up there?

The sense of danger was intense.

One slow step at a time, pausing often, Odrade climbed. She emerged into a larger passage hewn through the native rock. More bodies greeted her. These had been abandoned in the disarray of their final moments. Again, she saw only mummified flesh stripped of clothing. They lay scattered along this wider passage--twenty of them. She wove her way around them. Some had been stabbed in the same way as the five on the lower level. Some had been slashed and hacked and burned by lasgun beams. One had been beheaded and the skin-masked skull lay against a wall of the passage like a ball abandoned from some terrible game.

This new passage led straight ahead past openings into small chambers on both sides. She saw nothing of value in the small chambers where she sent her probing light: a few scattered strands of spice fiber, small spills of melted rock, melt bubbles occasionally on floors, walls, and ceilings.

What violence was this?

Suggestive stains could be seen on some of the chamber floors. Spilled blood? One chamber had a tiny mound of brown cloth in a corner. Scraps of torn fabric scattered under Odrade's foot.

There was dust. Dust everywhere. Her feet stirred it up in passing.

The passage ended at an archway that gave onto a deep ledge. She sent her light beyond the ledge: an enormous chamber, far larger than the one down below. Its curved ceiling went so high she knew it must extend into the rock base of the great wall. Wide, shallow steps led down from the ledge onto the chamber floor. Hesitantly, Odrade went down the steps and out onto the floor. She sent her light sweeping all around. Other passages led out of the great chamber. Some, she saw, had been blocked by stone and the stones torn away to be left scattered on the ledge and on this great floor.

Odrade sniffed the air. Carried on the dust stirred up by her feet there was a definite smell of melange. The smell wove through her sense of peril. She wanted to leave, hurry back to the others. But the danger was a beacon. She had to learn where that beacon led.

She knew where she was now, though. This was the great gathering chamber of Sietch Tabr, site of countless Fremen spice orgies and tribal convocations. Here, the Naib Stilgar had presided. Gurney Halleck had been here. The Lady Jessica. Paul Muad'Dib. Chani, mother of Ghanima. Here, Muad'Dib trained his fighters. The original Duncan Idaho was here . . . and the first Idaho ghola!

Why have we been brought here? What is the danger?

It was here, right here! She could feel it.

In this place, the Tyrant had concealed a spice hoard. Bene Gesserit records said the hoard had filled this entire chamber to the ceiling and into many of the surrounding passages as well.

Odrade pivoted, her gaze following the path of her light. Over there was the ledge of the Naibs. And there, the deeper Royal Ledge Muad'Dib had commissioned.

And there is the archway where I entered.

She sent her light along the floor, noting places where searchers had chipped and burned the rock seeking more of the Tyrant's fabulous hoard. Fish Speakers had taken most of that melange, its hiding place revealed by the Idaho ghola who had been consort of the famed Siona. The records said subsequent searchers had found more caches hidden behind false walls and floors. There were many authenticated accounts and the verifications of Other Memories. The Famine Times had seen violence here when desperate searchers won through to this place. That might explain the bodies. Many had fought just for the chance to search Sietch Tabr.

As she had been taught, Odrade tried to use her sense of danger as a guide. Did the miasma of past violence cling to these stones after all of those millennia? That was not her warning. Her warning was something immediate. Odrade's left foot encountered an uneven place on the floor. Her light picked out a dark line in the dust. She scattered the dust with a foot, revealing a letter and then an entire word burned in a flowing script.

Odrade read the word silently and then aloud.

"Arafel."

She knew this word. Reverend Mothers of the Tyrant's time had impressed it into the Bene Gesserit consciousness, tracing its roots out to the most ancient sources.

"Arafel: the cloud darkness at the end of the universe."

Odrade felt the gasping accumulation of her warning sense. It focused on that single word.

"The Tyrant's holy judgment," the priests called that word. "The cloud darkness of holy judgment!"

She moved out along the word, staring down at it, noting the curling at the end that trailed off into a small arrow. She looked where the arrow pointed. Someone else had seen the arrow and had cut into the ledge where it pointed. Odrade crossed to where the searcher's burner had left a darker pool of melted rock on the chamber floor. Streams of melted stone ran out in fingers away from the ledge, each finger trailing from a deep hole burned into the rock of the ledge.

Bending, Odrade peered into each hole with her light: Nothing. She sensed the treasure hunter's excitement riding on her warning-fear. The extent of the wealth this chamber had once held staggered imagination. In the worst of the old times, a hand-carried luggage case could hold enough spice to buy a planet. And the Fish Speakers had squandered this hoard, losing it in squabbles and shattering misjudgments and ordinary foolishness too picayune for history to record. They had been glad to accept Ixian alliance when the Tleilaxu broke the melange monopoly.

Did the searchers find it all? The Tyrant was superbly clever.

Arafel.

At the end of the universe.

Had he sent a message down the eons to the Bene Gesserit of today?

She cast the beam of her light once more around the chamber and then upward.

The ceiling described an almost perfect half globe overhead. It had been intended, she knew, as a model of the night sky seen from the entrance to Sietch Tabr. But even by the time of Liet Kynes, the first planetologist here, the original stars painted on that ceiling had been gone, lost in the tiny rock chippings of small quakes and the everyday abrasions of life.

Odrade's breath quickened. The sense of peril had never been greater. The danger beacon shone within her! Quickly, she trotted directly across to the steps where she had descended to this floor. Turning there, she cast backward in her mind for Other Memories to limn this place. They came slowly, forcing past that heart-pounding sense of doom. Pointing the beam of her light upward and peering along it, Odrade placed those ancient memories over the scene in front of her.

Bits of reflected brilliance!

Other Memories positioned them: indicators of the stars in a long-gone sky and right there! The silvery-yellow half circle of the Arrakeen sun. She knew it for a sunset sign.

The Fremen day starts at night.

Arafel!

Keeping her light on that sunset marker, she mounted the steps backward and went around the chamber on the ledge to the exact position she had seen in Other Memories.

Nothing remained of that ancient sun arc.

Searchers had chipped at the wall where it had been. Stone bubbles glistened where a burner had been passed along the wall. No breaks entered the original rock.

By the tightness in her chest, Odrade knew she teetered on the edge of a dangerous discovery. The beacon had led her here!

Arafel . . . at the edge of the universe. Beyond the setting sun!

She swept her light right and left. Another passage entrance opened on her left. Stones that had blocked it lay scattered on the ledge. Her heart pounding, Odrade slipped through the opening and found a short hall plugged with melted stone at the end. On her right, directly behind where the sunset marker had been, she found a small room thick with the smell of melange. Odrade entered the room and saw more signs of chipping and burning on walls and ceiling. The danger sense was oppressive here. She chanted the Litany Against Fear silently while she swept the beam of her light over the room. The place was almost square, about two meters on a side. The ceiling was less than half a meter above her head. Cinnamon pulsed in her nostrils. She sneezed and, blinking, saw a tiny discoloration on the floor beside the threshold.

More marks of that ancient search?

Bending close with her light held at a sharp angle on one side, she saw that she had glimpsed only the shadow of something etched deeply into the rock. Dust concealed most of it. She knelt and brushed the dust aside. Very thin etching and very deep. Whatever this was, it had been meant to endure. The last message of a lost Reverend Mother? This was a known Bene Gesserit artifice. She pressed sensitive fingertips against the etching and reconstructed its tracery in her mind.

Recognition leaped into her awareness: one word—inscribed in ancient Chakobsa, "Here."

This was no ordinary "here" to mark an ordinary place but the accented and emphatic "here" that said: "You have found me!" Her hammering heart emphasized it.

Odrade rested her handlight on the floor near her right knee and let her fingers explore the threshold beside that ancient summons. The stonework appeared unbroken to the eye but her fingers detected a tiny discontinuity. She pressed the discontinuity, twisted, turned, changed the angle of pressure several times and repeated her effort.

Nothing.

Sitting back on her heels, Odrade studied the situation. "Here."

The warning sense had grown even more acute. She could feel it as a pressure on her breathing.

Withdrawing slightly, she pulled her light back and lay full length on the floor to stare narrowly along the base of the threshold. *Here!* Could she place a tool there beside that word and lever the threshold? No . . . a tool was not indicated. This thing had the smell of the Tyrant, not of a Reverend Mother. She tried to push the threshold sideways. Nothing moved.

Feeling the tensions and danger sense accentuated by frustration, Odrade stood and kicked at the threshold beside the etched word. It moved! Something grated roughly against sand over her head.

Odrade dodged backward as sand cascaded onto the floor in front of her. A deep rumbling sound filled the tiny chamber. The stones shook under her feet. The floor tipped downward in front of her toward the doorway, opening a space under the door and its wall.

Once more, Odrade found herself precipitated forward and down into an unknown. Her light tumbled with her, its beam rolling over and over. She saw mounds of dark reddish brown in front of her. Cinnamon filled her nostrils.

She fell beside her light onto a soft mounding of melange. The opening through which she had fallen lay out of reach some five meters overhead. She grabbed up her light. Its beam picked out wide stone steps cut into the rock beside the opening. Something written on the risers but she saw only that there was a way out. Her first panic subsided, but the sense of danger left her almost breathless, forcing the movements of her chest muscles.

Left and right she sent the beam of her light into this place where she had fallen. It was a long room directly beneath the passage she had taken from the great chamber. The entire length of it was piled with melange!

Odrade probed upward with her light and saw why no searcher tapping on that passage floor overhead had detected this chamber. Criss-crossed rock bracings transferred all strain deep into the stone walls. Anyone tapping overhead would get back the sounds of solid rock.

Once more, Odrade looked at the melange around her. Even at today's tank-deflated prices, she knew she was standing on a treasure. This hoard would measure many long tons.

Is that the danger?

The warning sense within her remained just as acute as ever. The Tyrant's melange was not what she should fear. The triumvirate would make an equitable distribution of this lot and that would be the end of it. A bonus in the ghola project.

Another danger remained. She could not avoid the warning.

Again, she sent the light beam along the mounded melange. Her attention was drawn to the strip of wall above the spice. More words! Still in Chakobsa, written with a cutter in a fine flowing script, there was another message:

"A REVEREND MOTHER WILL READ MY WORDS!"

Something cold settled in Odrade's guts. She moved to her right with the light, plowing through an empire's ransom in melange. There was more to the message:

"I BEQUEATH TO YOU MY FEAR AND LONE-LINESS. TO YOU I GIVE THE CERTAINTY THAT THE BODY AND SOUL OF THE BENE GESSERIT WILL MEET THE SAME FATE AS ALL OTHER BODIES AND ALL OTHER SOULS."

Another paragraph of the message beckoned to the right of this one. She plowed through the cloying melange and stopped to read.

"WHAT IS SURVIVAL IF YOU DO NOT SUR-
VIVE WHOLE? ASK THE BENE TLEILAX THAT!
WHAT IF YOU NO LONGER HEAR THE MUSIC
OF LIFE? MEMORIES ARE NOT ENOUGH UN-
LESS THEY CALL YOU TO NOBLE PURPOSE!"

There was more of it on the narrow end wall of the
long chamber. Odrade stumbled through the melange
and knelt to read:

"WHY DID YOUR SISTERHOOD NOT BUILD
THE GOLDEN PATH? YOU KNEW THE NECES-
SITY. YOUR FAILURE CONDEMNED ME, THE
GOD EMPEROR, TO MILLENNIA OF PERSONAL
DESPAIR."

The words "God Emperor" were not in Chakobsa but
in the language of the Islamiyat, where they conveyed an
explicit second meaning to any speaker of that tongue:

"Your God and Your Emperor because you made
me so."

Odrade smiled grimly. *That* would drive Waff into a
religious frenzy! The higher he went, the easier to shatter
his security.

She did not doubt the accuracy of the Tyrant's accusation, nor the potential in his prediction that the Sisterhood could end. The sense of danger had led her to this
place unerringly. Something more had been at work, too.
The worms of Rakis still moved to the Tyrant's ancient
beat. He might slumber in his endless dream but monstrous life, a pearl in each worm to remind it, carried on
as the Tyrant had predicted.

What was it he had told the Sisterhood in his own
time? She recalled his words:

"When I am gone, they must call me Shaitan,

Emperor of Gehenna. The wheel must turn and turn along the Golden Path."

Yes—that was what Taraza had meant. *"But don't you see? The common people of Rakis have been calling him Shaitan for more than a thousand years!"*

So Taraza had known this thing. Without ever seeing these words, she had known.

I see your design, Taraza. And now I know the burden of fear you have carried all these years. I can feel it every bit as deeply as you do.

Odrade knew then that this warning sense would not leave until she ended, or the Sisterhood vanished from existence, or the peril was resolved.

Odrade lifted her light, got to her feet and slogged through the melange to the wide steps out of this place. At the steps, she recoiled. More of the Tyrant's words had been cut into each riser. Trembling, she read them as they moved upward to the opening.

"MY WORDS ARE YOUR PAST,

"MY QUESTIONS ARE SIMPLE:

"WITH WHOM DO YOU ALLY?

"WITH THE SELF IDOLATORS OF TLEILAX?

"WITH MY FISH SPEAKER BUREAUCRACY?

"WITH THE COSMOS-WANDERING GUILD?

"WITH HARKONNEN BLOOD SACRIFICERS?

"WITH A DOGMATIC SINK OF YOUR OWN CREATION?

"HOW WILL YOU MEET YOUR END?

"AS NO MORE THAN A SECRET SOCIETY?"

Odrade climbed past the questions, reading them a second time as she went. *Noble purpose?* What a fragile thing that always was. And how easily distorted. But the power

was there immersed in constant peril. It was all spelled out
on the walls and stairs of that chamber. Taraza knew without having it explained. The Tyrant's meaning was clear:

"Join me!"

As she emerged into the small room, finding a narrow
ledge along which she could swing herself to the door,
Odrade looked down at the treasure she had found. She
shook her head in wonder at Taraza's wisdom. So that
was how the Sisterhood might end. Taraza's design was
clear, all the pieces in place. Nothing certain. Wealth and
power, it was all the same in the end. The noble design
had been started and it must be completed even if that
meant the death of the Sisterhood.

What poor tools we have chosen!

That girl waiting back there in the deep chamber below the desert, that girl and the ghola being prepared on
Rakis.

*I speak your language now, old worm. It has no words
but I know the heart of it.*

Our fathers ate manna in the desert,
In the burning place where whirlwinds came.
Lord, save us from that horrible land!
Save us, oh-h-h-h-h save us
From that dry and thirsty land.

—SONGS OF GURNEY HALLECK, MUSEUM OF DAR-ES BALAT

Teg and Duncan, both heavily armed, emerged from the no-globe with Lucilla into the coldest part of the night. The stars were like needlepoints overhead, the air absolutely still until they disturbed it.

The dominant smell in Teg's nostrils was the brittle mustiness of snow. The odor infused every breath and when they exhaled, fat clouds of vapor puffed around their faces.

Tears of cold started in Duncan's eyes. He had been thinking much of old Gurney as they prepared to leave the no-globe, Gurney with his cheek scarred by a Harkonnen inkvine whip. Trusted companions would be needed now, Duncan thought. He did not trust Lucilla much and Teg was old, old. Duncan could see Teg's eyes glinting in the starlight.

Slinging a heavy antique lasgun over his left shoulder, Duncan thrust his hands deep into his pockets for warmth. He had forgotten how cold this planet could get. Lucilla seemed impervious to it, obviously drawing warmth from one of her Bene Gesserit tricks.

Looking at her, Duncan realized he had never trusted the witches much, not even the Lady Jessica. It was easy to think of them as traitors, devoid of any loyalty except to their own Sisterhood. They had so damned *many* secret tricks! Lucilla had given up her seductive ways, though. She knew he meant what he had said. He could feel her anger simmering. *Let her simmer!*

Teg stood quite still, his attention focused outward, listening. Was it right to trust the single plan he and Burzmali had worked out? They had no backup. Was it only eight days ago they had settled on it? It felt longer despite the press of preparations. He glanced at Duncan and Lucilla. Duncan carried a heavy old Harkonnen lasgun, the long field model. Even the extra charge cartridges were heavy. Lucilla had refused to carry more than a single tiny lasgun in her bodice. One small burst was all it held. An assassin's toy.

"We of the Sisterhood are noted for going into battle with only our skills as weapons," she said. "It diminishes us to change that pattern."

She had knives in her leg sheaths, though. Teg had seen them. Poison on them, too, he suspected.

Teg hefted the long weapon in his own hands: a modern field-style lasgun he had brought from the Keep. Over his shoulder, a mate to Duncan's weapon hung from its sling.

I must rely on Burzmali, Teg told himself. *I trained him; I know his qualities. If he says we trust these new allies, we trust them.*

Burzmali had been obviously overjoyed to find his old commander alive and safe.

But it had snowed since their last encounter and the

snow lay all around them, a tabula rasa upon which all tracks would be written. They had not counted on snow. Were there traitors in Weather Management?

Teg shivered. The air was cold. It felt like the chill of off-planet space, empty and giving starlight free access to the forest glade around them. The thin light reflected cleanly off the snow-covered ground and the white dusting on the rocks. Dark outlines of conifers and the leafless branches of deciduous trees displayed only their whitely diffused edges. All else was deepest shadow.

Lucilla blew on her fingers and leaned close to Teg to whisper "Shouldn't he be here by now?"

He knew that was not her real question. *"Can Burzmali be trusted?"* That was her question. She had been asking it one way and another ever since Teg had explained the plan to her eight days ago.

All he could say was: "I have staked my life on it."

"Our lives, too!"

Teg too disliked the accumulated uncertainties, but all plans relied ultimately on the skills of those who executed them.

"You're the one who insisted we must get out of there and go on to Rakis," he reminded her. He hoped she could see his smile, a gesture to take the sting out of his words.

Lucilla was not placated. Teg had never seen a Reverend Mother this obviously nervous. She would be even more nervous if she knew of their new allies! Of course, there was the fact that she had failed to carry out her full assignment from Taraza. How that must gall her!

"We took an oath to protect the ghola," she reminded him.

"Burzmali has taken that same oath."

Teg glanced at Duncan standing silently between them. Duncan gave no sign that he heard the argument or shared the nervousness. An ancient composure held his features motionless. He was listening to the night, Teg realized, doing what all three of them should be doing just now. There was an odd look of ageless maturity on his young features.

If ever I needed trusted companions, it's now! Duncan thought. His mind had gone questing backward into the Giedi Prime days of his pre-ghola roots. This was what they had called "a Harkonnen night." Safe within the warm shielding of their suspensor-buoyed armor, the Harkonnens had enjoyed hunting their subjects on such nights. A wounded fugitive could die of the cold. *The Harkonnens knew! Damn their souls!*

Predictably, Lucilla caught Duncan's attention with a look that said: *"We have unfinished business, you and I."*

Duncan turned his face up into the starlight, making sure she could see his smile, an offensive and knowing look that caused Lucilla to stiffen inwardly. He slipped the heavy lasgun from his shoulder and checked it. She noted the ornate scrollwork on its stock and along the barrel. It was an antique but still it gave off a deadly sense of purpose. Duncan rested it over his left arm, right hand on the grip, finger on the trigger, exactly as Teg was carrying his own modern weapon.

Lucilla turned her back on her companions and sent her senses probing onto the hillside above them and below. Even as she moved, sound erupted all around. Globs of sound filled their night—a great burst of rumblings off to the right, then silence. Another burst from downslope. Silence. From upslope! On all sides!

At the first sound, all three of them crouched into the shelter of the rocks outside the no-globe's cave entrance.

The sounds filling their night carried little definition: intrusive racketing, partly mechanical, partly squeaks and wails and hisses. Intermittently, a subterranean drumming made the ground vibrate.

Teg knew these sounds. There was a battle going on out there. He could hear the background hissing of burners and, in the distant sky, the lancing beams of armored lasguns.

Something flashed overhead trailing blue and red sparks. Another and another! The earth trembled. Teg inhaled through his nose: burned acid and a suggestion of garlic.

No-ships! Many of them!

They were landing in the valley below the ancient no-globe.

"Back inside!" Teg ordered.

As he spoke, he saw it was too late. People were moving in from all around them. Teg lifted his long lasgun and aimed it downslope toward the loudest of the intrusive noises and the nearest detectable movement. Many people could be heard shouting down there. Free glowglobes moved among the screening trees, set loose by whoever came from there. The dancing lights drifted upslope on a cold breeze. Dark figures moved in the shifting illumination.

"Face Dancers!" Teg grunted, recognizing the attackers. Those drifting lights would be clear of the trees within seconds and on his position in less than a minute!

"We've been betrayed!" Lucilla said.

A great shout roared from the hill above them: "Bashar!" Many voices!

Burzmali? Teg asked himself. He glanced back in that direction and then down at the steadily advancing Face Dancers. No time to pick and choose. He leaned toward Lucilla. "That's Burzmali above us. Take Duncan and run!"

"But what if—"

"It's your only chance!"

"You fool!" she accused, even as she turned to obey.

Teg's "Yes!" did nothing to ease her fears. This was what came of depending on the plans of others!

Duncan had other thoughts. He understood what Teg was about to do—sacrifice himself that two might escape. Duncan hesitated, looking at the advancing attackers below them.

Seeing the hesitation, Teg blared at him: "This is a battle order! I am your commander!"

It was the closest thing to Voice Lucilla had ever heard from a man. She gaped at Teg.

Duncan saw only the face of the Old Duke telling him to obey. It was too much. He grabbed Lucilla's arm, but before hustling her up the slope, he said: "We'll lay down a covering fire once we're clear!"

Teg did not respond. He crouched against a snow-dusted rock as Lucilla and Duncan scrambled away. He knew he must sell himself dearly now. And there must be something else: *the unexpected*. A final signature from the old Bashar.

The advancing attackers were coming up faster, exchanging excited shouts.

Setting his lasgun on maxibeam, Teg pressed the trigger. A fiery arc swept across the slope below him. Trees burst into flame and crashed. People screamed. The weapon would not perform long at this discharge level but while it did the carnage produced its desired effect.

In the abrupt silence after that first sweep, Teg shifted his position to another screening rock on his left and again sent a flaming lance down the dark slope. Only a few of the drifting glowglobes had survived that first slashing violence with its falling trees and dismembered bodies.

More screams greeted his second counterattack. He turned and scrambled across the rocks to the other side of the no-globe's access cave. There, he sent sweeping fire down the opposite slope. More screams. More flames and crashing trees.

No answering fire came back.

They want us alive!

The Tleilaxu were prepared to spend whatever number of Face Dancer lives it required to run his lasgun out of its charges!

Teg shifted the sling of the old Harkonnen weapon to a better position on his shoulder, getting it ready to swing into action. He discarded the almost empty charge in his modern lasgun, recharged it and rested the weapon across the rocks. Teg doubted he would get the chance to recharge the second weapon. Let them think down there that he had run out of charge cartridges. But there were two Harkonnen handguns in his belt as a last resort. They would be potent at close range. Some of the

Tleilaxu Masters, the ones who ordered such carnage, let *them* come closer!

Cautiously, Teg lifted his long lasgun from the rock and moved backward, drifting up into the higher rocks, slipping left and then right. He paused twice to sweep the slopes below him with short bursts as though conserving the gun's charge. There was no sense in trying to conceal his movements. They would have a life-tracer on him by now and, besides, there were the tracks in the snow.

The unexpected! Could he suck them in close?

Well above the no-globe's access cave he found a deeper pocket in the rocks, its bottom filled with snow. Teg dropped into this position, admiring the fine field of fire this new vantage provided. He studied it briefly: protected behind him by higher crags and open downslope on three sides. He lifted his head cautiously and tried to see around the screening rocks upslope.

Only silence there.

Had that shout come from Burzmali's people? Even so, there was no guarantee that Duncan and Lucilla could escape in these circumstances. It depended on Burzmali now.

Is he as resourceful as I always thought?

There was no time to consider the possibilities or change a single element of the situation. Battle had been joined. He was committed. Teg drew a deep breath and peered downslope over the rocks.

Yes, they had recovered and were resuming the advance. Without telltale glowglobes this time and silently now. No more shouts of encouragement. Teg rested the long lasgun on a rock in front of him and swept a burning arc from left to right in one long burst, letting it fade out at the end in an obvious loss of charge.

Unslinging the old Harkonnen weapon, he readied it, waiting in silence. They would expect him to flee up the hill. He crouched behind the screening rocks, hoping there was enough movement above him to confuse the life-tracers. He still heard people below him on that fire-wracked slope. Teg counted silently to himself, spacing out the distance, knowing from long experience how much time the attackers would require to come within deadly range. And he listened carefully for another sound he knew from previous encounters with the Tleilaxu: the sharp barking of commands in high-pitched voices.

There they were!

The Masters were spread out farther downslope than he had anticipated. Fearful creatures! Teg set the old lasgun on maxibeam and lifted himself suddenly from his protective cradle in the rocks.

He saw the arc of advancing Face Dancers in the light of burning trees and brush. The high-pitched voices of command came from behind the advance, well out of the dancing orange light.

Aiming over the heads of the nearest attackers, Teg sighted beyond the jumble of flames and pressed the trigger: two long bursts, back and forth. He was momentarily surprised by the extent of the destructive energy in the antique weapon. The thing obviously was the product of superb craftsmanship but there had been no way to test it in the no-globe.

This time, the screams carried a different pitch: high and frantic!

Teg lowered his aim and cleared the immediate slope

of Face Dancers, letting them feel the full force of the beam, revealing that he carried more than one weapon. Back and forth he swept the deadly arc, giving the attackers plenty of time to see the charge ebb into a final sputter.

Now! They had been sucked in once and would be more cautious. There just might be a chance to join Duncan and Lucilla. This thought full in his mind, Teg turned and scrambled out of his shelter across the upslope rocks. At his fifth step, he thought he had run into a hot wall. There was time for his mind to recognize what had happened: the shocking blast of a stunner full into his face and chest! It came from directly upslope where he had sent Duncan and Lucilla. Chagrin filled Teg as he fell into darkness.

Others could do the unexpected, too!

All organized religions face a common problem, a ten
der spot through which we may enter and shift them to
our designs: How do they distinguish hubris from
revelation?

—MISSIONARIA PROTECTIVA, THE INNER TEACHINGS

Odrade kept her gaze carefully away from the cool
green of the quadrangle below her where Sheeana
sat with one of the teaching Sisters. The teaching Sister
was the best, precisely fitted to this next phase in Sheeana's education. Taraza had chosen them all with care.

We proceed with your plan, Odrade thought. *But did
you anticipate, Mother Superior, how we might be marked
by a chance discovery here on Rakis?*

Or was it chance?

Odrade sent her gaze over the lower rooftops to the
spread of the Sisterhood's central stronghold on Rakis.
Rainbow tiles baked out there in glaring noon light.

All of this ours.

This was, she knew, quite the largest embassy the
priests permitted in their holy city of Keen. And her presence in this Bene Gesserit stronghold defied the agreement she had made with Tuek. But that had been before
the discoveries at Sietch Tabr. Besides, Tuek no longer
really existed. The Tuek who marched the priestly

precincts was a Face Dancer living out a precarious charade.

Odrade brought her thoughts back to Waff, who stood with two guardian Sisters, behind her, waiting near the door of this penthouse sanctuary with its fine view through armor-plaz windows and its impressive black furnishings into which a robed Reverend Mother might blend with only the lighter shades of her face visible to a visitor.

Had she gauged Waff correctly? Everything had been done precisely according to Missionaria Protectiva teachings. Had she opened the crack in his psychic armor sufficiently? He should be goaded to speak soon. Then she would know.

Waff stood back there calmly enough. She could see his reflection in the plaz. He gave no sign of understanding that the two tall, dark-haired Sisters flanking him were there to prevent his possible violence. But he certainly knew.

My guardians, not his.

He stood with his head bent to conceal his features from her but she knew he was uncertain. That part was sure. Doubts could be like a starving animal and she had fed those hungry doubts well. He had been so sure that their venture into the desert would be the occasion for his death. His Zensunni and Sufi beliefs were telling him now that God's will preserved him there.

Surely, though, Waff was reviewing now his agreement with the Bene Gesserit, seeing at last the ways he had compromised his people, how he had put his precious Tleilaxu civilization in terrible jeopardy. Yes, his composure was wearing thin, but only Bene Gesserit

eyes detected this. It would be time soon to begin rebuilding his awareness into a pattern more amenable to
the Sisterhood's needs. Let him stew a bit longer.

Odrade returned her attention to the view, loading the
suspense of this delay. The Bene Gesserit had chosen
this embassy location because of the extensive rebuilding
that had changed the entire northeastern quarter of the
old city. They could build and remodel here in their own
way and for their own purposes. Ancient structures designed for easy access by people on foot, wide lanes for
official groundcars and occasional squares in which ornithopters might land—all of that had been changed.

Keeping up with the times.

These new buildings stood much closer to the green-
planted avenues whose tall and exotic trees flaunted their
enormous water consumption. 'Thopters were relegated to
rooftop landing pads on selected buildings. Pedestrian
lanes clung to narrow elevations attached to the buildings.
Coin-operated, key-operated and palm-identification liftslots had been inset into the new buildings, their glowing
energy fields masked by dark brown, vaguely transparent
covers. The liftslots were spines of darker color in the flat
gray of plascrete and plaz. Humans dimly seen in the
tubes gave the effect of impurities moving up and down in
otherwise pure mechanical sausages.

All in the name of modernization.

Waff stirred behind her and cleared his throat.

Odrade did not turn. The two guardian Sisters knew
what she was doing and gave no sign. Waff's mounting
nervousness was merely confirmation that all went well.

Odrade did not feel that all was going truly well.

She interpreted the view out her window as just

another disquieting symptom of this disquieting planet. Tuek, she recalled, had not liked this modernization of his city. He had complained that some way must be found to stop it and preserve the old landmarks. His Face Dancer replacement continued that argument.

How like Tuek himself this new Face Dancer was. Did such Face Dancers think for themselves or just play out their parts in accordance with a Master's orders? Were they still mules, these new ones? How much different were these Face Dancers from the fully human?

Things about the deception worried Odrade.

The false Tuek's councillors, the ones fully involved in what they thought of as "the Tleilaxu plot," spoke of public support for modernization and openly gloated that they had their way at last. Albertus regularly reported everything to Odrade. Each new report worried her more. Even the obvious subservience of Albertus bothered her.

"Of course, the councillors do not mean *public* public support," Albertus said.

She could only agree. The behavior of the councillors signaled that they had powerful backing among the middle echelons of the priesthood, among the climbers who dared joke about their Divided God at weekend parties . . . among those being soothed by the hoard Odrade had found at Sietch Tabr.

Ninety thousand long tons! Half a year's harvest from the deserts of Rakis. Even a third of it represented a significant bargaining chip in the new balances.

I wish I had never met you, Albertus.

She had wanted to restore in him *the one who cares.*

What she had actually done was easily recognized by one trained in the Missionaria Protectiva's ways.

A groveling sycophant!

It made no difference now that his subservience was driven by an absolute belief in her holy association with Sheeana. Odrade had never before focused on how easily the Missionaria Protectiva's teachings destroyed human independence. That was always the goal, of course: *Make them followers, obedient to our needs.*

The Tyrant's words in that secret chamber had done more than ignite her fears for the Sisterhood's future.

"I bequeath to you my fear and loneliness."

From that millennial distance, he had planted doubts in her as surely as she had planted them in Waff.

She saw the Tyrant's questions as though they had been limned with glowing light on her inner eye.

"WITH WHOM DO YOU ALLY?"

Are we no more than a secret society? How will we meet our end? In a dogmatic stink of our own creation?

The Tyrant's words had been burned into her consciousness. Where was the "noble purpose" in what the Sisterhood did? Odrade could almost hear Taraza's sneering response to such a question.

"Survival, Dar! That's all the noble purpose we need. Survival! Even the Tyrant knew that!"

Perhaps even Tuek had known it. And what had that bought him in the end?

Odrade felt a haunting sympathy for the late High Priest. Tuek had been a superb example of what a tightly knit family could produce. Even his name was a clue: unchanged from Atreides days on this planet. The founding ancestor had been a smuggler, confidant of the first Leto. Tuek had come from a family that held firmly to its roots, saying: "There is something worth preserving in our past." The example this set for descendants was not lost on a Reverend Mother.

But you failed, Tuek.

These blocks of modernization visible out her window were a sign of that failure—sops to the rising power elements in Rakian society, those elements that the Sisterhood had worked so long to foster and strengthen. Tuek had seen this as a harbinger of the day when he would be too weak politically to prevent the things implied by such modernization:

A shorter and more upbeat ritual.

New songs, more in the modern manner.

Changes in the dancing. ("Traditional dances take so long!")

Above all, fewer ventures into the dangerous desert for the young postulants from the powerful families.

Odrade sighed and glanced back at Waff. The little Tleilaxu chewed his lower lip. Good!

Damn you, Albertus! I would welcome your rebellion!

Behind the closed doors of the Temple, the transition of the High Priesthood already was being debated. The new Rakians spoke of the need "to keep up with the times." They meant: "Give us more power!"

It has always been this way, Odrade thought. *Even in the Bene Gesserit.*

Still, she could not escape the thought: *Poor Tuek.*

Albertus reported that Tuek, just before his death and replacement by the Face Dancer, had warned his kin they might not retain familial control of the High Priesthood when he died. Tuek had been more subtle and resourceful than his enemies expected. His family already was calling in its debts, gathering its resources to retain a power base.

And the Face Dancer in Tuek's place revealed much by his mimic performance. The Tuek family had not yet learned of the substitution and one might almost believe the original High Priest had not been replaced, so good was this Face Dancer. Observing that Face Dancer in action betrayed much to the watchful Reverend Mothers. That, of course, was one of the things that had Waff squirming now.

Odrade turned abruptly on one heel and strode across to the Tleilaxu Master. *Time to have at him!*

She stopped two paces from Waff and glared down at him. Waff met her gaze with defiance.

"You've had enough time to consider your position," she accused. "Why do you remain silent?"

"My position? You think you give us a choice?"

"Man is but a pebble dropped in a pool," she quoted at him from his own beliefs.

Waff took a trembling breath. She spoke the proper words, but what lay behind such words? They no longer sounded right coming from the mouth of a powindah woman.

When Waff did not respond, Odrade continued her quotation: "And if man is but a pebble, then all his works can be no more."

An involuntary shudder swept through Odrade, causing a look of carefully masked surprise in the watchful guardian Sisters. That shudder was not part of the required performance.

Why do I think of the Tyrant's words at this moment? Odrade wondered.

"THE BODY AND SOUL OF THE BENE GESSE-RIT WILL MEET THE SAME FATE AS ALL OTHER BODIES AND ALL OTHER SOULS."

His barb had gone deep into her.

How was I made so vulnerable? The answer leaped into her awareness: *The Atreides Manifesto!*

Composing those words under Taraza's watchful guidance opened a flaw within me.

Could that have been Taraza's purpose: to make Odrade vulnerable? How could Taraza have known what would be found here on Rakis? The Mother Superior not only displayed no prescient abilities, she tended to avoid this talent in others. On the rare occasions when Taraza had demanded such a performance of Odrade herself, the reluctance had been obvious to the trained eye of a Sister.

Yet she made me vulnerable.

Had it been an accident?

Odrade sank into a swift recital of the Litany Against Fear, only a few eyeblinks but in that time Waff visibly came to a decision.

"You would force it upon us," he said. "But you do not know what powers we have reserved for such a moment." He lifted his sleeves to show where the dart throwers had been. "These were but paltry toys by comparison with our real weapons."

"The Sisterhood has never doubted this," Odrade said.

"Is it to be violent conflict between us?" he asked.

"It is your choice to make," she said.

"Why do you court violence?"

"There are those who would love to see Bene Gesserit and Bene Tleilax at each other's throats," Odrade said. "Our enemies would enjoy stepping in to pick up the pieces after we had weakened ourselves sufficiently."

"You state the argument for agreement but you give my people no room to negotiate! Perhaps your Mother Superior gave you no authority to negotiate!"

How tempting it was to pass it all back into Taraza's hands, just as Taraza wanted. Odrade glanced at the guardian Sisters. The two faces were masks betraying nothing. What did they really know? Would they realize if she went against Taraza's orders?

"Do you have such authority?" Waff persisted.

Noble purpose, Odrade thought. *Surely, the Tyrant's Golden Path demonstrated at least one quality of such purpose.*

Odrade decided on a creative truth. "I have such authority," she said. Her own words made it true. Having taken the authority, she made it impossible for Taraza to deny it. Odrade knew, though, that her own words committed her to a course sharply divergent from the sequential steps of Taraza's design.

Independent action. The very thing *she* had desired of Albertus.

But I am on the scene and know what is needed.

Odrade glanced at the guardian Sisters. "Remain here, please, and see that we are not disturbed." To Waff, she said: "We might as well be comfortable." She indicated two chairdogs set at right angles to each other across the room.

Odrade waited until they were seated before resuming

the conversation. "We require a degree of candor between us that diplomacy seldom allows. Too much hangs in the balance for us to engage in shallow evasions."

Waff looked at her strangely. He said: "We know there is dissension in your highest councils. Subtle overtures have been made to us. Is this part of . . ."

"I am loyal to the Sisterhood," she said. "Even those who approached you had no other loyalty."

"Is this another trick of—"

"No tricks!"

"With the Bene Gesserit there are always tricks," he accused.

"What is it you fear from us? Name it."

"Perhaps I have learned too much from you for you to allow me to go on living."

"Could I not say the same of you?" she asked. "Who else knows of our secret affinity? This is no *powindah* female talking to you here!"

She had ventured the word with some trepidation, but the effect could not have been more revealing. Waff was visibly shaken. He was a long minute recovering. Doubts remained, though, because she had planted them in him.

"What do words prove?" he asked. "You might still take the things you have learned from me and leave my people nothing. You still hold the whip over us."

"I carry no weapons in *my* sleeves," Odrade said.

"But in your mind is knowledge that could ruin us!" He glanced back at the guardian Sisters.

"They are part of my arsenal," Odrade agreed. "Shall I send them away?"

"And in their minds everything they have heard here,"

he said. He returned his wary gaze to Odrade. "Better if you all sent your memories away!"

Odrade pitched her voice in its most reasonable tones. "What would we gain by exposing your missionary zeal before you are ready to move? Would it serve us to blacken your reputation by revealing where you have placed your new Face Dancers? Oh, yes, we know about Ix and the Fish Speakers. Once we had studied your new ones, we went searching for them."

"You see!" His voice was dangerously edged.

"I see no other way to prove our affinity than to reveal something equally damaging about ourselves," Odrade said.

Waff was speechless.

"We would plant the worms of the Prophet on uncounted planets of the Scattering," she said. "What would the Rakian priesthood say and do if you revealed that?"

The guardian Sisters looked at her with thinly masked amusement. They thought she was lying.

"I have no guards with *me*," Waff said. "When only one person knows a dangerous thing, how easy it is to gain that person's eternal silence."

She lifted her empty sleeves.

He looked at the guardian Sisters.

"Very well," Odrade said. She glanced at the Sisters and gave a subtle handsign to reassure them. "Wait outside, please, Sisters."

When the door closed behind them, Waff returned to his doubts. "My people have not searched these rooms. What do I know of the things that could be hidden here to record our words?"

Odrade shifted into the language of the Islamiyat. "Then perhaps we should speak another tongue, one known only to us."

Waff's eyes glittered. In the same tongue, he said: "Very well! I will gamble on it. And I ask you to tell me the real cause of dissension among the . . . the Bene Gesserit."

Odrade allowed herself a smile. With the change of language, Waff's entire personality, his whole manner, changed. He was performing exactly as expected. None of his doubts had been reinforced in *this* tongue!

She responded with an equal confidence: "Fools fear that we may bring back another Kwisatz Haderach! That is what a few of my Sisters argue."

"There is no more need of such a one," Waff said. "The one who could be many places simultaneously has been and he has gone. He came only to bring the Prophet."

"God would not send such a message twice," she said.

It was the very sort of thing Waff had heard often in this tongue. He no longer thought it strange that a woman could utter such words. The language and the familiar words were enough.

"Has Schwangyu's death restored unity among your Sisters?" he asked.

"We have a common enemy," Odrade said.

"The Honored Matres!"

"You were wise to kill them and learn from them."

Waff leaned forward, completely caught up in his familiar tongue and the flow of their conversation. "They rule with sex!" he exulted. "Remarkable techniques of orgasmic amplification! We—" Belatedly, he became aware of who was sitting in front of him hearing all of this.

"We already know such techniques," Odrade reassured him. "It will be interesting to compare, but there are obvious reasons why we have never tried to ride to power on such a dangerous conveyance. Those whores are just stupid enough to make that mistake!"

"Mistake?" He was clearly puzzled.

"They are holding the reins in their own hands!" she said. "As the power grows, their control of it must grow. The thing will shatter of its own momentum!"

"Power, always power," Waff muttered. Another thought struck him. "Are you saying this was how the Prophet fell?"

"He knew what he was doing," she said. "Millennia of enforced peace followed by the Famine Times and the Scattering. A message of direct results. Remember! He did not destroy the Bene Tleilax or the Bene Gesserit."

"For what do you hope from an alliance between our two peoples?" Waff asked.

"Hope is one thing, survival another," she said.

"Always pragmatism," Waff said. "And some among you fear that you may restore the Prophet on Rakis with all of his powers intact?"

"Did I not say it?" The language of the Islamiyat was particularly potent in this questioning form. It placed the burden of proof on Waff.

"So they doubt God's hand in the creation of your Kwisatz Haderach," he said. "Do they also doubt the Prophet?"

"Very well, let us have it all out in the open," Odrade

said, and launched herself on the chosen course of deception: "Schwangyu and those who supported her broke away from the Great Belief. We harbor no anger toward any Bene Tleilax for having killed them. They saved us the trouble."

Waff accepted this utterly. Given the circumstances, it was precisely what could be expected. He knew he had revealed much here that might better have been held in reserve but there were still things the Bene Gesserit did not know. And the things he had learned!

Odrade shocked him totally then by saying: "Waff, if you think your descendants from the Scattering have returned to you unchanged, then foolishness has become your way of life."

He held himself silent.

"You have all of the pieces in your hands," she said. "Your descendants belong to the whores of the Scattering. And if you think any of *them* will abide by an agreement, then your stupidity goes beyond description!"

Waff's reactions told her she had him. The pieces were clicking into place. She had told him truth where it was required. His doubts were refocused where they belonged: against the people of the Scattering. And it had been done in his own tongue.

He tried to speak past a constriction in his throat and was forced to massage his throat before speech returned. "What can we do?"

"It's obvious. The Lost Ones have their eyes on us as just one more conquest. They think of it as cleaning up behind them. Common prudence."

"But they are so many!"

"Unless we unite in a common plan to defeat them, they will chew us up the way a slig chews up its dinner."

"We cannot submit to powindah filth! God will not permit it!"

"Submit? Who suggests that we submit?"

"But the Bene Gesserit always use that ancient excuse: 'If you can't beat them, join them.'"

Odrade smiled grimly. "God will not permit you to submit! Do you suggest He would permit it of us?"

"Then what is your plan? What would you do against such numbers?"

"Exactly what you plan to do: convert them. When you say the word, the Sisterhood will openly espouse the true faith."

Waff sat in stunned silence. So she knew the heart of the Tleilaxu plan. Did she know also how the Tleilaxu would enforce it?

Odrade stared at him, openly speculative. *Grasp the beast by the balls if you must,* she thought. But what if the projection by the Sisterhood's analysts was wrong? This whole *negotiation* would be a joke in that case. And there was that look in the back of Waff's eyes, that suggestion of older wisdom . . . much older than his flesh. She spoke with more confidence than she felt:

"What you have achieved with gholas from your tanks and kept secretly for yourselves alone, others will pay a great price to achieve."

Her words were sufficiently cryptic (Were others listening?) but Waff did not doubt for an instant that the Bene Gesserit knew even this thing.

"Will you demand a share in that as well?" he asked. The words rasped in his dry throat.

"Everything! We will share everything."

"What will you bring to this great sharing?"

"Ask."

"All of your breeding records."

"They are yours."

"Breeding mothers of our choice."

"Name them."

Waff gasped. This was far more than the Mother Superior had offered. It was like a blossom opening in his awareness. She was right about the Honored Matres, naturally—and about the Tleilaxu descendants from the Scattering. He had never completely trusted them. Never!

"You will want an unrestricted source of melange, of course," he said.

"Of course."

He stared at her, hardly believing the extent of his good fortune. The axlotl tanks would offer immortality only to those who espoused the Great Belief. No one would dare attack and attempt to seize a thing they knew the Tleilaxu would destroy rather than lose. And now! He had gained the services of the most powerful and enduring missionary force known. Surely, the hand of God was visible here. Waff was first awed and then inspired. He spoke softly to Odrade.

"And you, Reverend Mother, how do you name our accord?"

"Noble purpose," she said. "You already know the Prophet's words from Sietch Tabr. Do you doubt him?"

"Never! But . . . but there is one thing: What do you

propose with that ghola of Duncan Idaho and the girl, Sheeana?"

"We will breed them, of course. And their descendants will speak for us to all of those descendants of the Prophet."

"On all of those planets where you would take them!"

"On all of those planets," she agreed.

Waff sat back. *I have you, Reverend Mother!* he thought. *We will rule this alliance, not you. The ghola is not yours; he is ours!*

Odrade saw the shadow of his reservations in Waff's eyes but knew she had ventured as much as she dared. More would reawaken doubts. Whatever happened, she had committed the Sisterhood to this course. Taraza could not escape this alliance now.

Waff squared his shoulders, a curiously juvenile gesture belied by the ancient intelligence peering from his eyes. "Ahhhh, one thing more," he said, every bit the Master of Masters speaking his own language and commanding all of those who heard him. "Will you also help spread this . . . this Atreides Manifesto?"

"Why not? I wrote it."

Waff jerked forward. "You?"

"Did you think someone of lesser abilities could have done it?"

He nodded, convinced without further argument. This was fuel for a thought that had entered his own mind, a final point in their alliance: The powerful minds of Reverend Mothers would advise the Tleilaxu at every turn! What did it matter that they were outnumbered by those whores of the Scattering? Who could match such combined wisdom and insurmountable weapons?

"The title of the Manifesto is valid, too," Odrade said. "I am a true descendant of the Atreides."

"Would you be one of our breeders?" he ventured.

"I am almost past the age of breeding, but I am yours to command."

I remember friends from wars all but we forgot.

All of them distilled into each wound we caught.

Those wounds are all the painful places where we fought.

Battles better left behind, ones we never sought.

What is it that we spent and what was it we bought?

—SONGS OF THE SCATTERING

Burzmali based his planning on the best of what he had learned from his Bashar, keeping his own counsel about multiple options and fallback positions. That was a commander's prerogative! Necessarily, he learned everything he could about the terrain.

In the time of the Old Empire and even under the reign of Muad'Dib, the region around the Gammu Keep had been a forest reserve, high ground rising well above the oily residue that tended to cover Harkonnen land. On this ground, the Harkonnens had grown some of the finest pilingitam, a wood of steady currency, always valued by the supremely rich. From the most ancient times, the knowledgeable had preferred to surround themselves with fine woods rather than with the mass-produced artificial materials known then as polastine, polaz, and pormabat (latterly: tine, laz, and bat). As far back as the Old Empire there had been a pejorative label for the small rich and Families Minor arising from the knowledge of a rare wood's value.

"He's a three P-O," they said, meaning that such a person surrounded himself with cheap copies made from déclassé substances. Even when the supremely rich were forced to employ one of the distressful three P-Os, they disguised it where possible behind O-P (the Only P), pilingitam.

Burzmali knew all of this and more as he set his people to searching for a strategically situated pilingitam near the no-globe. The wood of the tree had many qualities that endeared it to master artisans: Newly cut, it worked like a softwood; dried and aged, it endured as a hardwood. It absorbed many pigments and the finish could be made to appear as though it occurred naturally within the grain. More important, pilingitam was anti-fungal and no known insect had ever considered it a suitable dinner. Lastly, it was fire-resistant, and aged specimens of the living tree grew outward from an enlarged and empty tube at the core.

"We will do the unexpected," Burzmali told his searchers.

He had noted the distinctive lime green of pilingitam leaves during his first overflight of the region. The forests of this planet had been raided and otherwise logged off during the Famine Times but venerable O-Ps were still nurtured among the evergreens and hardwoods replanted at the Sisterhood's orders.

Burzmali's searchers found one such O-P dominating a ridge above the no-globe site. It spread its leaves over almost three hectares. On the afternoon of the critical day, Burzmali placed decoys at a distance from this position and opened a tunnel from a shallow swale into the pilingitam's roomy core. There, he set up his command post and the backup necessities for escape.

"The tree is a life form," he explained to his people. "It will mask us from tracers."

The unexpected.

Nowhere in his planning did Burzmali assume that all of his actions would go undetected. He could only spread his vulnerability.

When the attack came, he saw that it appeared to follow a predicted pattern. He had anticipated that attackers would rely on no-ships and great numbers as they had in the assault on the Gammu Keep. The Sisterhood's analysts assured him that the major threat was from forces out of the Scattering—descendants of the Tleilaxu deployed by wildly brutal women calling themselves Honored Matres. He saw this as overconfidence and not audacity. A real audacity was in the arsenal of every student taught by the Bashar Miles Teg. It also helped that Teg could be relied upon to improvise within the limits of a plan.

Through his relays, Burzmali followed the scrambling escape of Duncan and Lucilla. Troopers with com-helmets and night lenses created a great display of activity at the decoy positions while Burzmali and his select reserves kept watch on the attackers, never betraying their position. Teg's movements were easily followed by his violent response to the attackers.

Burzmali noted with approval that Lucilla did not pause when she heard the battle sounds intensify. Duncan, however, tried to stop and almost ruined the plan. Lucilla saved the moment by jabbing Duncan in a sensitive nerve and barking: "You can't help him!"

Hearing her voice clearly through his helmet amplifiers, Burzmali cursed under his breath. Others would hear her, too! No doubt they already were tracking her, though.

Burzmali issued a subvocal command through the microphone implanted in his neck and prepared to abandon his post. He kept most of his attention on the approach of Lucilla and Duncan. If all went as planned, his people would bring down the pair of them while two helmetless and suitably garbed troopers continued the flight toward the decoy positions.

In the interim, Teg was creating an admirable path of destruction through which a groundcar might escape.

An aide intruded on Burzmali: "Two attackers are closing in behind the Bashar!"

Burzmali waved the man aside. He could give little thought to Teg's chances. Everything had to be focused on saving the ghola. Burzmali's thoughts were intense as he watched:

Come on! Run! Run, damn you!

Lucilla held a similar thought as she urged Duncan forward, keeping herself close behind him to shield him from the rear. Everything about her was marshaled for ultimate resistance. Everything in her breeding and training came to the fore in these moments. *Never give up!* To give up was to pass her consciousness into the Memory Lives of a Sister or into oblivion. Even Schwangyu had redeemed herself in the end by reverting to total resistance and had died admirably in the Bene Gesserit tradition, resisting to the last. Burzmali had reported it through Teg. Lucilla, assembling her uncounted lives, thought: *I can do no less!*

She followed Duncan down into a shallow swale beside the bole of a giant pilingitam and, when people arose out of the darkness to drag them down, she almost responded in berserker mode but a voice speaking Chakobsa in her ear said: "Friends!" This delayed her response for a heartbeat while she saw the decoys continue the flight out of the swale. That more than anything else revealed the plan and the identity of the people holding them against the rich leafy smells of the earth. When the people slid Duncan ahead of her into a tunnel aimed at the giant tree and (still in Chakobsa) cautioned speed, Lucilla knew she was caught in a typical Teg-style audacity.

Duncan saw it, too. At the stygian outlet of the tunnel, he identified her by smell and tapped out a message against her arm in the old Atreides silent battle language.

"Let them lead."

The form of the message startled her momentarily until she realized that the ghola of course would know this communication method.

Without speaking, the people around them removed Duncan's bulky antique lasgun and hustled the fugitives into the hatch of a vehicle that she did not identify. A brief red light flared in the darkness.

Burzmali spoke subvocally to his people: "There they go!"

Twenty-eight groundcars and eleven flitter-thopters scrambled from the decoy positions. *A proper diversion,* Burzmali thought.

Pressure in Lucilla's ears told her a hatch had been sealed. Again the red light flared and went dark.

Explosives shattered the great tree around them and their vehicle, now identifiable as an armored groundcar, surged up and out on suspensors and jets. Lucilla could follow their course only by flashes of fire and the twisting patterns of stars visible through frames of oval plaz. The enclosing suspensor field made the motions eerie, sensed only by the eyes. They sat cradled in plasteel seats while their car rocketed downslope directly across Teg's holdout position, shifting and darting in violent changes of direction. None of this wild motion transmitted itself to the flesh of the occupants. There were only the dancing blurs of trees and brush, some of them burning, and then the stars.

They were hugging the tops of the forest wreckage left by Teg's lasguns! Only then did she dare to hope that they might win free. Abruptly, their vehicle trembled into slow flight. The visible stars, framed by the tiny ovals of plaz, tipped and were obscured by a dark obstruction. Gravity returned and there was dim light. Lucilla saw Burzmali fling open a hatch on her left.

"Out!" he snapped. "Not a second to spare!"

Duncan ahead of her, Lucilla scrambled out of the hatch onto damp earth. Burzmali thumped her back, grabbed Duncan's arm and hustled them away from the car. "Quick! This way!" They crashed through tall bushes onto a narrow paved roadway. Burzmali, a hand on each of them now, rushed them across the road and pushed them flat in a ditch. He whipped a life-shield blanket over them and lifted his head to look back in the direction from which they had come.

Lucilla peered past him and saw starlight on a snowy slope. She felt Duncan stir beside her.

Far up the slope, a speeding groundcar, its jet-pod modifications visible against the stars, lifted on a plume of red, climbing, climbing . . . climbing. Suddenly, it darted off to the right.

"Ours?" Duncan whispered.

"Yes."

"How did it get up there without showing a . . ."

"An abandoned aqueduct tunnel," Burzmali whispered. "The car was programed to go on automatic." He continued to stare at the distant red plume. Abruptly, a gigantic burst of blue light rolled outward from the faraway red tracery. The light was followed immediately by a dull thump.

"Ahhhhh," Burzmali breathed.

Duncan, his voice low, said: "They are supposed to think you overloaded your drive."

Burzmali shot a startled look at the young face, ghostly gray in starlight.

"Duncan Idaho was one of the finest pilots in Atreides service," Lucilla said. It was an esoteric bit of knowledge and it served its purpose. Burzmali saw immediately that he was not just guardian of two fugitives. His charges possessed abilities that could be used if needed.

Blue and red sparks flashed across the sky where the modified groundcar had exploded. The no-ships were sniffing that distant globe of hot gases. What would the sniffers decide? The blue and red sparks slipped down behind the starlit bulges of the hills.

Burzmali whirled at the sound of footsteps on the roadway. Duncan had a handgun out so swiftly that Lucilla gasped. She put a restraining hand on his arm but he shook it off. Didn't he see that Burzmali had accepted this intrusion?

A voice called softly from the roadway above them: "Follow me. Hurry."

The speaker, a moving blot of darkness, jumped down beside them and went crashing through a gap in the bushes lining the road. Dark spots on the snowy slope beyond the screening bushes resolved themselves into at least a dozen armed figures. Five of this party grouped themselves around Duncan and Lucilla and urged them silently along a snow-covered trail beside the bushes. The rest of the armed party ran openly down across the snow-slope into a dark line of trees.

Within a hundred paces, the five silent figures formed their party into single file, two of their number ahead, three behind, the fugitives sheltered between them with Burzmali leading and Lucilla close behind Duncan. They came presently to a cleft in dark rocks and under a ledge where they waited, listening to more modified ground-cars thunder into the air behind them.

"Decoys upon decoys," Burzmali whispered. "We overload them with decoys. They *know* we must flee in panic as fast as possible. Now, we will wait nearby in concealment. Later, we will proceed slowly . . . on foot."

"The unexpected," Lucilla whispered.

"Teg?" It was Duncan, his voice little more than a breath.

Burzmali leaned close to Duncan's left ear: "I think they got him." Burzmali's whisper carried a deep tone of sadness.

One of their dark companions said: "Quickly now. Down here."

They were herded through the narrow cleft. Something emitted a creaking sound nearby. Hands hustled them into an enclosed passage. The creaking sounded from behind them.

"Get that door fixed," someone said.

Light flared around them.

Duncan and Lucilla stared around at a large, richly furnished room apparently cut into rock. Soft carpets covered the floor—dark reds and golds with a figured pattern like repetitive battlements worked in pale green. A bundle of clothing lay in a jumble on a table near Burzmali, who was in low-voiced conversation with one of their escort: a fair-haired man with high forehead and piercing green eyes.

Lucilla listened carefully. The words were understandable, relating how guards had been posted, but the green-eyed man's accent was one she had never before heard, a tumble of gutturals and consonants clicked off with surprising abruptness.

"Is this a no-chamber?" she asked.

"No." The answer was supplied by a man behind her speaking in that same accent. "The algae protect us."

She did not turn toward the speaker but looked up instead at the light yellow-green algae thick on the ceiling and walls. Only a few patches of dark rock were visible near the floors.

Burzmali broke off his conversation. "We are safe here. The algae is grown especially for this. Life scanners report only the presence of plant life and nothing else that the algae shields."

Lucilla pivoted on one heel, sorting the room's details: that Harkonnen griffin worked into a crystal table, the exotic fabrics on chairs and couches. A weapons rack against one wall held two rows of long field-style lasguns of a design she had never before seen. Each was bell-mouthed and with a curling gold guard over the trigger.

Burzmali had returned to his conversation with the green-eyed man. It was an argument over how they would be disguised. She listened with part of her mind while she studied the two members of their escort remaining in the room. The other three from the escort had filed out through a passage near the weapons cabinet, an opening covered by a thick hanging of shimmering silvery threads. Duncan, she saw, was watching her responses with care, his hand on the small lasgun in his belt.

People of the Scattering? Lucilla wondered. *What are their loyalties?*

Casually, she crossed to Duncan's side and, using the finger-touch language on his arm, relayed her suspicions. Both of them looked at Burzmali. *Treachery?*

Lucilla went back to her study of the room. Were they being watched by unseen eyes?

Nine glowglobes lighted the space, creating their own peculiar islands of intense illumination. It reached outward into a common concentration near where Burzmali still talked to the green-eyed man. Part of the light came directly from the drifting globes, all of them tuned into rich gold, and part of it was reflected more softly off the algae. The result was a lack of dark shadows, even under the furnishings.

The shimmering silver threads of the inner doorway

parted. An old woman entered the room. Lucilla stared at her. The woman had a seamed face as dark as old rosewood. Her features were sharply defined in a narrow frame of straggling gray hair that fell almost to her shoulders. She wore a long black robe worked with golden threads in a pattern of mythological dragons. The woman stopped behind a settee and placed her deeply veined hands on the back.

Burzmali and his companion broke off their conversation.

Lucilla looked from the old woman down to her own robe. Except for the golden dragons, the garments were similar in design, the hoods draped back onto the shoulders. Only in the side cut and the way it opened down the front was the design of the dragon robe different.

When the woman did not speak, Lucilla looked to Burzmali for explanation. Burzmali stared back at her with a look of intense concentration. The old woman continued to study Lucilla silently.

The intensity of attention filled Lucilla with disquiet. Duncan felt it, too, she saw. He kept his hand on the small lasgun. The long silence while eyes examined her amplified her unease. There was something almost Bene Gesserit about the way the old woman just stood there looking.

Duncan broke the silence, demanding of Burzmali: "Who is she?"

"I'm the one who'll save your skins," the old woman said. She had a thin voice that crackled weakly, but that same strange accent.

Lucilla's Other Memories brought up a suggestive

comparison for the old woman's garment: *Similar to that worn by ancient playfems.*

Lucilla almost shook her head. Surely this woman was too old for such a role. And the shape of the mythic dragons worked into the fabric differed from those supplied by memory. Lucilla returned her attention to the old face: eyes humid with the illnesses of age. A dry crust had settled into the creases where each eyelid touched the channels beside her nose. Far too old for a playfem.

The old woman spoke to Burzmali. "I think she can wear it well enough." She began divesting herself of her dragon robe. To Lucilla she said: "This is for you. Wear it with respect. We killed to get it for you."

"Who did you kill?" Lucilla demanded.

"A postulant of the Honored Matres!" There was pride in the old woman's husky tone.

"Why should I wear that robe?" Lucilla demanded.

"You will trade garments with me," the old woman said.

"Not without explanation." Lucilla refused to accept the robe being extended to her.

Burzmali took one step forward. "You can trust her."

"I am a friend of your friends," the old woman said. She shook the robe in front of Lucilla. "Here, take it."

Lucilla addressed Burzmali. "I must know your plan."

"We both must know it," Duncan said. "On whose authority are we asked to trust these people?"

"Teg's," Burzmali said. "And mine." He looked at the old woman. "You can tell them, Sirafa. We have time."

"You will wear this robe while you accompany Burzmali into Ysai," Sirafa said.

Sirafa, Lucilla thought. The name had almost the sound of a Bene Gesserit Lineal Variant.

Sirafa studied Duncan. "Yes, he is small enough yet. He will be disguised and conveyed separately."

"No!" Lucilla said. "I am commanded to guard him!"

"You are being foolish," Sirafa said. "They will be looking for a woman of your appearance accompanied by someone of this young man's appearance. They will not be looking for a playfem of the Honored Matres with her companion of the night — nor for a Tleilaxu Master and his entourage."

Lucilla wet her lips with her tongue. Sirafa spoke with the confident assurance of a House Proctor.

Sirafa draped the dragon robe over the back of the settee. She stood revealed in a clinging black leotard that concealed nothing of a body still lithe and supple, even well rounded. The body looked much younger than the face. As Lucilla looked at her, Sirafa passed her palms across her forehead and cheeks, smoothing them backward. Age lines grew shallow and a younger face was revealed.

A Face Dancer?

Lucilla stared hard at the woman. There were none of the other Face Dancer stigmata. Still . . .

"Get your robe off!" Sirafa ordered. Now her voice was younger and even more commanding.

"You must do it," Burzmali pleaded. "Sirafa will take your place as another decoy. It's the only way we'll get through."

"Get through to what?" Duncan asked.

"To a no-ship," Burzmali said.

"And where will that take us?" Lucilla demanded.

"To safety," Burzmali said. "We will be loaded with shere but I cannot say more. Even shere wears off in time."

"How will I be disguised as a Tleilaxu?" Duncan asked.

"Trust us that it will be done," Burzmali said. He kept his attention on Lucilla. "Reverend Mother?"

"You give me no choice," Lucilla said. She undid the quick fasteners and dropped her robe. She removed the small handgun from her bodice and tossed it onto the settee. Her own leotard was light gray and she saw Sirafa making note of this and of the knives in their leg sheaths.

"We sometimes wear black undergarments," Lucilla said as she slipped into the dragon robe. The fabric looked heavy but felt light. She pivoted in it, sensing the way it flared and fitted itself to her body almost as though it had been made just for her. There was a rough spot at the neck. She reached up and ran a finger along it.

"That is where the dart struck her," Sirafa said. "We moved fast but the acid scarred the fabric slightly. It is not visible to the eye."

"Is the appearance correct?" Burzmali asked Sirafa.

"Very good. But I will have to instruct her. She must make no mistakes or they will have both of you like that!" Sirafa clapped her hands for emphasis.

Where have I seen that gesture? Lucilla asked herself.

Duncan touched the back of Lucilla's right arm, his fingers secretly quick-talking: *"That hand clap! A mannerism of Giedi Prime."*

Other Memories confirmed this for Lucilla. Was this

woman part of an isolated community preserving archaic ways?

"The lad should go now," Sirafa said. She gestured to the two remaining members of the escort. "Take him to the place."

"I don't like this," Lucilla said.

"We have no choice!" Burzmali barked.

Lucilla could only agree. She was relying on Burzmali's oath of loyalty to the Sisterhood, she knew. And Duncan was not a child, she reminded herself. His prana-bindu reactions had been conditioned by the old Bashar and herself. There were abilities in the ghola that few people outside of the Bene Gesserit could match. She watched silently as Duncan and the two men left through the shimmering curtain.

When they were gone, Sirafa came around the settee and stood in front of Lucilla, hands on hips. Their gazes met at a level.

Burzmali cleared his throat and fingered the rough pile of clothing on the table beside him.

Sirafa's face, especially the eyes, held a remarkably compelling quality. The eyes were light green with clear whites. No lens or other artifice masked them.

"You have the right look about you," Sirafa said. "Remember that you are a special kind of playfem and Burzmali is your customer. No ordinary person would interfere with that."

Lucilla heard a veiled hint in this. "But there are those who might interfere?"

"Embassies from great religions are on Gammu now," Sirafa said. "Some you have never encountered. They are from what you call the Scattering."

"And what do you call it?"

"The Seeking." Sirafa raised a placating hand. "Do not fear! We have a common enemy."

"The Honored Matres?"

Sirafa turned her head to the left and spat on the floor. "Look at me, Bene Gesserit! I was trained only to kill them! That is my only function and purpose!"

Lucilla spoke carefully: "From what we know, you must be very good."

"In some things, perhaps I am better than you. Now listen! You are a sexual adept. Do you understand?"

"Why would priests interfere?"

"You call them priests? Well . . . yes. They would not interfere for any reason you might imagine. Sex for pleasure, the enemy of religion, eh?"

"Accept no substitutes for holy joy," Lucilla said.

"Tantrus protect you, woman! There are different *priests* from the Seeking, ones who do not mind offering immediate ecstasy instead of a promised hereafter."

Lucilla almost smiled. Did this self-styled killer of Honored Matres think she could advise a Reverend Mother on religions?

"There are people here who go about disguised as *priests*," Sirafa said. "Very dangerous. The most dangerous of all are those who follow Tantrus and claim that sex is the exclusive worship of their god."

"How will I know them?" Lucilla heard sincerity in Sirafa's voice and a sense of foreboding.

"That is not a concern. You must never act as though you recognize such distinctions. Your first concern is to make sure of your pay. You, I think, should ask fifty solari."

"You have not told me why they would interfere." Lucilla glanced back at Burzmali. He had laid out the rough clothing and was taking off his battle fatigues. She returned her attention to Sirafa.

"Some follow an ancient convention that grants them the right to disrupt your arrangement with Burzmali. In actuality, some will be testing you."

"Listen carefully," Burzmali said. "This is important."

Sirafa said: "Burzmali will be dressed as a field worker. Nothing else could disguise his weapon's calluses. You will address him as Skar, a common name here."

"But how do I deal with a priest's interruption?"

Sirafa produced a small pouch from her bodice and passed it to Lucilla, who hefted it in one hand. "That contains two hundred and eighty-three solari. If someone identifying himself as a divine . . . You remember that? Divine?"

"How could I forget it?" Lucilla's voice was almost a sneer but Sirafa paid no heed.

"If such a one interferes, you will return fifty solari to Burzmali with your regrets. Also, in that pouch is your playfem card in the name of Pira. Let me hear you say your name."

"Pira."

"No! Accent much harder on the 'a'!"

"Pira!"

"That is passable. Now listen to me with extreme care. You and Burzmali will be on the streets late. It will be expected that you have had previous customers. There must be evidence. Therefore, you will . . . ahhh, entertain Burzmali before leaving here. You understand?"

"Such delicacy!" Lucilla said.

Sirafa took it as a compliment and smiled, but it was a tightly controlled expression. Her reactions were so alien!

"One thing," Lucilla said. "If I must *entertain* a divine, how will I find Burzmali afterward?"

"Skar!"

"Yes. How will I find Skar?"

"He will wait nearby wherever you go. Skar will find you when you emerge."

"Very well. If a *divine* interrupts, I return one hundred solari to Skar and—"

"Fifty!"

"I think not, Sirafa." Lucilla shook her head slowly from side to side. "After being *entertained* by me, the divine will know that fifty solari is too small a sum."

Sirafa pursed her lips and glanced past Lucilla at Burzmali. "You warned me about her kind but I did not suppose that . . ."

Using only a touch of Voice, Lucilla said: "You suppose *nothing* unless you hear it from me!"

Sirafa scowled. She was obviously startled by Voice, but her tone was just as arrogant when she resumed. "Do I presume that you need no explanation of sexual variations?"

"A safe assumption," Lucilla said.

"And I do not need to tell you that your robe identifies you as a fifth-stage adept in the Order of Hormu?"

It was Lucilla's turn to scowl. "What if I show abilities beyond this fifth stage?"

"Ahhhhh," Sirafa said. "You will continue to heed my words, then?"

Lucilla nodded curtly.

"Very good," Sirafa said. "May I presume you can administer vaginal pulsing?"

"I can."

"From any position?"

"I can control any muscle in my body!"

Sirafa glanced past Lucilla at Burzmali. "True?"

Burzmali spoke from close behind Lucilla: "Or she would not claim it."

Sirafa looked thoughtful, her focus on Lucilla's chin. "This is a complication, I think."

"Lest you get the wrong idea," Lucilla said, "the abilities I was taught are not usually marketed. They have another purpose."

"Oh, I'm sure they do," Sirafa said. "But sexual agility is a—"

"Agility!" Lucilla allowed her tone to convey the full weight of a Reverend Mother's outrage. No matter that this might be what Sirafa hoped to achieve, she had to be put in her place! "Agility, you say? I can control genital temperature. I know and can arouse the fifty-one excitation points. I—"

"Fifty-one? But there are only—"

"Fifty-one!" Lucilla snapped. "And the sequencing plus the combinations number two thousand and eight. Furthermore, in combination with the two hundred and five sexual positions—"

"Two hundred and five?" Sirafa was clearly startled. "Surely, you don't mean—"

"More, actually, if you count minor variations. I am an Imprinter, which means I have mastered the three hundred steps of orgasmic amplification!"

Sirafa cleared her throat and wet her lips with her tongue. "I must warn you then to restrain yourself. Keep your full abilities unexpressed or . . ." Once more, she looked at Burzmali. "Why didn't you warn me?"

"I did."

Lucilla clearly heard amusement in his voice but did not look back to confirm it.

Sirafa inhaled and expelled two hard breaths. "If any questions are asked, you will say you are about to undergo testing for advancement. That may quiet suspicion."

"And if I'm asked about the test."

"Oh, that is easy. You smile mysteriously and remain silent."

"What if I'm asked about this Order of Hormu?"

"Threaten to report the questioner to your superiors. The questions should stop."

"And if they don't?"

Sirafa shrugged. "Make up any story you like. Even a Truth-sayer would be amused by your evasions."

Lucilla held her face in repose while she thought about her situation. She heard Burzmali—Skar!—stirring directly behind her. She saw no serious difficulties in carrying out this deception. It might even provide an amusing interlude she could recount later at Chapter House. Sirafa, she noted, was grinning at Burz—Skar! Lucilla turned and looked at her *customer*.

Burzmali stood there naked, his battle garb and helmet neatly stacked beside the small mound of rough clothing.

"I can see that Skar does not object to your preparations for this venture," Sirafa said. She waved a hand at his stiffly upcocked penis. "I will leave you, then."

Lucilla heard Sirafa depart through the shimmering curtain. Filling Lucilla's thoughts was an angry realization:

"This should be the ghola here now!"

It is your fate, forgetfulness. All of the old lessons of life, you lose and gain and lose and gain again.

—LETO II, THE VOICE OF DAR-ES-BALAT

"In the name of our Order and its unbroken Sisterhood, this account has been judged reliable and worthy of entry into the Chronicles of Chapter House."

Taraza stared at the words on her display projection with an expression of distaste. Morning light painted a fuzz of yellow reflections in the projection, making the words there appear dimly mysterious.

With an angry motion, Taraza pushed herself back from the projection table, arose and went to a south window. The day was young yet and the shadows long in her courtyard.

Shall I go in person?

Reluctance filled her at this thought. These quarters felt so . . . so secure. But that was foolishness and she knew it in every fiber. The Bene Gesserit had been here more than fourteen hundred years and still Chapter House Planet must be considered only temporary.

She rested her left hand on the smooth frame of the window. Each of her windows had been positioned to focus the attention on a splendid view. The room—its proportions, furnishing, colors—all reflected architects and builders who had worked single-mindedly to create a sense of support for the occupants.

Taraza tried to immerse herself in that supportive feeling and failed.

The arguments she had just experienced left a bitterness in this room even though the words had been voiced in the mildest tones. Her councillors had been stubborn and (she agreed without reservation) for understandable reasons.

Make ourselves into missionaries? And for the Tleilaxu?

She touched a control plate beside the window and opened it. A warm breeze perfumed by spring blossoms from the apple orchards wafted into the room. The Sisterhood was proud of the fruit they grew here at the power center of all their strongholds. No finer orchards existed at any of the Keeps and Dependent Chapters that wove the Bene Gesserit web through most of the planets humans had occupied under the Old Imperium.

"By their fruits, ye shall know them," she thought. *Some of the old religions can still produce wisdom.*

From her high vantage, Taraza could see the entire southern sprawl of Chapter House buildings. The shadow of a nearby watchtower drew a long uneven line across rooftops and courtyards.

When she thought about it, she knew this was a surprisingly small establishment to contain so much power. Beyond the ring of orchards and gardens lay a careful checkerboard of private residences, each with its surrounding plantation. Retired Sisters and selected loyal families occupied these privileged estates. Sawtoothed mountains, their tops often brilliant with snow, drew the

western limits. The spacefield lay twenty kilometers eastward. All around this core of Chapter House were open
plains where grazed a peculiar breed of cattle, a cattle so
susceptible to alien odors they would stampede in raucous bellowing at the slightest intrusion of people not
marked by the local smell. The innermost homes with
their pain-fenced plantings had been sited by an early
Bashar in such a way that no one could move through
the twisting ground-level channels day or night without
being observed.

It all appeared so haphazard and casual, yet there was
harsh order in it. And that, Taraza knew, personified the
Sisterhood.

The clearing of a throat behind her reminded Taraza
that one of those who had argued most vehemently in
Council remained waiting patiently in the open doorway.

Waiting for my decision.

The Reverend Mother Bellonda wanted Odrade
"killed out of hand." No decision had been reached.

*You've really done it this time, Dar. I expected your wild
independence. I even wanted it. But this!*

Bellonda, old, fat and florid, cold-eyed and valued for
her natural viciousness, wanted Odrade condemned as a
traitor.

"The Tyrant would have crushed her immediately!"
Bellonda argued.

Is that all we learned from him? Taraza wondered.

Bellonda argued that Odrade was not only an Atreides
but also a Corrino. There were emperors and vice-
regents and powerful administrators to a very large number in her ancestry.

With all of the power hunger this implies.

"Her ancestors survived Salusa Secundus!" Bellonda kept repeating. "Have we learned nothing from our breeding experiences?"

We learned how to create Odrades, Taraza thought.

After surviving the spice agony, Odrade had been sent to Al Dhanab, an equivalent of Salusa Secundus, there to be conditioned deliberately on a planet of constant testing: high cliffs and dry gorges, hot winds and frigid winds, little moisture and too much. It was judged a suitable proving ground for someone whose destiny might take her to Rakis. Tough survivors emerged from such conditioning. The tall, supple, and muscular Odrade was one of the toughest.

How can I salvage this situation?

Odrade's most recent message said that any peace, even the Tyrant's millennia of suppression, radiated a false aura that could be fatal to those who trusted it too much. That was both the strength and flaw in Bellonda's argument.

Taraza lifted her gaze to Bellonda waiting in the doorway. *She is too fat! She flaunts that before us!*

"We can no more eliminate Odrade than we can eliminate the ghola," Taraza said.

Bellonda's voice came low and level: "Both are now too dangerous to us. Look how Odrade weakens you with her account of those words at Sietch Tabr!"

"Has the Tyrant's message weakened me, Bell?"

"You know what I mean. The Bene Tleilax have no morals."

"Quit changing the subject, Bell. Your thoughts are darting around like an insect among the blossoms. What is it you really smell here?"

"The Tleilaxu! They made that ghola for their own purposes. And now Odrade wants us to—"

"You're repeating yourself, Bell."

"The Tleilaxu take shortcuts. Their view of genetics is not our view. It is not a *human* view. They make monsters."

"Is that what they do?"

Bellonda came into the room, walked around the table and stood close to Taraza, blocking the Mother Superior's view of the niche and its statuette of Chenoeh.

"Alliance with the priests of Rakis, yes, but not with the Tleilaxu." Bellonda's robes rustled as she gestured with a clenched fist.

"Bell! The High Priest is now a mimic Face Dancer. Ally with him, you mean?"

Bellonda shook her head angrily. "Believers in Shaihulud are legion! You find them everywhere. What will be their reaction to us if our part in the deception is ever exposed?"

"No you don't, Bell! We have seen to it that only the Tleilaxu are vulnerable there. In that, Odrade's right."

"Wrong! If we ally with them we are both vulnerable. We will be forced to serve the Tleilaxu design. It will be worse than our long subservience to the Tyrant."

Taraza saw the vicious glinting of Bellonda's eyes. Her reaction was understandable. No Reverend Mother could contemplate the special bondage they had endured under the God Emperor without at least some chilling remembrances. Whipped along against their will, never sure of Bene Gesserit survival from one day to the next.

"You think we assure our spice supply by such a stupid alliance?" Bellonda demanded.

It was the same old argument, Taraza saw. Without melange and the agony of its transformation, there could be no Reverend Mothers. The whores from the Scattering surely had melange as one of their targets—the spice and the Bene Gesserit mastery of it.

Taraza returned to her table and sank into her chairdog, leaning back while it molded itself to her contours. It was a problem. A peculiar Bene Gesserit problem. Although they searched and experimented constantly, the Sisterhood had never found a substitute for the spice. The Spacing Guild might want melange to trance-form its navigators, but *they* could substitute Ixian machinery. Ix and its subsidiaries competed in the Guild's markets. *They* had alternatives.

We have none.

Bellonda crossed to the other side of Taraza's table, put both fists on the smooth surface and leaned forward to look down at the Mother Superior.

"And we still don't know what the Tleilaxu did to our ghola!"

"Odrade will find out."

"Not reason enough to forgive her treachery!"

Taraza spoke in a low voice: "We waited for this moment through generation after generation and you would abort the project just like that." She slapped a palm lightly against the table.

"The precious Rakian project is no longer our project," Bellonda said. "It may never have been."

All of her considerable mental powers in hard focus, Taraza reexamined the implications of this familiar argument. It was a thing spoken frequently in the wrangling session they had concluded earlier.

Was the ghola scheme something set in motion by the Tyrant? If so, what could they do about it now? What *should* they do about it?

During the long dispute, the Minority Report had been in all of their minds. Schwangyu might be dead but her faction survived and it looked now as though Bellonda had joined them. Was the Sisterhood blinding itself to a fatal possibility? Odrade's report of that hidden message on Rakis could be interpreted as an ominous warning. Odrade emphasized this by reporting how she had been alerted by her inner sense of alarm. No Reverend Mother could treat such an event lightly.

Bellonda straightened and folded her arms across her breast. "We never completely escape the teachers of our childhood nor any of the patterns that formed us, do we?"

That was an argument peculiar to Bene Gesserit disputes. It reminded them of their own particular susceptibility.

We are the secret aristocrats and it is our offspring who inherit the power. Yes, we are susceptible to that and Miles Teg is a superb example.

Bellonda found a straight chair and sat down, bringing her eyes level with Taraza's. "At the height of the Scattering," she said, "we lost some twenty percent of our failures."

"It is not failures who are coming back to us."

"But the Tyrant surely knew this would happen!"

"The Scattering was his goal, Bell. That was his Golden Path, humankind's survival!"

"But we know how he felt about the Tleilaxu and yet

he did not exterminate them. He could have and he did not!"

"He wanted diversity."

Bellonda pounded a fist on the table. "He certainly got that!"

"We've been through all of these arguments over and over, Bell, and I still see no way to escape what Odrade has done."

"Subservience!"

"Not at all. Were we ever totally subservient to one of the pre-Tyrant emperors? Not even to Muad'Dib!"

"We're still in the Tyrant's trap," Bellonda accused. "Tell me, why have the Tleilaxu continued to produce his favorite ghola? Millennia, and still that ghola keeps coming out of their tanks like a dancing doll."

"You think the Tleilaxu still follow a secret order from the Tyrant? If so, then you argue for Odrade. She has created admirable conditions for us to examine this."

"He ordered nothing of the kind! He merely made that particular ghola deliciously attractive to the Bene Tleilax."

"And not to us?"

"Mother Superior, we must get ourselves out of the Tyrant's trap now! And by the most direct method."

"The decision is mine, Bell. I still lean toward a cautious alliance."

"Then at the very least let us kill the ghola. Sheeana can have children. We could—"

"This is not now and never was purely a breeding project!"

"But it could be. What if you're wrong about the power behind the Atreides prescience?"

"All of your proposals lead to alienation from Rakis and from the Tleilaxu, Bell."

"The Sisterhood could weather fifty generations on our present stockpiles of melange. More with rationing."

"You think fifty generations is a long time, Bell? Don't you see that this very attitude is why you are not sitting in my chair?"

Bellonda pushed herself back from the table, her chair scraping harshly against the floor. Taraza could see that she was not convinced. Bellonda no longer could be trusted. She might be the one who would have to die. And where was the noble purpose in that?

"This gets us nowhere," Taraza said. "Leave me."

When she was alone, Taraza once more considered Odrade's message. Ominous. It was easy to see why Bellonda and others reacted violently. But that showed a dangerous lack of control.

It is not yet time to write the Sisterhood's final will and testament.

In an odd way, Odrade and Bellonda shared the same fear but came to different decisions because of that fear. Odrade's interpretation of that message in the stones of Rakis conveyed an old warning:

This, too, shall pass away.

Are we to end now, crushed by ravenous hordes from the Scattering?

But the secret of the axlotl tanks was almost within the Sisterhood's grasp.

If we gain that, nothing can stop us!

Taraza swung her gaze around the details of her room. The Bene Gesserit power was still here. Chapter House remained concealed behind a moat of no-ships, its location unrecorded except in the minds of her own people. Invisibility.

Temporary invisibility! Accidents occurred.

Taraza squared her shoulders. *Take precautions but don't live in their shadows, constantly furtive.* The Litany Against Fear served a useful purpose when avoiding shadows.

From anyone but Odrade, the warning message with its disturbing implications that the Tyrant still guided his Golden Path would have been far less fearsome.

That damnable Atreides talent!

"No more than a secret society?"

Taraza gritted her teeth in frustration.

"Memories are not enough unless they call you to noble purpose!"

And what if it was true that the Sisterhood no longer heard the music of life?

Damn him! The Tyrant could still touch them.

What is he trying to tell us? His Golden Path could not be in peril. The Scattering had seen to that. Humans had spread their kind outward on uncounted courses like the spines of a hedgehog.

Had he seen a vision of the Scattered Ones returning? Could he possibly have anticipated this bramble patch at the foot of his Golden Path?

He knew we would suspect his powers. He knew it!

Taraza thought about the mounting reports of the Lost Ones who were returning to their roots. A remarkable diversity of people and artifacts accompanied by a remarkable degree of secrecy and wide evidence of conspiracy. No-ships of a peculiar design, weapons and artifacts of breathtaking sophistication. Diverse peoples and diverse ways.

Some, astonishingly primitive. At least on the surface.

And they wanted much more than melange. Taraza recognized the peculiar form of mysticism that drove the Scattered Ones back: *"We want your elder secrets!"*

The message of the Honored Matres was clear enough, too: "We will take what we want."

Odrade has it all right in her hands, Taraza thought. She had Sheeana. Soon, if Burzmali succeeded, she would have the ghola. She had the Tleilaxu Master of Masters. She could have Rakis itself!

If only she were not an Atreides.

Taraza glanced at the projected words still dancing above her tabletop: a comparison of this newest Duncan Idaho with all of the slain ones. Each new ghola had been slightly different from its predecessors. That was clear enough. The Tleilaxu were perfecting something. But what? Was the clue hidden in these new Face Dancers? The Tleilaxu obviously sought an undetectable Face Dancer, mimics whose mimicry reached perfection, shape-copiers who copied not only the surface memories of their victims but the deepest thoughts and identity as well. It was a form of immortality even more enticing than the one the Tleilaxu Masters used at present. That obviously was why they followed this course.

Her own analysis agreed with the majority of her advisors: Such a mimic would *become* the copied person. Odrade's reports on the Face Dancer–Tuek were highly suggestive. Even the Tleilaxu Masters might not be able to shake such a Face Dancer out of its mimic shape and behavior.

And its beliefs.

Damn Odrade! She had painted her Sisters into a corner. They had no choice except to follow Odrade's lead and Odrade knew it!

How did she know it? Was it that wild talent again?

I cannot act blindly. I must know.

Taraza went through the well-remembered regimen to restore a sense of calm. She dared not make momentous decisions in a frustrated mood. A long look at the statuette of Chenoeh helped. Lifting herself from the chairdog, Taraza returned to her favorite window.

It often soothed her to stare out at this landscape, observing how the distances changed with the daily movement of sunlight and shifts in the planet's well-managed weather.

Hunger prodded her.

I will eat with the acolytes and lay Sisters today.

It helped at times to gather the young around her and remember the persistence of the eating rituals, the daily timing—morning, noon, and evening. That formed a reliable cement. She enjoyed watching her people. They were like a tide speaking of deeper things, of unseen forces and greater powers that persisted because the Bene Gesserit had found the ways of flowing with that persistence.

These thoughts renewed Taraza's balance. Nagging questions could be placed temporarily at a distance. She could look at them without passion.

Odrade and the Tyrant were right: *Without noble purpose we are nothing.*

One could not escape, though, the fact that critical decisions were being made on Rakis by a person who suffered from those recurring Atreides flaws. Odrade had always displayed typical Atreides weakness. She had been positively benevolent to erring acolytes. Affections developed out of such behavior!

Dangerous and mind-clouding affections.

This weakened others, who then were required to compensate for such laxity. More competent Sisters were called upon to take erring acolytes in hand and correct the weaknesses. Of course, Odrade's behavior had exposed these flaws in acolytes. One must admit this. Perhaps Odrade reasoned thus.

When she thought this way, something subtle and powerful shifted in Taraza's perceptions. She was forced to put down a deep sense of loneliness. It rankled. Melancholy could be quite as mind-clouding as affection . . . or even love. Taraza and her watchful Memory Sisters ascribed such emotional responses to awareness of mortality. She was forced to confront the fact that one day she would be no more than a set of memories in someone else's living flesh.

Memories and accidental discoveries, she saw, had made her vulnerable. And just when she needed every available faculty!

But I am not yet dead.

Taraza knew how to restore herself. And she knew the consequences. Always after these bouts of melancholy she regained an even firmer grip on her life and its purposes. Odrade's flawed behavior was a source of her Mother Superior's strength.

Odrade knew it. Taraza smiled grimly at this awareness. The Mother Superior's authority over her Sisters
always became stronger when she returned from melancholy. Others had observed this but only Odrade knew
about the rage.

There!

Taraza realized that she had confronted the distressful
seeds of her frustration.

Odrade had clearly recognized on several occasions
what sat at the core of the Mother Superior's behavior. A
giant howl of rage against the uses others had made of
her life. The power of that suppressed rage was daunting
even though it could never be expressed in a way that
vented it. That rage must never be allowed to heal. How
it hurt! Odrade's awareness made the pain even more
intense.

Such things did what they were supposed to do, of
course. Bene Gesserit impositions developed certain
mental muscles. They built up layers of callousness that
could never be revealed to outsiders. Love was one of the
most dangerous forces in the universe. They had to protect themselves against it. A Reverend Mother could
never become intimately personal, not even in the services of the Bene Gesserit.

*Simulation: We play the necessary role that saves us. The
Bene Gesserit will persist!*

How long would they be subservient this time? Another thirty-five hundred years? Well, damn them all! It
would still be only a temporary thing.

Taraza turned her back on the window and its restor-
ative view. She *did* feel restored. New strength flowed

into her. There was strength enough to overcome that gnawing reluctance which had kept her from making the essential decision.

I will go to Rakis.

She no longer could evade the source of her own reluctance.

I may have to do what Bellonda wants.

Survival of self, of species, and of environment, these are what drive humans. You can observe how the order of importance changes in a lifetime. What are the things of immediate concern at a given age? Weather? The state of the digestion? Does she (or he) really care? All of those various hungers that flesh can sense and hope to satisfy. What else could possibly matter?

—LETO II TO HWI NOREE, HIS VOICE: DAR-ES-BALAT

Miles Teg awoke in darkness to find himself being carried on a litter sling supported by suspensors. By their faint energy glow, he could see the tiny suspensor bulbs in an updangling row around him.

There was a gag in his mouth. His hands were securely tied behind his back. His eyes remained uncovered.

So they don't care what I see.

Who *they* were he could not tell. The bobbing motions of the dark shapes around him suggested they were descending uneven terrain. A trail? The litter sling rode smoothly on its suspensors. He could sense the faint humming from the suspensors when his party stopped to negotiate the turn of a difficult passage.

Now and then through some intervening obstruction, he saw the flickering of a light ahead. They entered the lighted area presently and stopped. He saw a single glow-globe about three meters off the ground, tethered on a pole and moving gently in a cold breeze. By its yellow glow he discerned a shack in the center of a muddy clearing, many tracks in trampled snow. He saw bushes and a few sparse trees around the clearing. Someone passed a brighter handlight across his face. Nothing was said but Teg saw a hand gesture toward the shack. He had seldom seen such a dilapidated structure. It looked ready to collapse at the slightest touch. He bet himself that the roof leaked.

Once more, his party lurched into motion, swinging him toward the shack. He studied his escort in the dim light—faces muffled to the eyes in a cover that obscured mouths and chins. Hoods hid their hair. The clothing was bulky and concealed body details except for the general articulation of arms and legs.

The pole-tethered glowglobe went dark.

A door opened in the shack, sending a brilliant glare across the clearing. His escort hustled him inside and left him there. He heard the door close behind them.

It was almost blindingly bright inside after the darkness. Teg blinked until his eyes adapted to the change. With an odd sense of displacement, he looked around him. He had expected the shack's interior to match its exterior but here was a neat room almost bare of furnishings—only three chairs, a small table and . . . he drew in a sharp breath: an Ixian Probe! Couldn't they smell the shere on his breath?

If they were that unaware, let them use the probe. It would be agony for him but they would get nothing from his mind.

Something clicked behind him and he heard motion. Three people came into his field of vision and ranged themselves around the foot of the litter. They stared at him silently. Teg moved his attention across the three. The one on his left wore a dark singlesuit with open lapels. Male. He had the squarish face Teg had seen on some Gammu natives—small, beady eyes that stared straight through Teg. It was the face of an inquisitor, one who would not be moved by your agony. The Harkonnens had imported a lot of those in their day. Single-purpose types who could create pain without the slightest change of expression.

The one directly at Teg's feet wore bulky clothing of black and gray similar to that of the escort but the hood was thrown back to reveal a bland face under closely cropped gray hair. The face gave nothing away and the clothing revealed little. No telling if this one was male or female. Teg recorded the face: wide forehead, square chin, large green eyes above a knife-ridged nose; a tiny mouth pursed around a moue of distaste.

The third member of this group held Teg's attention longest: tall, a tailored black singlesuit with a severe black jacket over it. Perfectly fitted. Expensive. No decorations or insignia. Male definitely. The man affected boredom and this gave Teg a tag for him. Narrow, supercilious face, brown eyes, thin-lipped mouth. Bored, bored, bored! All of this in here was an unwarranted demand on his very important time. He had vital business elsewhere and these other two, these *underlings*, must be made to realize that.

That one, Teg thought, *is the official observer.*

The bored one had been sent by the masters of this place to watch and report what he saw. Where was his datacase? Ahhhh, yes: There it was, propped against a wall behind him. Those cases were like a badge for such functionaries. On his inspection tour, Teg had seen these people walking the streets of Ysai and other Gammu cities. Small, thin cases. The more important the functionary, the smaller the case. This one's case would barely contain a few dataspools and a tiny comeye. He would never be without an 'eye to link him with his superiors. Thin case: This was an important functionary.

Teg found himself wondering what the observer would say if Teg asked: "What will you tell them about my composure?"

The answer was already there on that bored face. He would not even answer. He was not here to answer. When this one leaves, Teg thought, he will walk with long strides. His attention will be on distances where only he knows what powers await him. He will slap that case against his leg to remind himself of his importance and to call the attention of these others to his badge of authority.

The bulky figure at Teg's feet spoke, a compelling voice and definitely female in those vibrant tones.

"See how he holds himself and watches us? Silence will not break him. I told you that before we entered. You are wasting our time and we do not have all that much time for such nonsense."

Teg stared at her. Something vaguely familiar in the voice. It had some of that compelling quality found in a Reverend Mother. Was that possible?

The heavy-faced Gammu type nodded. "You are right, Materly. But I do not give the orders here."

Materly? Teg wondered. *Name or title?*

Both of them looked at the functionary. That one

turned and bent to his datacase. He removed a small comeye from it and stood with the screen concealed from his companions and Teg. The 'eye came alight with a green glow, which cast a sickly illumination over the observer's features. His self-important smile vanished. He moved his lips silently, words formed only for someone on that 'eye to see.

Teg hid his ability to read lips. Anyone trained by the Bene Gesserit could read lips from almost any angle where they were visible. This man spoke a version of Old Galach.

"It is the Bashar Teg for sure," he said. "I have made identification."

The green light danced on the functionary's face while he stared into the 'eye. Whoever communicated with him was in agitated movement if that light meant anything.

Again, the functionary's lips moved soundlessly: "None of us doubts that he has been conditioned against pain and I can smell shere on him. He will . . ."

He fell silent as the green light once more danced on his face.

"I do not make excuses." His lips shaped the Old Galach words with care. "You know we will do our best but I recommend that we pursue with vigor all other means of intercepting the ghola."

The green light winked off.

The functionary clipped the 'eye to his waist, turned toward his companions and nodded once.

"The T-probe," the woman said.

They swung the probe over Teg's head.

She called it a T-probe, Teg thought. He looked up at

the hood as they brought it over him. There was no Ixian stamp on the thing.

Teg experienced an odd sense of déjà vu. He had the feeling that his own captivity here had occurred many times before. No single-incident déjà vu, it was a deeply familiar recognition: the captive and the interrogators—these three . . . the probe. He felt emptied. How could he know this moment? He had never personally employed a probe but he had studied their use thoroughly. The Bene Gesserit often used pain but relied mostly on Truthsayers. Even more than that, the Sisterhood believed that some equipment could put them too much under Ixian influence. It was an admission of weakness, a sign that they could not do without such despicable devices. Teg had even suspected there was something in this attitude of a hangover from the Butlerian Jihad, rebellion against machines that could copy out the essence of a human's thoughts and memories.

Déjà vu!

Mentat logic demanded of him: *How do I know this moment?* He *knew* that he had never before been a captive. It was such a ridiculous switch of roles. The great Bashar Teg a captive? He could almost smile. But that deep sense of familiarity persisted.

His captors positioned the hood directly over his head and began releasing the medusa contacts one at a time, fixing them to his scalp. The functionary watched his companions work, producing small signs of impatience on an otherwise emotionless face.

Teg moved his attention across the three faces. Which one of these would act the part of "friend"? Ahhhh, yes: the one called Materly. Fascinating. Was it a form of

Honored Matre? But neither of the others deferred to her as one would expect from what Teg had heard of those returning Lost Ones.

These were people from the Scattering, though—except possibly for the square-faced male in the brown singlesuit. Teg studied the woman with care: the mat of gray hair, the quiet composure in those widely spaced green eyes, the slightly protruding chin with its sense of solidity and reliability. She had been chosen well for "friend." Materly's face was a map of respectability, someone you could trust. Teg saw a withdrawn quality in her, though. She was one who would also observe carefully to catch the moment when she must become involved. Surely, she was Bene Gesserit–trained at the very least.

Or trained by the Honored Matres.

They finished attaching the contacts to his head. The Gammu type swung the probe's console into position where all three could watch the display. The probe's screen was concealed from Teg.

The woman removed Teg's gag, confirming his judgment. She would be the source of comfort. He moved his tongue around in his mouth, restoring sensation. His face and chest still felt a bit numb from the stunner that had brought him down. How long ago had that been? But if he was to believe the silent words of the functionary, Duncan had escaped.

The Gammu type looked to the observer.

"You may begin, Yar," the functionary said.

Yar? Teg wondered. *Curious name.* Almost had a Tleilaxu sound. But Yar was not a Face Dancer . . . or a Tleilaxu Master. Too big for one and no stigmata of the other. As one trained by the Sisterhood, Teg felt confident of this.

Yar touched a control on the probe's console.

Teg heard himself grunt with pain. Nothing had prepared him for that much pain. They must have turned their devil's machine to maximum for the first thrust. No question about it! They knew he was a Mentat. A Mentat could remove himself from some demands of flesh. But this was excruciating! He could not escape it. Agony shivered through his entire body, threatening to blank out his consciousness. Could shere shield him from this?

The pain diminished gradually and went away, leaving only quivering memories.

Again!

He thought suddenly that the spice agony must be like this for a Reverend Mother. Surely, there could be no greater pain. He fought to remain silent but heard himself grunting, moaning. Every ability he had ever learned, Mentat and Bene Gesserit, was called into play, keeping him from forming words, from begging for surcease, from promising to tell them anything if they would only stop.

Once more the agony receded and then surged back.

"Enough!" That was the woman. Teg groped for her name. *Materly?*

Yar spoke in a sullen voice: "He's loaded with shere, enough to last him a year at least." He gestured at his console. "Blank."

Teg breathed in shallow gasps. The agony! It continued to increase despite Materly's demand.

"I said enough!" Materly snapped.

Such sincerity, Teg thought. He felt the pain recede, withdrawing as though every nerve were being removed from his body, pulled out like threads of the remembered agony.

"It is wrong what we're doing," Materly said. "This man is—"

"He is like any other man," Yar said. "Shall I attach the special contact to his penis?"

"Not while I'm here!" Materly said.

Teg felt himself almost taken in by her sincerity. The last of the agony threads left his flesh and he lay there with a feeling that he had been suspended off the surface that supported him. The sense of déjà vu remained. He was here and not here. He had been here and he had not.

"They will not like it if we fail," Yar said. "Are you prepared to face them with another failure?"

Materly shook her head sharply. She bent over to bring her face into Teg's line of vision through the medusa tangle of probe contacts. "Bashar, I am sorry for what we do. Believe me. This is not of my making. Please, I find all of this disgusting. Tell us what we need to know and let me make you comfortable."

Teg formed a smile for her. She was good! He shifted his gaze to the watchful functionary. "Tell your masters for me. She is very good at this."

Blood darkened the functionary's face. He scowled "Give him the maximum, Yar." His voice was a clipped tenor without any of the deep training apparent in Materly's voice.

"Please!" Materly said. She straightened but kept her attention on Teg's eyes.

Teg's Bene Gesserit teachers had taught him that: "Watch the eyes! Observe how they change focus. As the focus moves outward, the awareness moves inward."

He focused deliberately on her nose. It was not an ugly face. Rather distinctive. He wondered what the figure might be under those bulky clothes.

"Yar!" That was the functionary.

Yar adjusted something on his console and pressed a switch.

The agony that surged through Teg now told him the previous level had, indeed, been lower. With the new pain came an odd clarity. Teg found himself almost capable of removing his awareness from this intrusion. All of that pain was happening to someone else. He had found a haven where little touched him. There was pain. Agony even. He accepted reports about these sensations. That was partly the shere's doing, of course. He knew that and was thankful.

Materly's voice intruded: "I think we're losing him. Better ease off."

Another voice responded but the sound faded into stillness before Teg could identify the words. He realized abruptly that he had no anchor point for his awareness. Stillness! He thought he heard his heart beating rapidly in fear but he was not sure. All was stillness, profound quiet with nothing behind it.

Am I still alive?

He found a heartbeat then, but no certainty that it was his own. *Thump-thump! Thump-thump!* It was a sensation of movement and no sound. He could not fix the source.

What is happening to me?

Words blazoned in brilliant white against a black background played across his visual centers:

"I'm back to one-third."

"Leave it at that. See if we can read him through his physical reactions."

"Can he still hear us?"

"Not consciously."

None of Teg's instructions had told him a probe could do its evil work in the presence of shere. But they called this a T-probe. Could bodily reactions provide a clue to suppressed thoughts? Were there revelations to be explored by physical means?

Again, words played against Teg's visual centers: "Is he still isolated?"

"Completely."

"Make sure. Take him a little deeper."

Teg tried to lift his awareness above his fears.

I must remain in control!

What might his body reveal if he had no contact with it? He could imagine what they were doing and his mind registered panic but his flesh could not feel it.

Isolate the subject. Give him nowhere to seat his identity.

Who had said that? Someone. The sense of déjà vu returned in full force.

I am a Mentat, he reminded himself. *My mind and its workings are my center.* He possessed experiences and memories upon which a center could rely.

Pain returned. Sounds. Loud! Much too loud!

"He's hearing again." That was Yar.

"How can that be?" The functionary's tenor.

"Perhaps you've set it too low." Materly.

Teg tried to open his eyes. The lids would not obey. He remembered then. They had called it a T-probe. This was no Ixian device. This was something from the Scattering. He could identify where it took over his muscles and senses. It was like another person sharing his flesh, preempting his own reactive patterns. He allowed himself to follow the workings of this machine's intrusions. It was a hellish device! It could order him to blink, fart, gasp, shit, piss—anything. It could command his body as though he had no thinking part in his own behavior. He was relegated to the role of observer.

Odors assailed him—disgusting odors. He would not command himself to frown but he thought of frowning. That was sufficient. These odors had been elicited by the probe. It was playing his senses, learning them.

"Do you have enough to read him?" The functionary's tenor.

"He's still hearing us!" Yar.

"Damn all Mentats!" Materly.

"Dit, Dat, and Dot," Teg said, naming the puppets of the Winter Show from his childhood on long-ago Lernaeus.

"He's talking!" The functionary.

Teg felt his awareness being blocked off by the machine. Yar was doing something at the console. Still, Teg knew his own Mentat logic had told him something vital: These three were puppets. Only the puppet masters were important. How the puppets moved—that told you what the puppet masters were doing.

The probe continued to intrude. Despite the force being applied, Teg felt his awareness matching the thing. It was learning him but he was also learning it.

He understood now. The whole spectrum of his senses could be copied into this T-probe and identified, tagged for Yar to call up when needed. An organic chain of responses existed within Teg. The machine could trace those out as though it made a duplicate of him. The shere and his Mentat resistance shunted the searchers away from his memories but everything else could be copied.

It will not think like me, he reassured himself.

The machine would not be the same as his nerves and flesh. It would not have Teg-memories or Teg-experiences. It had not been born of woman. It had never traveled down a birth canal and emerged into this astonishing universe.

Part of Teg's awareness applied a memory marker, telling him that this observation revealed something about the ghola.

Duncan was decanted from an axlotl tank.

The observation came to Teg with a sudden sharp biting of acid on his tongue.

The T-probe again!

Teg allowed himself to flow through a multiple simultaneous awareness. He followed the T-probe's workings and continued to explore this observation about the ghola, all the while listening for Dit, Dat, and Dot. The three puppets were oddly silent. Yes, waiting for their T-probe to complete its task.

The ghola: Duncan was an extension of cells that *had* been born of a woman impregnated by a man.

Machine and ghola!

Observation: *The machine cannot share that birth experience except in a remotely vicarious way sure to miss important personal nuances.*

Just as it was missing other things in him right now.

The T-probe was replaying smells. With each induced odor, memories revealed their presence in Teg's mind. He felt the great speed of the T-probe but his own awareness lived outside of that headlong rushing search, able to entangle him for as long as he desired in the memories being called up here.

There!

That was the hot wax he had spilled on his left hand when only fourteen and a student in the Bene Gesserit school. He recalled school and laboratory as though his only existence were there at this moment. *The school is attached to Chapter House.* By being admitted here, Teg knew he had the blood of Siona in his veins. No prescient could track him here.

He saw the lab and smelled the wax—a compound of artificial esters and the natural product of bees kept by failed Sisters and their helpers. He turned his memory to a moment when he watched bees and people at their labors in the apple orchards.

The workings of the Bene Gesserit social structure appeared so complicated until you saw through to the necessities: food, clothing, warmth, communication, learning, protection from enemies (a subset of the survival drive). Bene Gesserit survival took some adjustments before it could be understood. They did not procreate for the sake of humankind in general. No unmonitored racial involvement! They procreated to extend their own powers, to continue the Bene Gesserit, deeming that a sufficient service to humankind. Perhaps it was. Procreative motivation went deep and the Sisterhood was so thorough.

A new smell assailed him.

He recognized the wet wool of his clothing as he came into the command pod after the Battle of Ponciard.

The smell filled his nostrils and elicited the ozone of the pod's instruments, the sweat of the other occupants. *Wool!* The Sisterhood had always thought it a bit odd of him, the way he preferred natural fabrics and shunned the synthetics turned out in captive factories.

No more did he care for chairdogs.

I don't like the smells of oppression in any form.

Did these puppets—Dit, Dat, and Dot—know how oppressed they were?

Mentat logic sneered at him. Were not wool fabrics also a product of captive factories?

It was different.

Part of him argued otherwise. Synthetics could be stored almost indefinitely. Look how long they had endured in the nullentropy bins of the Harkonnen no-globe.

"I still prefer woolens and cottons!"

So be it!

"But how did I come by such a preference?"

It is an Atreides prejudice. You inherited it.

Teg shunted the smells aside and concentrated on the total movement of the intrusive probe. He found presently that he could anticipate the thing. It was a new muscle. He allowed himself to flex it while he continued to examine the induced memories for valuable insights.

I sit outside my mother's door on Lernaeus.

Teg removed part of his awareness and watched the scene: age eleven. He is talking to a small Bene Gesserit acolyte who came as part of the escort for Somebody Important. The acolyte is a tiny thing with red-blond hair and a doll's face. Upturned nose, green-gray eyes. The SI is a black-robed Reverend Mother of truly ancient appearance. She has gone behind that nearby door with Teg's mother. The acolyte, who is named Carlana, is trying her fledgling skills on the young son of the house.

Before Carlana utters twenty words, Miles Teg recognizes the pattern. She is trying to pry information out of him! This was one of the first lessons in delicate dissembling taught by his mother. There were, after all, people who might question a young boy about a Reverend Mother's household, hoping thereby to gain salable information. There is always a market for data about Reverend Mothers.

His mother explained: "You judge the questioner and fit your responses according to the susceptibilities." None of this would have served against a full Reverend Mother, but against an acolyte, especially this one!

For Carlana, he produces an appearance of coy reluctance. Carlana has an inflated view of her own attractions. He allows her to overcome his reluctance after a suitable marshaling of her forces. What she gets is a handful of lies, which, if she ever repeats them to the SI behind that closed door, are sure to win Carlana a severe censuring if not something more painful.

Words from Dit, Dat, and Dot: "I think we have him now."

Teg recognized Yar's voice yanking him out of old memories. *"Fit your responses according to the susceptibilities."* Teg heard the words in his mother's voice.

Puppets.

Puppet masters.

The functionary speaks: "Ask the simulation where they have taken the ghola."

Silence and then a faint humming.

"I'm not getting anything." Yar.

Teg hears their voices with painful sensitivity. He forces his eyes to open against the opposing commands of the probe.

"Look!" Yar says.

Three sets of eyes stare back at Teg. How slowly they move. Dit, Dat, and Dot: the eyes go blink . . . blink . . . at least a minute between blinks. Yar is reaching for something on his console. His fingers will take a week to reach their destination.

Teg explores the bindings on his hands and arms. Ordinary rope! Taking his time, he squirms his fingers into contact with the knots. They loosen, slowly at first, and then flying apart. He moves on to the straps holding him to the sling litter. These are easier: simple slip locks. Yar's hand is not even a fourth of the way to the console.

Blink . . . blink . . . blink . . .

The three sets of eyes show faint surprise.

Teg releases himself from the medusa tangle of probe contacts. *Pop-pop-pop!* The grippers fly away from him. He is surprised to notice a slow start of bleeding on the back of his right hand where it has brushed the probe contacts aside.

Mentat projection: *I am moving with dangerous speed.*

But now he is off the litter. Functionary is reaching a slow-slow hand toward a bulge in a side pocket. Teg's hand crushes the functionary's throat. Functionary will never again touch that little lasgun he always carries. Yar's outstretched hand is still not a third of the way to the probe console. There is definite surprise in his eyes, though. Teg doubts that the man even sees the hand that breaks his neck. Materly is moving a bit faster. Her left foot is coming toward where Teg had been just the flick of an instant previously. Still too slow! Materly's head is thrown back, the throat exposed for Teg's down-chopping hand.

How slowly they fall to the floor!

Teg became aware of perspiration pouring from him but he could not spare time to worry about this.

I knew every move they would make before they made it! What has happened to me?

Mentat projection: *The probe agony has lifted me to a new level of ability.*

Intense hunger pangs made him aware of the energy drain. He pushed the sensation aside, feeling himself re-turn to a normal time-beat. Three dull sounds: bodies falling to the floor.

Teg examined the probe console. Definitely not Ixian. Similar controls, though. He shorted out the data stor-age system, erasing it.

Room lights?

Controls beside the door from the outside. He extin-guished the lights, took three deep breaths. A whirling blur of motion erupted into the night.

The ones who had brought him here, clad in their bulky clothing against the winter chill, barely had time to turn toward the odd sound before the whirling blur struck them down.

Teg returned to normal time-beat more quickly. Star-light showed him a trail leading downslope through thick brush. He slipped and slid on the snow-churned mud for a space and then found the way to balance himself, anticipating the terrain. Each step went where he knew it must go. He found himself presently in an open space that looked out across a valley.

The lights of a city and a great black rectangle of building near the center. He knew this place: Ysai. The puppet masters were there.

I am free!

There was a man who sat each day looking out through a narrow vertical opening where a single board had been removed from a tall wooden fence. Each day a wild ass of the desert passed outside the fence and across the narrow opening—first the nose, then the head, the forelegs, the long brown back, the hindlegs, and lastly the tail. One day, the man leaped to his feet with the light of discovery in his eyes and he shouted for all who could hear him: "It is obvious! The nose causes the tail!"

—STORIES OF THE HIDDEN WISDOM,
FROM THE ORAL HISTORY OF RAKIS

Several times since coming to Rakis, Odrade had found herself caught in the memory of that ancient painting which occupied such a prominent place on the wall of Taraza's Chapter House quarters. When the memory came, she felt her hands tingle to the touch of the brush. Her nostrils swelled to the induced smells of oils and pigments. Her emotions assaulted the canvas. Each time, Odrade emerged from the memory with new doubts that Sheeana was her canvas.

Which of us paints the other?

It had happened again this morning. Still dark outside the Rakian Keep's penthouse where she quartered with Sheeana: An acolyte entered softly to waken Odrade and tell her that Taraza would arrive shortly. Odrade looked up at the softly illuminated face of the dark-haired acolyte and immediately that memory-painting flashed into her awareness.

Which of us truly creates another?

"Let Sheeana sleep a bit longer," Odrade said before dismissing the acolyte.

"Will you breakfast before the Mother Superior's arrival?" the acolyte asked.

"We will wait upon Taraza's pleasure."

Arising, Odrade went through a swift toilet and donned her best black robe. She strode then to the east window of the penthouse common room and looked out in the direction of the spacefield. Many moving lights cast a glow on the dusty sky there. She activated all of the room's glowglobes to soften the exterior view. The globes became reflected golden starbursts on the thick armor-plaz of the windows. The dusky surface also reflected a dim outline of her own features, showing the fatigue lines clearly.

I knew she would come, Odrade thought.

Even as she thought this, the Rakian sun came over the dust-blurred horizon like a child's orange ball thrust into view. Immediately, there was the heat-bounce that so many observers of Rakis had mentioned. Odrade turned away from the view and saw the hall door open.

Taraza entered with a rustle of robes. A hand closed the door behind her, leaving the two of them alone. The Mother Superior advanced on Odrade, black hood up and the cowl framing her face. It was not a reassuring sight.

Recognizing the disturbance in Odrade, Taraza

played on it. "Well, Dar, I think we finally meet as strangers."

The effect of Taraza's words startled Odrade. She correctly interpreted the threat but fear left her, spilling out as though it were water poured from a jug. For the first time in her life, Odrade recognized the precise moment of crossing a dividing line. This was a line whose existence she thought few of her Sisters suspected. As she crossed it, she realized that she had always known it was there: a place where she could enter the void and float free. She no longer was vulnerable. She could be killed but she could not be defeated.

"So it's not Dar and Tar anymore," Odrade said.

Taraza heard the clear, uninhibited tone of Odrade's voice and interpreted this as confidence. "Perhaps it never was Dar and Tar," she said, her voice icy. "I see that you think you have been extremely clever."

The battle has been joined, Odrade thought. *But I do not stand in the path of her attack.*

Odrade said: "The alternatives to alliance with the Tleilaxu could not be accepted. Especially when I recognized what it was you truly sought for us."

Taraza felt suddenly weary. It had been a long trip despite the space-folding leaps of her no-ship. The flesh always knew when it had been twisted out of its familiar rhythms. She chose a soft divan and sat down, sighing in the luxurious comfort.

Odrade recognized the Mother Superior's fatigue and felt immediate sympathy. They were suddenly two Reverend Mothers with common problems.

Taraza obviously sensed this. She patted the cushion beside her and waited for Odrade to be seated.

"We must preserve the Sisterhood," Taraza said. "That is the only important thing."

"Of course."

Taraza fixed her gaze searchingly on Odrade's familiar features. *Yes, Odrade, too, is weary.* "You have been here, intimately touching the people and the problem," Taraza said. "I want . . . no, Dar, I *need* your views."

"The Tleilaxu give the appearance of full cooperation," Odrade said, "but there is dissembling in this. I have begun to ask myself some extremely disturbing questions."

"Such as?"

"What if the axlotl tanks are not . . . tanks?"

"What do you mean?"

"Waff reveals the kinds of behavior you see when a family tries to conceal a deformed child or a mad uncle. I swear to you, he is embarrassed when we begin to touch on the tanks."

"But what could they possibly . . ."

"Surrogate mothers."

"But they would have to be . . ." Taraza fell silent, shocked by the possibilities this question opened.

"Who has ever seen a Tleilaxu female?" Odrade asked.

Taraza's mind was filled with objections: "But the precise chemical control, the need to limit variables . . ." She threw her hood back and shook her hair free. "You are correct: we must question everything. This, though . . . this is monstrous."

"He is still not telling the full truth about our ghola."

"What does he say?"

"No more than what I have already reported: a variation on the original Duncan Idaho and meeting all of the prana-bindu requirements we specified."

"That does not explain why they killed or tried to kill our previous purchases."

"He swears the holy oath of the Great Belief that they acted out of shame because the eleven previous gholas did not live up to expectations."

"How could they know? Does he suggest they have spies among . . ."

"He swears not. I taxed him with this and he said that a successful ghola would be sure to create a visible disturbance among us."

"What visible disturbance? What is he . . ."

"He will not say. He returns each time to the claim that they have met their contractual obligations. Where is the ghola, Tar?"

"What . . . oh. On Gammu."

"I hear rumors of . . ."

"Burzmali has the situation well in hand." Taraza closed her mouth tightly, hoping that was the truth. The most recent report did not fill her with confidence.

"You obviously are debating whether to have the ghola killed," Odrade said.

"Not just the ghola!"

Odrade smiled. "Then it's true that Bellonda wants me permanently eliminated."

"How did you . . ."

"Friendships can be a very valuable asset at times, Tar."

"You tread on dangerous ground, Reverend Mother Odrade."

"But I am not stumbling, Mother Superior Taraza. I am thinking long hard thoughts about the things Waff has revealed about those Honored Matres."

"Tell me some of your thoughts." There was implacable determination in Taraza's voice.

"Let us make no mistakes about this," Odrade said. "They have surpassed the sexual skills of our Imprinters."

"Whores!"

"Yes, they employ their skills in a way ultimately fatal to themselves and others. They have been blinded by their own power."

"Is that the extent of your long hard thoughts?"

"Tell me, Tar, why did they attack and obliterate our Keep on Gammu?"

"Obviously they were after our Idaho ghola, to capture him or kill him."

"Why would that be so important to them?"

"What are you trying to say?" Taraza demanded.

"Could the *whores* have been acting upon information revealed to them by the Tleilaxu? Tar, what if this secret thing Waff's people have introduced into our ghola is something that would make the ghola a male equivalent of the Honored Matres?"

Taraza put a hand to her mouth and dropped it quickly when she saw how much the gesture revealed. It was too late. No matter. They were still two Reverend Mothers together.

Odrade said: "And we have ordered Lucilla to make him irresistible to most women."

"How long have the Tleilaxu been dealing with those whores?" Taraza demanded.

Odrade shrugged. "A better question is this: How long have they been dealing with their own Lost Ones returned from the Scattering? Tleilaxu speak to Tleilaxu and many secrets could be revealed."

"A brilliant projection on your part," Taraza said. "What probability value do you attach to it?"

"You know that as well as I do. It would explain many things."

Taraza spoke bitterly. "What do you think of your alliance with the Tleilaxu now?"

"More necessary than ever. We must be on the inside. We must be where we can influence those who contend."

"Abomination!" Taraza snapped.

"What?"

"This ghola is like a recording device in human shape. They have planted him in our midst. If the Tleilaxu get their hands on him they will know many things about us."

"That would be clumsy."

"And typical of them!"

"I agree that there are other implications in our situation," Odrade said. "But such arguments only tell me that we dare not kill the ghola until we have examined him ourselves."

"That might be too late! Damn your alliance, Dar! You gave them a hold on us . . . and us a hold on them— and neither of us dares let go."

"Is that not the perfect alliance?"

Taraza sighed. "How soon must we give them access to our breeding records?"

"Soon. Waff is pressing the matter."

"Then, will we see their axlotl . . . tanks?"

"That is, of course, the lever I am using. He has given his reluctant agreement."

"Deeper and deeper into each other's pockets," Taraza growled.

Her tone all innocence, Odrade said: "A perfect alliance, just as I said."

"Damn, damn, damn," Taraza muttered. "And Teg has reawakened the ghola's original memories!"

"But has Lucilla . . ."

"I don't know!" Taraza turned a grim expression on Odrade and recounted the most recent reports from Gammu: Teg and his party located, the briefest of accounts about them and nothing from Lucilla; plans made to bring them out.

Her own words produced an unsettling picture in Taraza's mind. What was this ghola? They had always known the Duncan Idahos were not ordinary gholas. But now, with augmented nerve and muscle capabilities plus this unknown thing the Tleilaxu had introduced—it was like holding a burning club. You knew you might have to use the club for your own survival but the flames approached at a terrifying speed.

Odrade spoke in a musing tone: "Have you ever tried to imagine what it must be like for a ghola suddenly to awaken in renewed flesh?"

"What? What are you . . ."

"Realizing that your flesh was grown from the cells of a cadaver," Odrade said. "He remembers his own death."

"The Idahos were never ordinary people," Taraza said.

"The same may be said for these Tleilaxu Masters."

"What are you trying to say?"

Odrade rubbed her own forehead, taking a moment to review her thoughts. This was so difficult with someone who rejected affection, with someone who thrust outward from a core of rage. Taraza had no . . . no *simpatico*. She could not assume the flesh and senses of another except as an exercise in logic.

"A ghola's awakening must be a shattering experience," Odrade said, lowering her hand. "Only the ones with enormous mental resilience would survive."

"We assume that the Tleilaxu Masters are more than they appear to be."

"And the Duncan Idahos?"

"Of course. Why else would the Tyrant keep buying them from the Tleilaxu?"

Odrade saw that the argument was pointless. She said: "The Idahos were notoriously loyal to the Atreides and we must remember that I am Atreides."

"You think loyalty will bind this one to you?"

"Especially after Lucilla—"

"That may be too dangerous!"

Odrade sat back into a corner of the divan. Taraza wanted certainty. And the lives of the serial gholas were like melange, presenting a different taste in different surroundings. How could they be sure of their ghola?

"The Tleilaxu meddle with the forces that produced our Kwisatz Haderach," Taraza muttered.

"You think that's why they want our breeding records?"

"I don't know! Damn you, Dar! Don't you see what you've done?"

"I think I had no choice," Odrade said.

Taraza produced a cold smile. Odrade's performance remained superb but she needed to be put in her place.

"You think I would have done the same?" Taraza asked.

She still does not see what has happened to me, Odrade thought. Taraza had expected her pliant Dar to act with independence but the extent of that independence had shaken the High Council. Taraza refused to see her own hand in this.

"Customary practice," Odrade said.

The words struck Taraza like a slap in the face. Only the hard training of a Bene Gesserit lifetime prevented her from striking out violently at Odrade.

Customary practice!

How many times had Taraza herself revealed this as a source of irritation, a constant goad to her carefully capped rage? Odrade had heard it often.

Odrade quoted the Mother Superior now: "Immovable custom is dangerous. Enemies can find a pattern and use it against you."

The words were forced from Taraza: "That is a weakness, yes."

"Our enemies thought they knew our way," Odrade said. "Even you, *Mother Superior,* thought you knew the limits within which I would perform. I was like Bellonda. Before she even spoke, you knew what Bellonda would say."

"Have we made a mistake, not elevating you above me?" Taraza asked. She spoke from her deepest allegiance.

"No, Mother Superior. We walk a delicate path but both of us can see where we must go."

"Where is Waff now?" Taraza asked.

"Asleep and well guarded."

"Summon Sheeana. We must decide whether to abort that part of the project."

"And take our lumps?"

"As you say, Dar."

Sheeana was still sleepy and rubbing her eyes when she appeared in the common room but she obviously had taken the time to splash water on her face and dress in a clean white robe. Her hair was still damp.

Taraza and Odrade stood near an eastern window with their backs to the light.

"This is Sheeana, Mother Superior," Odrade said.

Sheeana came fully alert with an abrupt stiffening of her back. She had heard of this powerful woman, this Taraza, who ruled the Sisterhood from a distant citadel called Chapter House. Sunlight was bright in the window behind the two women, shining full into Sheeana's face, dazzling her. It left the faces of the two Reverend Mothers partly obscured, the black outlines of their figures fuzzy in the brilliance.

Acolyte instructors had prepared her against this encounter: "You stand at attention before the Mother Superior and speak respectfully. Respond only when she speaks to you."

Sheeana stood at rigid attention the way she had been told.

"I am informed that you may become one of us," Taraza said.

Both women could see the effect of this on the girl. By now, Sheeana was more fully aware of a Reverend Mother's accomplishments. The powerful beam of truth had been focused on her. She had begun to grasp at the enormous body of knowledge the Sisterhood had accumulated over the millennia. She had been told about selective memory transmission, about the workings of

Other Memories, about the spice agony. And here before her stood the most powerful of all Reverend Mothers, one from whom nothing was hidden.

When Sheeana did not respond, Taraza said: "Have you nothing to say, child?"

"What is there to say, Mother Superior? You have said it all."

Taraza sent a searching glance at Odrade. "Have you any other little surprises for me, Dar?"

"I told you she was superior," Odrade said.

Taraza returned her attention to Sheeana. "Are you proud of that opinion, child?"

"It frightens me, Mother Superior."

Still holding her face as immobile as she could, Sheeana breathed more easily. *Say only the deepest truth you can sense,* she reminded herself. Those warning words from a teacher carried more meaning now. She kept her eyes slightly unfocused and aimed at the floor directly in front of the two women, avoiding the worst of the brilliant sunlight. She still felt her heart beating too rapidly and knew the Reverend Mothers would detect this. Odrade had demonstrated it many times.

"Well it should frighten you," Taraza said.

Odrade asked: "Do you understand what is being said to you, Sheeana?"

"The Mother Superior wishes to know if I am fully committed to the Sisterhood," Sheeana said.

Odrade looked at Taraza and shrugged. There was no need for more discussion of this between them. That was the way of it when you were part of one family as they were in the Bene Gesserit.

Taraza continued her silent study of Sheeana. It was a

heavy gaze, energy-draining for Sheeana, who knew she must remain silent and permit that scorching examination.

Odrade put down feelings of sympathy. Sheeana was like herself as a young girl, in so many ways. She had that globular intellect which expanded on all surfaces the way a balloon expanded when filled. Odrade recalled how her own teachers had been admiring of this, but wary, just the way Taraza was now wary. Odrade had recognized this wariness while even younger than Sheeana and held no doubts that Sheeana saw it here. Intellect had its uses.

"Mmmmmm," Taraza said.

Odrade heard the humming sound of the Mother Superior's internal reflections as part of a simulflow. Odrade's own memory had surged backward. The Sisters who had brought Odrade her food when she studied late had always loitered to observe her in their special way, just as Sheeana was watched and monitored at all times. Odrade had known about those special ways of observing from an early age. That was, after all, one of the great lures of the Bene Gesserit. You wanted to be capable of such esoteric abilities. Sheeana certainly possessed this desire. It was the dream of every postulant.

That such things might be possible for me!

Taraza spoke finally: "What is it you think you want from us, child?"

"The same things you thought you wanted when you were my age, Mother Superior."

Odrade suppressed a smile. Sheeana's wild sense of independence had skated close to insolence there and Taraza certainly recognized this.

"You think that is a proper use for the gift of life?" Taraza asked.

"It is the only use I know, Mother Superior."

"Your candor is appreciated but I warn you to be careful in your use of it," Taraza said.

"Yes, Mother Superior."

"You already owe us much and you will owe us more," Taraza said. "Remember that. Our gifts do not come cheaply."

Sheeana has not the vaguest appreciation of what she will pay for our gifts, Odrade thought.

The Sisterhood never let its initiates forget what they owed and must repay. You did not repay with love. Love was dangerous and Sheeana already was learning this. *The gift of life?* A shudder began to course through Odrade and she cleared her throat to compensate.

Am I alive? Perhaps when they took me away from Mama Sibia I died. I was alive there in that house but did I live after the Sisters removed me?

Taraza said: "You may leave us now, Sheeana."

Sheeana turned on one heel and left the room but not before Odrade saw the tight smile on the young face. Sheeana knew she had passed the Mother Superior's examination.

When the door closed behind Sheeana, Taraza said: "You mentioned her natural ability with Voice. I heard it, of course. Remarkable."

"She kept it well bridled," Odrade said. "She has learned not to try it on us."

"What do we have there, Dar?"

"Perhaps someday a Mother Superior of extraordinary abilities."

"Not too extraordinary?"

"We will have to see."

"Do you think she is capable of killing for us?"

Odrade was startled and showed it. "Now?"

"Yes, of course."

"The ghola?"

"Teg would not do it," Taraza said. "I even have doubts about Lucilla. Their reports make it clear that he is capable of forging powerful bonds of . . . of affinity."

"Even as I?"

"Schwangyu herself was not completely immune."

"Where is the noble purpose in such an act?" Odrade asked. "Isn't this what the Tyrant's warning has—"

"Him? He killed many times!"

"And paid for it."

"We pay for everything we take, Dar."

"Even for a life?"

"Never forget for one instant, Dar, that a Mother Superior is capable of making any necessary decision for the Sisterhood's survival!"

"So be it," Odrade said. "Take what you want and pay for it."

It was the proper reply but it reinforced the new strength Odrade felt, this freedom to respond in her own way within a new universe. Where had such toughness originated? Was it something out of her cruel Bene Gesserit conditioning? Was it from her Atreides ancestry? She did not try to fool herself that this came from a decision never again to follow another's moral guidance rather than her own. This inner stability upon which she now stationed herself was not a pure morality. Not bravado, either. Those were never enough.

"You are very like your father," Taraza said. "Usually, it's the dam who provides most of the courage but this time I think it was the father."

"Miles Teg is admirably courageous but I think you oversimplify," Odrade said.

"Perhaps I do. But I have been right about you at every turn, Dar, even back there when we were student postulants."

She knows! Odrade thought.

"We don't need to explain it," Odrade said. And she thought: *It comes from being born who I am, trained and shaped the way I was . . . the way we both were: Dar and Tar.*

"It's something in the Atreides line that we have not fully analyzed," Taraza said.

"No genetic accidents?"

"I sometimes wonder if we've suffered any real accidents since the Tyrant," Taraza said.

"Did he stretch out back there in his citadel and look across the millennia to this very moment?"

"How far back would you reach for the roots?" Taraza asked.

Odrade said: "What really happens when a Mother Superior commands the Breeding Mistresses: 'Have that one go breed with that one'?"

Taraza produced a cold smile.

Odrade felt herself suddenly at the crest of a wave, awareness pushing all of her over into this new realm. *Taraza wants my rebellion! She wants me as her opponent!*

"Will you see Waff now?" Odrade asked.

"First, I want your assessment of him."

"He sees us as the ultimate tool to create the 'Tleilaxu Ascendancy.' We are God's gift to his people."

"They have been waiting a long time for this," Taraza said. "To dissemble so carefully, all of them for all of those eons!"

"They have our view of time," Odrade agreed. "That was the final thing to convince them we share their Great Belief."

"But why the clumsiness?" Taraza asked. "They are not stupid."

"It diverted our attention from how they were really using their ghola process," Odrade said. "Who could believe stupid people would do such a thing?"

"And what have they created?" Taraza asked. "Only the *image* of evil stupidity?"

"Act stupid long enough and you become stupid," Odrade said. "Perfect the mimicry of your Face Dancers and . . ."

"Whatever happens, we must punish them," Taraza said. "I see that clearly. Have him brought up here."

After Odrade had given the order and while they waited, Taraza said: "The sequencing of the ghola's education became a shambles even before they escaped from the Gammu Keep. He leaped ahead of his teachers to grasp things that were only implied and he did this at an alarmingly accelerated rate. Who knows what he has become by now?"

Historians exercise great power and some of them know it. They re-create the past, changing it to fit their own interpretations. Thus, they change the future as well.

—LETO II, HIS VOICE, FROM DAR-ES BALAT

Duncan followed his guide through the dawn light at a punishing clip. The man might look old but he was as springy as a gazelle and seemed incapable of tiring.

Only a few minutes ago they had put aside their night goggles. Duncan was glad to be rid of them. Everything outside the reach of the glasses had been black in the dim starlight filtering through heavy branches. There had been no world ahead of him beyond the range of the glasses. The view at both sides jerked and flowed—now a clump of yellow bushes, now two silver-bark trees, now a stone wall with a plasteel gate cut into it and guarded by the flickering blue of a burn-shield, then an arched bridge of native rock, all green and black underfoot. After that, an arched entry of polished white stone. The structures all appeared very old and expensive, maintained by costly handwork.

Duncan had no idea where he was. None of this terrain recalled his memories of the long-lost Giedi Prime days.

Dawn revealed that they were following a tree-shielded animal track up a hillside. The climb became steep. Occasional glimpses through trees on their left revealed a valley. A hanging mist stood guard over the sky, hiding the distances, enclosing them as they climbed. Their world became progressively a smaller place as it lost its connection with a larger universe.

At one brief pause, not for rest but for listening to the forest around them, Duncan studied his mist-capped surroundings. He felt dislodged, removed from a universe that possessed sky and the open features that linked it to other planets.

His disguise was simple: Tleilaxu cold-weather garments and cheek pads to make his face appear rounder. His curly black hair had been straightened by some chemical applied with heat. The hair was then bleached to a sandy blond and hidden under a dark watchcap. All of his genital hair had been shaved away. He hardly recognized himself in the mirror they held up for him.

A dirty Tleilaxu!

The artisan who created this transformation was an old woman with glittering gray-green eyes. "You are now a Tleilaxu Master," she said. "Your name is Wose. A guide will take you to the next place. You will treat him like a Face Dancer if you meet strangers. Otherwise, do as he commands."

They led him out of the cave complex along a twisting passage, its walls and ceiling thick with the musky green algae. In starlighted darkness, they thrust him from the passage into a chilly night and the hands of an unseen man—a bulky figure in padded clothing.

A voice behind Duncan whispered: "Here he is, Ambitorm. Get him through."

The guide spoke in an accent of gutturals: "Follow me." He clipped a lead cord to Duncan's belt, adjusted the night goggles and turned away. Duncan felt the cord tug once and they were off.

Duncan recognized the use of the cord. It was not something to keep him close behind. He could see this Ambitorm clearly enough with the night goggles. No, the cord was to spill him quickly if they met danger. No need for a command.

For a long time during the night they crisscrossed small ice-lined watercourses on a flatland. The light of Gammu's early moons penetrated the covering growth only occasionally. They emerged finally onto a low hill with a view of bushy wasteland all silvery with snow cover in the moonlight. Down into this they went. The bushes, about twice the height of the guide, arched over muddy animal passages little larger than the tunnels where they had begun this journey. It was warmer here, the warmth of a compost heap. Almost no light penetrated to a ground spongy with rotted vegetation. Duncan inhaled the fungal odors of decomposing plant life. The night goggles showed him a seemingly endless repetition of thick growth on both sides. The cord linking him to Ambitorm was a tenuous grip on an alien world.

Ambitorm discouraged conversation. He said "Yes," when Duncan asked confirmation of the man's name, then: "Don't talk."

The whole night was a disquieting traverse for Duncan. He did not like being thrown back into his own thoughts. Giedi Prime memories persisted. This place was like nothing he remembered from his pre-ghola youth. He wondered how Ambitorm had learned the way through here and how he remembered it. One animal tunnel appeared much like another.

In the steady, jogging pace there was time for Duncan's thoughts to roam.

Must I permit the Sisterhood to use me? What do I owe them?

And he thought of Teg, that last gallant stand to permit two of them to escape.

I did the same for Paul and Jessica.

It was a bond with Teg and it touched Duncan with grief. Teg was loyal to the Sisterhood. *Did he buy my loyalty with that last brave act?*

Damn the Atreides!

The night's exertions increased Duncan's familiarity with his new flesh. How young this body was! A small lurch of recollection and he could see that last pre-ghola memory; he could feel the Sardaukar blade strike his head—a blinding explosion of pain and light. Knowledge of his certain death and then . . . nothing until that moment with Teg in the Harkonnen no-globe.

The gift of another life. Was it more than a gift or something less? The Atreides were demanding another payment from him.

For a time just before dawn, Ambitorm led him at a sloshing run along a narrow stream whose icy chill penetrated the waterproof insulated boots of Duncan's Tleilaxu garments. The watercourse reflected bush-shadowed silver from the light of the planet's pre-dawn moon setting ahead of them.

Daylight saw them come out into the larger, tree-shielded animal track and up the steep hill. This passage emerged onto a narrow rocky ledge below a ridgetop of sawtoothed boulders. Ambitorm led him behind a screen of dead brown bushes, their tops dirty with wind-blown snow. He released the cord from Duncan's belt. Directly in front of them was a shallow declivity in the rocks, not quite a cave, but Duncan saw that it would offer some protection unless they got a hard wind over the bushes behind them. There was no snow on the floor of the place.

Ambitorm went to the back of the declivity and carefully removed a layer of icy dirt and several flat rocks, which concealed a small pit. He lifted a round black object from the pit and busied himself over it.

Duncan squatted under the overhang and studied his guide. Ambitorm had a dished-in face with skin like dark brown leather. Yes, those could be the features of a Face Dancer. Deep creases cut into the skin at the edges of the man's brown eyes. Creases radiated from the sides of the thin mouth and lined the wide brow. They spread out beside the flat nose and deepened the cleft of a narrow chin. Creases of time all over his face.

Appetizing odors began to arise from the black object in front of Ambitorm.

"We will eat here and wait a bit before we continue," Ambitorm said.

He spoke Old Galach but with that guttural accent which Duncan had never heard before, an odd stress on adjacent vowels. Was Ambitorm from the Scattering or a Gammu native? There obviously had been many linguistic drifts since the Dune days of Muad'Dib. For that matter, Duncan recognized that all of the people in the Gammu Keep, including Teg and Lucilla, spoke a Galach that had shifted from the one he had learned as a pre-ghola child.

"Ambitorm," Duncan said. "Is that a Gammu name?"

"You will call me Tormsa," the guide said.

"Is that a nickname?"

"It is what you will call me."

"Why did those people back there call you Ambitorm?"

"That was the name I gave them."

"But why would you . . ."

"You lived under the Harkonnens and you did not learn how to change your identity?"

Duncan fell silent. Was that it? Another disguise. Ambi . . . Tormsa had not changed his appearance. Tormsa. Was it a Tleilaxu name?

The guide extended a steaming cup toward Duncan. "A drink to restore you, *Wose*. Drink it fast. It will keep you warm."

Duncan closed both hands around the cup. *Wose. Wose and Tormsa. Tleilaxu Master and his Face Dancer companion.*

Duncan lifted the cup toward Tormsa in the ancient gesture of Atreides battle comrades, then put it to his lips. Hot! But it warmed him as it went down. The drink had a faintly sweet flavor over some vegetable tang. He blew on it and drank it down as he saw Tormsa was doing.

Odd that I should not suspect poison or some drug, Duncan thought. But this Tormsa and the others last night had something of the Bashar about them. The gesture to a battle comrade had come naturally.

"Why are you risking your life this way?" Duncan asked.

"You know the Bashar and you have to ask?"

Duncan fell silent, abashed.

Tormsa leaned forward and recovered Duncan's cup. Soon, all evidence of their breakfast lay hidden under the concealing rocks and dirt.

That food spoke of careful planning, Duncan thought. He turned and squatted on the cold ground. The mist was still out there beyond the screening bushes. Leafless limbs cut the view into odd bits and pieces. As he watched, the mist began to lift, revealing the blurred outlines of a city at the far edge of the valley.

Tormsa squatted beside him. "Very old city," he said. "Harkonnen place. Look." He passed a small monoscope to Duncan. "That is where we go tonight."

Duncan put the monoscope to his left eye and tried to focus the oil lens. The controls felt unfamiliar, not at all like those he had learned as a pre-ghola youth or had been taught at the Keep. He removed it from his eye and examined it.

"Ixian?" he asked.

"No. We made it." Tormsa reached over and pointed out two tiny buttons raised above the black tube. "Slow, fast. Push left to cycle out, right to cycle back."

Again, Duncan lifted the scope to his eye.

Who were the *we* who had made this thing?

A touch of the fast button and the view leaped into his gaze. Tiny dots moved in the city. People! He increased the amplification. The people became small dolls. With them to give him scale, Duncan realized that the city at the valley's edge was immense . . . and farther away than he had thought. A single rectangular structure stood in the center of the city, its top lost in the clouds. Gigantic.

Duncan knew this place now. The surroundings had changed but that central structure lay fixed in his memory.

How many of us vanished into that black hellhole and never returned?

"Nine hundred and fifty stories," Tormsa said, seeing where Duncan's gaze was directed. "Forty-five kilometers long, thirty kilometers wide. Plasteel and armor-plaz, all of it."

"I know." Duncan lowered the scope and returned it to Tormsa. "It was called Barony."

"Ysai," Tormsa said.

"That's what they call it now," Duncan said. "I have some different names for it."

Duncan took a deep breath to put down the old hatreds. Those people were all dead. Only the building remained. And the memories. He scanned the city around that enormous structure. The place was a sprawling mass of warrens. Green spaces lay scattered throughout, each of them behind high walls. Single residences with private parks, Teg had said. The monoscope had revealed guards walking the wall tops.

Tormsa spat on the ground in front of him. "Harkonnen place."

"They built to make people feel small," Duncan said.

Tormsa nodded. "Small, no power in you."

The guide had become almost loquacious, Duncan thought.

Occasionally during the night, Duncan had defied the order for silence and tried to make conversation.

"What animals made these passages?"

It had seemed a logical question for people trotting along an obvious animal track, even the musty smell of beasts in it.

"Do not talk!" Tormsa snapped.

Later, Duncan asked why they could not get a vehicle of some sort and escape in that. Even a groundcar would be preferable to this painful march across country where one route felt much like another.

Tormsa stopped them in a patch of moonlight and looked at Duncan as though he suspected his charge had suddenly become bereft of sense.

"Vehicles can follow!"

"No one can follow us when we're on foot?"

"Followers also must be on foot. Here, they will be killed. They know."

What a weird place! What a primitive place.

In the shelter of the Bene Gesserit Keep, Duncan had not realized the nature of the planet around him. Later, in the no-globe, he had been removed from contact with the outside. He had pre-ghola and ghola memories, but how inadequate those were! When he thought about it now, he realized there had been clues. It was obvious that Gammu possessed rudimentary weather control. And Teg had said that the orbiting monitors that guarded the planet from attack were of the best.

Everything for protection, damned little for comfort! It was like Arrakis in that respect.

Rakis, he corrected himself.

Teg. Did the old man survive? A captive? What did it mean to be captured here in this age? It had meant brutal slavery in the old Harkonnen days. Burzmali and Lucilla . . . He glanced at Tormsa.

"Will we find Burzmali and Lucilla in the city?"

"If they get through."

Duncan glanced down at his clothing. Was it a sufficient disguise? A Tleilaxu Master and companion? People would think the companion a Face Dancer, of course. Face Dancers were dangerous.

The baggy trousers were of some material Duncan had never before seen. It felt like wool to the hand, but he sensed that it was artificial. When he spat on it, spittle did not adhere and the smell was not of wool. His fingers detected a uniformity of texture that no natural material could present. The long soft boots and watchcap were of the same fabric. The garments were loose and puffy except at the ankles. Not quilted, though. Insulated by some trick of manufacture that trapped dead air between the layers. The color was a mottled green and gray— excellent camouflage here.

Tormsa was dressed in similar garments.

"How long do we wait here?" Duncan asked.

Tormsa shook his head for silence. The guide was seated now, knees up, arms wrapped around his legs, head cradled against his knees, eyes looking outward over the valley.

During the night's trip, Duncan had found the clothing remarkably comfortable. Except for that once in the water, his feet stayed warm but not too warm. There was plenty of room in trousers, shirt, and jacket for his body to move easily. Nothing abraded his flesh.

"Who makes clothing such as this?" Duncan asked.

"We made it," Tormsa growled. "Be silent."

This was no different than the pre-awakening days at the Sisterhood's Keep, Duncan thought. Tormsa was saying: "No need for you to know."

Presently, Tormsa stretched out his legs and straightened. He appeared to relax. He glanced at Duncan. "Friends in the city signal that there are searchers overhead."

"'Thopters?"

"Yes."

"Then what do we do?"

"You must do what I do and nothing else."

"You're just sitting there."

"For now. We will go down into the valley soon."

"But how—"

"When you traverse such country as this you become one of the animals that live here. Look at the tracks and see how they walk and how they lie down for a rest."

"But can't the searchers tell the difference between . . ."

"If the animals browse, you make the motions of browsing. If searchers come, you continue to do what it was you were doing, what any animal would do. Searchers will be high in the air. That is lucky for us. They cannot tell animal from human unless they come down."

"But won't they—"

"They trust their machines and the motions they see. They are lazy. They fly high. That way, the search goes faster. They trust their own intelligence to read their instruments and tell which is animal and which is human."

"So they'll just go by us if they think we're wild animals."

"If they doubt, they will scan us a second time. We must not change the pattern of movements after being scanned."

It was a long speech for the usually taciturn Tormsa. He studied Duncan carefully now. "You understand?"

"How will I know when we're being scanned?"

"Your gut will tingle. You will feel in your stomach the fizz of a drink that no man should swallow."

Duncan nodded. "Ixian scanners."

"Let it not alarm you," Tormsa said. "Animals here are accustomed to it. Sometimes, they may pause, but only for an instant and then they go on as if nothing has happened. Which, for them, is true. It is only for us that something evil may happen."

Presently, Tormsa stood. "We will go down into the valley now. Follow closely. Do exactly what I do and nothing else."

Duncan fell into step behind his guide. Soon, they were under the covering trees. Sometime during the night's passage, Duncan realized, he had begun to accept his place in the schemes of others. A new patience was taking over his awareness. And there was excitement goaded by curiosity.

What kind of a universe had come out of the Atreides times? *Gammu*. What a strange place Giedi Prime had become.

Slowly but distinctly, things were being revealed and each new thing opened a view to more that could be learned. He could feel patterns taking shape. One day, he thought, there would be a single pattern and then he would know why they had brought him back from the dead.

Yes, it was a matter of opening doors, he thought. You

opened one door and that let you into a place where there were other doors. You chose a door in this new place and examined what that revealed to you. There might be times when you were forced to try all of the doors but the more doors you opened, the more certain you became of which door to open next. Finally, a door would open into a place you recognized. Then you could say: "Ahhhh, this explains everything."

"Searchers come," Tormsa said. "We are browsing animals now." He reached up to a screening bush and tore down a small limb.

Duncan did the same.

I must rule with eye and claw—as the hawk among lesser birds.

—ATREIDES ASSERTION (REF: BG ARCHIVES)

At daybreak, Teg emerged from the concealing wind-breaks beside a main road. The road was a wide, flat thoroughfare—beam-hardened and kept bare of plant life. Ten lanes, Teg estimated, suitable for both vehicle and foot traffic. There was mostly foot traffic on it at this hour.

He had brushed most of the dust off his clothing and made sure there were no signs of rank on it. His gray hair was not as neat as he usually preferred but he had only his fingers for a comb.

Traffic on the road was headed toward the city of Ysai many kilometers across the valley. The morning was cloudless with a light breeze in his face moving toward the sea somewhere far behind him.

During the night he had come to a delicate balance with his new awareness. Things flickered in his second vision: knowledge of things around him before those things occurred, awareness of where he must put his foot in the next step. Behind this lay the reactive trigger that he knew could snap him into the blurring responses that flesh should not be able to accommodate. Reason could not explain the thing. He felt that he walked precariously along the cutting edge of a knife.

Try as he might, he could not resolve what had happened to him under the T-probe. Was it akin to what a Reverend Mother experienced in the spice agony? But he sensed no accumulation of Other Memories out of his past. He did not think the Sisters could do what he did. The doubled vision that told him what to anticipate from every movement within the range of his senses seemed a new kind of truth.

Teg's Mentat teachers had always assured him there was a form of living-truth not susceptible to proof by the marshaling of ordinary facts. It was carried sometimes in fables and poetry and often went contrary to desires, so he had been told.

"The most difficult experience for a Mentat to accept," they said.

Teg had always reserved judgment on this pronouncement but now he was forced to accept it. The T-probe had thrust him over a threshold into a new reality.

He did not know why he chose this particular moment to emerge from hiding, except that it fitted him into an acceptable flow of human movement.

Most of that movement on the road was composed of market gardeners towing panniers of vegetables and fruit. The panniers were supported behind them on cheap suspensors. Awareness of that food sent sharp hunger pains through him but he forced himself to ignore them. With experience of more primitive planets in his long service to the Bene Gesserit, he saw this human activity as little different from that of farmers leading loaded animals. The foot traffic struck him as an odd mixture of ancient and modern—farmers afoot, their produce floating behind them on perfectly ordinary technological devices. Except for the suspensors this scene was very like a similar day in humankind's most ancient past. A draft animal was a draft animal, even if it came off an assembly line in an Ixian factory.

Using his new second vision, Teg chose one of the farmers, a squat, dark-skinned man with heavy features and thickly calloused hands. The man walked with a defiant sense of independence. He towed eight large panniers piled with rough-skinned melons. The smell of them was a mouth-watering agony to Teg as he matched his stride to that of the farmer. Teg strode for a few minutes in silence, then ventured: "Is this the best road to Ysai?"

"It is a long way," the man said. He had a guttural voice, something cautious in it.

Teg glanced back at the loaded panniers.

The farmer looked sidelong at Teg. "We go to a market center. Others take our produce from there to Ysai."

As they talked, Teg realized the farmer had guided (almost herded) him close to the edge of the road. The man glanced back and jerked his head slightly, nodding forward. Three more farmers came up beside them and closed in around Teg and his companion until tall panniers concealed them from the rest of the traffic.

Teg tensed. What were they planning? He sensed no menace, though. His doubled vision detected nothing violent in his immediate vicinity.

A heavy vehicle sped past them and on ahead. Teg knew of its passage only by the smell of burned fuel, the wind that shook the panniers, the thrumming of a powerful engine and sudden tension in his companions. The high panniers completely hid the passing vehicle.

"We have been looking for you to protect you, Bashar," the farmer beside him said. "There are many who hunt you but none of them with us along here."

Teg shot a startled glance at the man.

"We served with you at Renditai," the farmer said.

Teg swallowed. *Renditai?* He was a moment recalling it—only a minor skirmish in his long history of conflicts and negotiations.

"I am sorry but I do not know your name," Teg said.

"Be glad that you do not know our names. It is better that way."

"But I'm grateful."

"This is a small repayment, which we are glad to make, Bashar."

"I must get to Ysai," Teg said.

"It is dangerous there."

"It is dangerous everywhere."

"We guessed you would go to Ysai. Someone will come soon and you will ride in concealment. Ahhhh, here he comes. We have not seen you here, Bashar. You have not been here."

One of the other farmers took over the towing of his companion's load, pulling two strings of panniers while the farmer Teg had chosen hustled Teg under a tow rope and into a dark vehicle. Teg glimpsed shiny plasteel and plaz as the vehicle slowed only briefly for the pickup. The door closed sharply behind him and he found himself on a soft upholstered seat, alone in the back of a groundcar. The car picked up speed and soon was beyond the marching farmers. The windows around Teg had been darkened, giving him a dusky view of the passing scene. The driver was a shaded silhouette.

This first chance to relax in warm comfort since his capture almost lured Teg into sleep. He sensed no threats. His body still ached from the demands he had made on it and from the agonies of the T-probe.

He told himself, though, that he must stay awake and alert.

The driver leaned sideways and spoke over his shoulder without turning: "They have been hunting for you for two days, Bashar. Some think you already off-planet."

Two days?

The stunner and whatever else they had done to him had left him unconscious for a long time. This only added to his hunger. He tried to make the flesh-embedded chrono play against his vision centers and it only flickered as it had done each time he consulted it since the T-probe. His time sense and all references to it were changed.

So some thought he had left Gammu.

Teg did not ask who hunted him. Tleilaxu and people from the Scattering had been in that attack and the subsequent torture.

Teg glanced around his conveyance. It was one of those beautiful old pre-Scattering groundcars, the marks of the finest Ixian manufacture on it. He had never before ridden in one but he knew about them. Restorers picked them up to renew, rebuild—whatever they did that brought back the ancient sense of quality. Teg had been told that such vehicles often were found abandoned in strange places—in old broken-down buildings, in culverts, locked away in machinery warehouses, in farm fields.

Again, his driver leaned slightly sideways and spoke

over one shoulder: "Do you have an address where you wish to be taken in Ysai, Bashar?"

Teg called up his memory of the contact points he had identified on his first tour of Gammu and gave one of these to the man. "Do you know that place?"

"It is mostly a meeting and drinking establishment, Bashar. I hear they serve good food, too, but anyone can enter if he has the price."

Not knowing why he had made that particular choice, Teg said: "We will chance it." He did not think it necessary to tell the driver that there were private dining rooms at the address.

The mention of food brought back sharp hunger cramps. Teg's arms began to tremble and he was several minutes restoring calmness. Last night's activities had almost drained him, he realized. He sent a searching gaze around the car's interior, wondering if there might be food or drink concealed here. The car's restoration had been accomplished with loving care but he saw no hidden compartments.

Such cars were not all that rare in some quarters, he knew, but all of them spoke of wealth. Who owned this one? Not the driver, certainly. That one had all the signs of a hired professional. But if a message had been sent to bring this car then others knew of Teg's location.

"Will we be stopped and searched?" Teg asked.

"Not this car, Bashar. The Planetary Bank of Gammu owns it."

Teg absorbed this silently. That bank had been one of his contact points. He had studied key branches carefully on his inspection tour. This memory drew him back into his responsibilities as guardian of the ghola.

"My companions," Teg ventured. "Are they . . ."

"Others have that in hand, Bashar. I cannot say."

"Can word be taken to . . ."

"When it is safe, Bashar."

"Of course."

Teg sank back into the cushions and studied his surroundings. These groundcars had been built with much plaz and almost indestructible plasteel. It was other things that went sour with age—upholstery, headliners, the electronics, the suspensor installations, the ablative liners of the turbofan ducts. And the adhesives deteriorated no matter what you did to preserve them. The restorers had made this one look as though it had just been cranked out of the factory—all subdued glowing in the metals, upholstery that molded itself to him with a faint sound of crinkling. And the smell: that indefinable aroma of newness, a mixture of polish and fine fabrics with just a hint of ozone bite underneath from the smoothly working electronics. Nowhere in it, though, was there the smell of food.

"How long to Ysai?" Teg asked.

"Another half hour, Bashar. Is there a problem that requires more speed? I don't want to attract . . ."

"I am very hungry."

The driver glanced left and right. There were no more farmers around them here. The roadway was almost empty except for two heavy transport pods with their tractors holding to the right verge and a large lorry hauling a towering automatic fruit picker.

"It is dangerous to delay for long," the driver said. "But I know a place where I think I can at least get you a quick bowl of soup."

"Anything would be welcome. I have not eaten for two days and there has been much activity."

They came to a crossroads and the driver turned left onto a narrow track through tall, evenly spaced conifers. Presently, he turned onto a one-lane drive through the trees. The low building at the end of this track was built of dark stones and had a blackplaz roof. The windows were narrow and glistened with protective burner nozzles.

The driver said: "Just a minute, sir." He got out and Teg had his first look at the man's face: extremely thin with a long nose and tiny mouth. The visible tracery of surgical reconstruction laced his cheeks. The eyes glowed silver, obviously artificial. He turned away and went into the house. When he returned, he opened Teg's door. "Please be quick, sir. The one inside is heating soup for you. I have said you are a banker. No need to pay."

The ground was icy crisp underfoot. Teg had to stoop slightly for the doorway. He entered a dark hallway, wood-paneled and with a well-lighted room at the end. The smell of food there drew him like a magnet. His arms were trembling once more. A small table had been set beside a window with a view of an enclosed and covered garden. Bushes heavy with red flowers almost concealed the stone wall that defined the garden. Yellow hotplaz gleamed over the space, bathing it in a summery artificial light. Teg sank gratefully into the single chair at the table. White linen, he saw, with an embossed edge. A single soup spoon.

A door creaked at his right and a squat figure entered carrying a bowl from which steam arose. The man hesitated when he saw Teg, then brought the bowl to the table and placed it in front of Teg. Alerted by that hesitation, Teg forced himself to ignore the tempting aroma drifting to his nostrils and concentrated instead on his companion.

"It is good soup, sir. I made it myself."

An artificial voice. Teg saw the scars at the sides of the jaw. There was the look of an ancient mechanical about this man—an almost neckless head attached to thick shoulders, arms that seemed oddly jointed at both shoulders and elbows, legs that appeared to swing only from the hips. He stood motionless now but he had entered here with a slightly jerking sway that said he was mostly replacement artificials. The look of suffering in his eyes could not be avoided.

"I know I'm not pretty, sir," the man rasped. "I was ruined in the Alajory explosion."

Teg had no idea what the Alajory explosion might have been but it obviously was presumed he knew. "Ruined," however, was an interesting accusation against Fate.

"I was wondering if I knew you," Teg said.

"No one here knows anyone else," the man said. "Eat your soup." He pointed upward at the coiled tip of quiescent snooper, the glow of its lights revealing that it read its surroundings and found no poison. "The food is safe here."

Teg looked at the dark brown liquid in his bowl. Lumps of solid meat were visible in it. He reached for the spoon. His trembling hand made two attempts before grasping the spoon and even then he sloshed most of the liquid out of the spoon before he could lift it a millimeter.

A steadying hand gripped Teg's wrist and the artificial voice spoke softly in Teg's ear: "I do not know what they did to you, Bashar, but no one will harm you here without crossing my dead body."

"You know me?"

"Many would die for you, Bashar. My son lives because of you."

Teg allowed himself to be helped. It was all he could do to swallow the first spoonful. The liquid was rich, hot and soothing. His hand steadied presently and he nodded to the man to release the wrist.

"More, sir?"

Teg realized then that he had emptied the bowl. It was tempting to say "yes" but the driver had said to make haste.

"Thank you, but I must go."

"You have not been here," the man said.

When they were once more back on the main road, Teg sat back against the groundcar's cushions and reflected on the curious echoing quality of what the *ruined* man had said. The same words the farmer had used: "You have not been here." It had the feeling of a common response and it said something about changes in Gammu since Teg had surveyed the place.

They entered the outskirts of Ysai presently and Teg wondered if he should attempt a disguise. The *ruined* man had recognized him quickly.

"Where do the Honored Matres hunt for me now?" Teg asked.

"Everywhere, Bashar. We cannot guarantee your safety but steps are being taken. I will make it known where I have delivered you."

"Do they say why they hunt me?"

"They never explain, Bashar."

"How long have they been on Gammu?"

"Too long, sir. Since I was a child and I was a baltern at Renditai."

A hundred years at least, Teg thought. *Time to gather many forces into their hands . . . if Taraza's fears were to be credited.*

Teg credited them.

"Trust no one those whores can influence," Taraza had said.

Teg sensed no threat to him in his present position, though. He could only absorb the secrecy that obviously enclosed him now. He did not press for more details.

They were well into Ysai and he glimpsed the black bulk of the ancient Harkonnen seat of Barony through occasional gaps between the walls that enclosed the great private residences. The car turned onto a street of small commercial establishments: cheap buildings constructed for the most part of salvaged materials that displayed their origins in poor fits and unmatched colors. Gaudy signs advised that the wares inside were the finest, the repair services better than those elsewhere.

It was not that Ysai had deteriorated or even gone to seed, Teg thought. Growth here had been diverted into something worse than ugly. Someone had chosen to make this place repellent. That was the key to most of what he saw in the city.

Time had not stopped here, it had retreated. This was no modern city full of bright transport pods and insulated usiform buildings. This was random jumbles, ancient structures joined to ancient structures, some built to individual tastes and some obviously designed with some long-gone necessity in mind. Everything about Ysai was joined

in a proximity whose disarray just managed to avoid chaos.
What saved it, Teg knew, was the old pattern of thorough-
fares along which this hodgepodge had been assembled.
Chaos was held at bay, although what pattern there was in
the streets conformed to no master plan. Streets met and
crossed at odd angles, seldom squared. Seen from the air,
the place was a crazy quilt with only the giant black rectangle of ancient Barony to speak of an organizing plan.
The rest of it was architectural rebellion.

Teg saw suddenly that this place was a lie plastered
over with other lies, based on previous lies, and such a
mad mixup that they might never dig through to a usable
truth. All of Gammu was that way. Where could such
insanity have had its beginnings? Was it the Harkonnens'
doing?

"We are here, sir."

The driver drew up to the curb in front of a window-
less building face, all flat black plasteel and with a single
ground-level door. No salvaged material in this construction. Teg recognized the place: the bolt hole he had chosen. Unidentified things flickered in Teg's second vision
but he sensed no immediate menace. The driver opened
Teg's door and stood to one side.

"Not much activity here at this hour, sir. I would get
inside quickly."

Without a backward glance, Teg darted across the
narrow walk and into the building—a small brightly
lighted foyer of polished white plaz and only banks of
comeyes to greet him. He ducked into a lift tube and
punched the remembered coordinates. This tube, he
knew, angled upward through the building to the fifty-
seventh floor rear where there were some windows. He

remembered a private dining room of dark reds and heavy brown furnishings, a hard-eyed female with the obvious signs of Bene Gesserit training, but no Reverend Mother.

The tube disgorged him into the remembered room but there was no one to receive him. Teg glanced around at the solid brown furnishings. Four windows along the far wall were concealed behind thick maroon draperies.

Teg knew he had been seen. He waited patiently, using his newly learned doubling-vision to anticipate trouble. There was no indication of attack. He took up a position to one side of the tube outlet and glanced around him once more.

Teg had a theory about the relationship between rooms and their windows—the number of windows, their placement, their size, height from the floor, relationship of room size to window size, the elevation of the room, windows curtained or draped, and all of this Mentat-interpreted against knowledge of the uses to which a room was put. Rooms could be fitted to a kind of pecking order defined with extreme sophistication. Emergency uses might throw such distinctions out the window but they otherwise were quite reliable.

Lack of windows in an aboveground room conveyed a particular message. If humans occupied such a room, it did not necessarily mean secrecy was the main goal. He had seen unmistakable signs in scholastic settings that window-less schoolrooms were both a retreat from the exterior world and a strong statement of dislike for children.

This room, however, presented something different: conditional secrecy plus the need to keep occasional watch on that exterior world. *Protective secrecy when required*. His opinion was reinforced when he crossed the room and twitched one of the draperies aside. The windows were tripled armor-plaz. So! Keeping watch on that world outside might draw attack. That was the opinion of whoever had ordered the room protected this way.

Once more, Teg twitched the drapery aside. He glanced at the corner glazing. Prismatic reflectors there amplified the view along the adjacent wall to both sides and from roof to ground.

Well!

His previous visit had not given him time for this closer examination but now he made a more positive assessment. A very interesting room. Teg dropped the drapery and turned just in time to see a tall man enter from the tube slot.

Teg's doubled vision provided a firm prediction on the stranger. This man brought concealed danger. The newcomer was plainly military—the way he carried himself, the quick eye for details that only a trained and experienced officer would observe. And there was something else in his manner that made Teg stiffen. This was a betrayer! A mercenary available to the highest bidder.

"Damned nasty the way they treated you," the man greeted Teg. The voice was a deep baritone with an unconscious assumption of personal power in it. The accent was one Teg had never before heard. This was someone from the Scattering! A Bashar or equivalent, Teg estimated.

Still, there was no indication of immediate attack.

When Teg did not answer, the man said: "Oh, sorry: I'm Muzzafar. Jafa Muzzafar, regional commander for the forces of Dur."

Teg had never heard of the forces of Dur.

Questions crowded Teg's mind but he kept them to himself. Anything he said here might betray weakness.

Where were the people who had met him here before? *Why did I choose this place?* The decision had been made with such inner assurance.

"Please be comfortable," Muzzafar said, indicating a small divan with a low serving table in front of it. "I assure you that none of what has happened to you was of my doing. Tried to put a stop to it when I heard but you'd already . . . left the scene."

Teg heard the other thing in this Muzzafar's voice now: caution bordering on fear. So this man had either heard about or seen the shack and the clearing.

"Damned clever of you," Muzzafar said. "Having your attack force wait until your captors were concentrating on trying to get information out of you. Did they learn anything?"

Teg shook his head silently from side to side. He felt on the edge of being ignited in a blurred response to attack, yet he sensed no immediate violence here. What were these Lost Ones doing? But Muzzafar and his people had made a wrong assessment of what had happened in the room of the T-probe. That was clear.

"Please, be seated," Muzzafar said.

Teg took the proffered seat on the divan.

Muzzafar sat in a deep chair facing Teg at a slight angle on the other side of the serving table. There was a crouching sense of alertness in Muzzafar. He was prepared for violence.

Teg studied the man with interest. Muzzafar had revealed no real rank—only commander. Tall fellow with a wide, ruddy face and a big nose. The eyes were gray-green and had the trick of focusing just behind Teg's right shoulder when either of them spoke. Teg had known a spy once who did that.

"Well, well," Muzzafar said. "I've read and heard a great deal about you since coming here."

Teg continued to study him silently. Muzzafar's hair had been cropped close and there was a purple scar about three millimeters long across the scalp line above the left eye. He wore an open bush jacket of light green and matching trousers—not quite a uniform but there was a neatness about him that spoke of customary spit and polish. The shoes attested to this. Teg thought he probably could see his own reflection in their light brown surfaces if he bent close.

"Never expected to meet you personally, of course," Muzzafar said. "Consider it a great honor."

"I know very little about you except that you command a force from the Scattering," Teg said.

"Mmmmmph! Not much to know, really."

Once more, hunger pangs gripped Teg. His gaze went to the button beside the tube slot, which, he remembered, would summon a waiter. This was a place where humans did the work usually assigned to automata, an excuse for keeping a large force assembled at the ready.

Misinterpreting Teg's interest in the tube slot, Muzzafar said: "Please don't think of leaving. Having my own medic come in to take a look at you. Shouldn't be but a moment. Appreciate it if you'd wait quietly until he arrives."

"I was merely thinking of placing an order for some food," Teg said.

"Advise you to wait until the doctor's had his look-see. Stunners leave some nasty aftereffects."

"So you know about that."

"Know about the whole damned fiasco. You and your man Burzmali are a force to be reckoned with."

Before Teg could respond, the tube slot disgorged a tall man in a jacketed red singlesuit, a man so bone-skinny that his clothing gaped and flapped about him. The diamond tattoo of a Suk doctor had been burned into his high forehead but the mark was orange and not the customary black. The doctor's eyes were concealed by a glistening orange cover that hid their true color.

An addict of some kind? Teg wondered. There was no smell of the familiar narcotics around him, not even melange. There was a tart smell, though, almost like some fruit.

"There you are, Solitz!" Muzzafar said. He gestured at Teg. "Give him a good scan. Stunner hit him day before yesterday."

Solitz produced a recognizable Suk scanner, compact and fitting into one hand. Its probe field produced a low hum.

"So you're a Suk doctor," Teg said, looking pointedly at the orange brand on the forehead.

"Yes, Bashar. My training and conditioning are the finest in our ancient tradition."

"I've never seen the identifying mark in that color," Teg said.

The doctor passed his scanner around Teg's head. "The color of the tattoo makes no difference, Bashar. What is behind it is all that matters." He lowered the scanner to Teg's shoulders, then down across the body.

Teg waited for the humming to stop.

The doctor stood back and addressed Muzzafar: "He is quite fit, Field Marshal. Remarkably fit, considering his age, but he desperately needs sustenance."

"Yes . . . well, that's fine then, Solitz. Take care of that. The Bashar is our guest."

"I will order a meal suited to his needs," Solitz said. "Eat it slowly, Bashar." Solitz did a smart about-face that set his jacket and trousers flapping. The tube slot swallowed him.

"Field Marshal?" Teg asked.

"A revival of ancient titles in the Dur," Muzzafar said.

"The Dur?" Teg ventured.

"Stupid of me!" Muzzafar produced a small case from a side pocket of his jacket and extracted a thin folder. Teg recognized a holostat similar to one he had carried himself during his long service—pictures of home and family. Muzzafar placed the holostat on the table between them and tapped the control button.

The full-color image of a bushy green expanse of jungle came alive in miniature above the tabletop.

"Home," Muzzafar said. "Frame bush in the center there." A finger indicated a place in the projection. "First one that ever obeyed me. People laughed at me for choosing the first one that way and sticking with it."

Teg stared at the projection, aware of a deep sadness in Muzzafar's voice. The indicated bush was a spindly grouping of thin limbs with bright blue bulbs dangling from the tips.

Frame bush?

"Rather thin thing, I know," Muzzafar said, removing his pointing finger from the projection. "Not secure at all. Had to defend myself a few times in the first months with it. Grew rather fond of it, though. They respond to that, you know. It's the best home in all the deep valleys now, by the Eternal Rock of Dur!"

Muzzafar stared at Teg's puzzled expression. "Damn! You don't have frame bushes, of course. You must forgive my crashing ignorance. We've a great deal to teach each other, I think."

"You called that home," Teg said.

"Oh, yes. With proper direction, once they learn to obey, of course, a frame bush will grow itself into a magnificent residence. It only takes four or five standards."

Standards, Teg thought. So the Lost Ones still used the Standard Year.

The tube slot hissed and a young woman in a blue serving gown backed into the room towing a suspensor-buoyed hotpod, which she positioned near the table in front of Teg. Her clothing was of the type Teg had seen during his original inspection but the pleasantly round face she turned to him was unfamiliar. Her scalp had been depilated, leaving an expanse of prominent veins. Her eyes were watery blue and there was something cowed in her posture. She opened the hotpod and the spicy odors of the food wafted across Teg's nostrils.

Teg was alerted but he sensed no immediate threat. He could see himself eating the food without ill effect.

The young woman put a row of dishes on to the table in front of him and arranged the eating implements neatly at one side.

"I've no snooper, but I'll taste the foods if you wish," Muzzafar said.

"Not necessary," Teg said. He knew this would raise questions but felt they would suspect him of being a Truthsayer. Teg's gaze locked onto the food. Without any conscious decision, he leaned forward and began eating. Familiar with Mentat-hunger, he was surprised at his own reactions. Using the brain in Mentat mode consumed calories at an alarming rate, but this was a new necessity driving him. He felt his own survival controlling his actions. This hunger went beyond anything of previous experience. The soup he had eaten with some caution at the house of the *ruined* man had not aroused such a demanding reaction.

The Suk doctor chose correctly, Teg thought. This food had been selected directly out of the scanner's summation.

The young woman kept bringing more dishes from hotpods ordered via the tube slot.

Teg had to get up in the middle of the meal and relieve himself in an adjoining washroom, conscious there of the hidden comeyes that were keeping him under surveillance. He knew by his physical reactions that his digestive system had speeded up to a new level of bodily necessity. When he returned to the table, he felt just as hungry as though he had not eaten.

The serving woman began to show signs of surprise and then alarm. Still, she kept bringing more food at his demand.

Muzzafar watched with growing amazement but said nothing.

Teg felt the supportive replacement of the food, the precise caloric adjustment that the Suk doctor had ordered. They obviously had not thought about quantity, though. The girl obeyed his demands in a kind of walking shock.

Muzzafar spoke finally. "Must say I've never before seen anyone eat that much at one sitting. Can't see how you do it. Nor why."

Teg sat back, satisfied at last, knowing he had aroused questions that could not be answered truthfully.

"A Mentat thing," Teg lied. "I've been through a very strenuous time."

"Amazing," Muzzafar said. He arose.

When Teg started to stand, Muzzafar gestured for him to remain. "No need. We've prepared quarters for you right next door. Safer not to move you yet."

The young woman departed with the empty hotpods.

Teg studied Muzzafar. Something had changed during the meal. Muzzafar watched him with a coldly measuring stare.

"You've an implanted communicator," Teg said. "You have received new orders."

"It would not be advisable for your friends to attack this place," Muzzafar said.

"You think that's my plan?"

"What is your plan, Bashar?"

Teg smiled.

"Very well." Muzzafar's gaze went out of focus as he listened to his communicator. When he once more concentrated on Teg, his gaze had the look of a predator. Teg felt himself buffeted by that gaze, recognizing that someone else was coming to this room. The Field Marshal thought of this new development as something extremely dangerous to his dinner guest but Teg saw nothing that could defeat his new abilities.

"You think I am your prisoner," Teg said.

"By the Eternal Rock, Bashar! You are not what I expected!"

"The Honored Matre who is coming, what does she expect?" Teg asked.

"Bashar, I warn you: Do not take that tone with her. You have not the slightest concept of what is about to happen to you."

"An Honored Matre is about to happen to me," Teg said.

"And I wish you well of her!"

Muzzafar pivoted and left via the tube slot.

Teg stared after him. He could see the flickering of second vision like a light blinking around the tube slot. The Honored Matre was near but not yet ready to enter this room. First, she would consult with Muzzafar. The Field Marshal would not be able to tell this dangerous female anything really important.

Memory never recaptures reality. Memory reconstructs. All reconstructions change the original, becoming external frames of reference that inevitably fall short.

—MENTAT HANDBOOK

Lucilla and Burzmali entered Ysai from the south into a lower-class quarter with widely spaced streetlights. It lacked only an hour of midnight and yet people thronged the streets in this quarter. Some walked quietly, some chatted with drug-enhanced vigor, some only watched expectantly. They wadded up at the corners and held Lucilla's fascinated attention as she passed.

Burzmali urged her to walk faster, an eager customer anxious to get her alone. Lucilla kept her covert attention on the people.

What did they do here? Those men waiting in the doorway: For what did they wait? Workers in heavy aprons emerged from a wide passage as Lucilla and Burzmali passed. There was a thick smell of rank sewage and perspiration about them. The workers, almost equally divided between male and female, were tall, heavy-bodied and with thick arms. Lucilla could not imagine what their occupation might be but they were of a single type and they made her realize how little she knew of Gammu.

The workers hawked and spat into the gutter as they

emerged into the night. *Ridding themselves of some contaminant?*

Burzmali put his mouth close to Lucilla's ear and whispered: "Those workers are the Bordanos."

She risked a glance back at them where they walked toward a side street. *Bordanos?* Ahhh, yes: people trained and bred to work the compression machinery that harnessed sewer gases. They had been bred to remove the sense of smell and the musculature of shoulders and arms had been increased. Burzmali guided her around a corner and out of sight of the Bordanos.

Five children emerged from a dark doorway beside them and wheeled into line following Lucilla and Burzmali. Lucilla noted their hands clutching small objects. They followed with a strange intensity. Abruptly, Burzmali stopped and turned. The children also stopped and stared at him. It was clear to Lucilla that the children were prepared for some violence.

Burzmali clasped both hands in front of him and bowed to the children. He said: "Guldur!"

When Burzmali resumed guiding her down the street, the children no longer followed.

"They would have stoned us," he said.

"Why?"

"They are children of a sect that follows Guldur—the local name for the Tyrant."

Lucilla looked back but the children were no longer in sight. They had set off in search of another victim.

Burzmali guided her around another corner. Now, they were in a street crowded with small merchants selling their wares from wheeled stands—food, clothing, small tools, and knives. A singsong of shouts filled the air as the merchants tried to attract buyers. Their voices had that end of the workday lift—a false brilliance composed of the hope that old dreams would be fulfilled, yet colored by the knowledge that life would not change for them. It occurred to Lucilla that the people of these streets pursued a fleeting dream, that the fulfillment they sought was not the thing itself but a myth they had been conditioned to seek the way racing animals were trained to chase after the whirling bait on the endless oval of the racetrack.

In the street directly ahead of them a burly figure in a thickly padded coat was engaged in loud-voiced argument with a merchant who offered a string bag filled with the dark red bulbs of a sweetly acid fruit. The fruit smell was thick all around them. The merchant complained: "You would steal the food from the mouths of my children!"

The bulky figure spoke in a piping voice, the accent chillingly familiar to Lucilla: "I, too, have children!"

Lucilla controlled herself with an effort.

When they were clear of the market street, she whispered to Burzmali: "That man in the heavy coat back there—a Tleilaxu Master!"

"Couldn't be," Burzmali protested. "Too tall."

"Two of them, one on the shoulders of the other."

"You're sure?"

"I'm sure."

"I've seen others like that since we arrived, but I didn't suspect."

"Many searchers are in these streets," she said.

Lucilla found that she did not much care for the everyday life of the gutter inhabitants on this gutter planet. She no longer trusted the explanation for bringing the ghola here. Of all those planets on which the precious ghola could have been raised, why had the Sisterhood chosen this one? Or was the ghola truly precious? Could it be that he was merely bait?

Almost blocking the narrow mouth of an alley beside them was a man plying a tall device of whirling lights.

"Live!" he shouted. "Live!"

Lucilla slowed her pace to watch a passerby step into the alleyway and pass a coin to the proprietor, then lean into a concave basin made brilliant by the lights. The proprietor stared back at Lucilla. She saw a man with a narrow dark face, the face of a Caladanian primitive on a body only slightly taller than that of a Tleilaxu Master. There had been a look of contempt on his brooding face as he took the customer's money.

The customer lifted his face from the basin with a shudder and then left the alley, staggering slightly, his eyes glazed.

Lucilla recognized the device. Users called it a hypnobong and it was outlawed on all of the more civilized worlds.

Burzmali hurried her out of the view of the brooding hypnobong proprietor.

They came to a wider side street with a corner doorway set into the building across from them. Foot traffic all around; not a vehicle in sight. A tall man sat on the first step in the corner doorway, his knees drawn up close to his chin. His long arms were wrapped around his knees, the thin-fingered hands clasped tightly together. He wore a wide-brimmed black hat that shaded his face from the streetlights, but twin gleams from the shadows under that brim told Lucilla that this was no kind of human she had ever before encountered. This was something about which the Bene Gesserit had only speculated.

Burzmali waited until they were well away from the seated figure before satisfying her curiosity.

"Futar," he whispered. "That's what they call themselves. They've only recently been seen here on Gammu."

"A Tleilaxu experiment," Lucilla guessed. And she thought: *A mistake that has returned from the Scattering.* "What are they doing here?" she asked.

"Trading colony, so the natives here tell us."

"Don't you believe it. Those are hunting animals that have been crossed with humans."

"Ahhh, here we are," Burzmali said.

He guided Lucilla through a narrow doorway into a dimly lighted eating establishment. This was part of their disguise, Lucilla knew: Do what others in this quarter did, but she did not relish eating in this place, not with what she could interpret from the smells.

The place had been crowded but it was emptying as they entered.

"This commerciel was recommended highly," Burzmali said as they seated themselves in a mechaslot and waited for the menu to be projected.

Lucilla watched the departing customers. Night workers from nearby factories and offices, she guessed. They appeared anxious in their hurry, perhaps fearful of what might be done to them if they were tardy.

How insulated she had been at the Keep, she thought. She did not like what she was learning of Gammu. What a scruffy place this commerciel was! The stools at the counter to her right had been scarred and chipped. The tabletop in front of her had been scored and rubbed with gritty cleaners until it no longer could be kept clean by the vacusweep whose nozzle she could see near her left elbow. There was no sign of even the cheapest sonic to maintain cleanliness. Food and other evidence of deterioration had accumulated in the table's scratches. Lucilla shuddered. She could not avoid the feeling that it had been a mistake to separate from the ghola.

The menu had been projected, she saw, and Burzmali already was scanning it.

"I will order for you," he said.

Burzmali's way of saying he did not want her to make a mistake by ordering something a woman of the Hormu might avoid.

It galled her to feel dependent. She was a Reverend Mother! She was trained to take command in any situation, mistress of her own destiny. How tiring all of this was. She gestured at the dirty window on her left where people could be seen passing on the narrow street.

"I am losing business while we dally, Skar."

There! That was in character.

Burzmali almost sighed. *At last!* he thought. She had begun to function once more as a Reverend Mother. He could not understand her abstracted attitude, the way she looked at the city and its people.

Two milky drinks slid from the slot onto the table. Burzmali drank his in one swallow. Lucilla tested her drink on the tip of her tongue, sorting the contents. An imitation caffiate diluted with a nut-flavored juice.

Burzmali gestured upward with his chin for her to

drink it quickly. She obeyed, concealing a grimace at the chemical flavors. Burzmali's attention was on something over her right shoulder but she dared not turn. That would be out of character.

"Come." He placed a coin on the table and hurried her out into the street. He smiled the smile of an eager customer but there was wariness in his eyes.

The tempo of the streets had changed. There were fewer people. The shadowy doors conveyed a deeper sense of menace. Lucilla reminded herself that she was supposed to represent a powerful guild whose members were immune to the common violence of the gutter. The few people on the street *did* make way for her, eyeing the dragons of her robe with every appearance of awe.

Burzmali stopped at a doorway.

It was like the others along this street, set back slightly from the walkway, so tall that it appeared narrower than it actually was. An old-fashioned security beam guarded the entrance. None of the newer systems had penetrated to the slum, apparently. The streets themselves were testimony to that: designed for groundcars. She doubted that there was a roofpad in the entire area. No sign of flitters or 'thopters could be heard or seen. There was music, though—a faint susurration reminiscent of semuta. Something new in semuta addiction? This would certainly be an area where addicts would go to ground.

Lucilla looked up at the face of the building as Burzmali moved ahead of her and made their presence known by breaking the doorway beam.

There were no windows in the building's face. Only the faint glitterings of surface 'eyes here and there in the dull sheen of ancient plasteel. They were old-fashioned comeyes, she noted, much bigger than modern ones.

A door deep in the shadows swung inward on silent hinges.

"This way." Burzmali reached back and urged her forward with a hand on her elbow.

They entered a dimly lighted hallway that smelled of exotic foods and bitter essences. She was a moment identifying some of the things that assailed her nostrils. Melange. She caught the unmistakable cinnamon ripeness. And yes, semuta. She identified burned rice, higet salts. Someone was masking another kind of *cooking*. There were explosives being made here. She thought of warning Burzmali but reconsidered. It was not necessary for him to know and there might be ears in this confined space to hear whatever she said.

Burzmali led the way up a shadowy flight of stairs with a dim glowstrip along the slanting baseboard. At the top he found a hidden switch concealed behind a patch in the patched and repatched wall. There was no sound when he pushed the switch but Lucilla felt a change in the movement all around them. Silence. It was a new kind of silence in her experience, a crouching preparation for flight or violence.

It was cold in the stairwell and she shivered, but not from the chill. Footsteps sounded beyond the doorway beside the patch-masked switch.

A gray-haired hag in a yellow smock opened the door and peered up at them past her straggling eyebrows.

"It's you," she said, her voice wavering. She stood aside for them to enter.

Lucilla glanced swiftly around the room as she heard the door close behind them. It was a room the unobservant might think shabby, but that was superficial. Underneath, it was quality. The shabbiness was another mask, partly a matter of this place having been fitted to a particularly demanding person: This goes here and nowhere else! That goes over there and it stays there! The furnishings and bric-a-brac looked a little worn but someone here did not object to that. The room felt better this way. It was that kind of room.

Who possessed this room? The old woman? She was making her painful way toward a door on their left.

"We are not to be disturbed until dawn," Burzmali said.

The old woman stopped and turned.

Lucilla studied her. Was this another who shammed advanced age? No. The age was real. Every motion was diffused by unsteadiness—a trembling of the neck, a failure of the body that betrayed her in ways she could not prevent.

"Even if it's somebody important?" the old woman asked in her wavering voice.

The eyes twitched when she spoke. Her mouth moved only minimally to emit the necessary sounds, spacing out her words as though she drew them from somewhere deep within. Her shoulders, curved from years of bending at some fixed work, would not straighten enough for her to look Burzmali in the eyes. She peered upward past her brows instead, an oddly furtive posture.

"What important person are you expecting?" Burzmali asked.

The old woman shuddered and appeared to take a long time understanding.

"Impor-r-rtant people come here," she said.

Lucilla recognized the body signals and blurted it because Burzmali must know:

"She's from Rakis!"

The old woman's curious upward gaze locked on Lucilla. The ancient voice said: "I was a priestess, Hormu Lady."

"Of course she's from Rakis," Burzmali said. His tone warned her not to question.

"I would not harm you," the hag whined.

"Do you still serve the Divided God?"

Again, there was that long delay for the old woman to respond.

"Many serve the Great Guldur," she said.

Lucilla pursed her lips and once more scanned the room. The old woman had been reduced greatly in importance. "I am glad I do not have to kill you," Lucilla said.

The old woman's jaw drooped open in a parody of surprise while spittle dripped from her lips.

This was a descendant of Fremen? Lucilla let her revulsion come out in a long shudder. This mendicant bit of flotsam had been shaped from a people who walked tall and proud, a people who died bravely. This one would die whining.

"Please trust me," the hag whined and fled the room.

"Why did you do that?" Burzmali demanded. "These are the ones who will get us to Rakis!"

She merely looked at him, recognizing the fear in his question. It was fear *for* her.

But I did not imprint him back there, she thought.

With a sense of shock she realized that Burzmali had

recognized hate in her. *I hate them!* she thought. *I hate the people of this planet!*

That was a dangerous emotion for a Reverend Mother. Still it burned in her. This planet had changed her in a way she did not want. She did not want the realization that such things could be. Intellectual understanding was one thing; experience was another.

Damn them!

But they already were damned.

Her chest pained her. Frustration! There was no escaping this new awareness. What had happened to these people?

People?

The shells were here but they no longer could be called fully alive. Dangerous, though. Supremely dangerous.

"We must rest while we can," Burzmali said.

"I do not have to earn my money?" she demanded.

Burzmali paled. "What we did was necessary! We were lucky and were not stopped but it could have happened!"

"And this place is safe?"

"As safe as I can make it. Everyone here has been screened by me or by my people."

Lucilla found a long couch that smelled of old perfumes and composed herself there to scour her emotions of the dangerous hate. Where hate entered, love might follow! She heard Burzmali stretching out to rest on cushions against a nearby wall. Soon, he was breathing deeply, but sleep evaded Lucilla. She kept sensing crowds of memories, things thrust forward by the Others who shared her inner storerooms of thinking. Abruptly, inner vision gave her a glimpse of a street and faces, people moving in bright sunlight. It took a moment for her to realize that she saw all of this from a peculiar angle—that she was being cradled in someone's arms. She knew then that this was one of her own personal memories. She could place the one who held her, feel the warm heartbeat next to a warm cheek.

Lucilla tasted the salt of her own tears.

She realized then that Gammu had touched her more deeply than any experience since her first days in the Bene Gesserit schools.

Concealed behind strong barriers the heart
becomes ice.

—DARWI ODRADE, ARGUMENT IN COUNCIL

It was a group filled with fierce tensions: Taraza (wearing secret mail under her robe and mindful of the other precautions she had taken), Odrade (certain that there could be violence and consequently wary), Sheeana (thoroughly briefed on the probabilities here and shielded behind three Security Mothers who moved with her like fleshly armor), Waff (worried that his reason might have been clouded by some mysterious Bene Gesserit artifice), the false Tuek (giving every evidence that he was about to erupt in rage), and nine of Tuek's Rakian counselors (each angrily engaged in seeking ascendancy for self or family).

In addition, five guardian acolytes, bred and trained by the Sisterhood for physical violence, stayed close to Taraza. Waff moved with an equal number of new Face Dancers.

They had convened in the penthouse atop the Dar-es-Balat Museum. It was a long room with a wall of plaz facing west across a roof garden of lacy greenery. The interior was furnished with soft divans and was decorated with artful displays from the Tyrant's no-room.

Odrade had argued against including Sheeana but Taraza remained adamant. The girl's effect on Waff and some of the priesthood represented an overwhelming advantage for the Bene Gesserit.

There were dolban screens over the long wall of windows to keep out the worst glare of a westering sun. That the room faced west said something to Odrade. The windows looked into the land of gloaming where Shai-hulud took his repose. It was a room focused on the past, on death.

She admired the dolbans in front of her. They were flat black slats ten molecules wide and rotating in a transparent liquid medium. Set automatically, the best Ixian dolbans admitted a predetermined level of light without much diminishing the view. Artists and antique dealers preferred them to polarizing systems, Odrade knew, because they admitted a full spectrum of available light. Their installation spoke of the uses to which this room was put—a display case for the best of the God Emperor's hoard. Yes—there was a gown that had been worn by his intended bride.

The priestly counselors were arguing fiercely among themselves at one end of the room, ignoring the false Tuek. Taraza stood nearby listening. Her expression said she thought the priests fools.

Waff stood with his Face Dancer entourage near the wide entrance door. His attention shifted from Sheeana to Odrade to Taraza and only occasionally to the arguing priests. Every movement Waff made betrayed his uncertainties. Would the Bene Gesserit really support him? Could they together override Rakian opposition by peaceful means?

Sheeana and her shielding escort came to stand beside Odrade. The girl still showed stringy muscles, Odrade observed, but she was filling out and the muscles had taken on a recognizable Bene Gesserit definition. The high planes of her cheekbones had grown softer under that olive skin, the brown eyes more liquid, but there were still red sunstreaks in her brown hair. The attention she spared for the arguing priests said she was assessing what had been revealed to her in the briefing.

"Will they really fight?" she whispered.

"Listen to them," Odrade said.

"What will the Mother Superior do?"

"Watch her carefully."

Both of them looked at Taraza standing in her group of muscular acolytes. Taraza now looked amused as she continued to observe the priests.

The Rakian group had started their argument out in the roof garden. They had brought it inside as the shadows lengthened. They breathed angrily, muttering sometimes and then raising their voices. Did they not see how the mimic Tuek watched them?

Odrade returned her attention to the horizon visible beyond the roof garden: not another sign of life out there in the desert. Any direction you looked outward from Dar-es-Balat showed empty sand. People born and raised here had a different view of life and their planet than most of those priestly counselors. This was not the Rakis of green belts and watered oases, which abounded in the higher latitudes like flowered fingers pointing into the long desert tracks. Out from Dar-es-Balat was the meridian desert that stretched like a cummerbund around the entire planet.

"I have heard enough of this nonsense!" the false Tuek exploded. He pushed one of the counselors roughly aside and strode into the middle of the arguing group, pivoting to stare into each face. "Are you all mad?"

One of the priests (It was old Albertus, by the gods!) looked across the room at Waff and called out: "Ser Waff! Will you please control your Face Dancer?"

Waff hesitated and then moved toward the disputants, his entourage close behind.

The false Tuek whirled and pointed a finger at Waff: "You! Stay where you are! I will brook no Tleilaxu interference! Your conspiracy is quite clear to me!"

Odrade had been watching Waff as the mimic Tuek spoke. Surprise! The Bene Tleilax Master had never before been addressed thus by one of his minions. What a shock! Rage convulsed his features. Humming sounds like the noises of angry insects came from his mouth, a modulated thing that clearly was some kind of language. The Face Dancers of his entourage froze but the false Tuek merely returned attention to his counselors.

Waff stopped humming. Consternation! His Face Dancer Tuek would not come to heel! He lurched into motion toward the priests. The false Tuek saw it and once more leveled a hand at him, the finger quivering.

"I told you to stay out of this! You might be able to do away with me but you'll not saddle me with your Tleilaxu filth!"

That did it. Waff stopped. Realization came over him. He shot a glance at Taraza, seeing her amused recognition of his predicament. Now, he had a new target for his rage.

"You knew!"

"I suspected."

"You . . . you . . ."

"You fashioned too well," Taraza said. "It's your own doing."

The priests were oblivious to this exchange. They shouted at the false Tuek, ordering him to shut up and remove himself, calling him a "damned Face Dancer!"

Odrade studied the object of this attack with care. How deep did the print go? Had he really convinced himself that he was Tuek?

In a sudden lull, the mimic drew himself up with dignity and sent a scornful glance at his accusers. "You all know me," he said. "You all know my years of service to the Divided God Who is One God. I will go to Him now if your conspiracy extends to that but remember this: He knows what is in your hearts!"

The priests looked as one man to Waff. None of them had seen a Face Dancer replace their High Priest. There had been no body to see. Every bit of evidence was the evidence of human voices saying things that might be lies. Belatedly, several looked at Odrade. Her voice was one of those that had convinced them.

Waff, too, was looking at Odrade.

She smiled and addressed herself to the Tleilaxu Master. "It suits our purposes that the High Priesthood not pass into other hands at this time," she said.

Waff immediately saw the advantage to himself. This was a wedge between priests and Bene Gesserit. This removed one of the most dangerous holds the Sisterhood had on the Tleilaxu.

"It suits my purposes, too," he said.

As the priests once more lifted their voices in anger,

Taraza came in right on cue: "Which of you will break our accord?" she demanded.

Tuek thrust two of his counselors aside and strode across the room to the Mother Superior. He stopped only a pace from her.

"What game is this?" he asked.

"We support you against those who would replace you," she said. "The Bene Tleilaxu join us in this. It is our way of demonstrating that we, too, have a vote in selecting the High Priest."

Several priestly voices were raised in unison: "Is he or is he not a Face Dancer?"

Taraza looked benignly at the man in front of her: "Are you a Face Dancer?"

"Of course not!"

Taraza looked at Odrade, who said: "There seems to have been a mistake."

Odrade singled out Albertus among the priests and locked eyes with him. "Sheeana," Odrade said, "what should the Church of the Divided God do now?"

As she had been briefed to do, Sheeana stepped out of her guardian enclosure and spoke with all of the hauteur she had been taught: "They shall continue to serve God!"

"The business of this meeting appears to have been concluded," Taraza said. "If you need protection, High Priest Tuek, a squad of our guardians awaits in the hall. They are yours to command."

They could see acceptance and understanding in him. He had become a creature of the Bene Gesserit. He remembered nothing of his Face Dancer origins.

When the priests and Tuek had gone, Waff sent a

single word at Taraza, speaking in the language of the Islamiyat: "Explain!"

Taraza stepped away from her guards, appearing to make herself vulnerable. It was a calculated move they had debated in front of Sheeana. In the same language, Taraza said: "We release our grip on the Bene Tleilax."

They waited while he weighed her words. Taraza reminded herself that the Tleilaxu name for themselves could be translated as "the un-nameable." That was a label often reserved for gods.

This *god* obviously had not extended the discovery in here to what might be happening with his mimics among Ixians and Fish Speakers. Waff had more shocks coming. He appeared quite puzzled, though.

Waff confronted many unanswered questions. He was not satisfied with his reports from Gammu. It was a dangerous double game he played now. Did the Sisterhood play a similar game? But the Tleilaxu Lost Ones could not be shunted aside without inviting attack by the Honored Matres. Taraza herself had warned of this. Did the old Bashar on Gammu still represent a force worthy of consideration?

He voiced this question.

Taraza countered with her own question: "How did you change our ghola? What did you hope to gain?" She felt certain she already knew. But the pose of ignorance was necessary.

Waff wanted to say: "The death of all Bene Gesserit!" They were too dangerous. Yet their value was incalculable. He sank into a sulking silence, looking at the Reverend Mothers with a brooding expression that made his elfin features even more childlike.

A petulant child, Taraza thought. She warned herself then that it was dangerous to underestimate Waff. You broke the Tleilaxu egg only to find another egg inside—ad infinitum! Everything circled back to Odrade's suspicions about the contentions that might still lead them to bloody violence in this room. Had the Tleilaxu really revealed what they had learned from the whores and the other Lost Ones? Was the ghola only a potential Tleilaxu weapon?

Taraza decided to prod him once more, using the approach of her Council's "Analysis Nine." Still in the language of the Islamiyat, she said: "Would you dishonor yourself in the land of the Prophet? You have not shared openly as you said you would."

"We told you the sexual—"

"You do not share all!" she interrupted. "It's because of the ghola and we know this."

She could see his reactions. He was a cornered animal. Such animals were dangerous in the extreme. She had once seen a mongrel hound, a feral and tail-tucked survivor of ancient pets from Dan, cornered by a pack of youths. The animal turned on its pursuers, slashing its way to freedom in totally unexpected savagery. Two youths crippled for life and only one without injuries! Waff was like that animal right now. She could see his hands longing for a weapon, but Tleilaxu and Bene Gesserit had searched one another with exquisite care before coming here. She felt sure he had no weapon. Still . . .

Waff spoke, baited suspense in his manner. "You think me unaware of how you hope to rule us!"

"And *there* is the rot that the people of the Scattering took with them," she said. "Rot at the core."

Waff's manner changed. It did not do to ignore the deeper implications of Bene Gesserit thought. But was she sowing discord?

"The Prophet set a locator ticking in the minds of every human, Scattered or not," Taraza said. "He has brought them back to us with all of the rot intact."

Waff ground his teeth. What was she doing? He entertained the mad thought that the Sisterhood had clogged his mind with some secret drug in the air. They *knew* things denied to others! He stared from Taraza to Odrade and back to Taraza. He knew he was old with serial ghola resurrections but not old in the way of the Bene Gesserit. These people were old! They seldom looked old but they were old, old beyond anything he dared imagine.

Taraza was having similar thoughts. She had seen the flash of deeper awareness in Waff's eyes. Necessity opened new doors of reason. How deep did the Tleilaxu go? His eyes were so old! She had the feeling that whatever had been a brain in these Tleilaxu Masters was now something else—a holo-recording from which all weakening emotions had been erased. She shared the distrust of emotions that she suspected in him. Was that a bond to unite them?

The tropism of common thoughts.

"You say you release your grip on us," Waff growled, "but I feel your fingers around my throat."

"Then here is a grip on our throat," she said. "Some of your Lost Ones have returned to you. Never has a Reverend Mother come back to us from the Scattering."

"But you said you knew all of the—"

"We have other ways of gaining knowledge. What do

you suppose happened to the Reverend Mothers we sent out into the Scattering?"

"A common disaster?" He shook his head. This was absolutely new information. None of the returned Tleilaxu had said anything at all about this. The discrepancy fed his suspicions. Whom was he to believe?

"They were subverted," Taraza said.

Odrade, hearing the general suspicion voiced for the first time by the Mother Superior, sensed the enormous power implicit in Taraza's simple statement. Odrade was cowed by it. She knew the resources, the contingency plans, the improvised ways a Reverend Mother might use to surmount barriers. Something Out There could stop *that*?

When Waff did not respond, Taraza said: "You come to us with dirty hands."

"You dare say this?" Waff asked. "You who continue to deplete our resources in the ways taught you by the Bashar's mother?"

"We knew you could afford the losses if you had resources from the Scattering," Taraza said.

Waff inhaled a trembling breath. So the Bene Gesserit knew even this. He saw in part how they had learned it. Well, a way would have to be found to bring the false Tuek back under control. Rakis was the prize the Scattered Ones really sought and it might yet be demanded of the Tleilaxu.

Taraza moved even closer to Waff, alone and vulnerable. She saw her guards grow tense. Sheeana took a small step toward the Mother Superior and was pulled back by Odrade.

Odrade kept her attention on the Mother Superior and

not on potential attackers. Were the Tleilaxu truly convinced that the Bene Gesserit would serve them? Taraza had tested the limits of it, no doubt of that. And in the language of the Islamiyat. But she looked very alone out there away from her guards and so near Waff and his people. Where would Waff's obvious suspicions lead him now?

Taraza shivered.

Odrade saw it. Taraza had been abnormally thin as a child and had never put on an excess ounce of fat. This made her exquisitely sensitive to temperature changes, intolerant of cold, but Odrade sensed no such change in the room. Taraza had made a dangerous decision then, so dangerous that her body betrayed her. Not dangerous to herself, of course, but dangerous to the Sisterhood. *There* was the most awful Bene Gesserit crime: disloyalty to their own order.

"We will serve you in all ways except one," Taraza said. "We will never become receptacles for gholas!"

Waff paled.

Taraza continued: "None of us is now nor will ever become . . ." she paused ". . . an axlotl tank."

Waff raised his right hand in the start of a gesture every Reverend Mother knew: the signal for his Face Dancers to attack.

Taraza pointed at his upraised hand. "If you complete that gesture, the Tleilaxu will lose everything. The messenger of God—" Taraza nodded over a shoulder toward Sheeana "—will turn her back upon you and the words of the Prophet will be dust in your mouths."

In the language of the Islamiyat, such words were too much for Waff. He lowered his hand but he continued to glower at Taraza.

"My ambassador said we would share everything we know," Taraza said. "You said you, too, would share. The messenger of God listens with the ears of the Prophet! What pours forth from the Abdl of the Tleilaxu?"

Waff's shoulders sagged.

Taraza turned her back on him. It was an artful move but both she and the other Reverend Mothers present knew she did it now in perfect safety. Looking across the room at Odrade, Taraza allowed herself a smile that she knew Odrade would interpret correctly. Time for a bit of Bene Gesserit punishment!

"The Tleilaxu desire an Atreides for breeding," Taraza said. "I give you Darwi Odrade. More will be supplied."

Waff came to a decision. "You may know much about the Honored Matres," he said, "but you—"

"Whores!" Taraza whirled on him.

"As you will. But there is a thing from them that your words reveal you do not know. I seal our bargain by telling you this. They can magnify the sensations of the orgasmic platform, transmitting this throughout a male body. They elicit the total sensual involvement of the male. Multiple orgasmic waves are created and may be continued by the . . . the female for an extended period."

"Total involvement?" Taraza did not try to hide her astonishment.

Odrade, too, listened with a sense of shock that she saw was shared by her Sisters present, even the acolytes. Only Sheeana seemed not to understand.

"I tell you, Mother Superior Taraza," Waff said, a gloating smile on his face, "that we have duplicated this with our own people. Myself even! In my anger, I caused the Face Dancer who played the . . . female part to destroy itself. No one . . . I say, no one! may have such a hold on me!"

"What hold?"

"If it had been one of these . . . these whores, as you call them, I would have obeyed her without question in anything." He shuddered. "I barely had the will to . . . to destroy . . ." He shook his head in bewilderment at the memory. "Anger saved me."

Taraza tried to swallow in a dry throat. "How . . ."

"How is it done? Very well! But before I share this knowledge I warn you: If one of you ever tries to use this power over one of us, bloody slaughter will follow! We have prepared our Domel and all of our people to respond by killing all Reverend Mothers they can find at the slightest sign that you seek this power over us!"

"None of us would do that, but not because of your threat. We are restrained by the knowledge that this would destroy us. Your bloody slaughter would not be necessary."

"Oh? Then why does it not destroy these . . . these whores?"

"It does! And it destroys everyone they touch!"

"It has not destroyed me!"

"God protects you, my Abdl," Taraza said. "As He protects all of the faithful."

Convinced, Waff glanced around the room and back to Taraza. "Let all know that I fulfill my bond in the land of the Prophet. This is the way of it, then . . ." He waved a hand to two of his Face Dancer guards. "We will demonstrate."

Much later, alone in the penthouse room, Odrade

wondered if it had been wise to let Sheeana see the whole performance. Well, why not? Sheeana already was committed to the Sisterhood. And it would have aroused Waff's suspicions to send Sheeana away.

There had been obvious sensual arousal in Sheeana as she watched the Face Dancer performance. The Training Proctors would have to call in their male assistants earlier than usual for Sheeana. What would Sheeana do then? Would she try this new knowledge on the men? Inhibitions must be raised in Sheeana to prevent that! She must be taught the dangers to herself.

The Sisters and acolytes present had controlled themselves well, storing what they learned firmly in memory. Sheeana's education must be built on that observation. Others mastered such internal forces.

The Face Dancer observers had remained inscrutable, but there had been things to see in Waff. He said he would destroy the two demonstrators but what would he do first? Would he succumb to temptation? What thoughts went through his mind as he watched the Face Dancer male squirm in mind-blanking ecstasy?

In a way, the demonstration reminded Odrade of the Rakian dance she had seen in the Great Square of Keen. In the short term, the dance had been deliberately unrhythmic but the progression created a long-term rhythm that repeated itself in some two hundred . . . steps. The dancers had stretched out their rhythm to a remarkable degree.

As had the Face Dancer demonstrators.

Siaynoq become a sexual grip on uncounted billions in the Scattering!

Odrade thought about the dance, the long rhythm followed by chaotic violence. Siaynoq's glorious focusing of religious energies had devolved into a different kind of exchange. She thought about Sheeana's excited response to her glimpses of that dance in the Great Square. Odrade remembered asking Sheeana: "What did they share down there?"

"The dancers, silly!"

That response had not been permissible. "I've warned you about that tone, Sheeana. Do you wish to learn immediately what a Reverend Mother can do to punish you?"

The words played themselves like ghost messages in Odrade's mind as she looked at the gathering darkness outside the Dar-es-Balat penthouse. A great loneliness welled up in her. All the others had gone from this room.

Only the punished one remains!

How bright-eyed Sheeana had been in that room above the Great Square, her mind so full of questions. "Why do you always talk about hurting and punishment?"

"You must learn discipline. How can you control others when you cannot control yourself?"

"I don't like that lesson."

"None of us does very much . . . until later when we've learned the value of it by experience."

As intended, that response had festered long in Sheeana's awareness. In the end, she had revealed all she knew about the dance.

"Some of the dancers escape. Others go directly to Shaitan. The priests say they go to Shai-hulud."

"What of the ones who survive?"

"When they recover, they must join a great dance in the desert. If Shaitan comes there, they die. If Shaitan does not come, they are rewarded."

Odrade had seen the pattern. Sheeana's explanatory words had not been necessary beyond that point, even though the recital had been allowed to continue. How bitter Sheeana's voice had been!

"They get money, space in a bazaar, that kind of reward. The priests say they have proved that they are human."

"Are the ones who fail not human?"

Sheeana had remained silent for a long time in deep thought. The track was clear to Odrade, though: the Sisterhood's test of humanity! Her own passage into the acceptable humanity of the Sisterhood had already been duplicated by Sheeana. How soft that passage seemed in comparison to the other pains!

In the dim light of the museum penthouse, Odrade held up her right hand, looking at it, remembering the agony box, and the gom jabbar poised at her neck ready to kill her if she flinched or cried out.

Sheeana had not cried out, either. But she had known the answer to Odrade's question even before the agony box.

"They are human but different."

Odrade spoke aloud in the empty room with its displays from the Tyrant's no-chamber hoard.

"What did you do to us, Leto? Are you only Shaitan talking to us? What would you force us to share now?"

Was the fossil dance to become fossil sex?

"Who are you talking to, Mother?"

It was Sheeana's voice from the open doorway across

the room. Her gray postulant's robe was only a faint shape there, growing larger as she approached.

"Mother Superior sent me for you," Sheeana said as she came to a stop near Odrade.

"I was talking to myself," Odrade said. She looked at the strangely quiet girl, remembering the gut-wrenching excitement of that moment when the Fulcrum Question had been asked of Sheeana.

Do you wish to be a Reverend Mother?

"Why are you talking to yourself, Mother?" There was a load of concern in Sheeana's voice. The Teaching Proctors would have their hands full removing those emotions.

"I was remembering when I asked you if you wished to be a Reverend Mother," Odrade said. "It prompted other thoughts."

"You said I must give myself to your direction in all things, holding back nothing, disobeying you in nothing."

"And you said: 'Is that all?'"

"I didn't know very much, did I? I still don't know very much."

"None of us does, child. Except that we're all in the dance together. And Shaitan will certainly come if the least of us fails."

When strangers meet, great allowance should be made
for differences of custom and training.

—THE LADY JESSICA, FROM "WISDOM OF ARRAKIS"

The last greenish line of light fell out of the horizon
before Burzmali gave the signal for them to move.
It was dark by the time they reached the far side of Ysai
and the perimeter road that was to lead them to Duncan.
Clouds covered the sky, reflecting the city's lights downward onto the shapes of the urban hovels through which
their guides directed them.

These guides bothered Lucilla. They appeared out of
side streets and from suddenly opened doorways to whisper new directions.

Too many people knew about the fugitive pair and
their intended rendezvous!

She had come to grips with her hatred but the residue
was a profound distrust of every person they saw. Hiding
this behind the mechanical attitudes of a playfem with
her customer had become increasingly difficult.

There was slush on the pedestrian way beside the
road, most of it scattered there by the passage of groundcars. Lucilla's feet were cold before they had gone half a

kilometer and she was forced to expend energy compensating for the added bloodflow in her extremities.

Burzmali walked silently, his head down, apparently lost in his own worries. Lucilla was not fooled. He heard every sound around them, saw every approaching vehicle. He hustled them off the pathway each time a groundcar approached. The cars went swishing past on their suspensors, the dirty slush flying from under their fanskirts and peppering the bushes along the road. Burzmali held her down beside him in the snow until he was sure the cars were out of sight and sound. Not that anyone riding in them could hear much except their own whirling passage.

They had been walking for two hours before Burzmali stopped and took stock of the way ahead. Their destination was a perimeter community that had been described to them as "completely safe." Lucilla knew better. No place on Gammu was completely safe.

Yellow lights cast an undershot glow on the clouds ahead of them, marking the location of the community. Their slushy progress took them through a tunnel under the perimeter road and up a low hill planted to some sort of orchard. The limbs were stark in the dim light.

Lucilla glanced upward. The clouds were thinning. Gammu had many small moons—fortress no-ships. Some of them had been placed by Teg but she glimpsed lines of new ones sharing the guardian role. They appeared to be about four times the size of the brightest stars and they often traveled together, which made their reflected light useful but erratic because they moved fast—up across the sky and below the horizon in only a few hours. She glimpsed a string of six such moons through a break in the clouds, wondering if they were part of Teg's defense system.

Momentarily, she reflected on the inherent weakness of the siege mentality that such defenses represented. Teg had been right about them. Mobility was the key to military success but she doubted that he had meant mobility on foot.

There were no easy hiding places on the snow-whitened slope and Lucilla felt Burzmali's nervousness. What could they do here if someone came? A snow-covered depression led down from their position to the left, angling toward the community. It was not a road but she thought it might be a path.

"Down this way," Burzmali said, leading them into the depression.

The snow came up to their calves.

"I hope these people are trustworthy," she said.

"They hate the Honored Matres," he said. "That's enough for me."

"The ghola had better be there!" She held back an even more angry response but could not keep herself from adding: "Their hatred isn't enough for me."

It was better to expect the worst, she thought.

She had come to a reassuring thought about Burzmali, though. He was like Teg. Neither of them pursued a course that would lead them into a dead end—not if they could help it. She suspected there were support forces concealed in the bushes around them even now.

The snow-covered trail ended in a paved pathway, gently curved inward from the edges and kept free of snow by a melt system. There was a trickle of dampness in the center. Lucilla was several steps onto this path before she recognized what it must be—a magchute. It was an ancient magnetic transport base that once had carried goods or raw materials to a pre-Scattering factory.

"It gets steeper here," Burzmali warned her. "They've carved steps in it but watch it. They're not very deep."

They came presently to the end of the magchute. It stopped at a decrepit wall—local brick atop a plasteel foundation. The faint light of stars in a clearing sky revealed crude workmanship in the bricks—typical Famine-Times construction. The wall was a mass of vines and mottled fungus. The growth did little to conceal the cracked courses of the bricks and the crude efforts to fill chinks with mortar. A single row of narrow windows looked down onto the place where the magchute debouched into a mass of bushes and weeds. Three of the windows glowed electric blue with some inner activity that was accompanied by faint crackling sounds.

"This was a factory in the old days," Burzmali said.

"I have eyes and a memory," Lucilla snapped. Did this grunting male think her completely devoid of intelligence?

Something creaked dismally off to their left. A patch of sod and weeds lifted atop a cellar door accompanied by an upward glow of brilliant yellow light.

"Quick!" Burzmali led her at a swift run across thick vegetation and down a flight of steps exposed by the lifting door. The door creaked closed behind them in a grumbling of machinery.

Lucilla found herself in a large space with a low ceiling. Light came from long lines of modern glowglobes strung along massive plasteel girders overhead. The floor was swept clean but showed scratches and indentations of activity, the locations no doubt of bygone machinery. She glimpsed movement far off across the open space. A young woman in a version of Lucilla's dragon robe trotted toward them.

Lucilla sniffed. There was a stink of acid in the room and undertones of something foul.

"This was a Harkonnen factory," Burzmali said. "I wonder what they made here?"

The young woman stopped in front of Lucilla. She had a willowy figure, elegant in shape and motion under the clinging robe. A subcutaneous glow came from her face. It spoke of exercise and good health. The green eyes, though, were hard and chilling in the way they measured everything they saw.

"So they sent more than one of us to watch this place," she said.

Lucilla put out a restraining hand as Burzmali started to respond. This woman was not what she seemed. *No more than I am!* Lucilla chose her words carefully. "We always know each other, it seems."

The young woman smiled. "I watched your approach. I could not believe my eyes." She swept a sneering glance across Burzmali. "This was supposed to be a customer?"

"And guide," Lucilla said. She noted the puzzlement on Burzmali's face and prayed he would not ask the wrong question. This young woman was danger!

"Weren't we expected?" Burzmali asked.

"Ahhhh, it speaks," the young woman said, laughing. Her laugh was as cold as her eyes.

"I prefer that you do not refer to me as 'it,'" Burzmali said.

"I call Gammu scum anything I wish," the young woman said. "Don't speak to me of your preferences!"

"What did you call me?" Burzmali was tired and his anger came boiling up at this unexpected attack.

"I call you anything I choose, scum!"

Burzmali had suffered enough. Before Lucilla could stop him, he uttered a low growl and aimed a heavy slap at the young woman.

The blow did not land.

Lucilla watched in fascination as the woman dropped under the attack, caught Burzmali's sleeve as one might catch a bit of fabric blowing in the wind and, in a blindingly fast pirouette whose speed almost hid its delicacy, sent Burzmali skidding across the floor. The woman dropped to a half crouch on one foot, the other prepared to kick.

"I shall kill him now," she said.

Lucilla, not knowing what might happen next, folded her body sideways, barely avoiding the woman's suddenly outthrust foot, and countered with a standard Bene Gesserit sabard that dumped the young woman on her back doubled up where the blow had caught her in the abdomen.

"A suggestion that you kill my guide is uncalled for, whatever your name is," Lucilla said.

The young woman gasped for breath, then, panting between words: "I am called Murbella, Great Honored Matre. You shame me by defeating me with such a slow attack. Why do you do that?"

"You needed a lesson," Lucilla said.

"I am only newly robed, Great Honored Matre. Please forgive me. I thank you for the splendid lesson and will thank you every time I employ your response, which I now commit to memory." She bowed her head, then leaped lightly to her feet, an impish grin on her face.

In her coldest voice, Lucilla asked: "Do you know who I am?" Out of the corners of her eyes, she saw Burzmali regain his feet with painful slowness. He remained at one side, watching the women, but anger burned his face.

"From your ability to teach me that lesson, I see that you are who you are, Great Honored Matre. Am I forgiven?" The impish grin had vanished from Murbella's face. She stood with head bowed.

"You are forgiven. Is there a no-ship coming?"

"So they say here. We are prepared for it." Murbella glanced at Burzmali.

"He is still useful to me and it is required that he accompany me," Lucilla said.

"Very good, Great Honored Matre. Does your forgiveness include your name?"

"No!"

Murbella sighed. "We have captured the ghola," she said. "He came as a Tleilaxu from the south. I was just about to bed him when you arrived."

Burzmali hobbled toward them. Lucilla saw that he had recognized the danger. This "completely safe" place had been infested by enemies! But the enemies still knew very little.

"The ghola was not injured?" Burzmali asked.

"It still speaks," Murbella said. "How odd."

"You will not bed the ghola," Lucilla said. "That one is my special charge!"

"Fair game, Great Honored Matre. And I marked him first. He is already partly subdued."

She laughed once more, with a callous abandonment that shocked Lucilla. "This way. There is a place where you can watch."

May you die on Caladan!

—ANCIENT DRINKING TOAST

Duncan tried to remember where he was. He knew Tormsa was dead. Blood had spurted from Tormsa's eyes. Yes, he remembered that clearly. They had entered a dark building and light had flared abruptly all around them. Duncan felt an ache in the back of his head. A blow? He tried to move and his muscles refused to obey.

He remembered sitting at the edge of a wide lawn. There was some kind of bowling game in progress—eccentric balls that bounced and darted with no apparent design. The players were young men in a common costume of . . . Giedi Prime!

"They are practicing to be old men," he said. He remembered saying that.

His companion, a young woman, looked at him blankly.

"Only old men should play these outdoor games," he said.

"Oh?"

It was an unanswerable question. She put him down with only the simplest of verbal gestures.

And betrayed me the next instant to the Harkonnens!

So that was a pre-ghola memory.

Ghola!

He remembered the Bene Gesserit Keep on Gammu. The library: holophotos and triphotos of the Atreides Duke, Leto I. Teg's resemblance was not an accident: a bit taller but otherwise it was all there—that long, thin face with its high-bridged nose, the renowned Atreides charisma . . .

Teg!

He remembered the old Bashar's last gallant stand in the Gammu night.

Where am I?

Tormsa had brought him here. They had been moving along an overgrown track on the outskirts of Ysai. *Barony*. It started to snow before they were two hundred meters up the track. Wet snow that clung to them. Cold, miserable snow that set their teeth chattering within a minute. They paused to bring up their hoods and close the insulated jackets. That was better. But it would be night soon. Much colder.

"There is a shelter of sorts up ahead," Tormsa said. "We will wait there for the night."

When Duncan did not speak, Tormsa said: "It won't be warm but it will be dry."

Duncan saw the gray outline of the place in about three hundred paces. It stood out against the dirty snow some two stories tall. He recognized it immediately: a Harkonnen counting outpost. Observers here had counted (and sometimes killed) the people who passed. It was built of native dirt turned into one giant brick by the simple expedient of preforming it in mud bricks and then superheating it with a wide-bore burner, the kind the Harkonnens had used to control mobs.

As they came up to it, Duncan saw the remains of a full-field defensive screen with fire-lance gaps aimed at the approaches. Someone had smashed the system a long time ago. Twisted holes in the field net were partly overgrown with bushes. But the fire-lance gaps remained open. Oh, yes—to allow people inside a view of the approaches.

Tormsa paused and listened, studying their surroundings with care.

Duncan looked at the counting station. He remembered them well. What confronted him was a thing that had sprouted like a deformed growth from an original tubular seed. The surface had been baked to a glassine finish. Warts and protrusions betrayed where it had been superheated. The erosion of eons had left fine scratches in it but the original shape remained. He looked upward and identified part of the old suspensor lift system. Someone had jury-rigged a block and tackle to the outbar.

So the opening through the full-field screen was of recent making.

Tormsa disappeared into this opening.

As though a switch had been thrown, Duncan's memory vision changed. He was in the no-globe's library with Teg. The projector was producing a series of views through modern Ysai. The idea of *modern* took on an odd overtone for him. Barony had been a modern city, if you thought of modern as meaning technologically uniform up to the norms of its time. It had relied exclusively on suspensor guide-beams for transport of people and material—all of them high up. No ground-level openings. He was explaining this to Teg.

The plan translated physically into a city that used every possible square meter of vertical and horizontal space for things other than movement of goods and humans. The guide-beam openings required only enough head room and elbow room for the universal transport pods.

Teg spoke: "The ideal shape would be tubular with a flat top for the 'thopters."

"The Harkonnens preferred squares and rectangles."

That was true.

Duncan remembered Barony with a clearness that made him shiver. Suspensor tracks shot through it like worm holes—straight, curved, flipping off at oblique angles . . . up, down, sideways. Except for the rectangular absolute imposed by Harkonnen whim, Barony was built to a particular population-design criterion: maximum stuffing with minimum expenditure of materials.

"The flat top was the only human-oriented space in the damned thing!" He remembered telling that to Teg and Lucilla both.

Up there on top were penthouses, guard stations at all the edges, at the 'thopter pads, at all the entries from below, around all of the parks. People living on the top could forget about the mass of flesh squirming in close proximity just below them. No smell or noise from that jumble was allowed on top. Servants were forced to bathe and change into sanitary clothing before emerging.

Teg had a question: "Why did that massed humanity permit itself to live in such a crush?"

The answer was obvious and he explained it. The

outside was a dangerous place. The city's managers made it appear even more dangerous than it actually was. Besides, few in there knew anything about a better life Outside. The only better life they knew about was on top. And the only way up there was through an absolutely abasing servility.

"It will happen and there's nothing you can do about it!"

That was another voice echoing in Duncan's skull. He heard it clearly.

Paul!

How odd it was, Duncan thought. There was an arrogance in the prescient like the arrogance of the Mentat seated in his most brittle logic.

I never before thought of Paul as arrogant.

Duncan stared at his own face in a mirror. He realized with part of his mind that this was a pre-ghola memory. Abruptly, it was another mirror, his own face but different. That darkly rounded face had begun to shape into the harsher lines it could have if it matured. He looked into his own eyes. Yes, those were his eyes. He had heard someone describe his eyes once as "cave sitters." They were deeply inset under the brows and riding atop high cheeks. He had been told it was difficult to determine if his eyes were dark blue or dark green unless the light were just right.

A woman said that. He could not remember the woman.

He tried to reach up and touch his hair but his hands would not obey. He remembered then that his hair had been bleached. Who did that? An old woman. His hair was no longer a cap of dark ringlets.

There was the Duke Leto staring at him in the doorway to the dining room on Caladan.

"We will eat now," the Duke said. It was a royal command saved from arrogance by a faint grin that said: "Somebody had to say it."

What is happening to my mind?

He remembered following Tormsa to the place where Tormsa said the no-ship would meet them.

It was a large building bulking in the night. There were several smaller outbuildings below the larger structure. They appeared to be occupied. Voices and machine sounds could be heard in them. No faces showed at the narrow windows. No door opened. Duncan smelled cooking as they passed the larger of the outbuildings. This reminded him that they had only eaten dry strips of leathery stuff that Tormsa called "travel food" that day.

They entered the dark building.

Light flared.

Tormsa's eyes exploded in blood.

Darkness.

Duncan looked at a woman's face. He had seen a face like this one before: a single *tride* taken from a longer holo sequence. Where was that? Where had he seen that? It was an almost oval face with just a small widening at the brow to mar its curved perfection.

She spoke: "My name is Murbella. You will not remember that but I share it now as I mark you. I have selected you."

I do remember you, Murbella.

Green eyes set wide under arched brows gave her features a focal region that left chin and small mouth for later examination. The mouth was full-lipped and he knew it could become pouting in repose.

The green eyes stared into his eyes. How cold that look. The power in it.

Something touched his cheek.

He opened his eyes. This was no memory! This was happening to him. It was happening now!

Murbella! She had been here and she had left him. Now she was back. He remembered awakening naked on a soft surface . . . a sleeping pad. His hands recognized it. Murbella unclothed just above him, green eyes staring at him with a terrible intensity. She touched him simultaneously in many places. A soft humming issued from between her lips.

He felt the swift erection, painful in its rigidity.

No power of resistance remained in him. Her hands moved over his body. Her tongue. The humming! All around him, her mouth touching him. The nipples of her breasts grazed his cheeks, his chest. When he saw her eyes, he saw conscious design.

Murbella had returned and she was doing it once more!

Over her right shoulder, he glimpsed a wide plaz window—Lucilla and Burzmali behind that barrier. *A dream?* Burzmali pressed his palms against the plaz. Lucilla stood with folded arms, a look of mingled rage and curiosity on her face.

Murbella murmured in his right ear: "My hands are fire."

Her body hid the faces behind the plaz. He felt the fire wherever she touched him.

Abruptly, the flame engulfed his mind. Hidden places within him came alive. He saw red capsules like a string of gleaming sausages passing before his eyes. He felt feverish. He was an engorged capsule, excitement flaring throughout his awareness. Those capsules! He knew them! They were himself . . . they were . . .

All of the Duncan Idahos, original and the serial gholas flowed into his mind. They were like bursting seedpods denying all other existence except themselves. He saw himself crushed beneath a great worm with a human face.

"Damn you, Leto!"

Crushed and crushed and crushed . . . time and again.

"Damn you! Damn you! Damn you! . . ."

He died under a Sardaukar sword. Pain exploded into a bright glare swallowed by darkness.

He died in a 'thopter crash. He died under the knife of a Fish Speaker assassin. He died and died and died.

And he lived.

The memories flooded him until he wondered how he could hold them all. The sweetness of a newborn daughter held in his arms. The musky odors of a passionate mate. The cascade of flavors from a fine Danian wine. The panting exertions of the practice floor.

The axlotl tanks!

He remembered emerging time after time: bright lights and padded mechanical hands. The hands rotated him and, in the unfocused blurs of the newborn, he saw a great mound of female flesh—monstrous in her almost immobile grossness . . . a maze of dark tubes linked her body to giant metal containers.

Axlotl tank?

He gasped in the grip of the serial memories that cascaded into him. *All of those lives! All of those lives!*

Now, he remembered what the Tleilaxu had planted in him, the submerged awareness that awaited only this moment of seduction by a Bene Gesserit Imprinter.

But this was Murbella and she was not Bene Gesserit.

She was here, though, ready at hand and the Tleilaxu pattern took over his reactions.

Duncan hummed softly and touched her, moving with an agility that shocked Murbella. *He should not be this responsive! Not this way!* His right hand fluttered against the lips of her vagina while his left hand caressed the base of her spine. At the same time, his mouth moved gently over her nose, down to her lips, down to the crease of her left armpit.

And all the time he hummed softly in a rhythm that pulsed through her body, lulling . . . weakening . . .

She tried to push away from him as he increased the pace of her responses.

How did he know to touch me there at just that instant? And there! And there! Oh, Holy Rock of Dur, how does he know this?

Duncan marked the swelling of her breasts and saw the congestion in her nose. He saw the way her nipples stood out stiffly, the areolae darkening around them. She moaned and spread her legs wide.

Great Matre, help me!

But the only Great Matre she could think of was locked securely away from this room, restrained by a bolted door and a plaz barrier.

Desperate energy flowed into Murbella. She responded

in the only way she knew: touching, caressing—using all of the techniques she had learned so carefully in the long years of her apprenticeship.

To each thing she did, Duncan produced a wildly stimulating countermove.

Murbella found that she no longer could control all of her own responses. She was reacting automatically from some well of knowledge deeper than her training. She felt her vaginal muscles tighten. She felt the swift release of lubricant fluid. When Duncan entered her she heard herself groan. Her arms, her hands, her legs, her entire body moved with both of the response systems— well-trained automation and the deeper, deeper plunging awareness of other demands.

How did he do this to me?

Waves of ecstatic contractions began in the smooth muscles of her pelvis. She sensed his simultaneous response and felt the hard slap of his ejaculation. This heightened her own response. Ecstatic pulsations drove outward from the contractions in her vagina . . . outward . . . outward. The ecstasy engulfed her entire sensorium. She saw a spreading blaze of whiteness against her eyelids. Every muscle quivered with an ecstasy she had not imagined possible for herself.

Again, the waves spread outward.

Again and again . . .

She lost count of the repetitions.

When Duncan moaned, she moaned and the waves swept outward once more.

And again . . .

There was no sensation of time or surroundings, only this immersion in a continuing ecstasy.

She wanted it to go on forever and she wanted it to stop. This should not be happening to a female! An Honored Matre must not experience this. These were the sensations by which men were governed.

Duncan emerged from the response pattern that had been implanted in him. There was something else he was supposed to do. He could not remember what it was.

Lucilla?

He imagined her dead in front of him. But this woman was not Lucilla; this was . . . this was Murbella.

There was very little strength in him. He lifted himself off Murbella and managed to sink back onto his knees. Her hands were fluttering in an agitation he could not understand.

Murbella tried to push Duncan away from her and he was not there. Her eyes snapped open.

Duncan knelt above her. She had no idea how much time had passed. She tried to find the energy to sit up and failed. Slowly, reason returned.

She stared into Duncan's eyes, knowing now who this man must be. Man? He was only a youth. But he had done things . . . things . . . All of the Honored Matres had been warned. There was a ghola armed with forbidden knowledge by the Tleilaxu. That ghola must be killed!

A small burst of energy surged into her muscles. She raised herself on her elbows. Gasping for breath, she tried to roll away from him and fell back to the soft surface.

By the Holy Rock of Dur! This male could not be permitted to live! He was a ghola and he could do things permitted only to Honored Matres. She wanted to strike out at him and, at the same time, she wanted to pull him back onto her body. *The ecstasy!* She knew that whatever he asked of her at this moment she would do. She would do it for him.

No! I must kill him!

Once more, she raised herself onto her elbows and, from there, managed to sit up. Her weakened gaze crossed the window where she had confined the Great Honored Matre and the guide. They still stood there looking at her. The man's face was flushed. The face of the Great Honored Matre was as unmoving as the Rock of Dur itself.

How can she just stand there after what she has seen here? The Great Honored Matre must kill this ghola!

Murbella beckoned to the woman behind the plaz and rolled toward the locked door beside the sleeping pad. She barely managed to unbolt and open the door before falling back. Her eyes looked up at the kneeling youth. Sweat glistened on his body. His lovely body . . .

No!

Desperation drove her off onto the floor. She was on her knees there and then, mostly by will power, she stood. Energy was returning but her legs trembled as she staggered around the foot of the sleeping pad.

I will do it myself without thinking. I must do it.

Her body swayed from side to side. She tried to steady herself and aimed a blow at his neck. She knew this blow from long hours of practice. It would crush the larynx. The victim would die of asphyxiation.

Duncan dodged the blow easily, but he was slow . . . slow.

Murbella almost fell beside him but the hands of the Great Honored Matre saved her.

"Kill him," Murbella gasped. "He's the one we were warned about. He's the one!"

Murbella felt hands on her neck, the fingers pressing fiercely at the nerve bundles beneath the ears.

The last thing Murbella heard before unconsciousness was the Great Honored Matre saying: "We will kill no one. This ghola goes to Rakis."

The worst potential competition for any organism can come from its own kind. The species consumes necessities. Growth is limited by that necessity which is present in the least amount. The least favorable condition controls the rate of growth. (Law of the Minimum)

—FROM "LESSONS OF ARRAKIS"

The building stood back from a wide avenue behind a screen of trees and carefully tended flowering hedges. The hedges had been staggered in a maze pattern with man-high white posts to define the planted areas. No vehicle entering or leaving could do so at any speed above a slow crawl. Teg's military awareness took all of this in as the armored groundcar carried him up to the door. Field Marshal Muzzafar, the only other occupant in the rear of the car, recognized Teg's assessment and said:

"We're protected from above by a beam enfilading system."

A soldier in camouflage uniform with a long lasgun on a sling over one shoulder opened the door and snapped to attention as Muzzafar emerged.

Teg followed. He recognized this place. It was one of the "safe" addresses Bene Gesserit Security had provided for him. Obviously, the Sisterhood's information was out of date. Recently out of date, though, because Muzzafar gave no indication that Teg might know this place.

As they crossed to the door, Teg noted that another protective system he had seen on his first tour of Ysai remained intact. It was a barely noticeable difference in the posts along the trees-and-hedges barriers. Those posts were scanlyzers operated from a room somewhere in the building. Their diamond-shaped connectors "read" the area between them and the building. At the gentle push of a button in the watchers' room, the scanlyzers would make small chunks of meat out of any living flesh crossing their fields.

At the door, Muzzafar paused and looked at Teg. "The Honored Matre you are about to meet is the most powerful of all who have come here. She does not tolerate anything but complete obedience."

"I take it that you are warning me."

"I thought you would understand. Call her Honored Matre. Nothing else. In we go. I've taken the liberty of having a new uniform made for you."

The room where Muzzafar ushered him was one Teg had not seen on his previous visit. Small and crammed with ticking black-paneled boxes, it left little room for the two of them. A single yellow glowglobe at the ceiling illuminated the place. Muzzafar crowded himself into a corner while Teg got out of the grimed and wrinkled singlesuit he had worn since the no-globe.

"Sorry I can't offer you a bath as well," Muzzafar said. "But we must not delay. She gets impatient."

A different personality came over Teg with the uniform. It was a familiar black garment, even to the starbursts at the collar. So he was to appear before this Honored Matre as the Sisterhood's Bashar. Interesting. He was once more completely the Bashar, not that this powerful sense of identity had ever left him. The uniform completed it and announced it, though. In this garment there was no need to emphasize in any other way precisely who he was.

"That's better," Muzzafar said as he led Teg out into the entry hallway and through a door Teg remembered. Yes, this was where he had met the "safe" contacts. He had recognized the room's function then and nothing appeared to have changed it. Rows of microscopic com-eyes lined the intersection of ceiling and walls, disguised as silver guide strips for the hovering glowglobes.

The one who is watched does not see, Teg thought. *And the Watchers have a billion eyes.*

His doubled vision told him there was danger here but nothing immediately violent.

This room, about five meters long and four wide, was a place for doing very high-level business. The merchandise would never be an actual exposure of money. People here would see only portable equivalents of whatever passed for currency—melange, perhaps, or milky soostones about the size of an eyeball, perfectly round, at once glossy and soft in appearance but radiant with rainbow changes directed by whatever light fell on them or whatever flesh they touched. This was a place where a danikin of melange or a small fold-pouch of soostones would be accepted as a natural occurrence. The price of a planet could be exchanged here with only a nod, an eyeblink or a low-voiced murmur. No wallets of currency would ever be produced here. The closest thing might be a thin case of translux out of whose poison-guarded interior would come thinner sheets of ridulian crystal with very large numbers inscribed on them by unforgeable dataprint.

"This is a bank," Teg said.

"What?" Muzzafar had been staring at the closed door in the opposite wall. "Oh, yes. She'll be along presently."

"She is watching us now, of course."

Muzzafar did not answer but he looked gloomy.

Teg glanced around him. Had anything been changed since his previous visit? He saw no significant alterations. He wondered if shrines such as this one had undergone much change at all over the eons. There was a dewcarpet on the floor as soft as brantdown and as white as the underbelly of a fur whale. It shimmered with a false sense of wetness that only the eye detected. A bare foot (not that this place had ever seen a bare foot) would feel caressing dryness.

There was a narrow table about two meters long almost in the center of the room. The top was at least twenty millimeters thick. Teg guessed it was Danian jacaranda. The deep brown surface had been polished to a sheen that drank the vision and revealed far underneath veins like river currents. There were only four admiral's chairs around the table, chairs crafted by a master artisan from the same wood as the table, cushioned on seat and back with lyrleather of the exact tone of the polished wood.

Only four chairs. More would have been an overstatement. He had not tried one of the chairs before and he did not seat himself now, but he knew what his flesh would find there—comfort almost up to the level of a despised chairdog. Not quite at that degree of softness and conformity to bodily shape, of course. Too much comfort could lure the sitter into relaxation. This room and its furnishings said: "Be comfortable here but remain alert."

You not only had to have your wits about you in this place but also a great power of violence behind you, Teg thought. He had summed it up that way before and his opinion had not changed.

There were no windows but the ones he had seen from the outside had danced with lines of light—energy barriers to repel intruders and prevent escape. Such barriers brought their own dangers, Teg knew, but the implications were important. Just keeping the energy flow in them would feed a large city for the lifetime of its longest-lived inhabitant.

There was nothing casual about this display of wealth.

The door that Muzzafar watched opened with a gentle click.

Danger!

A woman in a shimmering golden robe swept into the room. Lines of red-orange danced in the fabric.

She is old!

Teg had not expected her to be this ancient. Her face was a wrinkled mask. The eyes were deeply set green ice. Her nose was an elongated beak whose shadow touched thin lips and repeated the sharp angle of the chin. A black skullcap almost covered her gray hair.

Muzzafar bowed.

"Leave us," she said.

He left without a word, going out through the door by which she had entered. When the door closed behind him, Teg said, "Honored Matre."

"So you recognize this as a bank." Her voice carried only a slight trembling.

"Of course."

"There are always means of transferring large sums or selling power," she said. "I do not speak of the power that runs factories but of the power that runs people."

"And that usually passes under the strange names of government or society or civilization," Teg said.

"I suspected you would be very intelligent," she said. She pulled out a chair and sat but did not indicate that Teg should seat himself. "I think of myself as a banker. That saves a lot of muddy and distressful circumlocutions."

Teg did not respond. There seemed no need. He continued to study her.

"Why are you looking at me like that?" she demanded.

"I did not expect you to be this old," he said.

"Heh, heh, heh. We have many surprises for you, Bashar. Later, a younger Honored Matre may murmur her name to mark you. Praise Dur if that happens."

He nodded, not understanding much of what she said.

"This is also a very old building," she said. "I watched you when you came in. Does that surprise you, too?"

"No."

"This building has remained essentially unchanged for several thousand years. It is built of materials that will last much longer still."

He glanced at the table.

"Oh, not the wood. But underneath, it's polastine, polaz, and pormabat. The three P-Os are never sneered at where necessity calls for them."

Teg remained silent.

"Necessity," she said. "Do you object to any of the necessary things that have been done to you?"

"My objections don't matter," he said. What was she getting at? Studying him, of course. As he studied her.

"Do you think others have ever objected to what you did to them?"

"Undoubtedly."

"You're a natural commander, Bashar. I think you'll be very valuable to us."

"I've always thought I was most valuable to myself."

"Bashar! Look at my eyes!"

He obeyed, seeing little flecks of orange drifting in across the whites. The sense of peril was acute.

"If you ever see my eyes fully orange, beware!" she said. "You will have offended me beyond my ability to tolerate."

He nodded.

"I like it that you can command but you cannot command me! You command the muck and that is the only function we have for such as you."

"The muck?"

She waved a hand, a negligent motion. "Out there. You know them. Their curiosity is narrow gauge. No great issues ever enter their awareness."

"I thought that was what you meant."

"We work to keep it that way," she said. "Everything goes to them through a tight filter, which excludes all but that which has immediate survival value."

"No great issues," he said.

"You are offended but it doesn't matter," she said. "To those out there, a great issue is: 'Will I eat today?' 'Do I have shelter tonight that will not be invaded by attackers or vermin?' Luxury? Luxury is the possession of a drug or a member of the opposite sex who can, for a time, keep the beast at bay."

And you are the beast, he thought.

"I am taking some time with you, Bashar, because I see that you could be more valuable to us even than Muzzafar. And he is extremely valuable indeed. Even now, we are repaying him for bringing you to us in a receptive condition."

When Teg still remained silent, she chuckled. "You do not think you are receptive?"

Teg held himself quiet. Had they given him some drug in his food? He saw the flickering of doubled vision but the movements of violence had receded as the orange flecks left the Honored Matre's eyes. Her feet were to be avoided, though. They were deadly weapons.

"It's just that you think of the muck in the wrong way," she said. "Luckily, they are most self-limiting. They know this somewhere in the damps of their deepest consciousness but cannot spare the time to deal with that or anything else except the immediate scramble for survival."

"They cannot be improved?" he asked.

"They must not be improved! Oh, we see to it that self-improvement remains a great fad among them. Nothing real about it, of course."

"Another luxury they must be denied," he said.

"Not a luxury! Nonexistent! It must be occluded at all times behind a barrier that we like to call protective ignorance."

"What you don't know cannot hurt you."

"I don't like your tone, Bashar."

Again, the orange flecks danced in her eyes. The sense of violence diminished, however, as she once more chuckled. "The thing you beware of is the opposite of *what-you-don't-know*. We teach that new knowledge can be dangerous. You see the obvious extension: All new knowledge is non-survival!"

The door behind the Honored Matre opened and Muzzafar returned. It was a changed Muzzafar, his face flushed, his eyes bright. He stopped behind the Honored Matre's chair.

"One day, I will be able to permit you behind me this way," she said. "It is in my power to do this."

What had they done to Muzzafar? Teg wondered. The man looked almost drugged.

"You do see that I have power?" she asked.

He cleared his throat. "That's obvious."

"I am a banker, remember? We have just made a deposit with our loyal Muzzafar. Do you thank us, Muzzafar?"

"I do, Honored Matre." His voice was hoarse.

"I'm sure you understand this kind of power generally, Bashar," she said. "The Bene Gesserit trained you well. They are quite talented but not, I fear, as talented as we are."

"And I am told you are quite numerous," he said.

"Our numbers are not the key, Bashar. Power such as ours has a way of becoming channeled so that it can be controlled by small numbers."

She was like a Reverend Mother, he thought, in the way she could appear to answer without revealing much.

"In essence," she said, "power such as ours is allowed to become the substance of survival for many people.

Then, the threat of withdrawal is all that's required for us to rule." She glanced over her shoulder. "Would you wish us to withdraw our favor from you, Muzzafar?"

"No, Honored Matre." He was actually trembling!

"You have found a new drug," Teg said.

Her laughter was spontaneous and loud, almost raucous. "No, Bashar! We have an old one."

"And you would make an addict of me?"

"Like all the others we control, Bashar, you have a choice: death or obedience."

"That is a rather old choice," he agreed. What was her immediate threat? He could sense no violence. Quite the contrary. His doubled vision showed him broken glimpses of extremely sensuous overtones. Did they think they could imprint him?

She smiled at him, a knowing expression with something frigid under it.

"Will he serve us well, Muzzafar?"

"I believe so, Honored Matre."

Teg frowned in thought. There was something deeply evil about this pair. They went against every morality by which he modeled his behavior. It was well to remember that neither of them knew this strange thing that had speeded his reactions.

They seemed to be enjoying his puzzled discomfiture.

Teg took some reassurance from the realization that neither of these two really enjoyed life. He could see that in them clearly with eyes the Sisterhood had educated. The Honored Matre and Muzzafar had forgotten or, most likely, abandoned everything that supported the survival of joyous humans. He thought they probably no longer were capable of finding a real wellspring of joy in their own flesh. Theirs would have to be mostly a voyeur's existence, the eternal observer, always remembering what it had been like before they had taken the turning into whatever it was they had become. Even when they wallowed in the performance of something that once had meant gratification, they would have to reach for new extremes each time just to touch the edges of their own memories.

The Honored Matre's grin widened, showing a line of gleaming white teeth. "Look at him, Muzzafar. He has not the slightest conception of what we can do."

Teg heard this but he also saw with eyes trained by the Bene Gesserit. Not a milligram of naivete remained in either of these two. Nothing was expected to surprise them. Nothing could be truly new for them. Still, they plotted and devised, hoping that *this* extreme would produce the remembered thrill. They knew it would not, of course, and they expected to carry away from the experience only more burning rage out of which to fashion another attempt at the unreachable. That was how their thinking went.

Teg designed a smile for them, using all of the skills he had learned at Bene Gesserit hands. It was a smile full of compassion, of understanding and real pleasure in his own existence. He knew it for the most deadly insult he could hurl at them and he saw it hit. Muzzafar glowered at him. The Honored Matre went from orange-eyed rage to an abrupt surprise and then, quite slowly, to dawning pleasure. She had not expected this! It was something new!

"Muzzafar," she said, the orange receding from her eyes, "bring the Honored Matre who has been chosen to mark our Bashar."

Teg, his doubled vision showing the immediate peril,

understood at last. He could feel awareness of his own future spreading outward like waves as the power grew in him. The wild change in him was continuing! He felt the energy expand. With it came understanding and choices. He saw himself as the whirlwind rampaging through this building—bodies scattered behind him (Muzzafar and the Honored Matre among them) and the whole complex looking like an abattoir when he departed.

Must I do that? he wondered.

For each one he killed, more would have to be killed. He saw the necessity of it, though, as he saw at last the Tyrant's design. The pain he could see for himself almost made him cry out but he held it back.

"Yes, bring this Honored Matre to me," he said, knowing that this would be one less for him to seek out and destroy elsewhere in the building. The room of the scanlyzer controls must be taken out first.

O you who know what we suffer here, do not forget us in your prayers.

—SIGN OVER ARRAKEEN LANDING FIELD
(HISTORICAL RECORDS: DAR-ES-BALAT)

Taraza watched a snow-flutter of falling blossoms against the silvery sky of a Rakian morning. There was an opalescent sheen to the sky that, despite all of her preparatory briefings, she had not anticipated. Rakis held many surprises. The smell of mock orange was powerful here at the edge of the Dar-es-Balat roof garden, overriding all other odors.

Never believe that you have plumbed the depths of any place . . . or of any human, she reminded herself.

Conversation was ended out here but not the echoes of the spoken thoughts they had exchanged only minutes ago. All agreed, though, that it was time for action. Soon, Sheeana would "dance a worm" for them and once more demonstrate her mastery.

Waff and a new priestly representative would share this "holy event" but Taraza was sure neither of them knew the real nature of what they were about to witness. Waff bore watching, of course. He still carried that air of irritated disbelief in everything he saw or heard. It was a strange mixture with his underlying awe at being on

Rakis. The catalyst was obviously his rage over the fact that fools ruled here.

Odrade returned from the meeting room and stopped beside Taraza.

"I am extremely disquieted by the reports from Gammu," Taraza said. "Do you bring something new?"

"No. Things are obviously still chaotic there."

"Tell me, Dar, what do you think we should do?"

"I keep remembering the Tyrant's words to Chenoeh: 'The Bene Gesserit are so close to what they should be, yet so far.'"

Taraza pointed at the open desert beyond the museum city's qanat. "He's still out there, Dar. I'm sure of it." Taraza turned to face Odrade. "And Sheeana speaks to him."

"He told so many lies," Odrade said.

"But he didn't lie about his own incarnation. Remember what he said. 'Every descendant part of me will carry some of my awareness locked away within it, lost and helpless—pearls of me moving blindly in the sand, caught in an endless dream.'"

"You bank a great deal on your belief in the power of that dream," Odrade said.

"We must recover the Tyrant's design! All of it!"

Odrade sighed but did not speak.

"Never underestimate the power of an idea," Taraza said. "The Atreides were ever philosophers in their governance. Philosophy is always dangerous because it promotes the creation of new ideas."

Still, Odrade did not respond.

"The worm carries it all within him, Dar! All of the forces he set in motion are still in him."

"Are you trying to convince me or yourself, Tar?"

"I am punishing you, Dar. Just as the Tyrant is still punishing us."

"For not being what we should be? Ahh, here come Sheeana and the others."

"The worm's language, Dar. That is the important thing."

"If you say so, Mother Superior."

Taraza sent an angry stare at Odrade, who moved forward to greet the newcomers. There was a disturbing gloom in Odrade.

The presence of Sheeana, though, restored Taraza's sense of purpose. An alert little thing, Sheeana. Very good material. Sheeana had demonstrated her dance the previous night, performing in the great museum room against a tapestry background, an exotic dance against an exotic spice-fiber hanging with its image of desert and worms. She appeared to be almost a part of the hanging, a figure projected forward from the stylized dunes and their elaborately detailed coursing worms. Taraza recalled how Sheeana's brown hair had been thrown outward by the whirling movements of the dance, swinging in a fuzzy arc. Side-lighting accented the reddish glints in her hair. Her eyes had been closed but it was not a face in repose. Excitement betrayed itself in the passionate set of her wide mouth, the flaring of her nostrils, the forward thrust of her chin. Her motions had conveyed an inner sophistication that belied her youth.

The dance is her language, Taraza thought. *Odrade is correct. Seeing it, we will learn it.*

Waff had something of a withdrawn look this morning.

It was difficult to determine if his eyes were looking out-ward or inward.

With Waff was Tulushan, a darkly handsome Rakian, the priesthood's chosen representative at today's "holy event." Taraza, meeting him at the demonstration dance, had found it extraordinary how Tulushan never needed to say "but," and yet the word was always there in every-thing he uttered. A perfect bureaucrat. He rightly ex-pected to go far but those expectations would soon encounter their ultimate surprise. She felt no pity for him at this knowledge. Tulushan was a soft-faced youth of too few standards for such a position of trust. There was more to him than met the eye, of course. And less.

Waff moved to one side in the garden, leaving Odrade and Sheeana with Tulushan.

The young priest was expendable, naturally. That explained much about why he had been chosen for this venture. It told her that she had achieved the proper level of potential violence. Taraza did not think, though, that any of the priestly factions would dare harm Sheeana.

We will stay close to Sheeana.

They had spent a busy week since the demonstration of the whores' sexual accomplishments. A very disturb-ing week, when it came to that. Odrade had been kept busy with Sheeana. Taraza would have preferred Lucilla for this educational chore but you made do with what was available and Odrade obviously was the best available on Rakis for such teaching.

Taraza looked back toward the desert. They were waiting for the 'thopters from Keen with their cargoes of

Very Important Observers. The VIOs were not yet late but crowding it as such people always did.

Sheeana seemed to be taking the sexual education well, although Taraza's estimation of the Sisterhood's available teaching males on Rakis was not high. Her first night here, Taraza had called in one of the servant males. Afterward, she had judged it too much trouble for the little joy and forgetfulness it provided. Besides, what was there to forget? To forget was to allow a weakness.

Never forget!

That's what the whores did, though. They traded in forgetfulness. And they had not the least awareness of the Tyrant's continuing viselike hold on human destiny nor of the need to break that hold.

Taraza had listened secretly to the previous day's session between Sheeana and Odrade.

What was I listening for?

Young girl and teacher had been out here in the roof garden, facing each other on two benches, a portable Ixian damper hiding their words from anyone who did not have the coded translator. The suspensor-buoyed damper hovered over the two like a strange umbrella, a black disc projecting distortions that hid the precise movements of lips and the sounds of voices.

To Taraza, standing within the long meeting room, the tiny translator in her left ear, the lesson had occurred like an equally distorted memory.

When I was taught these things, we had not seen what the whores of the Scattering could do.

"Why do we say it's the complexity of sex?" Sheeana asked. "The man you sent last night kept saying that."

"Many believe they understand it, Sheeana. Perhaps

no one has ever understood it, because such words require more of the mind than they do of the flesh."

"Why must I not use any of the things we saw the Face Dancers do?"

"Sheeana, complexity hides within complexity. Great deeds and foul ones have been done at the goading of sexual forces. We speak of 'sexual strength' and 'sexual energies' and such things as 'the overmounting urge of desire.' I don't deny that such things are observable. But what we are looking at here is a force so powerful that it can destroy you and everything you hold worthwhile."

"That's what I'm trying to understand. What is it the whores are doing wrong?"

"They ignore the species at its work, Sheeana. I think you can already sense this. The Tyrant certainly knew about it. What was his Golden Path but a vision of sexual forces at work recreating humankind endlessly?"

"And the whores don't create?"

"They mostly try to control their worlds with this force."

"They seem to be doing that."

"Ahhh, but what counterforces do they call forth?"

"I don't understand."

"You know about Voice and how it can control some people?"

"But not control everybody."

"Exactly. A civilization subjected to Voice over a long period develops ways of adapting to this force, preventing manipulation by those who use Voice."

"So there are people who know how to resist the whores?"

"We see unmistakable signs of it. And that is one of the reasons we are here on Rakis."

"Will the whores come here?"

"I'm afraid so. They want to control the core of the Old Empire because they see us as an easy conquest."

"Aren't you afraid they'll win?"

"They won't win, Sheeana. Depend on it. But they are good for us."

"How is that?"

Sheeana's tone echoed Taraza's own shock at hearing such words from Odrade. How much did Odrade suspect? In the next instant, Taraza understood and she wondered if the lesson was equally understandable to the young girl.

"The core is static, Sheeana. We have been almost at a standstill for thousands of years. Life and movement are 'out there' with the people of the Scattering who resist the whores. Whatever we do, we must make that resistance even stronger."

The sound of approaching 'thopters broke Taraza from her reverie of remembrance. The VIOs were arriving from Keen. Still at some distance, but the sound carried far in the clear air.

Odrade's teaching method was a good one, Taraza had to admit as she scanned the sky for a first glimpse of the 'thopters. Apparently they were coming in low and from the other side of the building. That was the wrong direction but perhaps they had taken the VIOs on a short excursion over the remains of the Tyrant's wall. Many people were curious about the place where Odrade had found the spice hoard.

Sheeana, Odrade, Waff, and Tulushan went back into the long meeting room. They had heard the 'thopters, too. Sheeana was anxious to show her power over the worms. Taraza hesitated. There was a laboring sound in the approaching 'thopters. Were they overloaded? How many observers had they brought?

The first 'thopter lifted over the penthouse roof and Taraza saw the armored cockpit. She recognized treachery even before the first beam arced out of the machine, slicing through her legs below the knees. She fell heavily against a potted tree, her legs completely severed. Another beam slashed out at her, slicing at an angle across her hip. The 'thopter swept over her in an abrupt roar of booster jets and banked away to the left.

Taraza clung to the tree, shunting the agony aside. She managed to cut off most of the bloodflow from her wounds but the pain was great. Not as great as the spice agony, though, she reminded herself. That helped but she knew she was doomed. She heard shouts and the multiple sounds of violence all around the museum now.

I have won! Taraza thought.

Odrade darted from the penthouse and bent over Taraza. They said nothing but Odrade showed that she understood by putting her forehead to Taraza's temple. It was the ages-old cue of the Bene Gesserit. Taraza began pouring her life into Odrade—Other Memories, hopes, fears . . . everything.

One of them might yet escape.

Sheeana watched from the penthouse, staying where she had been ordered to wait. She knew what was happening out there in the roof garden. This was the ultimate mystery of the Bene Gesserit and every postulant was aware of it.

Waff and Tulushan, already out of the room when the attack came, did not return.

Sheeana shuddered with apprehension.

Abruptly, Odrade stood and ran back into the penthouse. There was a wild look in her eyes but she moved with purpose. Leaping up, she gathered glowglobes, grabbing them in bundles by their toggle cords. She thrust several bundles into Sheeana's hands and Sheeana felt her body grow lighter with the lift of the globes' suspensor fields. Trailing more clusters of the globes beyond their field range, Odrade hurried across to the narrow end of the room where a grill in the wall indicated what she sought. With Sheeana's help, she lifted the grill out of its slots, revealing a deep airshaft. The light of the clustered glowglobes showed rough walls inside.

"Hold the globes close to get the maximum field effect," Odrade said. "Push them away to lower yourself. In you go."

Sheeana clutched the toggle cords in a sweaty hand and hopped over the sill. She let herself fall, then fearfully clutched the globes close. Light from above told her Odrade was following.

At the bottom, they emerged into a pump room, the susurrations of many fans a background for the sounds of violence from outside.

"We must get to the no-room and then to the desert," Odrade said. "All of these machinery systems are interconnected. There will be a passage."

"Is she dead?" Sheeana whispered.

"Yes."

"Poor Mother Superior."

"I am the Mother Superior now, Sheeana. At least temporarily." She pointed upward. "Those were the whores attacking us. We must hurry."

The world is for the living. Who are they?
We dared the dark to reach the white and warm.
She was the wind when the wind was in my way.
Alive at noon, I perished in her form.
Who rise from the flesh to spirit know the fall:
The word outleaps the world and light is all.

—THEODORE ROETHKE
(HISTORICAL QUOTATIONS: DAR-ES-BALAT)

It required little conscious volition for Teg to become the whirlwind. He had recognized at last the nature of the threat from the Honored Matres. Recognition fitted itself into the blurred requirements made upon him by the new Mentat awareness that went with his magnified speed.

Monstrous threat required monstrous countermeasures. Blood spattered him as he drove himself through the headquarters building, slaughtering everyone he met.

As he had learned from his Bene Gesserit teachers, the great problem of the human universe lay in how you managed procreation. He could hear the voice of his first teacher as he carried destruction through the building.

"You may think of this only as sexuality but we prefer the more basic term: procreation. It has many facets and offshoots and it has apparently unlimited energy. The emotion called 'love' is only one small aspect."

Teg crushed the throat of a man standing rigidly in his path and, at last, found the control room for the building's defenses. Only one man was seated in it, his right hand almost touching a red key on the console in front of him.

With a slashing left hand, Teg almost decapitated the man. The body tipped backward in slow motion, blood welling from the gaping neck.

The Sisterhood is right to call them whores!

You could drag humankind almost anywhere by manipulating the enormous energies of procreation. You could goad humans into actions they would never have believed possible. One of his teachers had said it directly:

"This energy must have an outlet. Bottle it up and it becomes monstrously dangerous. Redirect it and it will sweep over anything in its path. This is an ultimate secret of all religions."

Teg was conscious of leaving more than fifty bodies behind him as he left the building. The last fatality was a soldier in camouflage uniform standing in the open doorway, apparently about to enter.

As he ran past apparently unmoving people and vehicles, Teg's revved-up mind had time to reflect on what he had left behind him. Was there any consolation, he wondered, in the fact that the old Honored Matre's last living expression was one of real surprise? Could he congratulate himself that Muzzafar would never again see his frame bush home?

The necessity for what he had accomplished in a few heartbeats was very clear, though, to one trained by the Bene Gesserit. Teg knew his history. There were many paradise planets in the Old Empire, probably many more among the people of the Scattering. Humans always seemed capable of trying that foolish experiment. People in such places mostly lazed along. A quick-smart analysis said this was because of the easy climates on such planets. He knew this for stupidity. It was because sexual energy was easily released in such places. Let the Missionaries of the Divided God or some denominational construct enter one of these paradises and you got outrageous violence.

"We of the Sisterhood know," one of Teg's teachers had said. "We have put a flame to that fuse more than once with our Missionaria Protectiva."

Teg did not stop running until he was in an alley at least five kilometers from the abattoir that had been the headquarters for the old Honored Matre. He knew that very little time had passed but there was something much more important upon which he had to focus. He had not killed every occupant of that building. There were eyes back there belonging to people who knew now what he could do. They had seen him kill Honored Matres. They had seen Muzzafar topple dead at his hands. The evidence of the bodies left behind and the slowed replay of recordings would tell it all.

Teg leaned against a wall. Skin was torn from his left palm. He let himself return to normal time as he watched blood oozing from the wound. The blood was almost black.

More oxygen in my blood?

He was panting but not as much as these exertions would seem to require.

What has happened to me?

It was something from his Atreides ancestry, he knew. Crisis had tipped him over into another dimension of human possibilities. Whatever the transformation, it was profound. He could see outward now into many necessities. And the people he had passed on his run to this alley had seemed like statues.

Will I ever think of them as muck?

It could only happen if he let it happen, he knew. But the temptation was there and he allowed himself a brief commiseration for the Honored Matres. Great Temptation had toppled them into their own muck.

What to do now?

The main line lay open to him. There was a man here in Ysai, one man who would be sure to know everyone Teg required. Teg looked around the alley. Yes, that man was near.

The fragrance of flowers and herbs wafted to Teg from somewhere down this alley. He moved toward this fragrance, aware that it led him where he needed to go and that no violent attack awaited him here. This was, temporarily, a quiet backwater.

He came to the fragrant source quickly. It was an inset doorway marked by a blue awning with two words on it in modern Galach: "Personal Service."

Teg entered and saw immediately what he had found. They were to be seen at many places in the Old Empire: eating establishments harking back to ancient times, eschewing automata from kitchen to table. Most of them were "in" establishments. You told friends about your latest "discovery" with an admonition to them not to spread the word.

"Don't want to spoil it with crowding."

This idea had always amused Teg. You spread the

word about such places but you did it under the guise of keeping a secret.

Mouth-watering odors of cooking emerged from the kitchen at the rear. A waiter passed bearing a tray from which steam lifted, carrying the promise of good things.

A young woman in a short black dress with a white apron came up to him. "This way, sir. We have a table open in the corner."

She held a chair for him to be seated with his back to the wall. "Someone will be with you in a moment, sir." She passed him a stiff sheet of cheap double-thickness paper. "Our menu is printed. I hope you won't mind."

He watched her leave. The waiter he had seen passed going the other way toward the kitchen. The tray was empty.

Teg's feet had led him here as though he had been running on a fixed track. And there was the man he required, dining nearby.

The waiter had stopped to talk to the man Teg knew held the answer to the next moves required here. The two were laughing together. Teg scanned the rest of the room: only three other tables occupied. An older woman sat at a table in the far corner nibbling at some frosty confection. She was dressed in what Teg thought must be the peak of current fashion, a clinging short red gown cut low at the neck. Her shoes matched. A young couple sat at a table off to his right. They saw no one except each other. An older man in a tightly fitted old-fashioned brown tunic ate sparingly of a green vegetable dish near the door. He had eyes only for his food.

The man talking to the waiter laughed loudly.

Teg stared at the back of the waiter's head. Tufts of blond hair sprang from the nape of the waiter's neck like broken bunches of dead grass. The man's collar was frayed beneath the tufted hair. Teg lowered his gaze. The waiter's shoes were run over at the heels. The hem of his black jacket had been darned. Was it thrift in this place? Thrift or some other form of economic pressure? The odors from the kitchen did not suggest any stinting there. The tableware was shining and clean. No cracked dishes. But the striped red and white cloth on the table had been darned in several places, care taken to match the original fabric.

Once more, Teg studied the other customers. They looked substantial. None of the starving poor in this place. Teg had it registered then. Not only was this an "in" place, somebody had designed it for just that effect. There was a clever mind behind such an establishment. This was the kind of restaurant that rising young executives revealed to make points with prospective customers or to please a superior. The food would be superb and the portions generous. Teg realized that his instincts had led him here correctly. He bent his attention to the menu then, allowing hunger to enter his consciousness at last. The hunger was at least as fierce as that which had astonished the late Field Marshal Muzzafar.

The waiter appeared beside him with a tray on which were placed a small open box and a jar from which wafted the pungent odor of newskin ointment.

"I see you have injured your hand, Bashar," the man said. He placed the tray on the table. "Allow me to dress the injury before you order."

Teg lifted the injured hand and watched the swift competence of the treatment.

"You know me?" Teg asked.

"Yes, sir. And after what I've been hearing, it seems strange to see you in full uniform. There." He finished the dressing.

"What have you been hearing?" Teg spoke in a low voice.

"That the Honored Matres hunt you."

"I've just killed some of them and many of their . . . What should we call them?"

The man paled but he spoke firmly. "Slaves would be a good word, sir."

"You were at Renditai, weren't you," Teg said.

"Yes, sir. Many of us settled here afterward."

"I need food but I cannot pay you," Teg said.

"No one from Renditai has need of your money, Bashar. Do they know you came this way?"

"I don't believe they do."

"The people here now are regulars. None of them would betray you. I will try to warn you if someone dangerous comes. What did you wish to eat?"

"A great deal of food. I will leave the choice to you. About twice as much carbohydrate as protein. No stimulants."

"What do you mean by a great deal, sir?"

"Keep bringing it until I tell you to stop . . . or until you feel I have overstepped your generosity."

"In spite of appearances, sir, this is not a poor establishment. The extras here have made me a rich man."

Score one for his assessment, Teg thought. The thrift here was a calculated pose.

The waiter left and again spoke to the man at the central table. Teg studied the man openly after the waiter went on into the kitchen. Yes, that was the man. The diner concentrated on a plate heaped with some green-garnished pasta.

There was very little sign in this man of a woman's care, Teg thought. His collar had been closed awry, the cling-straps tangled. Spots of the greenish sauce soiled his left cuff. He was naturally righthanded but ate while his left hand remained in the path of spillage. Frayed cuffs on his trousers. One trouser hem, partly released from its threaded bondage, dragged at the heel. Stockings mismatched—one blue and one pale yellow. None of this appeared to bother him. No mother or other woman had ever dragged this one back from a doorway with orders to make himself presentable. His basic attitude was announced in his whole appearance:

"What you see is as presentable as it gets."

The man looked up suddenly, a jerking motion as though he had been goosed. He sent a brown-eyed gaze around the room, pausing at each face in turn as though he looked for a particular visage. This done, he returned his attention to his plate.

The waiter returned with a clear soup in which shreds of egg and some green vegetables could be seen.

"While the rest of your meal is being prepared, sir," he said.

"Did you come here directly after Renditai?" Teg asked.

"Yes, sir. But I served with you also at Acline."

"The sixty-seventh Gammu," Teg said.

"Yes, sir!"

"We saved a good many lives that time," Teg said. "Theirs and ours."

When Teg still did not begin eating, the waiter spoke in a rather cold voice, "Would you require a snooper, sir?"

"Not while you're serving me," Teg said. He meant what he said but he felt a bit of a fraud because doubled vision told him the food was safe.

The waiter started to turn away, pleased.

"One moment," Teg said.

"Sir?"

"The man at that central table. He is one of your regulars?"

"Professor Delnay? Oh, yes, sir."

"Delnay. Yes, I thought so."

"Professor of martial arts, sir. And the history of same."

"I know. When it comes time to serve my dessert, please ask Professor Delnay if he would join me."

"Shall I tell him who you are, sir?"

"Don't you think he already knows?"

"That would seem likely, sir, but still . . ."

"Caution where caution belongs," Teg said. "Bring on the food."

Delnay's interest was fully aroused long before the waiter relayed Teg's invitation. The professor's first words as he seated himself across from Teg were: "That was the most remarkable gastronomic performance I have ever seen. Are you sure you can eat a dessert?"

"Two or three of them at least," Teg said.

"Astonishing!"

Teg sampled a spoonful of a honey-sweetened confection. He swallowed it, then: "This place is a jewel."

"I have kept it a careful secret," Delnay said. "Except for a few close friends, of course. To what do I owe the honor of your invitation?"

"Have you ever been . . . ah, *marked* by an Honored Matre?"

"Lords of perdition, no! I'm not important enough for that."

"I was hoping to ask you to risk your life, Delnay."

"In what way?" No hesitation. That was reassuring.

"There is a place in Ysai where my old soldiers meet. I want to go there and see as many of them as possible."

"Through the streets in full regalia the way you are now?"

"In any way you can arrange it."

Delnay put a finger to his lower lip and leaned back to stare at Teg. "You're not an easy figure to disguise, you know. However, there may be a way." He nodded thoughtfully. "Yes." He smiled. "You won't like it, I'm afraid."

"What do you have in mind?"

"Some padding and other alterations. We will pass you off as a Bordano overseer. You'll smell of the sewer, of course. And you'll have to carry it off that you don't notice."

"Why do you think that will succeed?" Teg asked.

"Oh, there's going to be a storm tonight. Regular thing this time of year. Laying down the moisture for next year's open crops. And filling the reservoirs for the heated fields, you know."

"I don't understand your reasoning, but when I've finished another of these confections, we'll go," Teg said.

"You'll like the place where we take refuge from the storm," Delnay said. "I'm mad, you know, to do this. But the proprietor here said I was to help you or never come here again."

It was an hour after dark when Delnay led him to the

rendezvous point. Teg, dressed in leathers and affecting a limp, was forced to use much of his mental power to ignore his own odors. Delnay's friends had plastered Teg with sewage and then hosed him off. The forced-air drying brought back most of the effluent aromas.

A remote-reading weather station at the door of the meeting place told Teg it had dropped fifteen degrees outside in the preceding hour. Delnay preceded him and hurried away into a crowded room where there was much noise and the sound of clinking glassware. Teg paused to study the doorside station. The wind was gusting to thirty klicks, he saw. Barometric pressure down. He looked at the sign above the station:

"A service to our customers."

Presumably, a service to the bar as well. Departing customers might well take one look at these readings and return to the warmth and camaraderie behind them.

In a large fireplace with inglenook at the far end of the bar there was a real fire burning. Aromatic wood.

Delnay returned, wrinkled his nose at Teg's smell and led him around the edge of the crowd into a back room, then through this into a private bathroom. Teg's uniform—cleaned and pressed—was laid out over a chair there.

"I'll be in the inglenook when you come out," Delnay said.

"In full regalia, eh?" Teg asked.

"It's only dangerous out in the streets," Delnay said. He went back the way they had come.

Teg emerged presently and found his way to the inglenook through groups that turned suddenly silent as people recognized him. Murmurous comments swept through the room. "The old Bashar himself." "Oh, yes, it's Teg. Served with him, I did. Know that face and figure anywhere."

Customers had crowded into the atavistic warmth of the fireside. There was a rich smell of wet clothing and drink-fogged breaths there.

So the storm had driven this crowd into the bar? Teg looked at the battle-hardened military faces all around him, thinking that this was not a usual gathering, no matter what Delnay said. The people here knew one another, though, and had expected to meet one another here at this time.

Delnay was sitting on one of the benches in the inglenook, a glass containing an amber drink in his hand.

"You put out the word to meet us here," Teg said.

"Isn't that what you wanted, Bashar?"

"Who are you, Delnay?"

"I own a winter farm a few klicks south of here and I have some banker friends who will occasionally loan me a groundcar. If you want me to be more specific, I'm like the rest of the people in this room—someone who wants the Honored Matres off our necks."

A man behind Teg asked: "Is it true that you killed a hundred of them today, Bashar?"

Teg spoke dryly without turning. "The number is greatly exaggerated. Could I have a drink, please?"

From his greater height, Teg scanned the room while someone was getting him a glass. When it was thrust into his hand, it was, as he expected, the deep blue of Danian Marinete. These old soldiers knew his preferences.

The drinking activity in the room continued but at a

more subdued pace. They were waiting for him to state his purpose.

Gregarious human nature got a natural boost on such a stormy night, Teg thought. Band together behind the fire in the mouth of the cave, fellow tribesmen! Nothing dangerous will get past us, especially when the beasts see our fire. How many other similar gatherings were there around Gammu on such a night? he wondered, sipping his drink. Bad weather could mask movements that the gathered companions did not want observed. The weather might also keep certain people inside who were otherwise not supposed to remain inside.

He recognized a few faces from his past—officers and ordinary soldiers—a mixed bag. For some of them, he had good memories: reliable people. Some of them would die tonight.

The noise level began to increase as people relaxed in his presence. No one pressed him for an explanation. They knew that about him, too. Teg set his own timetable.

The sounds of conversation and laughter were of a kind he knew must have accompanied such gatherings since the dawn times when humans clustered for mutual protection. Clinking of glassware, sudden bursts of laughter, a few quiet chuckles. Those would be the ones more conscious of their personal power. Quiet chuckles said you could be amused but you did not have to make a guffawing fool of yourself. Delnay was a quiet chuckler.

Teg glanced up and saw that the beamed ceiling had been built conventionally low. It made the enclosed space seem at once more extended and yet more intimate. Careful attention to human psychology here. It was a thing he had observed many places on this planet. It was a care to keep a damper on unwanted awareness. Make them feel comfortable and secure. They were not, of course, but don't let that get through to them.

For a few moments longer, Teg watched the drinks being distributed by the skilled waiting staff: dark local beers and some expensive imports. Scattered along the bar and on the softly illuminated tables were bowls containing crisp-fried local vegetables, heavily salted. Such an obvious move to heighten thirst apparently offended no one. It was merely expected in this trade. The beers would be heavily salted, too, of course. They always were. Brewers knew how to kick off the thirst response.

Some of the groups were getting louder. The drinks had begun to work their ancient magic. Bacchus was here! Teg knew that if this gathering were allowed to run its natural course, the room would reach a crescendo later in the night and then gradually, very gradually, the noise level would subside. Someone would go look at the doorside weather station. Depending on what that one saw, the place might wind down immediately or continue at the more subdued pace for some time. He realized then that somewhere behind the bar there would be a way to distort the weather station's readouts. This bar would not overlook such a way of extending its trade.

Get 'em inside and keep 'em here by any means they don't find objectionable.

The people behind this institution would fall in with the Honored Matres and not blink an eye.

Teg put his drink aside and called out: "May I have your attention, please?"

Silence.

Even the waiting staff stopped in what they were doing.

"Some of you guard the doors," Teg said. "No one goes in or out until I give the order. Those back doors, too, if you please."

When this had been sorted out, he stared carefully around the room, picking the ones his doubled vision and old military experience told him could be most trusted. What he had to do now had become quite plain to him. Burzmali, Lucilla, and Duncan were out there at the edge of his new vision, their needs easily seen.

"I presume you can get your hands on weapons rather quickly," he said.

"We came prepared, Bashar!" Someone out in the room shouted. Teg heard the drink in that voice but also the old adrenaline pumping that would be so dear to these people.

"We are going to capture a no-ship," Teg said.

That grabbed them. No other artifact of civilization was as closely guarded. These ships came to the landing fields and other places and they left. Their armored surfaces bristled with weapons. Crews were on constant alert in vulnerable locations. Trickery might succeed; open assault stood little chance. But here in this room Teg had reached a new awareness, driven by necessity and the wild genes in his Atreides ancestry. The positions of the no-ships on and around Gammu were visible to him. Bright dots occupied his inner vision and, like threads leading from one bauble to another, his doubled vision saw the way through this maze.

Oh, but I do not want to go, he thought.

The thing driving him would not be denied.

"Specifically, we are going to capture a no-ship from the Scattering," he said. "They have some of the best. You, you and you and you." He pointed, singling out individuals. "You will stay here and see that no one leaves or communicates with anyone outside of this establishment. I think you will be attacked. Hold out as long as you can. The rest of you, get your weapons and let's go."

Justice? Who asks for justice. We make our own justice.
We make it here on Arrakis—win or die. Let us not rail
about justice as long as we have arms and the freedom
to use them.

—LETO I; BENE GESSERIT ARCHIVES

The no-ship came in low over the Rakian sands. Its
passage stirred up dusty whirlwinds that drifted
around it as it settled in a crunching disturbance of the
dunes. The silvered yellow sun was sinking into a hori
zon disturbed by the heat devils of a long hot day. The
no-ship sat there creaking, a glistening steely ball whose
presence could be detected by the eyes and ears but not
by any prescient or long-range instrument. Teg's doubled
vision made him confident that no unwanted eyes saw his
arrival.

"I want the armored 'thopters and cars out there in no
more than ten minutes," he said.

People stirred into action behind him.

"Are you certain they're here, Bashar?" The voice was
that of a drinking companion from the Gammu bar, a
trusted officer from Renditai whose mood no longer was
that of someone recapturing the thrills of his youth. This
one had seen old friends die in the battle on Gammu. As
with most of the others who survived to come here, he
had left a family whose fate he did not know. There was

a touch of bitterness in his voice, as though he were trying to convince himself that he had been tricked into this venture.

"They will be here soon," Teg said. "They will arrive riding on the back of a worm."

"How do you know that?"

"It was all arranged."

Teg closed his eyes. He did not need eyes to see the activity all around him. This was like so many command posts he had occupied: an oval room of instruments and people who operated them, officers waiting to obey.

"What is this place?" someone asked.

"Those rocks to the north of us," Teg said. "See them? They were a high cliff once. It was called Wind Trap. There was a Fremen sietch there, little more than a cave now. A few Rakian pioneers live in it."

"Fremen," someone whispered. "Gods! I want to see that worm coming. I never thought I'd ever see such a thing."

"Another one of your unexpected arrangements, eh?" asked the officer of the growing bitterness.

What would he say if I revealed my new abilities? Teg wondered. *He might think I concealed purposes that would not bear close examination. And he would be right. That man is on the edge of a revelation. Would he remain loyal if his eyes were opened?* Teg shook his head. The officer would have little choice. None of them had much choice except to fight and die.

It was true, Teg thought then, that the process of arranging conflicts involved the hoodwinking of large masses. How easy it was to fall into the attitude of the Honored Matres.

Muck!

The hoodwinking was not as difficult as some supposed. Most people wanted to be led. That officer back there had wanted it. There were deep tribal instincts (powerful unconscious motivations) to account for this. The natural reaction when you began to recognize how easily you were led was to look for scapegoats. That officer back there wanted a scapegoat now.

"Burzmali wants to see you," someone off to Teg's left said.

"Not now," Teg said.

Burzmali could wait. He would have his day of command soon enough. Meanwhile, he was a distraction. There would be time later for him to skirt dangerously near the role of scapegoat.

How easy it was to produce scapegoats and how readily they were accepted! This was especially true when the alternative was to find yourself either guilty or stupid or both. Teg wanted to say for all of those around him:

"Look to the hoodwinking! Then you'll know our true intentions!"

The communications officer on Teg's left said: "That Reverend Mother is with Burzmali now. She insists they be allowed in to see you."

"Tell Burzmali I want him to go back and stay with Duncan," Teg said. "And have him look in on Murbella, make sure she's secured. Lucilla can come in."

It had to be, Teg thought.

Lucilla was increasingly suspicious about the changes in him. Trust a Reverend Mother to see the difference.

Lucilla swept in, her robes swishing to accent her vehemence. She was angry but concealing it well.

"I demand an explanation, Miles!"

That was a good opening line, he thought. "Of what?" he said.

"Why didn't we just go in at the—"

"Because the Honored Matres and their Tleilaxu companions from the Scattering hold most of the Rakian centers."

"How . . . how do you . . ."

"They've killed Taraza, you know," he said.

That stopped her, but not for long. "Miles, I insist that you tell me—"

"We don't have much time," he said. "The next satellite passage will show us on the surface here."

"But the defenses of Rakis—"

"Are as vulnerable as any other defenses when they become static," he said. "The families of the defenders are down here. Take the families and you have effective control of the defenders."

"But why are we out here in—"

"To pick up Odrade and that girl with her. Oh, and their worm, too."

"What will we do with a—"

"Odrade will know what to do with the worm. She's your Mother Superior now, you know."

"So you're going to whisk us off into—"

"You'll whisk yourselves! My people and I will remain to create a diversion."

That brought a shocked silence throughout the command station.

Diversion, Teg thought. *What an inadequate word.*

The resistance he had in mind would create hysteria among the Honored Matres, especially when they were made to believe the ghola was here. Not only would they counterattack, they eventually would resort to sterilization procedures. Most of Rakis would become a charred ruin. There was little likelihood that any humans, worms, or sandtrout would survive.

"The Honored Matres have been trying to locate and capture a worm without success," he said. "I really don't understand how they could be so blind in their concept of how you transplant one of them."

"Transplant?" Lucilla was floundering. Teg had seldom seen a Reverend Mother at such a loss. She was trying to assemble the things he had said. The Sisterhood had some of the Mentats' capabilities, he had observed. A Mentat could come to a qualified conviction without sufficient data. He thought that he would be long out of her reach (or the reach of any other Reverend Mother) before she assembled this data. Then there would be a scrambling for his offspring! They would pick up Dimela for their Breeding Mistresses, of course. And Odrade. She would not escape.

They had the key to the Tleilaxu axlotl tanks, too. It would be only a matter of time now until the Bene Gesserit overcame its scruples and mastered that source of the spice. A human body produced it!

"We're in danger here, then," Lucilla said.

"Some danger, yes. The trouble with the Honored Matres is that they're too wealthy. They make the mistakes of the wealthy."

"Depraved whores!" she said.

"I suggest you get to the entry port," he said. "Odrade will be here soon."

She left him without another word.

"Armor is all out and deployed," the communications officer said.

"Alert Burzmali to be ready for command here," Teg said. "The rest of us will be going out soon."

"You expect all of us to join you?" That was the one who looked for a scapegoat.

"I am going out," Teg said. "I will go alone if necessary. Only those who wish need join me."

After that, all of them would come, he thought. Peer pressure was little understood by anyone except those trained by the Bene Gesserit.

It grew silent in the command station except for the faint hummings and clicks of instruments. Teg fell to thinking about the "depraved whores."

It was not correct to call them depraved, he thought. Sometimes, the supremely rich did become depraved. That came from believing that money (power) could buy anything and everything. And why shouldn't they believe this? They saw it happening every day. It was easy to believe in absolutes.

Hope springs eternal and all of that gornaw!

It was like another faith. Money would buy the impossible.

Then came depravity.

It was not the same for the Honored Matres. They were, somehow, beyond depravity. They had come through it; he could see that. But now they were into something else so far beyond depravity that Teg wondered if he really wanted to know about it.

The knowledge was there, though, inescapable in his new awareness. Not one of those people would hesitate an instant before consigning an entire planet to torture if that meant personal gain. Or if the payoff were some imagined pleasure. Or if the torture produced even a few more days or hours of living.

What pleased them? What gratified? They were like semuta addicts. Whatever simulated pleasure for them, they required more of it every time.

And they know this!

How they must rage inside! Caught in such a trap! They had seen it all and none of it was enough—not good enough nor evil enough. They had entirely lost the knack of moderation.

They were dangerous, though. And perhaps he was wrong about one thing: Perhaps they no longer remembered what it had been like before the awful transformation of that strange tart-smelling stimulant that painted orange in their eyes. Memories of memories could become distorted. Every Mentat was sensitized to this flaw in himself.

"There's the worm!"

It was the communications officer.

Teg swiveled in his chair and looked at the projection, a miniature holo of the exterior to the southwest. The worm with its two tiny dots of human passengers was a distant sliver of wriggling movement.

"Bring Odrade in here alone when they arrive," he said. "Sheeana—that's the young girl—will remain behind to help herd that worm into the hold. It will obey her. Be sure Burzmali is standing ready nearby. We won't have much time for the transfer of command."

When Odrade entered the command station she was still breathing hard and exuding the smells of the desert, a compound of melange, flint, and human perspiration.

Teg sat in his chair apparently resting. His eyes remained closed.

Odrade thought she had caught the Bashar in an uncharacteristic attitude of repose, almost pensive. He opened his eyes then and she saw the change about which Lucilla had only been able to blurt a small warning—along with a few hasty words about the ghola's transformation. What was it that had happened to Teg? He was almost posing for her, daring her to see it in him. The chin was firm and held slightly upthrust in his normal attitude of observation. The narrow face with its webwork of age lines had lost none of its alertness. The long, thin nose so characteristic of the Corrinos and Atreides in his ancestry had grown a bit longer with advancing years. But the gray hair remained thick and that small peak at the forehead centered the observing gaze . . .

On his eyes!

"How did you know to meet us here?" Odrade demanded. "We had no idea where the worm was taking us."

"There are very few inhabited places here in the meridian desert," he said. "Gambler's choice. This seemed likely."

Gambler's choice? She knew the Mentat phrase but had never understood it.

Teg lifted himself from his chair. "Take this ship and go to the place you know best," he said.

Chapter House? She almost said it but thought of the others around her, these military strangers Teg had assembled. Who were they? Lucilla's brief explanation did not satisfy.

"We change Taraza's design somewhat," Teg said. "The ghola does not stay. He must go with you."

She understood. They would need Duncan Idaho's new talents to counter the whores. He was no longer merely bait for the destruction of Rakis.

"He will not be able to leave the no-ship's concealment, of course," Teg said.

She nodded. Duncan was not shielded from prescient searchers . . . such as the Guild navigators.

"Bashar!" It was the communications officer. "We've been bleeped by a satellite!"

"All right, you ground hogs!" Teg shouted. "Everybody outside! Get Burzmali in here."

A hatch at the rear of the station flew open. Burzmali lunged through. "Bashar, what are we—"

"No time! Take over!" Teg lifted himself from his command chair and waved for Burzmali to take it. "Odrade here will tell you where to go." On an impulse that he knew was partly vindictive, Teg grasped Odrade's left arm, leaned close, and kissed her cheek. "Do what you must, daughter," he whispered. "That worm in the hold may soon be the only one in the universe."

Odrade saw it then: Teg knew Taraza's complete design and intended to carry out his Mother Superior's orders to the very end.

Do what you must. That said it all.

We are not looking at a new state of matter but at a newly recognized relationship between consciousness and matter, which provides a more penetrating insight into the workings of prescience. The oracle shapes a projected inner universe to produce new external probabilities out of forces that are not understood. There is no need to understand these forces before using them to shape the physical universe. Ancient metal workers had no need to understand the molecular and submolecular complexities of their steel, bronze, copper, gold, and tin. They invented mystical powers to describe the unknown while they continued to operate their forges and wield their hammers.

—MOTHER SUPERIOR TARAZA, ARGUMENT IN COUNCIL

The ancient structure in which the Sisterhood secreted its Chapter House, its Archives, and the offices of its most sacrosanct leadership did not just make sounds in the night. The noises were more like signals. Odrade had learned to read those signals over her many years here. That particular sound there, that strained creaking, was a wooden beam in the floor not replaced in some eight hundred years. It contracted in the night to produce those sounds.

She had Taraza's memories to expand on such signals.

The memories were not fully integrated; there had been very little time. Here at night in Taraza's old working room, Odrade used a few available moments to continue the integration.

Dar and Tar, one at last.

That was a quite identifiable Taraza comment.

To haunt the Other Memories was to exist on several planes simultaneously, some of them very deep, but Taraza remained near the surface. Odrade allowed herself to sink farther into the multiple existences. Presently, she recognized a self who was currently breathing but remote while others demanded that she plunge into the all-enfolding visions, everything complete with smells, touches, emotions—all of the originals held intact within her own awareness.

It is unsettling to dream another's dreams.

Taraza again.

Taraza who had played such a dangerous game with the future of the entire Sisterhood hanging in the balance! How carefully she had timed the leaking of word to the whores that the Tleilaxu had built dangerous abilities into the ghola. And the attack on the Gammu Keep confirmed that the information had reached its source. The brutal nature of that attack, though, had warned Taraza that she had little time. The whores would be sure to assemble forces for the total destruction of Gammu—just to kill that one ghola.

So much had depended on Teg.

She saw the Bashar there in her own assemblage of Other Memories: the father she had never really known.

I didn't know him at the end, either.

It could be weakening to dig into those memories, but she could not escape the demands of that luring reservoir.

Odrade thought of the Tyrant's words: "The terrible field of my past! Answers leap up like a frightened flock blackening the sky of my inescapable memories."

Odrade held herself like a swimmer balanced just below the water's surface.

I most likely will be replaced, Odrade thought. *I may even be reviled.* Bellonda certainly was not giving easy agreement to the new state of command. No matter. Survival of the Sisterhood was all that should concern any of them.

Odrade floated up out of the Other Memories and lifted her gaze to look across the room into the shadowy niche where the bust of a woman could be discerned in the low light of the room's glowglobes. The bust remained a vague shape in its shadows but Odrade knew that face well: Chenoeh, guardian symbol of Chapter House.

"There but for the grace of God . . ."

Every sister who came through the spice agony (as Chenoeh had not) said or thought that same thing, but what did it really mean? Careful breeding and careful training produced the successful ones in sufficient numbers. Where was the hand of God in that? God certainly was not the worm they had brought from Rakis. Was the presence of God felt only in the successes of the Sisterhood?

I fall prey to the pretensions of my own Missionaria Protectiva!

She knew that these were similar to thoughts and questions that had been heard in this room on countless occasions. Bootless! Still, she could not bring herself to remove that guardian bust from the niche where it had reposed for so long.

I am not superstitious, she told herself. *I am not a compulsive person. This is a matter of tradition. Such things have a value well known to us.*

Certainly, no bust of me will ever be so honored.

She thought of Waff and his Face Dancers dead with Miles Teg in the terrible destruction of Rakis. It did not do to dwell on the bloody attrition being suffered in the Old Empire. Better to think about the muscles of retribution being created by the blundering violence of the Honored Matres.

Teg knew!

The recently concluded Council session had subsided in fatigue without firm conclusions. Odrade counted herself lucky to have diverted attention into a few immediate concerns dear to them all.

The punishments: Those had occupied them for a time. Historical precedents fleshed out the Archival analyses to a satisfying form. Those assemblages of humans who allied themselves with the Honored Matres were in for some shocks.

Ix would certainly overextend itself. They had not the slightest appreciation of how competition from the Scattering would crush them.

The Guild would be shunted aside and made to pay dearly for its melange and its machinery. Guild and Ix, thrown together, would fall together.

The Fish Speakers could be mostly ignored. Satellites of Ix, they were already fading into a past that humans would abandon.

And the Bene Tleilax. Ah, yes, the Tleilaxu. Waff had succumbed to the Honored Matres. He had never admitted it but the truth was plain. *"Just once and with one of my own Face Dancers."*

Odrade smiled grimly, remembering her father's bitter kiss.

I will have another niche made, she thought. *I will commission another bust: Miles Teg, the Great Heretic!*

Lucilla's suspicions about Teg were disquieting, though. Had he been prescient at last and able to *see* the no-ships? Well, the Breeding Mistresses could explore those suspicions.

"We have laagered up!" Bellonda accused.

They all knew the meaning of that word: they had retreated into a fortress position for the long night of the whores.

Odrade realized she did not much care for Bellonda, the way she laughed occasionally to expose those wide, blunt teeth.

They had discussed the cell samples from Sheeana for a long time. The "proof of Siona" was there. She had the ancestry that shielded her from prescience and could leave the no-ship.

Duncan was an unknown.

Odrade turned her thoughts to the ghola out there in the grounded no-ship. Lifting herself from the chair, she crossed to the dark window and looked in the direction of the distant landing field.

Did they dare risk releasing Duncan from the shielding of that ship? The cell studies said he was a mixture of many Idaho gholas—some descendant of Siona. But what of the taint from the original?

No. He must remain confined.

And what of Murbella?—*pregnant* Murbella? An Honored Matre dishonored.

"The Tleilaxu intended for me to kill the Imprinter," Duncan said.

"Will you try to kill the whore?" That was Lucilla's question.

"She is not an Imprinter," Duncan said.

The Council had discussed at length the possible nature of the bonding between Duncan and Murbella. Lucilla maintained there was no bonding at all, that the two remained wary opponents.

"Best not to risk putting them together."

The sexual prowess of the whores would have to be studied at length, though. Perhaps a meeting between Duncan and Murbella in the no-ship could be risked. With careful protective measures, of course.

Lastly, she thought about the worm in the no-ship's hold—a worm nearing the moment of its metamorphosis. A small earth-dammed basin filled with melange awaited that worm. When the moment came, it would be lured out by Sheeana into the bath of melange and water. The resulting sandtrout could then begin their long transformation.

You were right, father. It was so simple when you looked at it clearly.

No need to seek a desert planet for the worms. The sandtrout would create their own habitat for Shai-hulud. It was not pleasant to think of Chapter House Planet transformed into vast areas of wasteland but it had to be done.

The "Last Will and Testament of Miles Teg," which he

had planted in the no-ship's submolecular storage systems, could not be discredited. Even Bellonda agreed to that.

Chapter House required a complete revision of all its historical records. A new look had been demanded of them by what Teg had seen of the Lost Ones—the whores from the Scattering.

"You seldom learn the names of the truly wealthy and powerful. You see only their spokesmen. The political arena makes a few exceptions to this but does not reveal the full power structure."

The Mentat philosopher had chewed deep into everything they accepted and what he disgorged did not agree with Archival dependence upon "our inviolate summations."

We knew it, Miles, we just never faced up to it. We're all going to be digging in our Other Memories for the next few generations.

Fixed data storage systems could not be trusted.

"If you destroy most copies, time will take care of the rest."

How Archives had raged at that telling pronouncement by the Bashar!

"The writing of history is largely a process of diversion. Most historical accounts divert attention from the secret influences around the recorded events."

That was the one that had brought down Bellonda. She had taken it up on her own, admitting: "The few histories that escape this restrictive process vanish into obscurity through obvious processes."

Teg had listed some of the processes: "Destruction of as many copies as possible, burying the too revealing accounts in ridicule, ignoring them in the centers of education, insuring that they are not quoted elsewhere and, in some cases, elimination of the authors."

Not to mention the scapegoat process that brought death to more than one messenger bearing unwelcome news, Odrade thought. She recalled an ancient ruler who kept a pikestaff handy with which to kill messengers who brought bad news.

"We have a good base of information upon which to build a better understanding of our past," Odrade had argued. "We've always known that what was at stake in conflicts was the determination of who would control the wealth or its equivalent."

Maybe it was not a real "noble purpose" but it would do for the time being.

I am avoiding the central issue, she thought.

Something would have to be done about Duncan Idaho and they all knew it.

With a sigh, Odrade summoned a 'thopter and prepared herself for the short trip to the no-ship.

Duncan's prison was at least comfortable, Odrade thought when she entered it. This had been the ship commander's quarters lately occupied by Miles Teg. There were still signs of his presence here—a small holo stat projector revealing a scene of his home on Lernaeus; the stately old house, the long lawn, the river. Teg had left a sewing kit behind on a bedside table.

The ghola sat in a sling chair staring at the projection. He looked up listlessly when Odrade entered.

"You just left him back there to die, didn't you?" Duncan asked.

"We do what we must," she said. "And I obeyed his orders."

"I know why you're here," Duncan said. "And you're not going to change my mind. I'm not a damned stud for the witches. You understand me?"

Odrade smoothed her robe and sat on the edge of the bed facing Duncan. "Have you examined the record my father left for us?" she asked.

"Your father?"

"Miles Teg was my father. I commend his last words to you. He was our eyes there at the end. He had to *see* the death on Rakis. The 'mind at its beginning' understood dependencies and key logs."

When Duncan looked puzzled, she explained: "We were trapped too long in the Tyrant's oracular maze."

She saw how he sat up more alertly, the feline movements that spoke of muscles well conditioned to attack.

"There is no way you can escape alive from this ship," she said. "You know why."

"Siona."

"You are a danger to us but we would prefer that you lived a useful life."

"I'm still not going to breed for you, especially not with that little twit from Rakis."

Odrade smiled, wondering how Sheeana would respond to that description.

"You think it's funny?" Duncan demanded.

"Not really. But we'll still have Murbella's child, of course. I guess that will have to satisfy us."

"I've been talking to Murbella on the com," Duncan said. "She thinks she's going to be a Reverend Mother, that you're going to accept her into the Bene Gesserit."

"Why not? Her cells pass the proof of Siona. I think she will make a superb Sister."

"Has she really taken you in?"

"You mean, have we failed to observe that she thinks she will go along with us until she learns our secrets and then she will escape? Oh, we know that, Duncan."

"You don't think she can get away from you?"

"Once we get them, Duncan, we never really lose them."

"You don't think you lost the Lady Jessica?"

"She came back to us in the end."

"Why did you really come out here to see me?"

"I thought you deserved an explanation of the Mother Superior's design. It was aimed at the destruction of Rakis, you see. What she really wanted was the elimination of almost all of the worms."

"Great Gods below! Why?"

"They were an oracular force holding us in bondage. Those pearls of the Tyrant's awareness magnified that hold. He didn't predict events, he created them."

Duncan pointed toward the rear of the ship. "But what about . . ."

"That one? It's just one now. By the time it reaches sufficient numbers to be an influence once more, humankind will have gone its own way beyond him. We'll be too numerous by then, doing too many different things on our own. No single force will rule all of our futures completely, never again."

She stood.

When he did not respond, she said: "Within the imposed limits, which I know you appreciate, please think about the kind of life you want to lead. I promise to help you in any way I can."

"Why would you do that?"

"Because my ancestors loved you. Because my father loved you."

"Love? You witches can't feel love!"

She stared down at him for almost a minute. The bleached hair was growing out dark at the roots and curling once more into ringlets, especially at his neck, she saw.

"I feel what I feel," she said. "And your water is ours, Duncan Idaho."

She saw the Fremen admonition have its effect on him and then turned away and was passed out of the room by the guards.

Before leaving the ship, she went back to the hold and stared down at the quiescent worm on its bed of Rakian sand. Her viewport looked down from some two hundred meters onto the captive. As she looked, she shared a silent laugh with the increasingly integrated Taraza.

We were right and Schwangyu and her people were wrong. We knew he wanted out. He had to want that after what he did.

She spoke aloud in a soft whisper, as much for herself as for the nearby observers stationed there to watch for the moment when metamorphosis began in that worm.

"We have your language now," she said.

There were no words in the language, only a moving, dancing adaptation to a moving, dancing universe. You could only *speak* the language, not translate it. To know the meaning you had to go through the experience and even then the meaning changed before your eyes. "Noble purpose" was, after all, an untranslatable experience. But when she looked down at the rough, heat-immune hide of that worm from the Rakian desert, Odrade knew what she saw: the visible evidence of noble purpose.

Softly, she called down to him: "Hey! Old worm! Was this your design?"

There was no answer but then she had not really expected an answer.

GOD EMPEROR OF DUNE

"Rich fare. . . . Heady stuff." —*Los Angeles Times*

"A fourth visit to distant Arrakis that is every bit as fascinating as the other three—every bit as timely." —*Time*

"Book four of the Dune series has many of the same strengths as the previous three, and I was indeed kept up late at night." —*Challenging Destiny*

HERETICS OF DUNE

"A monumental piece of imaginative architecture . . . indisputably magical." —*Los Angeles Herald Examiner*

"Appealing and gripping. . . . Fascinating detail, yet cloaked in mystery and mysticism." —*The Milwaukee Journal*

"Herbert works wonders with some new speculation and an entirely new batch of characters. He weaves together several fascinating story lines with almost the same mastery as informed *Dune*, and keeps the reader intent on the next revelation or twist." —*Challenging Destiny*

CHAPTERHOUSE: DUNE

"Compelling . . . a worthy addition to this durable and deservedly popular series." —*The New York Times*

"The vast and fascinating Dune saga sweeps on—as exciting and gripping as ever." —*Kirkus Reviews*

The Dune Chronicles by Frank Herbert

DUNE
DUNE MESSIAH
CHILDREN OF DUNE
GOD EMPEROR OF DUNE
HERETICS OF DUNE
CHAPTERHOUSE: DUNE

Other Books by Frank Herbert

THE BOOK OF FRANK HERBERT
DESTINATION: VOID (revised edition)
DIRECT DESCENT
THE DOSADI EXPERIMENT
EYE
THE EYES OF HEISENBERG
THE GODMAKERS
THE GREEN BRAIN
THE MAKER OF DUNE
THE SANTAROGA BARRIER
SOUL CATCHER
WHIPPING STAR
THE WHITE PLAGUE
THE WORLDS OF FRANK HERBERT
MAN OF TWO WORLDS (with Brian Herbert)

Books by Frank Herbert and Bill Ransom

THE JESUS INCIDENT
THE LAZARUS EFFECT
THE ASCENSION FACTOR

Books by Brian Herbert

DREAMER OF DUNE: THE BIOGRAPHY OF FRANK HERBERT

Books Edited by Brian Herbert

THE NOTEBOOKS OF FRANK HERBERT'S DUNE
SONGS OF MUAD'DIB

Books by Brian Herbert and Kevin J. Anderson

DUNE: HOUSE ATREIDES
DUNE: HOUSE HARKONNEN
DUNE: HOUSE CORRINO
DUNE: THE BUTLERIAN JIHAD
DUNE: THE MACHINE CRUSADE
DUNE: THE BATTLE OF CORRIN
THE ROAD TO DUNE
(also by Frank Herbert; includes the novel *Spice Planet*)
HUNTERS OF DUNE
SANDWORMS OF DUNE
PAUL OF DUNE
THE WINDS OF DUNE
SISTERHOOD OF DUNE
MENTATS OF DUNE
NAVIGATORS OF DUNE
DUNE: THE DUKE OF CALADAN
DUNE: THE LADY OF CALADAN